**Sharon Kendrick** ~~writing~~
competition by describing her ideal date: being flown
to an exotic island by a gorgeous and powerful man.
Little did she realise that she'd just wandered into her
dream job! Today she writes for Mills & Boon, and
her books feature often stubborn but always *to-die-for*
heroes and the women who bring them to their knees.
She believes that the best books are those you never
want to end. Just like life…

**Maisey Yates** is a *New York Times* bestselling author
of over one hundred romance novels. She has a coffee
habit she has no interest in kicking, and a slight
Pinterest addiction. She lives with her husband and
children in the Pacific Northwest. When Maisey isn't
writing she can be found singing in the grocery store,
shopping for shoes online, and probably not doing
dishes. Check out her website: maiseyyates.com.

# CINDERELLA'S CHRISTMAS SECRET

## SHARON KENDRICK

# HIS MAJESTY'S FORBIDDEN TEMPTATION

## MAISEY YATES

MILLS & BOON

First Published in Great Britain 2020
by Mills & Boon, an imprint of HarperCollins*Publishers*
1 London Bridge Street, London, SE1 9GF

Cinderella's Christmas Secret © 2020 Sharon Kendrick

His Majesty's Forbidden Temptation © 2020 Maisey Yates

ISBN: 978-0-263-27841-5

MIX
Paper from
responsible sources
FSC C007454

This book is produced from independently certified FSC™ paper
to ensure responsible forest management.
For more information visit www.harpercollins.co.uk/green.

Printed and bound in Spain
by CPI, Barcelona

# CINDERELLA'S CHRISTMAS SECRET

**SHARON KENDRICK**

In memory of my dearest friend
Mandy 'Gregoire' Morris, who was clever, cultured,
kind, and possessed a wicked sense of humour—
qualities which live on in her four amazing children,
Simon, Katy, Robin and Guy.

# CHAPTER ONE

'I CAN'T...' HOLLIE's words came out as a strangled squeak as she held the dress up.

It was very Christmassy. In fact, it *screamed* Christmas—and not in a good way. Short, bright and very green, it gleamed beneath the garish lights of the hotel where the party was being held. She tried again. 'I can't possibly wear this, Janette.'

Her boss's perfectly plucked brows were elevated. 'Why not?'

'Because it's...' Hollie hesitated. Normally, she was the most accommodating of employees. She was a peacemaker. A facilitator. She worked very hard and did what was asked of her, but surely there was a limit. 'A little on the small side...'

But her boss wasn't interested in her objections. In fact, she was even more self-absorbed than usual and had been in a particularly vile mood since her fingernail had chipped that morning and subsequently snagged one of her super-fine stockings.

'Someone of your age can get away with wearing something as daring as that,' Janette clipped out as she adjusted a low-hanging bunch of mistletoe. 'You might find it suits you, Hollie—it'll certainly make a change from your usual wardrobe choices.'

'But—'

'No buts,' continued her boss smoothly. 'We're sponsoring this party, just in case you'd forgotten. And since one of the waitresses is a no-show and with so many VIPs coming, we can't possibly be short-staffed. All you have to do is to turn up dressed as an elf for a couple of hours and hand out a few canapés. Why, if I were a few years younger I would have worn the outfit myself! Especially as Maximo Diaz has agreed to come.' She flashed a veneer-capped smile. 'Potentially the most valuable client we've ever had. Mr Big. Mr Limitless Bank Account. And if his hotel purchase goes through before Christmas, you're looking at a big fat bonus. Surely you haven't forgotten that, have you?'

Hollie shook her head. No, of course she hadn't. How could she have forgotten Maximo Diaz and all the fuss which surrounded him whenever he made an appearance in the small Devon town where she'd moved after her life's savings had become someone else's pocket money? How could *anyone* ever forget a man who resembled a dark, avenging angel who had tumbled to earth in a custom-made suit? A man who made her heart race with uncomfortable excitement whenever he caught her in the hard, black spotlight of his gaze so that she felt like a butterfly pinned to a piece of card.

She swallowed. She guessed every woman felt that way about him. She'd seen the way he was watched by every female who happened to be in the vicinity, whenever he walked into the estate agency where Hollie worked. She'd noticed the way their eyes were drawn—

reluctantly or otherwise—to the powerful muscularity of his body and the glow of his olive-dark skin. He was a man who seemed to have taken up stubborn residence in her imagination. A man who symbolised a simmering sexuality and virility which scared her and excited her in equal measure—and no matter how hard she tried, she found it impossible to remain neutral to him.

Not that she would have made very much of a mark on *his* radar. Powerful Spanish billionaires tended not to take much notice of nondescript women who beavered away quietly in the background of large offices. Occasionally she'd made him a cup of coffee, accompanied by one of the home-made biscuits she sometimes brought to the office, if her boss wasn't on one of her rigid diets. She remembered him absently taking a bite from a piece of featherlight shortbread and then looking at it in surprise, as if the taste of something sweet was something he wasn't used to. He probably wasn't. Because 'sweet' wasn't really a word you associated with the rugged tycoon. Hard and dark were words which sprang more readily to mind.

But she shouldn't be thinking about Maximo Diaz— not when Janette was still fixing her with that expectant stare, and automatically Hollie smiled back.

'Of course I haven't forgotten Señor Diaz,' she said. 'He's a very important client.'

'Yes, he is. Which is why all the local bigwigs and politicians are so eager to meet him,' Janette said eagerly. 'He's going to have a big impact on this area, Hollie. Especially if he turns the old castle into a hotel like it was before, back in the day. It means we won't have to use this eyesore of a place any more for our official functions—and not before time.'

'Yes, I do realise that.'

'So you'll do it?'

Hollie nodded. It seemed she didn't have a choice and therefore she would accept the situation gracefully. Wasn't that one of life's most important lessons? 'Yes, Janette, I'll do it.'

'Excellent. Run along and get changed. I've popped in a pair of my own shoes—I think we're the same size. You'll never fit into the other ones. Oh, and wear your hair down for once, will you? I don't know why you always insist on hiding away your best feature!'

Tucking the outfit under her arm, Hollie slipped from the room, dodging gaudy streamers along the way, trying to concentrate on the evening ahead rather than her boss's rather overbearing manner. Despite being a whole two months until the holidays, the hotel was decked out with yuletide sparkle, which didn't quite manage to disguise the ugly fittings which had seen better days. Yet she wasn't going to complain about the fact that the festival seemed to come earlier every year, because Christmas was a welcome break in the normal routine. A time for candles and carols and twinkling lights. For pine-scented trees and bells and snow. She might not have any family of her own to celebrate with but somehow that didn't matter. It was a time when strangers talked to one another and it brought with it the indefinable sense of hope that, somehow, things were going to get better—and Hollie loved that feeling.

Fluorescent lights lit the way to a gloomy subterranean cloakroom, which was a bit like descending into hell, but Hollie remained determinedly positive as she shook out the fur-trimmed green dress, the red and white striped tights and Janette's scarlet stilettos, which were scarily high.

Peeling off her shirt dress, flesh-coloured tights and sensible court shoes, she stood shivering in her underwear as she struggled into her elf costume. But by the time she had managed to zip it up, she realised her reservations had been well founded because the person who stared back at her from the mirror was...

*Unrecognisable.*

She blinked, finding it hard to reconcile this new image of herself—and not just because she was wearing what amounted to fancy dress. The no-show waitress must have been much shorter, because the hem of fake white fur swung to barely mid-thigh—a super-short length, which was exaggerated by Janette's skyscraper heels. The other waitress must have been slimmer too, because the green velvet was clinging to every pore of Hollie's body, like honey on the back of a teaspoon. The rich material moulded itself to her breasts and hugged her waist in a style which was as far from her usual choice of outfit as it was possible to imagine.

She looked...

She cleared her throat, hating the sudden nerves and fear which slammed through her body and made her heart race like a train. She looked like a stranger, that was for sure. The way her mother used to look when she was expecting a visit from her father. As if tight clothes could mask a basic incompatibility—as if adornment were the only thing a woman needed to make a man love her. And it hadn't worked, had it? She remembered the bitterness which used to distort her mother's features after she had slammed the door in his wake.

*'You can never make a man love you, Hollie, because men aren't capable of love!'*

It was a lesson she'd never forgotten—her mum had made sure of that—but not one she particularly wanted to remember, especially now. She wished she could strip off these stupid clothes and the too-high heels. Skip the party and go home to her rented cottage. She could study that new cake recipe she was planning to try out on the weekend and dream about the time when she could finally open her own business and be independent at last. One more year of frugality and she should have amassed the funds she needed. Only this time she would be sure to go it alone, in a part of the world which she found manageable. A picturesque little Devon town called Trescombe—not some big, anonymous city like London, where it was all too easy for a person like her to slip off the radar and become invisible.

Was it that erosion of her confidence which had led to her not paying attention to what was going on around her—until one day Hollie had discovered that nearly all the money had gone and her supposedly best friend had ripped her off? It had been a harsh and hurtful lesson, but she had learnt from it. Never again would she put herself in the position of being conned by someone she'd thought of as a friend, and have her trust in human nature eroded yet again.

And wasn't that another reason for making sure this party was a success? Because Maximo Diaz's purchase of the old castle on top of the big hill outside town had the potential to herald a new golden age in local tourism and Hollie wanted to be part of it. It hadn't been a hotel for years but was crying out for some love and attention. And if the enigmatic Spaniard was an unlikely candidate to play the part of neighbourhood saviour—well, that was what life was like. Sometimes it threw up surprises and you discovered that people didn't always fit into the little boxes you tried to squeeze them into. Just because a man was an impossibly wealthy global superstar, didn't mean he couldn't also be a good man, did it?

Remembering Janette's parting words, Hollie pulled the scrunchy from her hair and shook her head to let her hair tumble down around her shoulders. It was a colour best described as light brown, though some of the bitchier girls at school used to call it 'mousy'. But it was clean and shiny and it streamed abundantly over her breasts, effectively hiding that rather scary glimpse of cleavage.

The final touch was a red and green hat with a bell on the end and the sound of it jangling like a cash register as she crammed it over her head made Hollie smile. One day soon she would open her very own tea shop and, although she wasn't planning on wearing quite such a revealing uniform, tonight's event would be perfect practice for her future career of serving the public. Wobbling a little in her spindly heels, she headed for the door.

Christmas elf?

How hard could it be?

He didn't want to be here.

Despite the fact that he was poised on the brink of a venture guaranteed to net him even more millions, Maximo Diaz was feeling even more detached than usual.

He looked around at a room which, bizarrely, was decorated with thick streamers of glittering tinsel—even though it was still only October. A giant fir dominated one wall and tiny golden and silver lights twinkled in every available corner of the room. Christmas had, it seemed, come ridiculously early to this one-horse town, with its distant glimpses of the sea and the bleak sweeping moorland which lay to the east.

His mouth hardened.

The truth was, he didn't want to be anywhere right now. Not at either of his homes in Madrid or New York and certainly not here in Devon. Because everywhere he went he took himself with him and 'here' was inside his head, listening to clamouring thoughts which would not be silenced. For the first time in his life, he was finding it difficult to switch off and that disturbed him.

In his past there had been troubles. Of course there had. Everyone had troubles and sometimes he felt as if he'd netted more than his fair share. Bleak, dark events which had come out of nowhere and threatened to blindside him, although in the end they had bounced off him like hailstones on a pavement because he had willed them to. He had schooled himself to cultivate a steely self-control and had always prided himself on his ability to shrug off hardship. To step away from chaos, resilient and untouched, like a phoenix rising from the ashes. But back then youth, hunger and ambition had been on his side, shielding him against hurt and shielding him against pain. He had come to the conclusion that he was one of those lucky few who were immune to hurt. And if that meant people—usually women—were prone to describe him as cold and unfeeling. Well, he could live with that.

Yet who would have thought the death of someone he'd despised could have pierced his heart so ragged? How was that even *possible*? He hadn't seen her in years. Hadn't wanted to—and with good reason. He should have felt anger or injustice or resentment—maybe all three—as he'd said goodbye to the woman who had given birth to him, summoned to her bedside by the nuns who had cared for her during her final days. Yet it hadn't been like that. He shook his head. His reaction had surprised him. And angered him too, because he hadn't wanted to feel that way. As he'd held her papery hand with its dark tracery of veins, he had felt a deep sorrow welling up inside him. He had been overwhelmed by a sense of something lost, which now eluded him for ever.

And he didn't do that kind of emotion. Not now and not ever.

But he had to carry on. To brush off pointless grief and make like it had never happened. What other choice was there for someone who had turned indifference into an art form? He would get over it because he always did. And he would forgive himself for that rare foray into the saccharine world of sentimentality, because that was a place which held no allure for him.

He would continue with his inexorable rise to the top. He would keep on making a fortune from fundamentally changing the infrastructure of different countries. Building roads and building railways and creating a turnover which caused his competitors to shake their heads with frustration and awe. He had added a luxury hotel chain to his portfolio now and was surrounded by the kind of wealth which, strangely and rather disturbingly, had not brought him the satisfaction he'd sought. But it certainly made women's eyes grow wide whenever they stepped over the threshold of one of his homes or slid into the leather-bound luxury of his private jet. And just because he had more money than he would ever need in several lifetimes, didn't mean he wanted to slow down. Because he liked success. He liked it a lot. Not because of the material rewards it reaped, but for the glow of achievement it provided, no matter how fleeting that feeling proved to be. It was as if he was intent on proving himself over and over again, if not to the father and mother who had rejected him, then maybe to himself.

'Can I tempt you with something to eat, Señor Diaz?'

A soft voice broke into Maximo's reverie and, glad to have the dark tangle of his thoughts interrupted, he turned his head to see a woman standing there, a tray of food in her hands. But it wasn't the unappetising fare which caught his attention and held it, as much as her appearance.

Tempt him? She most certainly could.

His narrowed his eyes, because the thought came out of nowhere, especially as she looked faintly ridiculous in her fancy-dress costume. A sudden pulse beat at his temple and he felt the inexplicable drying of his mouth. Ridiculous, yes—but kind of sexy, too. No. Scrub that. *Very* sexy.

For a moment he thought she seemed faintly familiar, but the thought instantly left him because he was finding it difficult not to stare. And difficult to breathe. Who wouldn't when she looked so...*spectacular*? He swallowed as he continued with his silent scrutiny. Rich green velvet emphasised the porcelain paleness of her skin and a band of white fur at her shoulders drew his attention to her creamy flesh—which was unfashionably soft and abundant. Maximo allowed his gaze to move down, distracted by long legs which seemed to go all the way up to her armpits, an illusion no doubt helped by her teetering shoes. Sexy, scarlet shoes—and most men didn't bother denying their reaction to *that* kind of footwear.

Yet, in direct contrast to the provocation of those killer heels, she wore not a scrap of make-up on her milk-pale face and the healthy sway of hair which gleamed beneath the fairy lights made Maximo experience something he hadn't felt in quite a while. A stealthy but insistent tug of desire, which pulsed through his veins like sweet, dark honey.

His mouth twisted self-deprecatingly. Surely the healthy libido which seemed to have deserted him of late hadn't been stirred by something as off-the-wall as a woman in fancy dress? Maybe his sexual appetite had become so jaded that he was being tempted by a little seasonal role play.

'Um...we have a selection of delicious canapés on offer,' she was saying, her words tumbling over themselves, and something about the softness of her voice made his skin prickle with recognition once more. 'We've got pineapple and cheese on sticks and vol-au-vents—or there's mini quiche, if you prefer.'

'Mini quiche?' he echoed sardonically, dropping his gaze to survey something unrecognisable which was stabbed unappetisingly onto the end of a cocktail stick, and maybe she picked up on his tone because when he looked up again, her face had turned very pink.

'I know they're not to everyone's taste—'

His mouth twisted. 'You can say that again.'

'But the tourist board suggested we go with a retro theme,' she defended.

He found himself unexpectedly charmed by her blush, for when was the last time *that* had happened? 'And why would that be, I wonder?'

'Because nostalgia is big, especially at Christmas.' She hesitated, as if establishing whether he really did want to talk to her or whether he was just being polite. 'Isn't that the whole point of it?'

'But it isn't Christmas,' he pointed out. 'Not for weeks.'

'Yes, I know. But the holiday always puts people in a good mood. And everywhere looks better with a few decorations and a Christmas tree.'

'I must beg to differ,' he commented, shooting a disparaging gaze at the glittering fir with its flashing fairy lights, which was nudging the hotel ceiling. He studied the fake presents he could see piled up at the base and couldn't repress a shudder. 'It looks monstrous.'

She hesitated again. 'You sound as if you don't like Christmas?'

'Something of an understatement,' he returned coolly. 'If you want the truth, I loathe it.'

'Oh. Right. Well, that's a shame,' she said and he could see her biting her lip as she struggled to think of a suitably compensatory response. 'In that case, would you like a glass of bubbly? There's plenty over on the bar—I can easily go and fetch you one.'

He could just imagine the quality of wine on offer but something about her worried expression made Maximo bite back the acerbic response which was hovering on his lips. Suddenly he realised it wasn't fair to take his mood out on her. For him, this party was nothing more than a social necessity—an opportunity to meet the local officials who would help facilitate his ambitious plans. It certainly wasn't what he'd call a pleasure, and she was only doing her job, after all.

And then that first faint flicker of recognition crystallised into something more solid, which made him examine her face more closely, because the dark-lashed beauty of her grey eyes had stirred more than a vague memory.

'Don't I know you?' he questioned suddenly.

She wriggled her milky shoulders a little awkwardly. 'You don't exactly *know* me, Signor Diaz,' she said. 'We've met a few times when you've been into the office. I work in the estate agency you're using to purchase the castle. I'm usually—'

'Sitting behind a desk. *Sí, sí*—of course, I remember,' he said, for hadn't she been an oasis of calm during his recent purchase, and as unlike her abrasive and predatory boss as it was possible to be? She'd made him coffee and served him with something delicious to accompany it. But usually her clothes were unremarkable and her thick hair always scraped back in a style so severe, he imagined even a nun might shun it as unflattering. He remembered thinking that if he were planning on moving his business here, she might make the perfect secretary, and perhaps he would have poached her and paid her twice as much as she was currently earning.

He'd had no idea that beneath her drab clothes was a body which was little short of sensational and he was finding it unexpectedly difficult to reconcile these two dramatically different images of the same woman. 'So why the sudden change of role—and the sudden change of outfit?'

'I know. It's awful, isn't it?' she whispered, her stricken gaze glancing down at the clashing colours of red and green.

'I don't know if that's the word I would have chosen,' he answered carefully. 'I think it suits you, if you want the truth.'

'Seriously?' She looked surprised and then shyly delighted.

And wasn't it strange how her obvious self-consciousness was playing sudden havoc with Maximo's senses? The way she was biting her bottom lip was drawing his attention to the cushion of pink flesh which curved so sweetly into a shy smile. Her mouth suddenly looked very inviting. And extremely kissable. Bizarre. He shook his head, reminding himself that there were plenty of women more suitable as recipients of his desire than an office junior in fancy dress. 'Are you moonlighting?'

'You could say that.'

She lowered her voice again so he had to lean closer to hear her, and as he did he caught the faint drift of her scent and wondered how something so light and delicate could smell so unbelievably provocative. 'The waitress who'd been hired to do this let them down at the last minute,' she confided. 'And I was asked to—'

'Ah! There you are, Maximo! Hiding away in the shadows, like some dashing conquistador!'

A shrill voice crashed into their conversation and Maximo looked up to see Janette James bearing down on them, her body language managing to be both sinuous yet determined at the same time. She wore a look on her face which he'd seen the first time he'd walked into her estate agency and every time since. It was an expression he'd encountered many times during his life, but especially from middle-aged divorcees.

'I do hope Hollie has been looking after you?' she was saying. 'I'm sure she has, judging by the amount of time she's been standing here.' She fluttered him another predatory smile before turning to the hapless waitress by his side. 'But there *are* other people in the room, Hollie dear, tempting as it must be to monopolise Señor Diaz. People who are very hungry. So run along, will you? The mayor keeps glancing in your direction and he looks as if he could murder a sausage roll.'

Hollie nodded, aware of Maximo Diaz's burning black gaze on her as she moved away and that the high heels were making her hips sway in a way she hoped wasn't drawing attention to her bottom. Finding the mayor waiting, she kept her smile intact as he popped an entire sausage roll into his mouth, and thought about what her boss had said. *Had* she been guilty of monopolising the Spaniard? Maybe she had. She'd certainly been transfixed by him. Lulled by the timbre of his richly accented voice, she had been unable to tear her eyes away from his darkly beautiful face. But for once it had been a two-way street, because tonight she sensed that she had captured his complete attention. Instead of flicking her his usual dismissive glance, he had been openly staring at her and talking to her and listening to her as if her opinion actually *mattered*.

Had she been gaping at him like a stranded fish in response to that and drinking in all that powerful mastery instead of 'working the room' as Janette had told her to? She turned her head and watched other people moving towards him, as if they too were being magnetised by all that unashamed masculinity.

'Good-looking fellow, isn't he?' observed the mayor wryly, noting the direction of her gaze as he reached for a second sausage roll. 'I've noticed every woman in the room can't seem to stop staring at him.'

Hollie winced. And she had been as guilty as the rest! She had drooled over him like some teenager at a pop concert.

'I guess everyone's interested because he's about to become a local landowner.'

'You think so? Wouldn't have anything to do with the size of his wallet or the fact that he looks like an old-fashioned matinee idol, would it?'

'Of course not,' she said primly, quickly excusing herself to continue her elfish duties with renewed fervour, in an attempt to redeem herself in her boss's eyes. She dispensed the gradually wilting selection left on her tray, topped up glasses and tried to keep busy, but, irritatingly, her thoughts kept flitting back to the man with the black eyes who was currently being monopolised by the local member of parliament. Maximo Diaz had unsettled her and made her feel distinctly disorientated because when he'd looked at her that way, she'd felt...

It was difficult to describe but she'd felt *different*. As if she weren't Hollie Walker at all, but as if another woman had taken over her body. During a brief conversation about the wisdom of serving throwback cocktail snacks, an entirely different narrative had been running through her head. Hadn't she found her gaze straying to the Spaniard's sensual lips, which looked like an invitation to sin, and wondered what it would be like to be kissed by him? Hadn't her curiosity been piqued about how it would feel to be held in the arms of someone who looked so unbelievably strong?

Which was crazy. A man like Maximo Diaz was about as far out of her reach as the cold stars in the heavens. He was an international playboy with girlfriends who featured regularly on the covers of glossy magazines, while she was a twenty-six-year-old virgin. In fact, sometimes Hollie thought she could be defined by all the things she *hadn't* done. Yes, she'd gone to live in London—and just look how *that* had ended—but she'd never been intimate with a man. She'd never lain naked in someone's arms, or shared a giggling breakfast with them next morning, or gone on a mini-break, or been given a sentimental piece of jewellery.

Maybe that was her own fault. She knew people thought she dressed too conservatively for her age, because they'd hinted at it more than once and Janette had come right out and said so on more than one occasion. But they hadn't grown up watching a woman who used sexual allure like a weapon, had they? Who'd painted her face like a courtesan and squeezed her body into clothes bought solely for the intention of showing off her fabulous physique. But it hadn't worked. Her mother had spent years making herself available to a man who didn't want her and, as Hollie had watched her repeat that humiliating spectacle over and over again, she had vowed she was never going to be like that. Women didn't need a man to define them any more and she was going to live her life on *her* terms.

She cleared away empty glasses and plates and the next time she looked, Maximo Diaz was nowhere to be seen and most of the other guests had begun to drift away. Her heart sank. And that was that. She hadn't even seen him go! Feeling curiously deflated, she brushed up the dropped cocktail sticks and pine needles which littered the floor before making her way back to the basement to change, and by the time she'd bagged up her elf costume, the place was almost empty.

Someone had turned off the flashing Christmas tree lights and the hotel seemed deserted as she left by the staff entrance at the back. But as Hollie stepped out into the dark night, she was unprepared for the rain— or rather, the sudden deluge which was tipping from the sky. With no umbrella and a coat which wasn't particularly waterproof, she was quickly soaked through and her windswept progress to the nearby bus stop didn't provide much in the way of shelter. She looked upwards. Why hadn't the council bothered to repair that gaping hole in the roof?

In vain she scanned the horizon for the welcoming light of the bus and was just contemplating digging out her phone to call a taxi—and to hell with the expense— or even braving the elements and walking home, when a large dark car purred soundlessly down the street and came to a gliding halt beside her.

It wasn't a car she recognised. It was sleek and gleaming and obviously very expensive. A car which looked totally out of place in this tiny Devon town, especially as it was being driven by a chauffeur who wore a peaked cap. But Hollie's heart missed a beat as she identified the powerful figure sitting in the back seat.

The electric window slid down and the shiver which rippled down her spine had less to do with the water slowly soaking through her jacket and more to do with the ebony gaze of Maximo Diaz, which was spearing through her like a dark sword. With a crashing heart she registered his thick black hair and the curve of his sensual mouth, which now twisted in what looked like resignation.

'Get in' was all he said.

# CHAPTER TWO

'WHERE TO?' MAXIMO demanded as the woman slid her damp and shivering body onto the seat beside him and his chauffeur shut the door on the howling night.

'I was on my way h-home.'

'I'd kind of worked that out for myself,' he said, steeling himself against the strangely seductive stumble of her words. 'Where do you live?'

'Right on the edge of town, towards the moors.' She turned her face towards his in the dim light of the limousine and he could hear the faint deference in her voice. 'It's very kind of you to give me a lift, Señor Diaz.'

'I'm not known for my kindness,' he told her, with impatient candour. 'But you'd have to be pretty hardhearted to drive past a woman standing alone at a rainy bus stop on a night like this.' He stared at the raindrops which glittered on her pale cheeks and lowered his voice. 'The question is whether you want me to drive you home, or did your mother warn you never to accept lifts from strangers?'

'You're not exactly a stranger, are you?' she answered primly. 'And since you're offering, then I'll ac-

cept. Thank you. It's a rotten night and it really is very...
nice of you.'

*Nice* as well as kind? Maximo almost laughed as he
leaned forward to tap the glass and the big car moved
forward. When was the last time he'd been described in
such glowing terms? The nurses who had cared for his
mother in her final days would certainly never have sub-
scribed to such a favourable opinion, but their views on
the world had been as black and white as the habits they
wore. Nice sons did not neglect their dying mother, nor
remain dry-eyed as she shuddered out her last breath.

'Anyway, you can call me Maximo. And put on your
seat belt,' he ordered, dragging his thoughts back from
the painful past to the woman still shivering beside him.

'I'm trying.'

Waving away her fumbling fingers, he leaned over
to slot in her seat belt and as he again caught a drift of
scent which was more soap than perfume, he wondered
if his behaviour really *was* motivated by a stab of chiv-
alry and nothing more. Because wasn't the truth that tonight he had wanted her—and not in some hypothetical
role as his ideal secretarial assistant? Hell, no. Tonight,
all the softness and sweetness he'd previously associated with her had collided with a totally unexpected
raunchy version, which had planted desire stubbornly
in his mind. And he hadn't seemed able to shift it...

Either way, he hadn't intended to take it any further,
for what would be the point? She was a small-town
woman and he was just...passing through. He didn't do
one-night stands. He never had, for all kinds of reasons.
They were too messy and had the potential to be complicated, and complicated was something he avoided

at all cost. So he had left the hotel and the humdrum party and convinced himself he would quickly forget her—at least until next time he ran into her, if indeed he did. Only by then, she would be back to normal. He wouldn't be dazzled by that very obvious visual stimulant of a short, figure-hugging dress, because she would be back in her drab clothes—barely meriting a second glance as he signed off on his castle purchase. And that would be an end to it. *Adios.* He wasn't intending to stay in this claustrophobic town for a second longer than he needed to. He would sign on the dotted line, put his deal into rapid motion—and nobody would see him for dust.

And then fate had conspired to put her directly in his path—quite literally. No longer a red-and-white-stockinged elf, but a wet and bedraggled woman standing by the roadside. Shivering.

'You're cold,' he observed.

'A bit.'

Commanding his driver in Spanish to increase the heat, he turned to her.

'How's that? Any better?'

'Much better.' She wriggled around in the seat a little. 'It's weird but even the seat feels warm.'

'That's because it's heated.'

'Your car seat has a *heater*?'

'It's hardly at the cutting edge of invention,' he said drily. 'Most new cars do.'

There was silence for a moment.

'I've never owned a car.'

'You're kidding?'

'No.' She shook her head and a few raindrops sprayed over in his direction. 'There's never really been any reason to have one. I used to live in London, where it's impossible to park, and I don't need one here. We need to turn left, please. Just there, past the lamp post.'

Maximo met his driver's eyes in the rear-view mirror and the man gave a barely perceptible nod of comprehension as he started to negotiate the turn. 'So how do you manage without one?'

'Oh, it's easy enough. I walk—when the weather's fine. Or I use my bike. These country roads around here are glorious in the springtime.'

Inadvertently, an image strayed into his mind of a woman on a bicycle, her long shiny hair flowing behind her, while pale flowers sprang in drifts along the hedgerows. He had just allowed this uncharacteristically romantic fantasy to incorporate an element of birdsong, when he heard her teeth begin to chatter.

'You're still cold,' he observed.

'Yes. But we're here now. It's the last house—just before the road turns into a mud track,' she was saying, pointing towards a small, darkened house in the distance. 'That's right. Stop just here.'

The car drew to a halt and Maximo saw the chauffeur unclip his seat belt, obviously intending to open the car door, but something compelled him to halt his action with a terse command.

'*Permitame...*' Maximo murmured, getting out and going to Hollie's side of the car. And even while he was opening the door for her, he was telling himself there was no need to behave like some old-fashioned doorman—not when he'd already played the Good Samaritan and given her a lift home. But somehow he wasn't interested in listening to reason and indeed, he seemed impervious to the hard lash of rain on his face.

'You're getting wet!' she protested.

'I'll survive.'

That look of hesitation was back on her face again. 'Would you…?' She glanced up at the darkened cottage and then back at him as if summoning up a courage she didn't normally call on. 'Would you like to come in, for a cup of coffee? Just as my way of saying thank you? No, that's an absolutely stupid suggestion. I don't know why I made it. Forget it. Forget I said anything.' She shook her head as if embarrassed. 'I'm sure you have somewhere else you need to be.'

He saw the doubt which crossed her face, echoing the ones which were proliferating inside his own head, because this wasn't his style. Not at all. He didn't frequent houses like this and he didn't know women like her. Not any more. He'd left the world of mediocrity behind him a long time ago and had never looked back.

'Actually, there's nowhere I need to be right now and I'd love a cup of coffee. But quickly,' he amended. 'Before both of us get any wetter.'

As he followed her up the narrow path Maximo told himself it wasn't too late to change his mind. He could get his driver to speed out of town, return to his luxury hotel and lose himself in some work—maybe even call that model who'd been texting him for months. The Christmas elf would let herself into her little home, take off her dripping coat—and that would be that. She would be a little disappointed, yes, and even he might experience the briefest of pangs himself, but it would soon pass. He'd never met a woman he would miss if he never saw her again.

Dipping his head to enter the tiny house, he felt the icy temperature hit him. Did she notice his shoulders bunch against the chilly blast as he closed the door behind him?

'I know. It's freezing. I keep the heating off when I'm not here,' she explained, giving a slightly nervous laugh as she switched on a tall lamp.

He didn't need to ask why. She might claim to be nobly conserving energy as everyone was supposed to be doing these days, but he suspected the real reason was a lack of cash. Why else would she be doing more than one job and living in such humble surroundings? He looked around the room, observing the faded rug on the hearth and noticing that the thin curtains she drew across the window didn't quite meet in the middle. Yet the cushions on the sofa looked home-made and a dark red lily in a pot on the table looked almost startling in its simple beauty. And something about the limitations of the room suddenly seemed achingly familiar to him, even though he had grown up in the north-west of Spain and this was England.

He felt the twist of his heart, for it was a long time since he had been anywhere which wasn't five-star. He had embraced luxury for so long that he'd thought those impoverished memories had vanished into the dark abyss of time. Forgotten. For a long time he'd wanted to forget them—no, had *needed* to forget them—but now they came rushing back in an acrid stream.

He remembered the cold and the hunger. The proud need to survive without letting people know your sweater wasn't thick enough, or that your boots had holes in them. He remembered the slow seep of water making his feet wet and cold. And wasn't that the craziest thing of all—that you sometimes found yourself hungering for the things you no longer had, even if they were bad things? So that when he'd been poor he had craved nothing but wealth and now he had all the money he could ever use, wasn't he guilty of sentimentalising the hardships of the past?

'I'll make you some coffee.'

Her soft words broke into his reverie, her expression criss-crossed with anxiety. Perhaps she'd seen the tension on his face and had interpreted it as disapproval. Maybe that was why she was looking as if she regretted her decision to invite him here. Had he appeared to be *judging* her, when he had no right to judge anyone?

Except maybe himself.

'No,' he said. 'Get yourself dry first. The coffee can wait.'

'But—'

'Just do it,' he reaffirmed harshly.

Unable—or unwilling—to ignore the deep mastery in the Spaniard's voice, Hollie nodded and ran upstairs, her heart pounding with excitement, and started stripping off her sodden clothes, bundling her damp tights into the laundry basket and searching around for something suitable to wear. As her fingertips halted on her best woollen dress, she thought how weird it was to think of Maximo Diaz downstairs, because the only men who ever stepped over the threshold were tradespeople commissioned by her landlord to repair the aging and rather dodgy appliances.

She knew her self-contained behaviour meant she was often regarded as something of an oddity and there were a million reasons she gave to herself and others when asked why she didn't socialise much. She didn't have a lot of spare cash, because she was saving up to start her own business. She hadn't lived here very long, so she didn't know many people. These things were true, but weren't the whole story. The real reason was that her solitary life made her feel safe and protected. It didn't leave her open to pain or deception, or having her life messed up by somebody else.

Yet she had broken the habit of a lifetime and invited Maximo Diaz into her home, hadn't she? A world-famous billionaire financier. She was surprised she'd had the nerve and even more surprised when he'd accepted. And now she had to go down and face him and say... *what*? What on earth did she have in common with the Spanish billionaire?

Yet even though part of her was regretting her impulsiveness, she couldn't deny the slow curl of excitement which was unfurling somewhere low in her stomach. Was it wrong to feel this way about someone she barely knew? She stared in the mirror, her hand automatically reaching for something to tie her hair up, but at the last minute her hand fell back and she left it loose and streaming down her back as she closed her bedroom door behind her.

The creak of the stairs should have warned him she was on her way back down but Maximo didn't appear to have heard her and for a moment Hollie stood immobile on the foot of the stairs. And suddenly it was as though someone had waved a magic wand and filled her ordinary little sitting room with unexpected life and colour, and Maximo Diaz was at the blazing heart of it.

He had lit the fire. Removed his smart suit jacket and put it on the sofa to coax a blaze from the sometimes stubborn little wood-burning stove. Behind the small glass doors, orange flames were licking upwards from the applewood logs and already a blanket of heat was beginning to seep out into the room. Had she thought that a man so rich and so privileged would be unwilling to get his hands dirty? Yes, she had. But it was his stance which surprised her most, for he was sitting back on his heels on the old hearthrug as if he were perfectly comfortable to find himself there. He seemed lost in thought as the flames flickered shadows over his aristocratic profile.

Hollie felt another ripple of excitement whispering over her skin—a sensation as unsettling as that low clench of heat unfurling inside her. She knew she ought to say something but she didn't want to break the spell. At least, not yet. Because surely any minute now he would come to his senses. He would suddenly realise that his driver was waiting in the car outside and it was time to excuse himself.

Silently, she went into the kitchen and made a pot of coffee, which she carried back into the sitting room, and when he glanced up and saw her, something unrecognisable gleamed in the ebony abyss of his eyes. Something which made her feel as shivery as before, as if she were standing outside in the rain again.

Was she imagining it?

Was she imagining the glint of approval as he ran his narrow-eyed gaze over her?

'Come and sit by the fire,' he said.

His rich voice washed over her like dark silk, as Hollie acknowledged what sounded like a direct order. Did he always assume such an air of rightful dominance, she wondered—and was it wrong to find that more than a little exciting? She put the tray down and sank onto the floor beside him and wondered if she was getting herself into something outside her experience, which a sensible person should steer clear of. But she was cold, the fire was hot and the coffee smelt unbearably good. And surely she wasn't misguided enough to think that Maximo Diaz was actually going to make a pass at her!

'Maybe I should have offered you wine,' she ventured.

'Is that what you want?'

She shook her head. She was already distracted by his proximity—wine was the last thing she needed. 'Good heavens, no,' she said briskly. 'This will be fine. Just so long as it doesn't keep you awake.'

His lips curved into a mocking smile. He looked as if he was about to make a comment, then seemed to change his mind, leaning back against the old armchair behind him and spreading his long legs out in front of him.

For a moment everything in the room became very still—like the preternatural calm which sometimes comes before a storm. The crackle of the fire and the pounding of her heart were the only sounds Hollie could hear and, in the soft light, his eyes looked ebony-dark as he turned his head to study her.

'Have you lived here long?' he questioned.

'Just over a year now. I lived in London before that.'

'Where you didn't have a car.'

She beamed, pleased he'd remembered. 'That's right.'

'So what was the lure of a place like Trescombe?'

Hollie wondered how to answer him. No need to tell him she'd been ripped off. Or that a supposed good friendship had hit the skids as a result. Nobody wanted to hear that kind of downbeat detail and she certainly didn't want to start re-evaluating whether she'd been a hopeless judge of character. And wasn't her new-found motto that she was going to look forward, not back?

'My dream has always been to run a traditional English tea shop,' she told him. 'And when London didn't work out, I heard about an opportunity opening up down here. There's a great site in the town but it won't be available until springtime and until that happens I need regular work so I can save up as much as possible. That's why I'm working for Janette. I'm sorry, I should have asked you before—would you like anything to eat to go with that?'

Reluctantly, Maximo smiled in response to her question. He could sense her eagerness to keep him entertained and knew he ought to cut the visit short rather than get her hopes up, yet he stayed exactly where he was. For the first time in a long time, he felt *comfortable*. Uncharacteristically comfortable. The simply furnished room and warm fire were strangely seductive and so too was her undemanding company. In fact, for someone who was notoriously restless, he might have been able to relax completely—were it not for the undeniable tension which had begun to build in the air between them.

His senses seemed heightened. He could see the

thrust of her breasts against the soft jersey of her dress and the pebbled outline of her nipples. He swallowed. It might have been a while since he'd been intimate with a woman but the subliminal message of desire which Little Miss Christmas was sending his way was unmistakable.

*And it was driving him crazy.*

Was she aware that her eyes grew dark whenever she looked his way, or that she kept trailing the tip of her tongue over her mouth, like an unobserved cat contemplating where its next meal was coming from? And didn't he want to pull her into his arms, to test if those lips tasted as sweet as they looked?

'Why don't you wear your hair down more often?' he said suddenly.

His question seemed to startle her, for she touched her fingers to the silky waves which rippled almost to her waist. 'Because it isn't…' She shrugged. 'I don't know. Practical, I guess.'

'And do you always have to be practical?'

'As much as possible, yes. Life is easier that way,' she asserted, when he continued to look at her. 'You know, more dependable.'

'Really?' he pondered reflectively, the pad of his thumb brushing over the beard-shadowed jut of his jaw—a movement which seemed to fascinate her. 'But surely dependability can get a little boring sometimes. How old are you?'

'Twenty-six,' she said, a little defiantly.

'Don't you ever want to throw caution to the wind and do something unpredictable?'

'I've never really thought about it much, to be honest.'

He noticed that her fingers were trembling, making her coffee cup rattle against the saucer as she quickly put it down on the hearth.

'Well, think about it now,' he said. 'What would you do, for example, if I were to acknowledge the unspoken desire in your eyes and touch you? If I were to brush my fingers against your hair, to discover whether it feels as soft as it looks in the firelight?'

'I can't…' Her words sounded husky and he could see the swallowing movement of her throat. 'I can't imagine you doing something like that.'

'No?' He heard the note of repressed hope in her voice and silently, he answered it, reaching out to imprison a single lock of hair and stroking it between his thumb and forefinger, like a merchant examining a piece of valuable cloth. 'The funny thing is neither can I. But I am. And it does. Like silk, I mean. Rich, dark golden silk.'

'Mr Diaz.'

'I've been thinking about touching you all night long,' he husked unsteadily, skating his palm down over the abundant waves. 'And you like it, don't you? You like me stroking your hair.'

Her shuddered word was barely audible. 'Y-yes.'

For a while he listened to her uneven breathing and felt his own corresponding leap of desire. 'And you know what comes next, don't you?'

She shook her head and gazed at him in silence.

'Yes, you do.'

'Tell me,' she whispered, like a child asking to be told a story.

'I kiss you,' he said, a note of urgency deepening his voice to a growl.

Their eyes met. 'Yes,' she whispered, nodding her head with eager assent. 'Yes, please.'

It was the most innocent yet the most provocative thing he'd ever heard.

And suddenly her hair was a rope and Maximo was using it to guide him towards her waiting lips and he felt his body tense with a sweet and tantalising hunger.

# CHAPTER THREE

MAXIMO WAS KISSING HER until she had started to make mewling little sounds of hunger. Until she was moving her body restlessly against him in a gesture of unspoken need.

She should have been nervous about what was about to happen, but fear was the last thing on Hollie's mind as the Spaniard drew away from her, his black eyes blazing with passion in the glow of the firelight.

He laced his fingers through the fall of her hair, and his breath was warm against her lips as he spoke. 'I think it's time we found ourselves somewhere more comfortable, don't you?'

'Yes, please,' she whispered again, and then wondered if she should at least have gone through the motions of pretending to give it more than a moment's consideration.

But that flicker of apprehension fled as soon as he picked her up and carried her upstairs, like the masterful embodiment of all her forbidden dreams. She could hear the powerful beat of her heart and the creak of the wood as he negotiated the narrow staircase.

'Where's your bedroom?' he demanded, once they'd reached the top.

She supposed now wasn't the time to tell him there was only one bedroom—instead she jerked her head in the direction of the nearest door, wishing she had tidied up a bit more. 'In there.'

But as he kicked it open, Maximo didn't seem to notice the cardigan lying on the chair or the pile of cookery books teetering in a haphazard pile on the bedside table. Instead, he set her down and spoke in a voice which suddenly seemed much more accented than before and more than a little unsteady.

'You are wearing far too many clothes,' he growled, skating his fingertips over her trembling body. 'And part of me wishes you'd kept that crazy costume on so I could have had the pleasure of removing it. I've never undressed an elf before.'

Did that mean he didn't like her woollen dress? Probably—it was undoubtedly very staid in comparison, though comparisons were never a good thing, certainly not in her case. But as he peeled it over her head before efficiently disposing of her tights, Hollie suddenly forgot about her insecurities.

'You're shivering,' he observed.

'The upstairs of this cottage is f-freezing.'

'And is that the only reason you're shivering?'

She liked the teasing note in his voice. Was it that which gave her the courage to hook her hand around the back of his head and brush her lips close to his?

'No,' she whispered. 'Not just that, no.'

His soft laugh was tinged with faint triumph as he

pulled back the duvet and pushed her down onto the mattress. 'So why don't you warm up the bed for me?' he suggested as he pulled the duvet over her. 'While I get out of these clothes.'

Hollie studied him hungrily as he peeled off his sweater, her mouth drying to dust as his fingers slipped to the button of his trousers. She was grateful that the room was in semi-darkness, which successfully hid the burn of her cheeks as, slowly, he slid the zip down. And she didn't avert her gaze, not once. Even when he kicked off his boxer shorts to reveal the powerful shaft of his erection, though it was the first time she had ever seen a naked man before.

He climbed into bed beside her and when he took her in his arms, she felt so warm and so…safe—that she buried her head in his shoulder, overcome by a sudden emotion she couldn't put a name to.

'Mi belleza…' he breathed, exploring her trembling flesh with his fingers until she felt as if she were melting, and then unclipping her bra so that her large breasts came tumbling out. And when he put his mouth to her puckered nipple and sucked, Hollie felt as if she were going to dissolve with pleasure.

How could it be that she wasn't feeling the slightest bit shy? Even though she was wearing nothing but a pair of panties, which were growing damper by the second as she clung to him as if her life depended on it. Because that was what it felt like. As if she hadn't known what it was to be properly alive before Maximo Diaz kissed her. As if she'd die if she didn't get more of him. More of *this*…this fierce flame of desire which was arrowing through her body and setting her on fire, making her feel as if she were on the verge of hurtling towards some place of unimaginable bliss.

'Maximo,' she breathed, her voice sounding slurred and nothing like her voice at all. 'That is so…so *incredible.*'

His dark head lifted its attention from her breast and his eyes grew smoky as he moved up the bed to kiss her again, his tongue nudging inside her parted lips. And Hollie let her tongue fence with his, loving this brand-new intimacy as her breasts pressed eagerly against his bare chest, as if her button-hard nipples were trying to communicate some unspoken need to him. And instantly he answered it, his hand reaching down to run his fingertip over the damp gusset of her panties. She quivered as he brushed against her swollen bud through the sodden material and felt the whisper of his words on her lip.

'And so are you.' He shook his head and swallowed. 'I never imagined you'd be so…'

'So, what?' she questioned breathlessly.

He seemed to recover some of his poise, tugging at the elasticated edge of her plain panties. 'Well, you're a little overdressed, for one thing.'

'Am I?'

'Mmm…' For a moment he grazed another teasing fingertip over her damp panties, which made her squirm with delight and frustration, before sliding them off and allowing them to join the tangle of other clothes which were scattered over the floor of her small bedroom. 'But you are also hot. Surprisingly hot. Like my every fantasy brought to life. Who knew?'

'So are you,' she whispered boldly, splaying her fingers over his bare chest and thinking how rich his olive skin looked in the soft lamplight. Tentatively she rubbed at one of *his* nipples, silently enjoying his corresponding shudder of pleasure which gave her the confidence to return the compliment. 'You are my every fantasy, too.'

For a moment he grew still, then drew his head away from hers. His black eyes were narrowed but there was no mistaking the sudden warning which glinted from their ebony depths. 'But fantasies aren't real,' he said silkily. 'We both know that, don't we?'

'No, of course they're not. Absolutely they're not.' Eager to convey her agreement, Hollie nodded, instinctively knowing what he wanted, or, more importantly, what he *didn't* want. He didn't want her reading too much into this and falling for him and, to be honest, that was the last thing she wanted either. She didn't know much about what made men tick but she'd recognised from the get-go that Maximo Diaz was the last person to hitch her star to. Yes, she'd had a crush on him since the first time they'd met and, yes, that feeling had just grown and grown—but she certainly wasn't alone in feeling that way. That she now found herself naked in bed with him wasn't something she'd imagined would happen, not in her wildest dreams. That it had happened in a way which seemed completely natural made her feel comfortable with her own body for the first time in her life and she was grateful to him for that. So why should she deny herself the inevitable outcome of them being here like this?

Why *should* she?

Always, she'd stuck rigidly to the path of convention, because life had felt safer that way. But nothing was ever completely safe and Maximo had been right. For once she wanted to dabble with impulsiveness instead of dependability. She'd never been in love—never wanted to be in love, for that matter—because she'd witnessed the fallout which could result from investing in such an unreliable emotion. She'd never had a boyfriend who had lasted longer than a month and she'd never been turned on enough to get any further than accepting a couple of mechanical fumbles, which had turned her stomach and made her call an instant halt to them.

She'd thought she was one of those women who just didn't feel physical desire. The kind of woman people used to mock and call frigid. But Maximo Diaz was in the process of demonstrating that there was nothing wrong with her body. Nothing at all. Just so long as she didn't start entertaining any unrealistic expectations of some kind of future with the Spanish tycoon. Because that wasn't just impractical—it was stupid.

She closed her eyes as he sank his lips to hers again and moved his hand between her thighs, and Hollie wrapped her arms tightly around his muscular shoulders as if he were her rock and her anchor. How was it possible to feel this good, with a man's tongue in her mouth and his finger strumming at her bare bud with sweetly accurate intensity? But idle reflection was no longer possible, not when a sudden clench of desire was making her heated body as taut as the string of a newly tuned violin.

'Maximo!' she gasped.

He lifted his head, mockery and passion glinting in his eyes. 'What is it?' he husked.

She wanted to tell him to stop. She wanted to tell him

never to stop. But then it was happening. Her body had started clenching around his finger, with swift and perfect spasms, and she was crying out something which sounded as if it had been torn from somewhere deep inside her, as the world splintered into a kaleidoscope of vivid rainbows.

Consciousness receded and then came back again in a slow and sensual comedown. She was dimly aware of him watching her and waiting for her body to grow still. He kissed each tingling nipple in turn and then reached for something he must have put on the locker, which she assumed must be a condom. Because Hollie knew the rules—even if she'd never had to follow them before now—and sex had to be safe.

But his hands seemed to be unsteady as he unpeeled the foil and she watched like a hungry voyeur as he slid the rubber down over his erect shaft. Part of her was wondering why she wasn't experiencing a faint wrench of embarrassment, or some element of misgiving at the reality of what was about to happen. But Hollie felt none of those things. Her current state of being was so dreamy and so...*complete* that she simply opened her arms wide as Maximo came to lie down on top of her, welcoming the warm weight of his body.

He was hard and honed and powerful, yet his skin was silky and warm. She was aware of his rigid hardness pressing against her belly and she could feel her thighs opening for him, as if some inner knowledge was orchestrating her movements, making someone with no experience seem as if she knew exactly what she was doing. He gave a low laugh as he positioned himself over her, his lips brushing over hers as she felt his hard tip seeking entry.

'Do you want me, *mi belleza*?'

'*Sí,*' she answered and this made him smile, but as he thrust inside her the smile faded, his eyes briefly closing before he opened them again.

She could feel the sudden tension in his body as he stared at her with a question furrowing his brow.

'Your first time?' he verified.

She nodded, wondering if she'd imagined the note of disbelief in his voice, the lump in her throat making words impossible, terrified he wouldn't want her now he knew that nobody else ever had.

But in that she was wrong.

Very wrong.

Very deliberately, he changed his position, reaching underneath her to cushion her fleshy buttocks with the palms of his hands and bring her thighs up to his hips, so that their bodies seemed even closer than before. He kissed her long and he kissed her hard and just the feel of his mouth on hers was enough to make her relax into what was happening as her body adjusted around him and his incredible width. He began to move again, each thrust seeming to fill her completely—and the sensation of his flesh inside her flesh, of somehow being at *one* with him, blew her mind as nothing ever had before.

Did she wrap her legs around his waist to make his penetration even deeper, or had he guided her into doing that? Hollie wasn't sure. The only thing she was sure of was that those feelings were building up inside her again, taking her higher and higher towards another incredible peak. And then she reached it. Almost without expecting to, she stumbled over the edge and went into free fall and Hollie screamed out her pleasure— she who had never screamed in her life. As she began to spasm around him, she could feel his body begin to buck with pleasure as he bit out words in fractured Spanish—harsh sounds which seemed to split the night.

His movements seemed to go on and on and never had she been so aware of each and every sensation. She could feel the ragged pull of oxygen into her lungs as she tried to steady her breathing. She could hear the muffled pounding of her heart. There was a fine sheen of sweat on Maximo's shoulders and she could detect a raw and very distinctive masculine scent in the air. And now he was heavy against her—as heavy as her eyelids, which felt as if they had been weighted with lead. A sigh fluttered from her lips as she snuggled into his arms and she must have dozed off. Perhaps he did too, for when she woke it was to the realisation that he was growing hard inside her again and Hollie gave a hungry little yelp of longing. Her arms tightened around him and as she began to writhe against him, she could hear herself making wordless sounds of demand against his skin.

'No.' Cutting short her next wriggle of anticipation with a curt order, he carefully withdrew from her.

She was aware of him rolling away and then, to her horror—he carefully peeled off the condom before getting out of bed. His black hair was ruffled as he stared down at her, his jet eyes unreadable as their gazes clashed.

'Where's the bathroom?'

Startled, Hollie searched her befuddled brain for a

coherent response. 'J-just along the corridor. You can't miss it.'

After he'd gone, she just lay there, her thoughts in a muddle. At first it shamed her to think she'd just been intimate with a man who didn't even know the layout of her house, but Hollie quickly remonstrated with herself. She wasn't going to feel *any* kind of shame—otherwise what would be the point? And she certainly wasn't going to start getting squeamish and wonder what he'd done with the condom. In fact, she refused to feel any negativity at all about what had just happened. She'd just had sex with a man she fancied very much and it had been amazing. Women the world over did this sort of thing all the time. She had joined the party at last—she certainly hadn't done anything *wrong*.

Sitting up in bed, she smoothed down the mussed tumble of her hair and then Maximo walked back into the room—or maybe she should say *sauntered*—looking totally comfortable with his own nakedness, in all its olive-dark gloriousness. She half expected him to reach for his clothes and start getting dressed, and she told herself she would be okay with that—because what choice did she have?—but to her astonishment, he climbed right back into bed beside her. And then Hollie experienced a little shiver of self-recrimination. Did she think so little of herself that she'd thought he would be out of there as fast as his legs could carry her?

She turned to face him, waiting for him to take the lead, because what did a woman *do* in a situation like this? She had no idea and no experience. Was she supposed to praise him, or thank him for the most incredible happening of her entire life? Or act all cool, as if it were no big deal? Why didn't some enterprising person write a sexual etiquette book for virgins? she wondered.

He lay down beside her and for a moment she thought he was about to lean over and kiss her again and, oh, how she wished he would. But instead, he pushed away some of the hair which had fallen into her face and let his gaze scan over her like a dark searchlight.

'Your first time,' he said again.

It was half statement and half question. 'That's right,' Hollie replied, swallowing down her sudden nervousness that this was going to turn into some sort of interrogation session and she would come over as a freak. 'Do you mind?'

'Mind?' He seemed to mull this over in his head. 'Why should I mind? You're an adult. You have free will. You came to a decision that you wanted to have sex with me. I'm flattered, of course, and more than a little interested to know why.'

She wondered if he was fishing for compliments. Did he want her to say he was so gorgeous that she hadn't been able to resist him? *And wouldn't that have been the truth?* But Maximo Diaz needed no boost for his ego, not from her. Certainly not when he was lying there, dissecting what had just happened between them with all the cool detachment of a scientist in the lab. 'Does there have to be a reason?'

He shrugged and the ripple of muscle beneath his broad shoulders was more than a little distracting.

'Most women wait—though I guess you've waited quite a long time already—for a long-term relationship in which they can feel comfortable. Something which has a little more depth.' He paused. 'And history.'

It sounded like an accusation. Or a reproach. Was he somehow *disappointed* that she hadn't made him wait?
'Maybe I'm not most women.'

'No. Maybe you're not. In fact, I would take that as a given. You are certainly very surprising. You confounded my expectations which, believe me, doesn't happen very often.' He gave a short laugh before fixing her with that glittering black gaze again, their bodies still very close, the slick of his sweat-sheened skin sticky against hers. 'So which is the real you, I wonder—the efficient mouse who slaves away behind her desk, or the minxy hostess in fancy dress who wiggles her bottom so provocatively when she walks?'

'It was the shoes which made me walk that way.'

'Ah, so we must blame the shoes, must we?' he questioned gravely.

'I borrowed them,' she explained, when she saw the glint of mockery in his eyes. 'Oh. I see. You're teasing me.'

'Yes, I am teasing you, *mia belleza*,' he said, and his voice suddenly deepened into a velvety note of intent. 'But not for very much longer, because teasing inevitably provokes desire. What I would most like to do to you right now is to kiss you again and then to—'

'Make love?' she put in eagerly, then could have kicked herself for her naivety, which was surely responsible for the sudden tension which had entered his body.

'Well, that is one way of describing what we are about to do, though you need to remember that this has nothing to do with love.' His golden olive features hardened. 'Love is a concept invented by society. As a bribe, or a threat. As a marketing tool used by big businesses. Or as a method of control—a way of regulating women's behaviour.'

Hollie opened her mouth to object to what sounded like pure cynicism, until she realised that she agreed with him. Every single word. Hadn't her own mother carried her supposed 'love' for her father around with her like some dark jewel pressed close to her heart—guarding it and polishing it and making it more important than anything else in her life, including her own daughter?

'What *does* it have to do with, then?' she questioned boldly, because why wouldn't she be bold when she had come this far? When she was naked and glowing with physical satisfaction, even though the turn of the conversation was proving a little too raw for her liking. But then the insistent little clench deep at her core made her realise that she would prefer to stop talking altogether, and start kissing...

Did he read her body language? Was that why he reached out to stroke her face, his thumb whispering to her neck, where it lingered on the frantic little pulse which was beating there? Hollie shivered as he continued with his journey and it seemed to take for ever before he reached her nipple, his eyes not leaving hers as he massaged its diamond hardness, a small smile playing at the edges of his lips as it pebbled beneath his thumb. And she realised he still hadn't answered her question.

'It has to do with sensation. With feeling,' he answered, as if he'd read her mind. 'And this is the best feeling in the world. Wouldn't you agree?'

'Yes.' There was a short silence while she fought and

lost the battle to let the subject go. 'But you've felt it before, I suppose? Probably lots of times.'

He didn't deny it. 'Of course. But not for a while.'

She wanted to ask, but Hollie told herself it was none of her business. That his answers might not be what she wanted to hear. And when she didn't say anything—which seemed to surprise him—he moved closer. So close that at the points where their bodies connected, she could feel goosebumps icing her skin.

'So why don't we enjoy what we have? Just for tonight,' he added softly. 'I could send my chauffeur home and we could enjoy a little more uncomplicated pleasure. I could show you many different ways to achieve orgasm. We could explore and enjoy each other's bodies, because yours is...'

Hollie felt a feeling of power as his finger drifted down over her sternum, to lie possessively on the soft flesh of her belly. 'Mine is what?' she questioned breathlessly, as if she had conversations about the nature of desire every day of the week.

'*Esta magnifica.* So soft, so womanly, so full,' he husked, beginning to knead her flesh with his fingers and making her want to moan with delight. 'I want to be inside you again. Deep inside you. As many times as I can. Do you want that, too?'

Of course she did and she nodded eagerly. Who wouldn't want it? But his husky question came with a coded warning. *Just for tonight*, he had emphasised. Which meant she mustn't expect anything more. His words weren't the stuff of dreams or fairy tales, but that didn't mean she had to shoot them down in flames. At least he was being honest with her. At least he wasn't playing games and messing with her head, which meant something to a person who had been brought up to believe that men were nothing but inveterate liars. And now he was reaching down for his discarded trousers and sliding his phone from the pocket to have a rapid conversation in Spanish, presumably with his chauffeur, laughing briefly before hanging up. What was he laughing about? she wondered. But suddenly her slight paranoia was forgotten because he was pulling another condom from his wallet and in that moment Hollie felt properly grown-up for the first time in her life.

She was having sex! The amazing Spaniard had already given her, not one, but two orgasms—and he was planning on giving her some more! Christmas really had come early!

She settled back against the pillows, anticipation shivering her skin as he began to stroke her, with that look of dark intent on his face which made her melt inside. And then he ruined it all, as he brushed his lips over hers.

'Do you realise,' he mused, his hand reaching comfortably for her breast, 'that I don't even know your name?'

# CHAPTER FOUR

HOLLIE'S MOUTH DRIED as she waited. She was trembling. Of course, she was trembling. Who wouldn't be in her situation?

She closed her eyes, uttering some kind of wordless prayer, but when her lids fluttered open, her wish had not been granted. Nothing had changed. She was still staring through the window of her tiny cottage at the dark night outside and the Christmas lights in the window of the house opposite. She was still exactly the same woman she'd been seconds ago.

She swallowed.

Pregnant.

Pregnant with the Spanish tycoon's baby.

Her heart pounding, she knew she couldn't keep putting off the inevitable. She needed to tell Maximo and the longer it went on, the harder it seemed to be.

She was still finding it hard to get her head around what she'd done. After a lifetime of being a virgin, she'd fallen into bed with a man who was practically a stranger. She couldn't have found a more unsuitable man to be her first lover, if she'd tried. An international playboy who had seemed all too eager to put distance between them once their brief encounter was over.

The night had not ended on a particularly good note. She'd hoped he might stay on for a while next morning. She'd thought about making him pancakes for breakfast, with honey or cheese. Or an omelette, maybe—because didn't the Spanish use a lot of eggs in their cooking? Perhaps she'd been secretly hoping to impress him with her undoubted skill at all things cuisine—the way to a man's heart and all that. But no. He had climbed out of bed, all glorious and glowing and naked, when the dawn light had been nothing but a glimmer on the horizon. She must have slipped back into sleep because the next time her eyelids had fluttered open, he had been fully dressed and maybe she should have guessed what was coming from the terse tone of his words.

'I'd better go.'

'Oh. Must you?' Her voice had been little more than a murmur, but afterwards she wondered if she'd sounded a little *needy*.

'I'm afraid I must. I've called my chauffeur to come and pick me up. I have a meeting.'

She remembered thinking it was very early to be having a meeting and then, drugged with satiation and satisfaction, she had fallen into a deep sleep and when she'd woken up, he had gone.

It had taken nearly a week for her to realise Maximo wasn't going to contact her again. He had told her he wouldn't but hadn't there been a stupid glimmer of hope which had taken up stubborn residence in her mind and made her hope he might change his mind? But there had been no phone call. No flowers. No unexpected dropping in at the estate agency to ask whether she might happen to be free for lunch—and of course she would have said yes, because her daily home-made sandwich, which reposed at the bottom of the office fridge, could easily be eaten another day.

But Maximo had done none of these things. The purchase of his castle was now complete and everyone in the town was breathlessly waiting for the refurbishment to begin, when he would turn it into the most talked about hotel in Devon to add to his prestigious group. She assumed that was why he was here today. She'd heard he was having high-powered meetings in the nearby city of Exeter and so, when Janette had left the office to have her nails painted, Hollie had hunted around for the tycoon's telephone number and had sent him a text, asking if she could see him.

His answer hadn't exactly boosted her confidence, or her resolve. It had been blunt and to the point. Some people might even have called it rude.

I'm very busy.

She wished she could have told him to take a running jump, but that was exactly what he would like her to do, she reminded herself bitterly. Her finger had been shaking with rage and she had wasted time correcting several typos as she had furiously tapped out a response.

I'm sure you are, but I need to see you.

She'd been forced to wait for a whole hour before the reluctant reply had come winging back.

I can give you half an hour at six p.m. Where?

That had made her hesitate. Neutral territory would be best. But she couldn't risk any kind of scene, not in a town this small where people would talk. And so even though uncomfortable memories of last time he had visited her cottage wouldn't seem to leave her alone, Hollie forced herself to reply.

Can you come to my cottage? I assume you remember where it is?

And the terse rejoinder.

I'll see you there.

It seemed insane to think about it now, but she'd actually made some biscuits in preparation for his visit, which were currently sitting on her best china plate in the kitchen. She'd told herself it was more to give herself something to do, rather than pacing the floor as she waited for the smooth purr of his limousine. But the insane truth was that she was making shortbread because she knew he liked it.

It was pathetic, really. Did she honestly imagine that the sugary cookie was going to make him smile and tell her everything was going to be okay, and he was fine with the fact that she was carrying his baby after what was only ever supposed to be a one-night stand?

She turned away from the window and glanced around the small sitting room, her gaze coming to rest on the miniature Christmas tree she'd forced herself to decorate, even though she hadn't been feeling remotely festive at the time. Its rainbow lights were pretty and the little baubles she'd crafted herself usually filled her heart with seasonal joy as she dangled them from the pine branches. But she had been so bogged down by a feeling of dread at what she was about to do that not even holiday decorations had been able to lighten her mood.

She heard the sound of a powerful engine and quickly ducked away from the window, not wanting to be seen watching and waiting, like some kind of crazed stalker from a horror film. She drew in a deep breath as she heard the approaching crunch of footsteps and slowly expelled it as the doorbell jangled.

Silently counting to three, Hollie walked calmly towards the door, trying to mentally prepare herself for the sight of Maximo Diaz as it swung open. And even though she had thought about him every single day since their night of passion, Hollie was still unprepared for the visceral impact of seeing him again.

He looked…

Her heart rate, which had already been elevated, now began to pick up into a deafening crescendo as she stared at him.

He looked…incredible.

Dressed entirely in black, he wore jeans and a buttery leather jacket, beneath which was a sweater so soft it could only have been made from cashmere. But that was the only soft thing about him. His body was hard and his face was even harder. Black eyes studied her as coldly as chips of jet and those wickedly sensual lips were set and unsmiling. How weird it was to think of all the pleasures those lips had showered on her while they'd been in bed together, when now they seemed to flatten at the edges with a look of faint disdain. Or was that her imagination?

Hollie knew she had to pull herself together. She couldn't keep catastrophising or trying to get inside his head. She had to act as normally as possible, although that was never going to be easy given what she was about to tell him. How would she have spoken to him if she hadn't had sex with him? How did she used to speak to him when he came into the office, during those easy, uncomplicated days before she'd been stupid enough to allow him to seduce her? With an enormous effort, she fixed a bright smile to her lips, aware of the stupidity of her greeting even as it tumbled from her.

'Good afternoon, Señor Diaz!'

Maximo tried very hard not to react to the instinctive punch to his gut as he studied the woman standing before him. He should be on his guard after her rather embarrassing determination to see him, yet all he could think about was her pale, soft flesh and the thickness of her shiny golden-brown hair as it had tumbled down over her bare breasts. Was that unwanted reaction responsible for his drawled words, which weren't the words he intended? 'Don't you think such formality is a little inappropriate, in view of what happened?'

'Even though you didn't even know my name at the time?' she answered quickly.

Maximo winced. She was right. How had that even *happened*? He still wasn't sure, and looking at her now provided no easy answers. The provocative minx in the towering red heels and thigh-skimming green dress was nothing but a distant memory, for she'd reverted back to her usual sensible look. Her magnificent hair was tied back into a tight bun and her lips were bare. She wore a neat skirt and forgettable sweater, which had obviously not been bought with the intention of emphasising her curves, and her brown leather boots had seen better days. They were obviously old boots which had been carefully polished—and something about that recognition of someone who was 'making do' struck a raw and distant chord deep inside him. She looked unremarkable, yet... He frowned. Wasn't there a glowing inner quality about her, which seemed to transcend her rather drab appearance?

'But I do know your name now,' he said, attempting a placatory smile. 'Hollie.'

'Hollie Walker,' she supplied crisply and then blushed, and that only seemed to emphasise her innocence.

Had he really had sex with her? Taken her virginity in one smooth and delicious thrust? Yes, he had. And it had been amazing. No. That wasn't quite accurate. It had been nothing short of sensational. Turned on and beguiled by those long legs and cascading hair and the startlingly dramatic change in her appearance, Maximo had succumbed to a one-night stand in a way he hadn't done since his teenage years. Her innocence had come as a shock and he still wasn't quite sure why he hadn't extricated himself from the situation as quickly as possible after that first time, doing them both a favour and recognising that someone like him was bad news for a small-town woman like her.

But he hadn't. He had carried on losing himself inside her sweet, tight body for most of the night, over and over again. And when they'd eventually run out of condoms—something which had never happened to him before—he had pleasured her in other ways. He had used his tongue and his fingers and, at one point, an ice cube from the freezer downstairs, he recalled—so that the memory of her shuddered cries of fulfilment had stubbornly lodged themselves in his brain for days afterwards. He'd had difficulty forgetting the way she'd cried out his name and the way her soft thighs had wrapped themselves around his thrusting back. He'd had difficulty concentrating on work too, drifting off into sensual daydreams at the slightest provocation, until he had forced himself to stop thinking about her.

But none of those things addressed his immediate concerns and now a feeling of wariness crept over him as he looked into Hollie Walker's face. Because, why had she asked to see him? Deliberately pushing away the brief cloud of darkness which hovered on the edge of his mind, he met her gaze with a look of polite enquiry.

'So. What can I do for you, Hollie? I meant it when I told you I was busy. There are things I need to get finished before Christmas, which is in a few days' time, as you clearly know.' He forced himself to give a curt nod of acknowledgement in the direction of the smallest tree he had ever seen.

Her mouth was working and her previously glowing complexion had paled. 'There's no easy way to say this. I wish there was.' She clenched her hands into two fists and squeezed them tight until the knuckles grew white. 'I'm pregnant, Maximo,' she husked. 'I'm going to have your baby.'

The world spun and a dull sound inside his head threatened to deafen him. For a minute Maximo thought he must be dreaming, but her trembling body and white face were real enough and told their own story.

For this was no dream. The nightmare had become real.

'You can't be.' His words were icy but the anger growing inside him felt hot and vital and all-consuming. 'We took precautions.'

'Well, obviously those precautions didn't work,' she said. 'Look, I realise this has come as a complete shock to you—'

'But clearly not to you.' He frowned as he did some rapid mental calculations. 'We had sex in—'

'October,' she supplied swiftly, her cheeks flaming. 'Just in case you're muddling me with someone else.'

'There hasn't been anyone else,' he snapped before wondering why on earth he had told her *that*. Because wouldn't it give her more power than she already had if she realised that every other woman had left him cold since he'd exited her bed, that wet dawn morning? Would she mistakenly start thinking she was special, or different?

'Oh. Right,' she said, looking startled.

His gaze skated over her as it had done with so many women in the past, but for once there was only one place it was focussed on. Not on her hair or lips or the curve of her breasts, but on her abdomen. 'Pregnant,' he repeated, as if affirming what his naked eye could not see.

'Eleven weeks.'

He felt as if he were speaking in a language he didn't really understand. As if he had entered a world which was now defined by dates. 'You certainly took your time telling me.'

She nodded. 'I know. I didn't realise for a while. At first I couldn't believe it, because I thought we were so careful. I made myself do three tests, until eventually I had to accept the evidence of what I found. And you weren't around to tell, Maximo. You were supposed to be coming back to Trescombe. Everyone thought work was going to start on the castle before Christmas—'

'What work?' he demanded.

'Well, you're turning it back into a hotel, aren't you? It's been the talk of the town for months. But you just… disappeared.'

'I have a global business,' he informed her coldly. 'Which seems to have gone into overdrive lately.'

'And was that…?' Her face was screwed up and she seemed to be forcing herself to ask the question. 'Was that the only reason?'

Maximo's mouth hardened. Wasn't it better she knew? Better to trample on her foolish dreams rather than to allow them to flourish unchecked? 'Not the only reason, no. If you must know I thought that creating space between us would ensure you didn't get the wrong idea about what had happened. I didn't want you building castles in the air.'

'You're the one with the interest in castles, Maximo,' she said coldly. 'I told you at the time I was okay with it.'

'Women say all kinds of things they don't mean, Hollie. They say them to save face, or sometimes to convince themselves that they actually believe them.'

She glared at him. 'And you were so certain I'd be a thorn in your side with my unwanted devotion that you didn't want to risk a return visit, is that it? Were you worried I'd believe I was hopelessly in love with you?'

'That was always a possibility.'

'Even though you're proving to be so arrogant and unlikeable?'

He shrugged. 'You were an innocent. A virgin. Sometimes a woman's first experience of sex can warp her judgement, particularly if it was as good as yours was. I'd warned you what kind of man I was but I wasn't sure whether you wanted to believe it. But all that is irrelevant now.'

He realised she was looking at him and the reproach on her flushed face suggested she had been hurt by his condemnatory assessment of their night together. But he wasn't going to tell lies in order to spare her feelings. She needed to know the truth, because surely that would limit the painful repercussions of a situation he had been so determined not to create during his own lifetime. The legacy of his upbringing was bitter enough to taint him for ever and he didn't want to feel trapped. Not ever again.

'I've never wanted marriage or children,' he bit out. 'And while the first is within my power to control, the second is clearly not.'

'But I'm not asking you for anything!' she declared furiously, her fists still clenched and looking as if she would like to use them to punch him. 'I can manage perfectly well on my own.'

He glanced around the small room. At the hand-knitted blanket on the battered sofa. At tired-looking walls, which even the rainbow glow from the fairy lights on the Christmas tree couldn't quite disguise.

He remembered the narrow bed in the cold bedroom upstairs, where he had torn the clothes from his body with the eagerness of a boy who had never had sex before. And the speed with which he had made his escape the following morning, issuing a terse directive to his chauffeur to get him the hell out of there when the car had arrived.

And all he could think was—what had he *done*?

'What, here?' he demanded. 'You think you can bring up this baby here, in a place like this?'

'Of course I can! It may not be grand and I may not have a lot of spare cash, but I will manage. I don't know how, but I will. I'm not deluding myself that it's going to be easy, but I'm not afraid of hard work. It won't hurt me to scrimp and save and go without—but there's one thing my baby will never go short of, and that's love!'

An expression of such fierce protectiveness came over her face, that Maximo found himself unexpectedly humbled by her fervour, until he reminded himself that words were cheap. 'Very admirable,' he drawled.

'I'm not seeking your approval.' Angrily, she shook her head. 'In fact, I don't want anything from you, Maximo Diaz. Because I don't need you! Do you understand?'

But he shook his head, as if she hadn't spoken. 'I am not dishonourable enough to desert you in your time of need, just as long as your expectations don't exceed what I am prepared to offer you,' he bit out, withdrawing his wallet from his inside pocket and extracting a business card. He slapped the card down beside the Christmas tree with more force than he had intended, causing the flimsy baubles to jangle before striding towards the front door, barely able to contain the anger which was simmering up inside him.

He pulled open the door. 'You can telephone my office and they will give you contact details of my lawyer, who will fine-tune all the necessary arrangements,' he concluded icily. 'You will have the necessary funds to employ nannies, chauffeurs, cleaners—whatever it is you think you might need to make your life easier once you have a child. But there is one thing you're never going to get, Hollie—at least, not from me—and that's a father for your baby.'

# CHAPTER FIVE

'HOLLIE, ARE YOU even listening to what I'm saying?'

Hollie swallowed. No, of course she wasn't listening—not properly, anyway. She hadn't been fully concentrating on Janette's words, just as she hadn't been concentrating on anything lately. Not the news, nor office views, or even the fact that it was Christmas tomorrow. The only thing which was eating up her mind was the terrible showdown she'd had with Maximo a couple of days ago, when she had told him she was expecting his baby and he had reacted with...

Anger?

Disbelief?

Yes, both those things—and more besides. He had been icy with her, and distant. He had seemed to go out of his way to push her away and to view her with coldly dispassionate eyes. Nobody would ever have guessed they'd been lovers. Although, if you didn't even get to share a whole night with a man—did that actually *count* as being a lover?

That had been bad enough but worse was to follow because when she'd arrived at work the next morning, Janette had asked could she make a cake for Maximo, to celebrate his completion on the purchase of the castle. It had been the last thing on earth Hollie had felt like doing, but what excuse could she possibly use for declining?

*I'm terribly sorry, Janette, but I'm pregnant with Maximo's baby and he's being so unreasonable that I'd be tempted to tip a dollop of arsenic into the mix.*

No, she had nodded her head submissively, even though her heart had wrenched with bitterness and shame. And as she had beaten the eggs and measured out the sugar, she had been unable to flush the image of Maximo's angry face from her mind and to wonder where they went from here. She still had the business card he'd given her, just before he'd made his arrogant assertion that she should contact his lawyers.

He had cold-bloodedly stated that his money would enable her to employ a whole stable of staff, and had ended the conversation by announcing that he had no intention of being a father to his child. Well, that suited her just fine. Did he really imagine she, or her baby, wanted *anything* to do with a man who hadn't bothered to hide his dismay when she'd told him her momentous news?

But surely the most important thing right now was to hang onto her job, at a time when she had never needed work more badly. Which was why she looked up at her boss and forced a weak smile. 'What were you saying, Janette?' she asked.

'I was congratulating you on your cake, Hollie, which is absolutely lovely—though I have to say that it's not quite up to your *usual* standard.'

Hollie nodded. Of course it wasn't. It was unfortunate that a huge salt tear had plopped onto the finished product at the very last minute and Hollie's subsequent attempts at repair work only seemed to have made it worse.

'I know it's not that good,' she said.

'It can't be helped.' Janette's words were brisk. 'I'm sure he won't notice. It's the thought that counts, and this will make him realise that our agency is always prepared to go the extra mile—just in case he's thinking of buying any more local property in the area. Just make sure you deliver it today, can you, dear?'

'D-deliver it?' Hollie could see from Janette's expression that she hadn't quite managed to hide the horror in her voice. 'You mean deliver the cake? To...to Maximo?'

'To *Señor Diaz*,' Janette corrected, frosting her a severe look. 'Since when did you start using first names with clients, Hollie? Of course, I mean you! I thought you'd be delighted to comply after the way you monopolised him at the party. And who else is going to do it?'

'But—'

'Most people are very busy this close to Christmas, but at least you haven't got any family. I'd do it myself except that I have a date through that new site—Flirty at Fifty. I mean, it sounds almost too good to be true, but, still...' Janette's steely-eyed look couldn't quite disguise the unmistakable glint of hope which lurked in her heavily made-up eyes. She shrugged. 'Mustn't look a gift horse in the mouth and all that. Just make sure the cake arrives at the castle this afternoon, will you? There are a few more papers he needs to sign at the same time. But you'd better get a move on.' She shot a quick glance out of the agency's big glass windows. 'I don't like the look of those clouds and they're forecasting snow over the holidays. Dave can drop you at the bottom of the lane on the way to his four o'clock appointment and you can easily walk back.'

Behind her frozen smile, Hollie felt as if she were in pieces, chewed up by a growing feeling of dread at the thought of seeing Maximo again. Their last meeting had been bad enough. The awkwardness and embarrassment of facing the reluctant father of her baby was an episode she wasn't eager to repeat. But without having to explain *why* she didn't want to go—and just imagine Janette's reaction if she did *that*—common sense told her that refusal simply wasn't an option.

Common sense.

How ironic that something she had relied on all her life had deserted her when she needed it most. If she'd been sensible she wouldn't have fallen into bed with him—seduced by a lazy smile and a hard body, and a smooth line in seduction.

She glanced out of the window, where the main street was bustling with last-minute shoppers, and as she looked up at the sky she could see that Janette hadn't been exaggerating. The heavy pewter clouds looked bloated and full and there was a strange saffron light radiating downwards, making the seasonal colours in the shop windows even more vivid than usual.

Christmas trees were laden with baubles and strings of fairy lights created magical grottos. Branches of greenery and berries were swathed in thick, fake snow—but occasionally a flake of the real stuff fluttered down to lie on the glittery pavement. Strings of tinsel sparkled as brightly as the midday sun and jolly figures of Santa were tempting little children to tug on their mother's hand to try to get them to linger.

Hollie's heart slammed against her ribcage.

Little children.

That was what she would have before too long. A child of her own. First there would be a baby and then the baby would grow into a toddler and then...

But, no. Before she started trying to imagine an unimaginable future, she needed to deal with the present and there was one thing which couldn't be put off any longer. She would deliver the wretched cake to Maximo and get him to sign the papers. She would do both these things in a calm and outwardly relaxed manner, and if he brought up the subject of his lawyer again, she would tell him that these things would probably be better addressed once the seasonal break was over and the dust had settled.

At just after three, Dave's rather beaten-up old car dropped her off at the bottom of the lane and, carefully clutching the cake box, Hollie began to climb the steep hill towards Kastelloes. From here the ancient grey castle looked faintly forbidding as it dominated the green landscape with its turrets and its towers. It hadn't been a hotel for a long time but Hollie's excitement at the thought of it being brought to life again had been somewhat dampened by the dramatic changes in her own fortune.

She tried to imagine bringing a new life into the world. Would she still be able to open her tea shop with a tiny infant in tow—was that going to be possible, despite all the proud protestations she'd made to Maximo?

As her reluctant steps carried her closer to the castle, she noticed that the snow was starting to fall more heavily and coating her cheeks with big white blobs.

There was no sign of life as she walked over the drawbridge and past the old gatehouse. No Maximo rushing out to relieve her of her burden as she came to a halt in front of the ancient oak door. If he wasn't in, then he wouldn't be able to sign the papers, would he? And Janette would just have to accept that. But an upwards glance showed a golden light gleaming through one of the mullioned windows, indicating that *someone* was home, and, although her heart was plummeting, Hollie knew she couldn't back out now.

She paid the driver and, after putting the cake box down on the doorstep, pulled the bell and heard a faint ringing from somewhere deep inside the castle. She looked around as she waited, trying to enjoy the vision of the falling snow covering the stone pots and statues with a fine layer of white. But more importantly, it allowed her to look away from the door, because she didn't want Maximo opening it and finding her staring up at him with anxiety written all over her face. She needed to show him she was in control, even if she didn't particularly feel that way.

Her hands were cold and she wished she'd remembered to bring gloves with her. Her coat felt inadequately thin and the breath leaving her mouth was coming out in big, white puffs. She was just beginning to wonder if anyone *was* at home when the door of the castle opened with a creak and she turned to see Maximo standing before her, his powerful frame outlined by its arching wooden frame. Hollie felt her stomach somersault and silently cursed—but what could she do about her instinctive reaction? Despite everything which had happened between them, she obviously hadn't acquired any immunity to him. And no wonder. Dressed in his habitual black, he looked as if he had arrived from another age. As if he were thoroughly at home in this windswept citadel, high on a hill. A conquistador, Janette had once called him and, with all that powerful and brooding darkness he exuded, didn't her boss have a point?

'Hollie,' he said. His rich Spanish accent filtered over her skin like velvet but there was a frown creasing his brow. 'This is a…surprise.'

And obviously an unwelcome one, judging by his acid tone. 'I have some papers for you to sign,' she said, instantly on the defensive, determined to ensure he understood she was there because she *had* to be and not because she wanted to be. 'Also…' flushing, she bent to retrieve the large white box from the doorstep, which she held towards him '… Janette wanted you to have this.'

'What is it?' he questioned, eying the box warily.

A few random snowflakes fluttered onto her cheeks and she shuffled from one foot to the other, feeling acutely embarrassed by the cold lack of welcome in his eyes. Suddenly she understood the expression about wishing the ground would open up and swallow you. 'It's a cake.'

'A cake?' he echoed.

'We wanted to…well, it was Janette's idea, actually. She wanted to celebrate the sale of Kastelloes and so she asked me to bake you a cake.'

'And does she ask you to do this for all your purchasers?' he questioned silkily as he took the box from her. 'Or should I be flattered?'

Something about the sarcastic way he said it made Hollie's temper suddenly erupt. She had tried doing this in a polite and professional manner yet he still seemed so full of himself. So full of arrogant provocation and mockery. Did he think she'd concocted some kind of flimsy excuse just in order to see him? She wasn't *that* desperate. 'Christmas is supposed to be a time for giving, isn't it?' she retorted. 'Perhaps that was one of the reasons she asked me to do it. And you don't have to eat it, you know,' she added. 'You can always feed it to the birds. I'm sure they'd appreciate something to line their stomachs in this cold weather.'

'I'm sure they would,' he said. As if on cue, a flurry of snow came cascading down from the straining sky, straight onto her sleek head, and Maximo reluctantly acknowledged the growing tension inside him.

He had come to this ancient castle specifically to escape Christmas, because it was a festival he avoided wherever possible. It provided the ideal bolt-hole and he'd planned to spend a few days there before he had the building razed to the ground. He hadn't imagined that anybody would come near him and he hadn't wanted them to. Yet now Hollie Walker had turned up, reminding him of his harsh new reality. Forcing him to acknowledge the child growing in her belly—a fact which was complicated by the realisation that he would like nothing better than to take her into his arms and kiss her again. To strip her of her drab clothing and reveal the luscious body which lay beneath. To lose himself in her sweetness as he had done on that rain-lashed night.

His mouth twisted, because what would be the point of that? He was not going to be a part of her life, or her child's. He had given her the details of his lawyer, so she could be in no doubt that he would be more than generous. Because providing financially for Hollie and her baby was something he could do. The *only* thing he could do. A child needed love and he did not know how to give love. His heart was damaged—his emotions shredded. He had accepted that a long time ago.

So why not just sign the damned papers, enthuse over the damned cake and then send her on her way, no matter how much he hungered to recreate that night he'd spent in her arms? If he was cold and indifferent towards her, she would soon realise how much better off she was without a man like him. 'You'd better come inside,' he said.

'Don't worry. I'll be sure not to keep you for any longer than I have to.'

'Let's go to the library,' he said, shutting the door on the icy blast outside. 'Unlike most of the castle, at least it's warm in there.'

'Whatever,' she said, with a shrug.

Hollie's heart was heavy as she followed Maximo through the wood-panelled corridors, thinking he couldn't have been more unwelcoming if he'd tried. She thought how abrupt he seemed and she wished she weren't here. In fact, she wished she were anywhere but here—but the instant she entered the library, her concerns were briefly forgotten.

She'd only ever seen the place deserted, when Janette had brought her round to view it just before it went on the market. The fire exit signs from its days as a hotel were faded and the place had always appeared so lacklustre and uninspiring. But not today. Today she found herself noticing the perfect proportions of the room—the intricate carvings of cherubs and sailing ships, and the huge mullioned windows which overlooked the grounds. Was that Maximo's influence? she found herself wondering. Did he have the ability to transmute dull surroundings and turn them into a place which breathed beauty, as he had done the night when she'd taken him home?

Maybe it was just the roaring fire in the grate which had brought the ancient room to vibrant life—illuminating the detailing on the stone fireplace and the bare wall above it, which was just crying out for a painting. A rich landscape in oil, Hollie thought longingly. Or a portrait. You could put a comfortable chair underneath—two chairs, maybe—and sit there in the evenings watching the shadows fall. She felt a wistful wrench of her heart. Couldn't someone turn this castle into a home?

It was unlikely to be Maximo.

She turned to find him studying her, his black gaze fixed on her intently, as if he had never really seen her before. Hollie's heart missed a beat, because wasn't she feeling a bit like that herself? As if this were the first time they'd ever been alone. She felt *awkward* in his presence, which was slightly ridiculous, when you considered all the things they'd done together.

Or maybe it wasn't ridiculous at all. What did she know? She'd thought that what they'd shared had been intimacy, but she had been wrong. In her innocence she had confused sex with real closeness. But you could be naked in a man's arms and it counted for nothing, because right now Maximo Diaz seemed like a stranger. A stranger whose child she carried.

'What exactly do you want me to sign?' he questioned, putting the unopened box down on the table.

'It's right here.' Her hands were trembling as she scrabbled around inside her briefcase and she wondered if he'd noticed as she walked across the room towards him. 'It's the release form concerning the fixtures and fittings. It's just a formality.'

He was reading it. Of course he was. He wasn't the kind of man who would put his signature to something he hadn't studied first. And because he was reading it, it was taking much longer than she had anticipated.

The silence in the room seemed immense and Hollie pulled out her phone and began to look at it, as if there were loads of missed calls she needed to attend to, though in truth the screen was just a blur of mangled words. As a distraction technique it was pretty useless because she couldn't escape the troubled whirl of her thoughts as the minutes ticked slowly by. His dark head was bent and when eventually she heard the scratch of his pen, he looked up, his smile brief and perfunctory.

'I think that's everything you need.'

*He can't wait to get rid of you.*

He was rising from the chair and Hollie couldn't hold back her shiver as he handed her the document.

'If there's nothing more, I'll see you out.'

'There's really no need. I know my way around.'

'I insist.' He shot her a brief look and something

like pain filtered through his black eyes. 'How are you feeling?'

It might have been funny if it hadn't been so sad and Hollie only just managed to keep a burst of hysterical laughter from her lips. To say there was an elephant in the room didn't come close to it. Was that to be his only reference to the fact that she was pregnant? Because if so she was just going to have to deal with it. From somewhere she managed to produce a smile. 'I'm fine, thanks,' she said. 'The doctor seems very pleased with my progress so far.'

There was a pause. 'Look, I'm aware that my reaction to your news wasn't great and I apologise for that.'

His words were grudging rather than heartfelt, but Hollie told herself she must be generous in her response. 'No, it was hardly the stuff of dreams,' she said drily. 'But that's okay. It must have come as a terrible shock and at least you were being honest. And I'm over it now.'

'My lawyers tell me you haven't made contact yet.'

'No. I thought I'd wait until after Christmas now.'

He inclined his head. 'As you wish.'

*As you wish?*

Hollie had a whole catalogue of wishes, most of which were never going to come true. She wished he had a heart instead of a lump of cold steel lodged somewhere deep in his chest. She wished...

No. Only a fool would ever wish for love from such an unsuitable candidate.

They had reached the hall and he was opening the door and all Hollie wanted was to get away from him and the way he was making her feel, when his terse exclamation startled her.

*'Es imposible!'*

Hollie followed his gaze and looked outside. Her Spanish was limited to about three words which involved asking for a beer, but even she understood that what he'd just said wasn't true, because it wasn't impossible at all. She felt the jump of her heart. She'd been so busy with her thoughts that she'd barely noticed the time passing, or the increased snowfall. But from here she was aware of how quickly the weather had closed in, and now they seemed to be in a complete white-out.

The landscape had been utterly transformed. Trees, grass and bushes were coated with a mantle of white, which sparkled like diamonds in the fading violet light. The thick fall had turned the place into a winter fairy tale—but one with an underlying threat because, outwardly, everything had changed. No footsteps up the lane. It was as if she'd never been there.

Hollie had only ever thought of snow as a positive thing—as pretty, white and fluffy—but now she saw it as an obstacle, barring her way out of there. And there was no sign of it stopping. She stared up into the darkening sky and uttered a soft curse beneath her breath. All she wanted was to get back to her little cottage because, although it might not amount to very much, at least it was *home.*

'Where's your taxi?' he demanded.

She shrugged. 'I got a lift here and I was planning to walk back.'

He made a soft curse beneath his breath. 'I would take you myself except that I've dismissed the chauffeur for the holidays and he's taken the car.'

'It's fine,' she said, between gritted teeth, thinking

that she'd rather walk home barefoot than be driven home by *him*. 'I've been cooped up in the office all morning, and a bit of snow won't kill me.' With a grimace of stark realisation, Hollie stared down at her feet. 'These boots weren't exactly made for walking, but I guess they'll have to do.'

'Are you out of your mind?' he snapped. 'You can't possibly walk home in this.'

'Watch me.'

'I don't think so. You're pregnant, remember?'

'I'm hardly likely to forget, am I?'

'Do you make a habit of being rescued from bad weather, Hollie?' he demanded. 'Don't you think it's time you invested in one of those clever phone apps?'

'Oh, go to hell!' she snapped back, taking a defiant step forward and immediately sinking into a deep white drift which came almost to the top of her boots. And suddenly Maximo's hands were on her waist and he was lifting her clean out of the snow, and she was staring up into the hard glitter of his black eyes. And wasn't it crazy that, in the midst of all her complicated emotions, her overriding feeling was the hungry throb of her blood in response to his touch? 'Go to hell,' she repeated weakly.

His velvety voice filtered over her skin. 'Even hell would reject a man like me.'

'Please put me down,' she said. 'I want to go home.'

'Well, you can't. You're not going anywhere right now. Not when it's like this. You're going to have to stay here for the time being.' He lowered her to her feet. 'Unless that's what you had in mind all along?'

She moved even further away from him, though that

did little to ease the furious punch of her heart. 'Are you serious? Are you arrogant enough to think I'd deliberately get myself stranded here like this?'

He shrugged. 'Only you know the answer to that, Hollie. But if you're asking whether I think a woman is capable of such manipulation, then I'm afraid the answer has to be yes.'

'Why, you...*cynic*,' she breathed.

'You think so? I prefer to call it realism. But that's irrelevant.' He moved towards the door, his muscular body all honed and rippling strength. 'And rather than standing here debating my perceived defects of character, you'd better come inside, out of the cold.'

# CHAPTER SIX

MAXIMO SHUT THE door with more force than he intended, his heart racing with…what? Anger at being stuck with an uninvited guest at the worst time of the year? Yes, there was that. But Hollie was not just any uninvited guest. He stared down at the mutinous tremble of her lips and felt the shimmer of something indefinable spearing at his heart. She was the mother of his child, he reminded himself grimly. A child he had never wanted. Because why would he wish to pass on his cold and emotionless genes to an innocent baby?

Yet his feelings of claustrophobia were complicated by a sensation which threatened to derail his intention to keep his distance from the woman he had seduced, and no matter how firmly he spoke to himself, it was having precisely no effect on him. Because every time he looked at Hollie Walker, he felt that same powerful kick of desire. In spite of everything, he still wanted her. He wanted her badly and yet he still couldn't work out why. He liked his women hard-edged. Tough and sexy. Women who knew the score—not wide-eyed innocents, with lips which trembled when you kissed them.

He preferred considered sex—a careful coupling

rather than wild passion which ran the risk of taking a man hostage. He drew his boundaries from the outset. He preferred to be in the driving seat when it came to relationships and women were so eager for his body and his company that they invariably acceded to his demands. Yet with Hollie Walker, hadn't he already broken one of his self-imposed rules? They said a woman was a mystery until you bedded her and once that happened, she inevitably lost some of that allure. That had always been the case before, so why wasn't it happening now?

Why did he want to discover more about her? And why the hell was he experiencing an overwhelming need to tumble her down and cover her soft body with the hot, hard heat of his own until she cried out his name? She might currently be glaring at him as if he were the devil incarnate, but her anger didn't quite mask her own desire. No. Not at all. The faint flush of her cheeks and the darkening of her spectacular grey eyes was a pretty reliable indicator that she was far from immune to *him*. And since they were stuck with each other until the snow melted, perhaps it might be a good idea to capitalise on that potent sexual chemistry.

They had to do *something* to occupy themselves during the long hours ahead and tomorrow was Christmas Day—a holiday which up until now had always been something he just needed to survive, but now he could see the possibility of transforming it into something else.

Something erotic.

The clench in his gut was sweetly pervasive until the split second when he noticed the flash of vulnerability which had crossed her pale face and silently he remonstrated with himself, forcing himself to listen to reason.

*You don't have to have sex with her. You just have to provide shelter until the weather breaks and get through the next few hours.*

'I'll show you where you can sleep,' he said tightly.

'I'm sure that won't be necessary,' she said, equally tightly. 'I'm not planning on staying any longer than I need to.'

'You'll stay until it's safe to return and that certainly won't be before nightfall.'

Their eyes met in a silent clash of wills, until eventually she backed down and nodded.

'Then it seems I have no choice.'

'That's right,' he agreed softly. 'You don't. Now come with me.'

Hollie felt chewed up as she trailed behind Maximo up the curving stone staircase which led to the upstairs floor of the chilly castle. She was scared. Scared of the way he made her feel. Scared of wanting to touch him instead of needing to push him away. Because he didn't want her. *He didn't want her.* And that was something she shouldn't forget. His dismay on discovering she was trapped here might have been almost comical to observe, if it hadn't been so hurtful. But she guessed that nobody could ever accuse Maximo Diaz of being duplicitous. He was honest to a fault, which had to be a good thing. And since she was here—maybe she just needed to make the best of it. To look on the bright side. She pressed her lips together.

For both their sakes.

He was pushing open the door of one of the bedrooms and as Hollie stepped inside she was aware of a further drop in temperature. The bed was bare and the room largely empty—there was nothing in the way of decorative furnishing to make it seem inviting or attractive. It certainly wasn't going to be a fairy-tale Christmas Eve, not by any stretch of the imagination.

'You'll find linen in the big wooden cupboard just along the corridor,' he advised, his dark brows knitting together, as if he had just noticed her shiver. 'You're cold?'

'A bit.'

'Let me see what I can do. I've never seen anything quite so archaic as what passes for a heating system here.'

'Don't you have any staff with you?' she questioned curiously.

Black eyebrows were elevated in mocking query. 'You think I travel around with a retinue of servants?'

She shrugged. 'You're a rich man. Apparently, that's what rich men do. And you *do* have a chauffeur.'

'*Sí.* I do. But the answer is no, I am completely on my own. Because surely a man is not a true man if he cannot fend for himself. If he cannot live independently of his staff.'

'Christmas is not a time for independence,' she said firmly. 'It's a time for family.'

'And will your family be missing you, Hollie?' he questioned suddenly. 'Is that why you are so eager to get back?'

'I have no family,' she said, deciding it wouldn't be diplomatic or wise to tell him that her desire to get away had been all about his effect on her. Baldly, she gave him the bare facts, the way she always did, just so they could get the inevitable mechanical sympathy out of the way. 'Both my parents are dead.'

'Snap,' he said softly.

It wasn't what she'd been expecting and Hollie almost wished he hadn't told her that, because that was the stupid thing about the mind—it took you down false paths, based on very flimsy evidence. If she wasn't careful it would be easy to start imagining they had something in common, because they were both orphans. When she knew and he knew that they had absolutely nothing in common, other than an inconvenient sexual chemistry and a baby neither of them had planned.

'At least nobody's going to miss us!' she observed brightly, wishing it didn't please her so much to see him smile in response. But the curve of his lips lasted only a second, as though this man was not comfortable with smiling.

'I'll leave you to get settled in,' he said abruptly. 'I'll be downstairs. Come and find me when you've finished. Take as long as you like.'

*Settling in* seemed a rather over-ambitious term for getting used to such spartan accommodation, but after Maximo had left, Hollie tried to make the bedroom as comfortable as possible. There were no sheets, but she hunted down several mismatched velvet throws and a thick eiderdown, which provided a colourful display against the quiet grey hues of the faded walls. And thankfully she was *used* to sleeping in a chilly bedroom.

The nearby bathroom was ancient, with a noisy cistern and a vast, old-fashioned bath—but the water was piping hot. She washed her hands with a bar of rock-hard soap then stared into the rather mottled mirror above the sink. She was expecting her appearance to come as a shock, but to her surprise her eyes were shining and her cheeks were pink and glowing. She brushed her hair, tempted to leave it loose because wouldn't that provide some essential warmth around her neck and shoulders? But something stopped her and it was the memory of Maximo using a single strand of it as a rope, just before he'd kissed her. Because those kinds of memories weren't helpful. Not helpful at all. Carefully, she wound it into a tight chignon and pinned it into place, before heading downstairs to find Maximo.

He wasn't in the library, but she could smell the aroma of food cooking and Hollie made her way through a series of maze-like corridors towards the kitchen. She could hear movement but when she walked in, the sight which greeted her was the last thing she had expected. What *had* she expected? She wasn't sure—but it certainly wasn't to see the Spanish tycoon with his back to her, his black sweater rolled up to his elbows as he stirred something.

Did she make a sound? Was that why he turned around, his olive skin gleaming from the heat of the hob? And Hollie could do nothing about the instant wrench of her heart, as if she were registering his gorgeousness for the very first time. Because Maximo, holding up a wooden spoon as the conductor of an orchestra might hold a baton, looked insanely sexy. Maybe her hormones were making her respond to him this way. Because right then he looked like the carer and provider. The alpha man. The hunter. The father of her baby. Beneath her sweater she felt her breasts tighten and wondered if he'd noticed. Would that account for the almost imperceptible narrowing of his eyes and the sudden tension which stilled his magnificent body so that he looked almost poised to strike?

'Gosh,' she said.

'*Gosh?*' he echoed, his sardonic tone easing a little of the tension in the air. 'Am I to take that as a very English word of surprise?'

'I suppose I am a bit surprised,' she admitted. 'I didn't have you down as a budding chef.'

'Less of the budding, more of the accomplished.'

'Of course. Silly of me to forget that you probably excel in everything you turn your hand to.'

'You're getting the hang of me, Hollie.'

'Who taught you to cook?'

'I'm self-taught.'

'Wow.' She blew a silent whistle. 'Now I'm even more impressed.'

'Why wouldn't I teach myself how to cook?' he questioned. 'As I told you, my independence is important to me.' His black eyes glittered a challenge at her. 'And isn't your assumption that I'm breaking some sort of mould rather sexist?'

Was it? Hollie wasn't sure. As he turned back to the hob, the only thing she was certain of was a stupid sense of yearning as she feasted her eyes on the black tendrils of hair which brushed against his neck. She didn't want to feel wistful but it was difficult not to. Because if they'd been a real couple they might have done stuff like this—cooked meals and flirted a little. They might have gone out on a few dates, instead of letting passion lead them to a one-night stand with massive consequences. But she wasn't the type of woman Maximo dated, she reminded herself fiercely. She'd seen photos of his girlfriends on the Internet and she was nothing like any of them. She just happened to be a warm and willing body who had made herself available on a night when he'd obviously wanted company.

But those were pointless thoughts. Negative thoughts she wasn't going to entertain. Instead Hollie watched as Maximo chopped onions with rather terrifying dexterity and realised he hadn't been exaggerating about his prowess in the kitchen. 'So what are you cooking?' she asked.

'It's a variation of a dish called *cocido montañéas*. Mountain stew. It comes from northern Spain. From Cantabria.'

'And is that where you come from?'

'It is.' He sliced a wooden spoon through the thick mixture, clearly more comfortable discussing the meal than details about his birthplace. 'It's more of a winter soup really, with pork and chorizo and beans and greens and wine and garlic and pretty much anything else you can find to throw in.'

'It's not...'

'Not?' He turned round again as her words tailed off, only this time his gleaming black gaze pierced through her like a sword. 'Not what, Hollie?'

'Well, it's not the kind of food I can imagine someone like you eating, let alone cooking.'

'Why not?'

Hollie traced her finger along a deep gouge in the ancient table and wondered how long ago it had been put there and by whom. 'It's more I imagine the food a labourer might eat.'

'And I'm no labourer?'

She smiled at the preposterousness of this. 'Obviously not.'

'Maybe,' he said softly. 'But once I was.'

She glanced up from the table, watching as he put a lid on the pot and turned the heat down low. 'You? A labourer?'

Maximo didn't answer immediately, amazed he'd given her an opening to pursue this particular topic because discussions about his past were something he vetoed. Especially with lovers. Women *always* asked questions and he understood why. Knowledge was power and the more you knew about someone, the closer you could presume your relationship to be. Except that any 'closeness' his lovers presumed was all inside their heads. Usually he recommended they consult the Internet if they wanted to discover more about him, confident they'd find out only what he wanted them to know—having successfully kept his online profile deliberately sparse, by employing an IT expert who made sure that happened.

His past was private and his alone—and the only time he connected with it was during this ritual he followed most Christmases, when he cooked up the kind of food which would never feature on the menu of any of the fancy restaurants he frequented these days. At Christmas he went back to basics. He did it because it reminded him of who he had been and where he had come from, and usually it was enough to make him satisfied with his lot and to remind him what he *didn't* want from life.

But something had happened which had changed the

way he thought about everything, and though it pained him to admit it—it all stemmed from his mother's recent passing. Didn't seem to matter that he didn't *want* to be affected by the death of a woman he had despised. Fact was, he was. Ever since it had happened he'd felt... disconnected. Like a tethered balloon whose string had just been cut, leaving him drifting aimlessly and without direction. As if all the money and power he had acquired along the way suddenly meant nothing. Was that why he had taken this provincial office worker to bed and lost himself in a storm of passion so all-pervasive that it had left him feeling dazed and confused the next morning? As if, for the first time in his life, it had felt as if he'd come home.

*Wasn't that why he hadn't contacted her again? Because he didn't like the way she made him feel, or because he didn't trust those feelings?*

He didn't know and he didn't care and that was why he had walked away. Why he had resisted the surprising desire to contact her again. And time was great for taking the urgency out of desire. It had been easy to lose himself in work and travel and to allow the many projects he juggled to take over his life. To forget about that night and the woman who had temporarily made him lose control.

Yet now, as he stared into the wide grey eyes which were fixed on his, he found himself wanting to tell her stuff. Nothing too deep. No, definitely not that. But it would amuse him to reveal his beginnings to her, to show her some of the real man beneath the fancy patina. Would take his mind off the persistent urge to pull her into his arms and start kissing her, which would complicate his life in a way it didn't need complicating.

'Yes, I was a labourer,' he said. 'And if you know my roots you might be able to understand why. I was the only child of a single mother, and money was scarce. I remember being hungry—always hungry. My need to get food took precedence over schoolwork and the local school wasn't up to much anyway. And when I was fourteen, I started working on the roads.'

'Fourteen?' she breathed, her eyes growing even wider. 'Wow. Is that even *legal*?'

'I doubt it.' He shrugged. 'But there weren't so many checks back then. It was a different kind of world. The guy who owned the construction site didn't know how old I was and if they had, they probably wouldn't have cared.'

'You mean you lied about your age?' she questioned, as if that were important to her.

'I let them believe what they wanted to believe. That's mostly what people do in life, Hollie—haven't you discovered that by now? I was big and strong for my age and looked much older than I was, and it was easy to let my work speak for itself. I started out with a pick and shovel. Breaking up rocks with a big hammer and trying not to inhale the dust. I learnt a lot about construction.' He gave a short laugh. 'But I learnt plenty more about human nature.'

'In what way?'

Her voice was soft. Way too soft to resist—and for some reason, Maximo didn't even try.

'I learnt how to fight,' he admitted. 'I learnt how a man can lose everything through drink, and that gambling is nothing but a short journey to ruin. But mostly I learnt that I didn't want to hang round doing that kind of work for ever.'

'No, I can imagine you didn't. So how did you make the leap, from being a—?'

'Labourer?' Her head was bent as she traced all the scratches on the table with the tip of her finger, as if she were trying not to meet his gaze. And wasn't there a bit of him which was glad about that? Because those beautiful grey eyes were cool and searching and it wasn't easy to ignore their candid gaze.

'It wasn't rocket science,' he continued. 'I made sure I was always the first to arrive and the last to leave and I saved every euro I could to buy my first digger. Eventually that one digger became five, and then twenty— and soon I was the sub-contractor of choice for the big boys.' He gave a short laugh. 'Until I became one of the big boys myself. I started building roads and then railways, and I never really looked back.' Most emphatically he had not looked back.

She absorbed all this in silence for a moment. 'It's not—'

'Not what you expected?' he supplied acidly. 'You imagined I was born with the Spanish equivalent of a silver spoon in my mouth? *Nacer en cuna de oro.* That I grew up with money?'

'Something like that. You seem very comfortable with your wealth. Comfortable in your own skin.'

'Thank you,' he said gravely, and was aware of the warm approbation in his voice as he said it. Her look of surprise indicated she'd heard it too, but then she was unaware that she had just paid him a great compliment—perhaps the greatest compliment of all. For hadn't that been what he had strived for above all else? *To feel comfortable in his own skin.*

But then she ruined it.

'And you have a kind of—I don't know.' She wriggled her shoulders. 'A kind of *aristocratic* look about you.'

Maximo's lips clamped shut, telling himself to be grateful that her perceptive observation had brought him to his senses at last. What was the *matter* with him? Hadn't he been just about to tell her the rest of his pitiful story, lulled by her soft voice and seeking eyes? And why—just because his estranged mother was dead and his equilibrium had temporarily been disturbed?

Hadn't he spent the last two decades eradicating those memories—only to almost blurt them out to a woman who already had too much power over him? Because her pregnancy gave Hollie Walker undue influence in his life, he recognised suddenly—and she could use that influence any way she saw fit.

He gave the pot another stir. He had carefully controlled his image for most of his life. He never gave interviews, never let people too close. He worked hard and played hard and donated generously to charity—and for these qualities he was mostly admired and envied in equal measure. But of himself he gave nothing away. Even during his longest relationships—and none of those had ever been what you'd call lengthy—he had never been anything less than guarded. Hadn't that been part of his appeal—that women saw him as an enigma and a challenge and themselves as the one who would break down those high barriers with which he had surrounded himself?

But Hollie was different. She couldn't help but be different. She was carrying his baby and, inevitably, that was going to cause ripples of curiosity in the circles in which he moved. Sooner or later people were going to find out that this unknown Englishwoman was pregnant with his child. She would be able to present herself to the world however she saw fit. As a victim, if she so desired. And he would have absolutely no control over that.

He felt the sudden knot in his stomach. He had already told her plenty about himself, but of her he knew nothing. Nothing at all. Wasn't it time he did? Not because he particularly cared what made her tick, but because he needed to redress that balance of knowledge.

He pulled out the stool opposite hers and sat down. 'What about you?' he questioned, carelessly.

'Me?'

'I've told you how I started out. Now it's your turn.'

Hollie hesitated. He had divulged much more than she'd expected, though she'd noticed that his story had stopped very abruptly. But he had still surprised her and maybe if he hadn't been so forthcoming she might have brushed over her own background, because it wasn't much to write home about, was it? Even so, it was more than a little distracting to have him sitting so close, making her acutely aware of all the latent power in his muscular body and the devilish gleam of his ebony eyes.

'I was the only child of a single mother, too,' she began and saw a muscle begin working at his temple, as if he thought she was grasping for things they had in common and was irritated by it. Instantly, she sought to emphasise the differences between them. 'We weren't exactly poor, but we weren't exactly rich either. My father...'

'What about your father?' he probed.

She shrugged. 'Well, to be honest, I never knew him very well. He was a bit of a womaniser, I guess. Good-looking. Easy company. One of those men who want to have their cake and eat it. He was a sales manager and so travelled around the area a lot. He had several different lovers, although only one child, as far as I know. He'd tell my mother he loved her and he'd move in with us for a bit and then...' She shrugged. 'I don't know if having a baby cramped his style, or whether he found it stultifying that the whole household always seemed to revolve around him. But the more my mother ran round after him, the more he seemed to despise her. So they'd have a big row and he'd move out and then the whole cycle would start again.'

'That must have been tough on you,' he observed slowly.

'Not really.' Hollie slipped into her best *every-cloud-has-a-silver-lining* attitude. 'It's true that Mum used to go to pieces every time, but it's how I taught myself how to cook, and...'

'Go on,' he said, the faintest of smiles touching the edges of his mouth.

She picked up the story again, thinking that nobody ever really asked her stuff like this. 'One day my father just stopped contacting her and we never found out what happened to him. Like you said, things were different in those days and there was no social media to be able to track someone down. My mum never really got over it and after she died, I sold her little house and went to catering college. Long story short, I made a friend there and used the rest of my savings to go into business with her—we opened a tea shop in London.'

'But? I sense there's a but coming.'

He was insightful, she thought—or maybe such a successful businessman was always going to have an instinct for a duff business venture. 'My partner borrowed a whole load of money on the business and couldn't pay it back.'

'That's theft,' he observed acidly.

'She *meant* to pay it back,' she defended. 'But that was never going to happen and I couldn't bear to waste any more time, or make any more bad memories by chasing her through the small courts. Anyway, we'd chosen a hopeless location. It was more a hip coffee shop sort of area and not really suited to a venue which was serving dinky plates of scones, with cream and jam. It's why I came to Devon, which *is* that kind of place. It's why, no matter what happens, I'm glad you came here too, Maximo.'

He looked startled. 'You are?'

'Yes, I am. Not because of the baby, because I know that's bad news for you.' She ignored the pained expression on his face but resolutely carried on. 'It wasn't meant to happen, but it did—and I will do everything to make sure our child has the best possible life I can give them. And I've lived with a man who didn't want to be a father, which is why I can cope with the fact you don't want to be involved. It's better that way. Better that we're upfront about things from the beginning so everyone knows where they stand—'

'Hollie—'

'No, please let me finish.' She drew a deep breath and stared straight into his fathoms-deep eyes, thinking how thick and black the lashes were. 'What makes me glad is the fact that you've bought Kastelloes, because you'll be injecting life back into this town and local community. So my business—and every other business in Trescombe—will benefit.' He got up quickly to attend to his cooking, an uncomfortable expression crossing his face, and she wondered if she was boring him. 'Gosh, it's seven o'clock already,' she observed, sneaking a glance at her watch. 'Only five more hours to go and it'll be Christmas Day!'

'I can hardly wait,' he said sarcastically.

She watched as he finished cooking the meal, wishing she could tear her eyes away from the graceful agility of his movements and the way his black jeans clung to the hard thrust of his buttocks. But she couldn't. And all the while she was becoming aware of the four walls which surrounded them and the fact that they were completely alone in this beautiful, desolate building. She could feel tension between them mounting—like dark layers of something tantalising, building and building into the promise of something unbearably sweet.

'Let's eat,' he said suddenly.

But his face was still tense as he began to serve up the soup, his shadow seeming to swamp her in an all-consuming darkness. And somehow his abrupt words managed to destroy the fragile harmony which had briefly existed between them.

# CHAPTER SEVEN

HOLLIE SHIVERED AS she lay huddled beneath the heap of the velvet throws, wiggling her toes to stop them from freezing. It was so *quiet*. Nothing to listen to except the sound of the distant church bells in nearby Trescombe. Nothing to distract her from the thought that Maximo was sleeping just along the corridor and that felt weird. Was he thinking about her and her predicament, or was he fast asleep and oblivious to the presence of his unwanted guest? She cocked her ear as the twelfth and final bell faded into the silent night, announcing to the world that Christmas day had finally arrived.

Some Christmas! She was stuck in a cold, almost empty castle with a man who didn't want her there. She turned her pillow over and bashed it with her fist. Didn't matter how many sheep she tried to count, she just couldn't sleep. In fact, she had dozed only fitfully since she'd retired to bed just after ten last night, leaving Maximo downstairs, working in the library.

Their shared supper had been *awkward*, to say the least. Oh, the food had been delicious—no doubt about that. Maximo's Cantabrian mountain stew had hit the spot and the tycoon had waited on her in a way she suspected was totally out of character. She had been impressed by his culinary skills and had said so. But Hollie hadn't been impervious to the unspoken words which had seemed to dangle in the air like invisible baubles. Just as she'd been unable to ignore the spiralling tension which curled like smoke in the base of her stomach whenever he came near.

But last night had been about more than sexual chemistry and, although his powerful presence had been impossible to ignore, Hollie had learnt a little more about the father of her child. It had been an illuminating insight to discover that his wealth hadn't been handed to him on a plate, but he was a self-made man, and that revelation had made her feel an undoubted respect towards him. Yet afterwards it was as if he regretted having told her anything at all, because when she had tried to ask him about growing up in those harsh circumstances, he had very firmly changed the subject. And after that, things had become a little stilted.

It hadn't exactly helped that she had nothing to sleep in and when she'd plucked up courage to ask Maximo if he had a pyjama top she could borrow, he had stared at her as if she had taken leave of her senses.

'Are you crazy?' he'd questioned, black eyes narrowed. 'I never wear anything in bed.'

It had proved yet one more awkward moment in a whole series of them and in Hollie's opinion, that was far too much information to take on board, in the circumstances. Berating her naïve stupidity and hiding her sudden blush by leaping to her feet, she had escaped upstairs and run herself a bath—more to get warm than anything else. But when she had returned to her room she had found a T-shirt lying on top of the velvet heap of bedcovers, which Maximo must have left there for her. A black T-shirt with the word *Legend* inscribed across the front. Pulling it on, she had momentarily revelled in the feel of the soft material against her clean skin— even though the garment had swamped her. And wasn't she aware—on some fundamental level—that she got a kick out of wearing it because *he* had worn it, too?

She tossed and turned as the minutes continued to tick slowly by. She looked at her watch to note that midnight had become one o'clock and she was as restless as before and so, wrapping one of the velvet throws around herself, she went to the window and gazed outside. And despite everything, she couldn't hold back the sigh of wonder which escaped from her lips because outside was the most perfect scene she could imagine—like an illustration from a book about winter.

The snow had stopped falling and the moon was huge in the sky, bathing the milky landscape in a bright and silvery light. Against the frosty stillness of the landscape, the tall shapes of the trees rose ghostly and beautiful and for a moment Holly just drank it all in until the dryness in her throat reminded her that she was thirsty. Why hadn't she thought to bring a drink to bed with her?

She stood very still and listened but could hear nothing and surely Maximo must be fast asleep by now. Carefully opening the door to avoid making any noise, she crept along the corridor, clutching her makeshift cloak around her. The whisper of velvet brushing against the stone steps was the only sound she could hear and quietly she made her way to the kitchen, turning the switch on so that it flooded with light. It was neat and clean, all the debris from dinner tidied away. Maximo had obviously cleared up after she went to bed. He really *was* independent she thought, scrolling back through those rare memories of her father to realise that not once had he ever lifted a finger to help her mother.

She poured herself a glass of water and thirstily gulped it down before pouring another and switching off the light. And although the castle was dark and very quiet, Hollie wasn't in the least bit spooked—because the walls felt friendly. She wondered if other women, like her, had wandered these stone corridors in the dead of night and wondered how they were going to cope with an unknown future.

Lost in thought, she had almost reached the end of the passageway when a figure suddenly emerged from the shadows and Hollie jumped. Water arced and splashed against the stone wall and as the glass slipped from her fingers Maximo lunged forward to catch it—cradling the intact vessel in the palm of his hand like a professional cricketer who had just made a sensational catch.

'You scared the life out of me!' she accused, aware that his hair was ruffled as if he'd hurriedly dragged his sweater over his head and that the top button of his jeans was undone.

'I didn't mean to alarm you. I couldn't sleep and I heard something moving downstairs, or rather someone, so I threw on some clothes and came down to investigate.' His shuttered gaze flicked over her. 'You'd better get back upstairs,' he added, and suddenly his voice was tinged with harshness. 'It's cold.'

Hollie nodded but she didn't move. She *couldn't* move. It was as if she had suddenly forgotten how to use her legs.

'It's cold everywhere,' she whispered. 'I've been awake for hours.'

His eyes narrowed and a look of intense calculation darkened his already shadowed features. He looked as if he were fighting some silent inner battle and when he nodded his head, Hollie couldn't decide whether he had won, or lost.

'Maybe we should try and do something about that,' he said. 'What do you think?'

His soft question slid over her skin, snaring her with threads of silk. And he was studying her with that absorbed and shadowed gaze, which was making her grow weak. And all the time, raw desire was pulsing around them, like a living being. Hollie felt breathless. Poised on the edge of something—but she didn't know the rules of this game. She didn't know how to play. 'That depends what you had in mind,' she stumbled.

He smiled. A slow and speculative smile. A smile no sane woman could have resisted. 'There are any number of options. We could go upstairs and I could lend you another T-shirt. We could see if we can find any more of those velvet wraps you seem so fond of. Or you could share my bed and get warm that way. It's up to you. It's your call, Hollie.'

Maybe if he'd asked that same question during daylight hours when he'd made it plain she was an unwelcome guest, then Hollie might have refused. But the darkness had added a strange layer of anonymity, as well as enhancing her already aroused senses. And it was Christmas morning, wasn't it? A time of magic and secret wishes, when anything could happen. She sensed he wouldn't judge her if she said yes, because this was a time out of life and she wanted it. She wanted it very badly.

'Yes, please,' she said simply.

'Which?'

'You know which.'

He made a low growling noise beneath his breath, as if her easy capitulation had pleased him. Then he put the empty glass down on the stone floor, very carefully, and took her in his arms. He brushed her hair from her cheeks, looking down at her for a moment, his gaze crystalline and hard. She'd thought he might kiss her, but he didn't. Instead, he laced his fingers through hers and led her towards the stairs. It felt very grownup but…it also felt very disappointing and it wasn't until they had reached the upstairs floor that Hollie raised her face to his in question. Because hadn't she secretly been longing for the ultimate castle fantasy of Maximo sweeping her up into his arms and carrying her to his lair?

'You want to know why I didn't carry you this time?' he guessed.

'Yes.' Hollie nodded, marvelling at his perception even as she resented it. Just how many women had he carried to his bed over the years? she wondered.

'Because you're pregnant,' he admitted. 'And I'm terrified of dropping you.'

It was a surprisingly tender admission and Hollie felt her skin grow warm. 'You're way too strong to drop me—and I'm not made of glass, Maximo.'

'I wouldn't bring up the subject of glass right now if I were you.'

His teasing broke a little of the tension until he stared down at her again, his expression dark and unfathomable, and she could see a pulse beating wildly at his temple. 'But since we're on the flat again...'

And this time he *did* pick her up, striding along the corridor to a room just beyond her own, kicking open the door and giving rampant life to her foolish fantasies. It was a room a little larger than her own and just as sparsely furnished, though the bed was much bigger. But Hollie barely noticed the equally haphazard bedclothes, or the thick paperback which was lying open on the locker. All she could see was the man who was lowering her onto the mattress, his aristocratic features dark and shuttered as he made sure she was covered by a feather-soft eiderdown, before stripping his clothes off.

She lay and watched as he peeled off his shirt, his skin gleaming like living metal in the bright moonlight which streamed in through the windows. She observed the line of black hair which arrowed down from his chest to his navel and as he began to slide the zip down, he lifted his head to slant her the sexiest smile she'd ever seen.

'Does it turn you on to watch me undress?' he murmured.

Hollie nodded. She liked that he wasn't treating her as a novice, which essentially she was. Last time they'd had sex it had all been so new and so incredible—as if she hadn't been able to believe that someone like Maximo was in bed with someone like her. But while she might be new to all this, even she could acknowledge the undeniable chemistry which burned between them and she was determined to enjoy every second of what came next. She wasn't going to long for the impossible or wish things had been different. That ship had sailed. She was going to live in the now.

The mattress dipped as he came to lie beside her, taking the baggy hem of the T-shirt she was still wearing and running the tip of his finger over it. 'You have me at something of a disadvantage,' he murmured. 'You're still wearing this, while I am completely naked.'

'Surely it's me that's at a disadvantage,' she returned, lifting her arms above her head without being asked so that he could peel off the offending garment and drop it to one side of the bed.

Maximo pulled her into his arms, brushing aside the thick fall of her silky hair as he pressed his lips into her neck. He hadn't thought this would happen. God knew, he hadn't intended for it to happen—but in the end she had proved too much of a temptation and, besides, which of them was he protecting by resisting something they obviously both wanted? Not her, who was so hungry for him that she was writhing against him like a siren, her breath warm and fast against his skin. Nor himself, either. After all, the damage had already been done and she was pregnant. And if that was a cynical way of looking at it, so what?

He began to explore her body, reacquainting himself with her soft curves and delicious flesh, his fingers sliding over her silky skin. He cupped her breasts in his palms, thinking how full they were—much fuller than last time.

Was that because of the baby?

A rush of something he didn't recognise roared through his blood but deliberately, he blocked it.

*He wasn't going to think about the baby. The only thing he was going to think about was pleasure.*

So he concentrated on employing every sensual skill he had learnt, tempering blatant provocation with the tantalising whisper of soft promise. So that while his rock-hard erection was pushing against her belly, he was kissing her eyelids, her cheeks, her neck and her ears, making her wait until finally he allowed his lips to plunder hers. Was it the little cry of bliss she gave which made him feel as if he were drowning? As if she were drawing him into some unknown place of dark, sweet honey.

'You are...*deliciosa.*'

'Delicious?' she guessed.

'You are fluent in Spanish now, are you, Hollie?' But as she opened her mouth to doubtless make some equally flippant reply, he kissed away the answer, reaching down to slide his finger between her silken folds, enjoying her gasped frustration as he brought her to the edge of orgasm, over and over again. Only when he could bear his own exquisite torture no longer did he position himself to enter her at last—though more slowly and carefully than he had ever done before. And didn't that make him feel...?

What?

He didn't know and he didn't care because his thoughts were being scatter-gunned by Hollie clenching hard around him, her back arching like a bow as she spasmed, and then he too was jerking helplessly in her arms.

For a while there was no sound other than their ragged sighs, and then she drifted her lips to his cheek.

'Maximo,' she murmured huskily.

'Don't move,' he instructed unsteadily, because already he was growing hard inside her again. 'Stay exactly where you are.'

'I have no intention of going anywhere.'

He gave a soft laugh as he began to move and, while the second time was just as amazing, the third almost defied definition, leaving him gloriously sated and replete.

'I've never done it without protection before,' he observed after a while, lying back against the rumpled bedclothes, his skin warm with satisfaction.

'So that's a first?'

'Well, by my reckoning, it's actually the second.'

His head tipped back against the pillow as she giggled and he must have slept, because when next he opened his eyes, the bright light of a winter's morning had replaced the silvery moonlight of the previous night. He lay there for a moment in silence, aware of Hollie's head on his shoulder—her hair spread out over his chest like satin. He stared down at the twin crescents of her lashes, dark and feathery against her pink cheeks. Her rosy lips were parted, her breathing slow and steady and he felt a twist of something unknown deep inside him.

She was so damned...*unexpected*.

He swallowed.

She had surprised him the first time around with her innocence and she had surprised him this time by being so gloriously accessible. Her body had opened up with a delicious familiarity. It was as if she instinctively knew what pleased him—as if they had been designed to fit together perfectly.

What was the *matter* with him? Almost imperceptibly he shook his head, trying to clear the thoughts which had obviously been skewed by the heady cocktail of hormones which were surging through his bloodstream. But the movement must have woken her, because Hollie's lashes fluttered open and Maximo found himself dazzled by the light shining from her wide grey eyes. He saw a flicker of confusion cross her face, as if she couldn't quite work out where she was, or who with— and then her lips curved into a smile which only made him want to kiss her.

'Happy Christmas!' she said.

'And to you,' he said, his swift smile intended to inform her that he hadn't had a complete personality change during the night. 'Hollie—'

'It's okay,' she said quickly, before moving away from him towards the other side of the bed. 'You don't have to say a word. I know the score.'

'You do?' he questioned.

Hollie couldn't miss the look of surprise which had darkened his features. Was he worried she was about to start planning some sort of future with him, just because they'd had amazing sex? Was he so arrogant as to imagine that a long night of love-making had turned her head?

*And wasn't he right to think that way when her heart was full of wonder at the beauty of what had happened? But Maximo would never know that. Not now and not ever—because if he did, it would destroy this fragile relationship of theirs.*

'Of course I do,' she answered, her staunch words helping disguise the distracting flutter of her emotions. 'We've already had the discussion. You don't want to be involved with family life and I'm cool with that, for all the reasons I gave before. Nothing has changed. I enjoyed last night and I hope you did too—'

'You know damned well I did,' he growled.

'Well, then.' She raised her eyebrows. 'What's not to like? Has the snow melted? Because if so, I can be on my way and out of your hair.'

Jumping out of bed, she grabbed the nearest velvet throw—which just happened to be scarlet—and wrapped it around herself, before padding over to the window, aware of Maximo's gaze burning into her, watching every move she made.

Part of her wondered if it had all been a dream and the snow nothing but a figment of her imagination. Hadn't she feared that this morning she would look out onto the dull greys and browns of a midwinter garden? But the scene which greeted her was as frozen and as beautiful as it had been the day before. A completely impenetrable world of white. Deep down Hollie knew it would probably be best for everyone if she could make her escape, but she couldn't help the sudden leap of her heart when she realised that wasn't going to be possible. Who could blame her for wanting to eke out this sensual liaison for as long as possible? 'Oh, dear.'

'Oh, dear what?'

'Bad news, I'm afraid. There's no sign of any thaw and it looks like there might even have been a fresh fall during the night. The road out of here is blocked, all right.' She turned back to face him, wondering what had caused his face to darken like that. 'Looks like my departure is going to have to be delayed.'

'You sound almost *disappointed*, Hollie. Are you so eager to get away?'

Hollie gave him the benefit of her brightest smile. Perhaps she was better at acting than she'd thought. Maybe her relationship with Maximo—if you could call it a relationship—was a bit like Christmas. There was all this amazing stuff on the surface, which made you feel fantastic at the time, but after a day or two it was all over, as if it had never happened.

And thinking of Christmas… Hollie sucked in a breath. Just because Maximo had set himself up as some kind of modern-day Scrooge, didn't mean she had to copy him, did it? They might not have a tree, or fancy baubles, but wasn't *adaptable* her middle name? She knew what the score was, which meant that she didn't have to try to impress him. She could just be herself, which she knew from some of her girlfriends wasn't always the case when you were with a man. Wasn't that a liberation of sorts?

So she shot him another smile. 'The only disappointment would be if we weren't going to celebrate Christmas, but that's not going to happen.'

'It isn't?' he questioned, with a frown.

'Certainly not.'

'But there's nothing here. The castle doesn't run to fairy lights,' he said sarcastically. 'And I told you. I don't like Christmas.'

'Maybe you don't, but I do. There's no need for us to

forgo the festivities, just because we're lacking a few resources—and I don't intend to. Just leave it to me.'

The darkness in his eyes had been replaced by a sudden smokiness which Hollie recognised and it was with a feeling of falling—or failing—that she felt her body's instant response.

'I don't care about the damned festivities,' he ground out. 'All I care about is having you back in my bed again. Now come over here, Hollie Walker, before I lose patience.'

Hollie had never been quite so aware of her own power and for a few brief moments she revelled in it. 'Why don't you come and get me?' she said.

# CHAPTER EIGHT

'OKAY. YOU CAN open them now.'

The soft hands which had been covering his eyes were removed and Maximo grew still as he stared at the scene in front of him, unable to believe what he was seeing. He shook his head a little, but nothing altered. What the hell had happened? The previously bare room now seemed like a distant memory, replaced by a glittering and shimmering spectacle. Because Hollie had decorated the long table in the castle library for a late Christmas lunch. No. She'd done much more than that. She had actually decorated the whole damned room so that it resembled something you might see on the movie channel throughout the month of December.

Gleaming silver discs and squares hung from the ceiling, suspended by almost invisible pieces of thread. More dangled from a large branch of conifer, which somehow managed to resemble a miniature Christmas tree. And there were sprigs of holly just about everywhere—lying on empty bookshelves and decorously placed on the mantelpiece—plus an enormous bunch which had been stuck into a pottery jug as a centrepiece for the table.

As for the table…

Maximo been entertained many times during his life with no expense spared, because when a woman made you dinner, she seemed to think she was auditioning for a permanent role in your life.

But this was different.

He narrowed his eyes. Echoing the bright holly berries, the table was spread with what looked like the scarlet velvet throw which had adorned her naked body that very morning. Matching red ribbons were tied in festive bows around two snowy linen napkins and everywhere there were candles. Tall candles and squat candles. Some which were near the end of their natural life and others which were clearly brand-new. Their flames flickered upwards and wove intricate shadows against the walls, while more flames came from the fire which was burning brightly in the grate. His gaze moved to the window where outside dusk was falling on the pristine snowy scene, and the contrast with the illuminated interior of the ancient room made the place look almost…magical.

'What have you done?' he husked.

She shrugged. 'I played around with what we had. The candles I found in the scullery. The shiny things hanging from the ceiling are cardboard, covered with silver foil which I discovered in a drawer in the kitchen—and the cotton comes from a sewing kit in my handbag. The napkins were in those hampers you ordered, as were the ribbons—and I found the rest of the stuff in the garden.' She chewed on her lip, anxiety suddenly creasing her brow. 'You do like it?'

'It's…it's a surprise,' he admitted at last. 'It's…well, it's remarkable.'

She looked at him a little uncertainly, as if unsure whether or not that was a compliment. 'Why don't you sit down?' she suggested. 'And I'll bring the food in.'

'I'll help.'

'No,' she said firmly. 'You won't. Humour me, Maximo. You waited on me at dinner last night and now it's my turn. I'm perfectly capable of carrying a dish or two. You can open the wine if you like and pour yourself a glass. I'm just having water—obviously. So let me go and fetch the food.'

Maximo uncorked the bottle and walked across to the fire to hurl an applewood log onto the already crackling blaze, more to distract himself from the spiky carousel of his thoughts than for any other reason. *This* was the reason he always turned down every damn Christmas invitation which ever came his way, because this kind of homely festivity mocked him. Every single time. It reminded him of the lives of others and all the things he'd never had. It made him think of families who cooked and ate together, laughing and talking as they sat around the table. And his discomfort was amplified by Hollie's presence, by her newly discovered sexuality coupled with the fact that she was pregnant with his child.

She returned to the room, carrying a large tray which he took from her, waving away her protests, and he watched while she left for a final journey to the kitchen. Her hips were swaying in unconscious invitation, and she looked almost unbearably sexy in a borrowed sweater of his, which came down to mid-thigh. When he had finally released her from his bed that morning she had bemoaned aloud the fact that she didn't have a change of knickers.

'Then don't wear any.'

'I can't do that!'

'Why not?' His query had been casual, but his heart had been racing like a schoolboy's. And she had looked at him, and he at her, and somehow their getting up had been delayed even further. She had straddled him with abandon and afterwards they had shared a bath and stayed there until their fingertips were wrinkled, and she had squealed with delight when he'd wrapped her in a bathrobe and carried her back into the bedroom.

He couldn't remember ever feeling quite so turned on by a woman and if she hadn't gone to so much trouble with the meal, he might have suggested they postpone it in favour of a far more sensual feast.

But Maximo couldn't shake off a lingering sense of disconnect as he sat down at the table. Because for some reason it felt as if ghosts were joining them and sitting at those empty chairs. The ghost of his mother, so recently dead. His father, too—though he'd only discovered his demise by reading about it in one of the national Spanish newspapers last year. He thought of Christmases past. He stared at Hollie's belly. Of Christmases future.

'There's some of your Cantabrian mountain stew, which I've reheated,' she was saying, shattering his troubled thoughts with her soft English chatter. 'And lots of lovely cheeses and meats from those fancy hampers. Shall I cut you a slice of this Iberico ham, Maximo?'

His tongue felt as if it wouldn't work, as if it were too big for his mouth. He shook his head, taking a sip of wine. Rich, red wine which warmed the blood like soup. He always drank this particular vintage during his preferred solitary Christmases, but tonight, he might as well have been drinking vinegar. Why was he so beset with the past tonight? he wondered with irritation—as if it were a heavy mantle around his shoulders which he couldn't shake off?

'Is something wrong?' she said as he put the barely touched glass down.

He shook his head. 'No, nothing's wrong.'

'Forgive me for contradicting you, Maximo, but something clearly *is*.'

'Let's eat,' he growled. Remembering that they'd missed breakfast, he forced himself to work his way through some of the food, though he noticed that Hollie was tucking into her own meal with a healthy appetite and, on some level, that pleased him. Eventually, she looked up from her plate of cheese and crackers, putting her knife down with a thoughtful expression on her face.

'You know, something has been puzzling me,' she observed slowly.

'Really?' he questioned, injecting a deliberate note of boredom into his voice because her analytical tone suggested she was intending to take the conversation somewhere he didn't want it to go.

'Any ideas?' she ventured.

'I have many attributes, Hollie,' he drawled, 'but mind-reading has never been one of them.'

But his sarcasm didn't deter her. She simply dabbed at the corners of her mouth with her napkin.

'When you told me about how you started in business, about breaking up big rocks in the road, there was something you failed to mention.'

'There were probably plenty of things I didn't mention.'

'Your parents, for one,' she said.

'Maybe that was a deliberate omission.'

'I mean, how did that happen?' she mused, as if he hadn't spoken. 'Because fourteen *is* very young, no matter how old you looked. You haven't explained what your parents had to say about you joining a construction team and working the roads.'

There was a pause. A pause which seemed to last for ever, giving him time to fall back on his familiar strategies for avoiding scrutiny. But something stopped him and he didn't know what. Was it the clearness of her grey eyes—or an expression of something like compassion which had softened her lovely face, rather than judgement? Almost as if she had guessed at the truth. He thought about what she'd told him about her own father—about his failure to be there for her. Maybe he and Hollie Walker had a lot more in common than he'd previously thought, and was it really such a big deal for the mother of his baby to discover a few truths about him?

'They didn't know,' he said.

'But they must have known. How could they not?'

'By that time in my life, my mother and I were estranged—'

'At *fourteen*?'

'Yes, Hollie. At fourteen. It happens.'

'And your father?'

He shrugged. 'He did not really deserve that title, for I only ever had the briefest of relationships with him.'

'Why?' she questioned quietly. 'What happened?'

His mouth tightened because this was the part which

was definitely off-limits. The part he had taken extra care to filter from his life and online presence—confident in the knowledge that nobody else in the picture would disclose it, because it didn't reflect well on them. Very few people knew who his father had been, and that had always suited him just fine.

Yet suddenly he remembered the nurses who had looked at him so contemptuously when he had stood by his mother's deathbed all those weeks ago. Was it that which made him want to break the habit of a lifetime and unburden himself to Hollie? Those nuns who had judged him and found him wanting for his seeming neglect. His mouth hardened. As if anyone who was old and a mother was automatically some kind of saint who deserved unconditional love from her child—a child she had shunned and rejected.

'My mother was never married to my father,' he said baldly. 'I was illegitimate. Not such a big deal now, but pretty big at the time, particularly in the part of the world where I grew up.' He saw her flinch and wondered if she was thinking about her own situation, wondering whether she too would be judged in this small part of Devon which was now her home. 'My father was one of Spain's wealthiest men. Have you heard of the clothes chain Estilo?' he questioned suddenly.

'Yes, of course I have. Practically every woman on the planet has an Estilo piece in her wardrobe.'

'He owned it,' he said and saw her eyes widen in shock. 'He was married, of course. He had any number of lovers—my mother being just one of them.'

'And was she…content with that?'

His narrowed his eyes. 'No woman is ever truly content with being a mistress, Hollie. Maybe that's why she became pregnant.'

'With you?'

He nodded. '*Sí.* With me. He had told her from the very start that he wanted no children, for he already had two daughters—and although he desperately wanted a son, he planned to conceive one with his similarly aristocratic wife. Outwardly, his life was a model of respectability and he had no intention of altering that state. When my mother went to him with news I was on the way, I think she was expecting him to change his mind and divorce his wife, but he didn't. He didn't want the scandal or the damage to his reputation as a family man. So he ordered her from the house and gave her nothing, not even after I was born.' His mouth thinned. 'There was no acknowledgement that I was his child and certainly no maintenance.'

'But…if he was so rich—'

'To have compensated her would have been an admission of liability and that was something he wasn't prepared to do.'

'She didn't go to the papers?'

'Like I said, it was a different world back then and he had most of the media in his pocket anyway.' His mouth hardened. 'So I lived from hand to mouth with a mother who was increasingly resentful that I had ruined her chances of having a "normal" life. Because where we lived, a woman who had a child out of wedlock was shunned.'

Her grey gaze was steady as she flicked her tongue over her lips. 'What happened?' she whispered.

He shrugged. 'My father had no other son and then

his wife died and, behind the scenes, my mother was concocting a plan. I only learned afterwards that she had gone to his home and confronted him. Told him I looked exactly like him—which was true—and that I had his mannerisms. In the extremely macho world in which he operated, she appealed to both his ego and his pride. She asked would he not prefer his only son to inherit his valuable business, rather than his daughters—two women who would be bound to go off and have families of their own. So he agreed to give me a home in his enormous mansion in the centre of Madrid.' He smiled bitterly. 'I guess you might describe it as a trial run. Like taking on an apprentice on a temporary basis, to see whether or not they fit in. To see if I was suitable to be recognised as his son.'

'And what did you do?' she questioned, when the silence which followed his disclosure became elongated. 'Did you go?'

'Life at home wasn't exactly wonderful and I can't pretend that the thought of inheriting one of Spain's most profitable companies didn't appeal to a boy who had known nothing but hardship. So I went to my father's house…' He shrugged as his voice tailed off. 'And quickly realised that the situation I found myself in was untenable.'

'How so?' she whispered.

He was lost now. Lost in the dark memories of the past. He remembered being bemused by the amount of cutlery beside his plate, and cramming food in his mouth as if he were a street urchin. Which was exactly how he had felt. Like a poor boy who had wandered into a parallel universe. He remembered being amazed at marble-decked bathrooms the size of ballrooms and lavish dinners which could have fed a whole village. His stepsisters laughing because he didn't know which knife to use. The servants looking at him with a scorn they hadn't bothered to hide, as if recognising that he was an outsider. *Un bastardo.* And that was never going to change—he'd recognised that instantly. He'd stuck it out for as long as he could but it had felt as if he were trapped inside his own private hell.

'I wasn't made to feel *welcome*,' he summarised acidly and although she looked as if she wanted him to elaborate, he was damned if he was going to do that, for any frailties he possessed, he showed to no one. Nobody would ever see him vulnerable—not even the mother of his child. 'As dawn broke on Christmas Eve, I left to return to my mother and managed to hitch rides from Madrid to A Coruña. I arrived not long before midnight when the night was bitterly cold and the snow was falling. I remember seeing the Belen in the town square… the traditional nativity scene,' he elaborated, when he saw her frown. 'I thought my mother might be out— although I certainly didn't think she'd be on her way to Mass. She was more likely to be drinking in a bar.' He gave a short laugh. 'But she'd gone.'

'Gone?' she echoed. 'Gone where?'

'I never found out. She had cleared out all her stuff the month before and left no word or forwarding address.' It shouldn't have come as a shock, but it did. Because deep down he had always believed that she loved him, because she was his mother. But she did not love him. She never had. He had fallen to his knees in the icy snow and wept and that was the last time he had ever wept. At least he'd had food in his rucksack—the only thing he had taken from his father's house. And then he had begun to walk, though he didn't know where. He had walked on through the night and on Christmas morning he had stumbled across the construction site and waited there for workers to return after the Christmas break. And he had vowed there and then that he would never let anyone close enough to hurt him again.

'She wiped me from her life as if I had never existed,' he continued, the words falling from his mouth like stones. 'It was only much later, when I had started to make money, that she contacted me again.'

'And were you ever…reconciled?'

'We met,' he said tersely, staring down at his fingernails. 'But her main focus was on what I could buy for her, rather than making up for all those lost years. I provided for her throughout the rest of her life but I never saw her again until a couple of months ago.'

'She…died?'

He looked up at her, feeling himself tense up. 'How the hell did you know that?' he demanded.

'Something in your face as you said it. I could see your pain.' Her voice was soft again. How did she make it so damned soft? 'I'm sorry for your loss, Maximo. I know she was cruel to you, but she was still your mother.'

He wanted to deny that he felt anything but she was getting up from the table and walking round to where he sat, sliding onto his lap to face him, one bare leg on either side of his. She looked at him for a long moment before resting her head on his in an age-old gesture which had never come his way before. Maybe he'd never needed it before. It had nothing to do with sex—and everything to do with comfort. And it was powerful, he realised. Unbelievably…powerful.

He wanted to shrug her off, to tell her he didn't need any clumsy attempts at sympathy—but the words remained unspoken, the gesture never made. He could smell her clean, soapy scent and right then she seemed to embody all the virtues he'd never really associated with the women in his life.

Innocence.

Decency.

Kindness.

Suddenly a tension which had been coiled so tightly inside him started unravelling, like a line spinning wildly from the fisherman's rod. Something he hadn't even realised had been stretched to breaking point now snapped and he held her tightly, losing himself in an embrace so close that you couldn't have fitted a hair between them.

He told himself it was desire.

Because it *was* desire. What else could it be? The powerful beat of his heart and the low clench of heat were familiar enough, but his urgent need to possess her was off the scale. With one hand he hooked the back of her neck and brought her face down to his, revelling in that first sweet taste of her lips as her satiny hair spilled over his hands. He deepened the kiss and deepened it still more, until she was writhing around on his lap—her lack of panties instantly apparent from the syrupy wetness which was seeping into his jeans.

'Unzip me,' he urged throatily.

Instantly, she complied, although her fingers were

trembling and it took some careful manoeuvring before he was free, and then at last he lowered her down onto his aching shaft, a ragged groan escaping from his lips as he filled her.

She rode him. She rode him as if she had been born to do just that. Was it instinct which made her so proficient at that age-old rhythm? Because it certainly wasn't experience. Yet she seemed to read him so well. As if she knew exactly when he wanted her to pull the borrowed sweater over her head so that he could drink in every second of her partial striptease and the luscious bounce of her breasts. She shook her hair, so that it moved around her bare shoulders like a shiny ripple of wheat. And then he was coming and so was she. Coming and coming and coming…and it was like no orgasm he'd ever experienced.

His shout of exclamation—or was it exultation?—was harsh. Imprecise. His body bucked helplessly beneath her. And when it was over she didn't say a word, and he was glad. He didn't want her attempting to give meaning to what had just taken place. Because it had no meaning. It was just a manifestation of their extraordinary physical chemistry.

He stirred, wanting to put a little distance between them. Needing space to order his befuddled thoughts. 'Don't you think maybe it's time for dessert?'

'But there isn't…' Her breath was warm against his neck, her words soporific and slightly slurred. 'I'm afraid there isn't any dessert.'

He pulled back from her and frowned. 'Really? I thought you brought cake with you?'

Unwillingly stirred from her sleepy state, Hollie

stared back at him in confusion, suddenly remembering the wretched cake which Janette had insisted on commissioning. 'You really want cake now?'

'Why not?'

Why *not*? She hadn't wanted to present it to him at the time and she was even less inclined to do so now, because it seemed to symbolise some of the things which had been so out of kilter between them. It reminded her of the speed with which he'd left her bed and the way he'd distanced himself afterwards. Worst of all was the memory of his reaction to her pregnancy when he'd been so angry and cold. And she was slightly irritated that he'd asked for it now, because it was hardly the most romantic way to end what had just been the most erotic encounter of her life. But Maximo doesn't do romance, she reminded herself fiercely. He does sex. And that's all he does. Better think about that before you start fabricating any more foolish dreams about him.

'Of course. How could I have forgotten? I'll go and fetch it,' she said, sliding from his lap and plucking his sweater from the floor, before wriggling it over her head. After a detour to the bathroom she hunted down the cake, and when she walked back into the library, she found Maximo still sitting at the table, seemingly lost in thought as he stared across the room at the crackling fire. He looked up as she put the cake on the table, but his expression was shadowed and indecipherable—their mood of lazy sensuality seemingly broken. She wanted to cut him a slice before he had seen it, but he had risen from his seat to look over her shoulder, at the Spanish word for congratulations, which she had laboriously piped onto the white icing.

'*"Felicidades",*' he read slowly, and then pointed to a fuzzy-looking shape beside the word. 'And what's this?'

Did he guess it was a teardrop, which had fallen straight onto the coloured icing at a critical moment? Yesterday she might have concocted some flimsy excuse and told him that she'd been trying to create a star, but not today. Because he had told her stuff. He'd confided in her. Hard, painful stuff. He'd let his guard down, presumably because he'd felt as if, on some level, he could trust her. So maybe she should trust him, too. And besides, it wasn't as if they had any shared illusions about the future which could be tarnished by the truth, was it?

'It was a tear,' she admitted, meeting the seeking expression in his black eyes with a shrug. 'I was feeling a bit sorry for myself.'

'But you're not now?'

'No, I'm not. There's no point. If life gives you lemons, you just have to make lemonade.'

Maximo took the slice she offered him, breaking off a fragment and putting it in his mouth so that it melted in a sugary rush against his tongue. He thought about the days which had led up to this moment, and the days which would follow. His mind began to compose an agenda, just like when he took on a new business deal and had to deal with facts methodically. Whatever happened he would support his child financially—in a way in which his own father had never supported him.

*Just* financially?

He stared across the table at Hollie, who was studiously picking frosting off her own piece of cake, though not actually eating any. And suddenly he realised that, despite all her outward simplicity, the package she presented was way more complex than he'd first imagined.

He had been the first man to have had sex with her. The only man. That shouldn't have meant anything but the truth was, it did. It made a primitive satisfaction pulse through his body. And although that realisation should have unsettled him, somehow it didn't because it had shone a light onto something else he'd only just realised.

Going forward, he didn't *want* her sleeping with other men. Just as he didn't want his child calling another man Papi. Maybe his attitude could be described as possession but could also be described as pragmatism. Because if the lack of a father had cast dark clouds over his life, hadn't she experienced something similar? And if that were the case, then wasn't it comparatively easy for them to do something about it, to spare their own child a similar kind of heartache?

'Marry me, Hollie.'

She looked up from her crumbled cake, her expression one of shock then confusion, as if she hadn't heard him properly. She knitted her brows together. 'What did you say?'

'I said, marry me, Hollie.'

'Is that an…order?'

'Does my method of asking offend you? Do you want me to pretend?' he demanded huskily. 'To go down on one knee with a ring-pull from a cola can and tell you I'll buy you a thirty-carat diamond ring when we hit the shops?'

'No, Maximo, I don't want you to pretend anything.

I want you to tell me why you've suddenly come out with this extraordinary proposal.'

There was a pause. She'd told him she didn't want him to pretend, so he wouldn't. 'Because I think it's the only sensible solution to our dilemma.'

'*Dilemma?* Is that what you call it?'

'Don't try to gilt-edge a situation which neither of us ever intended to happen,' he said roughly. 'But instead, let's try to make the best of what we have. To make the lemonade, as you said. I don't want this child to grow up thinking his father didn't want him.'

'But you don't, do you?' she questioned baldly. 'Want him. Or her, for that matter.'

He shook his head. 'Now that the shock has worn off, I find that I do.'

'But that isn't enough to justify marriage, Maximo.'

'*No lo es*—I agree. And if it were someone else, I suspect I would not be having this conversation. But I find you easy company, Hollie, and that is rare—for my past relationships with women have not been easy. And believe me, our sexual chemistry is even more rare.'

'But…marriage,' she said. 'Isn't that a rather extreme solution?'

Her continued opposition rather than the instant capitulation he'd been anticipating only spurred Maximo on—because never did he feel quite so alive as when he was having to fight for something. 'I don't think I'll have a problem living with you. Plus my work takes me away a lot, which would give us both space. You will never have to worry about money. Ever. And that will still apply even if you find the situation intolerable and ask me for a divorce.'

He looked at her, his eyes cool and expectant, and Hollie felt the lurch of something she couldn't quite define. Or maybe she just didn't dare to. Because surely she should be feeling offended by his rather brutal words. Surely she shouldn't be excited about the thought of getting wed to a man who was clearly offering marriage out of some archaic form of *duty*? But she was. She couldn't help herself. She might try to talk herself out of her feelings by applying logic, but they were still her feelings.

The truth was that she found him easy company, too. And while she had no experience of sexual chemistry, she didn't imagine it was possible for that side of their relationship to get any better.

But the main thing to consider was her baby.

Their baby.

She touched her fingers to her belly and felt a little spark of hope flickering inside her. Didn't she owe it to this innocent life inside her to offer their child the best possible start in life? To not have to worry about spiralling childcare costs, or the fact that her baby had no contact with a single other blood relative than her. Hadn't she grown up that way and found it lonely and miserable? And Maximo had experienced that too— he'd effectively admitted it to her earlier.

Yet she didn't have a clue about what passed for normal behaviour in the world of this privileged billionaire. For all she knew, he might want what she believed was called an 'open' marriage and some instinct deep in her gut told her she would find that intolerable.

'What about fidelity?' she blurted out. 'Are you intending to be faithful to me?'

'I am and I will,' he said, his voice suddenly growing harsh. 'But I will also be truthful, Hollie. And if ever I meet a woman I desire more than you, then I will tell you so immediately and we will dissolve our marriage.'

It wasn't the answer she'd wanted, but she guessed it would have to do. Because although once again his words were brutal, at least they were true. She thought of the story he had told her and the bitter sadness she had seen in his eyes as he'd recounted it. Maximo had his vulnerabilities too, she realised, just like her. Couldn't they be there for each other—to reach out to each other in times of need—united against a sometimes cruel world?

So Hollie nodded as a sudden sense of calm filled her and the smile she gave him came straight from the heart. 'Then I will,' she said softly. 'I will marry you, Maximo.'

# CHAPTER NINE

THE THAW SET in and it was as if the snow had never existed. As if it had all been nothing but a dream. As if Christmas Day and the four days which followed had never actually happened.

Except that they had. At the end of that delicious and sensual sojourn in the ancient castle Kastelloes, Maximo Diaz had asked Hollie Walker to marry him. And her future had changed in an instant. Her image of herself as a plucky but sometimes lonely single mother had crumbled away and instead she was having to get her head around the fact that soon she was going to be the wife of the sexy Spanish tycoon.

Maximo was still sleeping as she slipped silently from the bed, wrapping herself in velvet—green today—before staring out of the window. Water was dripping from branches, from bushes—drip-drip-drip. The dark turrets of the castle were no longer topped by a crown of white and nor did the bushes look like giant white stones. The magic had gone, she realised, a sudden whisper of apprehension prickling over her as she studied Maximo's tousled black head lying against the pillow and all her suppressed fears were suddenly given life.

Would he wake up and regret the resolution they'd come to at the end of Christmas Day, when—possibly affected by the emotional aftermath of the things he'd told her—he had asked her to be his wife? Perhaps it would be better if she gave him the opportunity to retract words he might have delivered too hastily, and she wondered if she could manage to do it in a way which meant that neither of them would lose face.

His lashes fluttered open—so dark against the silken olive of his skin—and mentally Hollie steeled herself against his beauty as he surveyed her through a shuttered gaze.

'The snow has melted,' she said baldly.

'That's good.'

'Good?'

'Sure. Unless you were planning to build a snowman. Don't you need a change of underwear, and don't we need to get to London? If the roads are clear, it means we can go.'

'London?' She looked at him blankly. 'You never said anything about London.'

'My jet is in an airfield on the outskirts of the city, Hollie.' His voice was soft but his words resolute. 'And I'm due back in Madrid for a New Year's party I've promised to attend under pain of death if I don't. As my future wife you'll be coming with me and there's no reason why you shouldn't move in straight away.'

She hadn't considered living in Madrid either. How stupid was that? 'But I thought...'

'What?' he prompted softly, throwing back the pile

of velvet throws to rise from the bed like a magnificent dark and golden statue brought to life, before walking towards her. 'What did you think?'

'That I'd…' It was difficult to think of anything when he was standing so close and so naked. 'Well, I'll have to work out my notice for Janette.'

'Seriously?'

She nodded. 'Of course.'

He shrugged, his eyes shards of glittering jet. 'Even though I could easily arrange for one of my staff to take your place?'

His suggestion made her feel dispensable. As if her job and her old life were of no consequence. And even though it *was* a simple office job which anyone could probably do, and even though Hollie had often found Janette difficult, she had no intention of disappearing in a puff of smoke simply because a rich man was snapping his fingers. If she fell in with his autocratic wishes so readily, it wouldn't bode well for the rest of their lives, would it?

'I'm afraid I can't do that, Maximo,' she said. 'I can't possibly break my contract. I don't want to sneak away from Trescombe under a black cloud.'

His face darkened, as if her determination surprised and slightly irked him. 'I am loath to be apart from you, Hollie—perhaps I've become a little too used to having you in my bed,' he murmured. 'But obviously we can work round it. We'll just have to jet between the two places until you're free to move, if that's what you want.'

Of course it wasn't what she *wanted*. In a way, she was terrified of being apart from him. Terrified that their affair and his subsequent proposal would get diluted by distance and prove as insubstantial as the Christmas snow itself. If she worked out her notice there was the very real possibility that Maximo would change his mind and Hollie didn't want him to change his mind.

She wanted this. Him. The whole package.

She wanted to be his wife. She wanted him to be a father to their baby.

But if Maximo was going to get cold feet, then surely it was better if they discovered it now rather than later.

'The month will soon pass,' she said, with a certainty she didn't feel.

'You think so?' He sighed. 'Then I guess I must be patient—which is not an attribute I've ever been particularly known for. I suppose I must admire your loyalty to your employer, Hollie—but that's all we're going to say on the subject, because I'm taking you back to bed.'

Hollie was still glowing when Maximo's limousine made its way up the hill towards the castle, and she began to get an idea how smoothly the world worked when it was powered by wealth. Decisions which might have taken weeks to evolve were enacted almost before you'd finished making them. Life became seamless and also a little bit scary as she was driven to her cottage and instructed to pack only the things she couldn't bear to be without.

'But we're not leaving Trescombe completely, are we?' she questioned. 'I mean, it's not like we're cutting ties with the place completely. Because when you start renovating the castle—'

'Let's just concentrate on the essentials for now, shall we, Hollie?'

And although his words were a little clipped, Hollie couldn't deny how comforting it was to have someone else make the decisions. She felt the tension leave her body, realising this was the first time she'd ever had someone to lean on. She had cared for her mother and supported her emotionally when she'd gone to pieces, and then she had cared for herself when her mother had died. Why wouldn't she? Yet she couldn't deny how great it was to let someone else take responsibility for a change.

'Okay,' she said. 'I'll go and get my things together. Would you like to come inside?'

'No. I'll wait here in the car. I have a few calls to make.'

It took her less than twenty minutes before Hollie rushed out of the door with her little suitcase, half imagining that the limousine might have disappeared in the interim, like Cinderella's fancy coach turning into a pumpkin. But, no, it was still there—and the six-year-old twin boys who lived in the house opposite were gazing at the shiny black livery as if Santa's reinvented sleigh had made a post-Christmas appearance. As the chauffeur shut the door behind her, Maximo lifted a narrow-eyed gaze from his computer and Hollie got the distinct feeling he had forgotten she was there.

Through towns decked with Christmas finery, they were driven at speed to London, where Maximo announced his intention to buy her a completely new wardrobe, so she could arrive in Madrid suitably clad.

Which left her wondering exactly what was the matter with the way she looked now.

She stared rather moodily at her well-polished brown

leather boots before lifting her gaze to his. 'Because I'll let you down, I suppose?'

'It's not a question of letting me down. You look like a college student,' he informed her, almost gently, his fingertips whispering over her mane of hair. 'Which is undoubtedly a wildly sexy look, just not one which is particularly appropriate for my future wife. If you aren't dressed suitably it will make you self-conscious, for you will be mixing with women who will undoubtedly be wearing very costly clothes.'

'Gosh, you're making our future union sound like it's going to be fun, Maximo.'

He smiled then—a slow, sensual smile which curled over her skin like a wisp of smoke. 'Oh, I can offer you fun, Hollie. Be in no doubt about that. Now wipe that apprehensive look from your face and kiss me instead.'

And wasn't it crazy how his kiss had the power to dissolve every last doubt?

The limousine dropped them at an expensive-looking department store in central London with doormen who looked as if they had stepped straight out of a Victorian novel. And although the post-Christmas sales had just started and there were stampedes of people buying sequinned dresses and puddings which would shortly reach their sell-by dates, Hollie was assigned a personal shopper all to herself, though Maximo's insistence on accompanying her took her a little by surprise.

He watched as she paraded before him in a variety of outfits and the molten smoulder of his eyes when he approved a particular article of clothing was flattering, yes—but his attention quickly turned back to his computer, as though his work was more engrossing than anything else. Of course it was. He was just dressing her up like a doll so that she wouldn't disappoint him in front of all his rich friends.

But she couldn't deny that the exquisite garments felt wonderful against her skin—more than that, they made her look like someone she'd never believed she could be. Why, at certain angles she looked almost…pretty.

'I suppose you've taken lots of women shopping in the past like this?' she probed.

'Not a single one,' he admitted. 'But then, I've never asked anyone to marry me before either. Just as I have never been quite so much in physical thrall to a woman as I am to you. And so, to avoid unnecessary repetition of predictable questions, shall I simply assure you that having my full attention like this is not the way I usually operate? Does that put your mind at rest, as well as flattering your ego, Hollie?'

It did. It made her feel…*special*. It made her want to whistle a tune, to sing out loud at the top of her voice. She felt as if she could conquer the world.

And when the shopping expedition was concluded and they had eaten lunch in a hushed restaurant with thick white tablecloths and women who watched him with predatory eyes, Maximo dropped her back at the store, where she was whisked off to a basement spa which smelt faintly of sandalwood and tuberose. There she had her first ever bikini wax, a pedicure and make-up lesson, though she begged them to go easy on the mascara. Next, a sweet girl in a white uniform took her to the hairdressing section to have a couple of inches snipped off her mane and some choppy layers added. And when it was all done, she stood in front of the full-length mirror in her new silk dress, with a shiny fall of hair shimmering around her shoulders, and her transformation seemed complete.

She didn't look like Hollie Walker any more.

Neither an uptight office girl nor a giddy Christmas elf stared back at her today.

She looked like an expensive glossy *stranger*.

And when Maximo came to collect her, he must have thought along similar lines because he appeared almost taken aback by her appearance.

'*Bien, bien, bien*—what have we here, *mia belleza*?' he mused, his black gaze travelling over every inch of her, before he slid onto the back seat of the car beside her.

'You don't like it?'

'I didn't say that.' His hand slid over her thigh, his fingers stroking over the navy silk. 'You look out of this world.'

'Like an alien, you mean?'

He laughed. 'No, not remotely like that. Why do you always put yourself down?'

'Perhaps I'm not used to compliments.'

'Then I shall have to make sure you get used to them. Like a beautiful woman at her peak, is that better? My only complaint is that there isn't time for me to prove just how much you have excited my senses, because we need to buy you a ring before the shop closes.'

'We don't really have to do that today, do we, Maximo? Haven't we shopped enough?'

'I'm afraid we do. I was given to understand that

women can never have too much shopping, although maybe you're the exception to the rule,' he added drily. 'But tomorrow, we fly to Madrid and I intend that you should arrive there wearing the biggest diamond in the world.'

Hollie supposed it would be churlish to object to having 'the biggest diamond in the world' on the grounds that she was feeling increasingly detached from reality with all this high-end purchasing power. Yet wasn't this just another example of making sure she was 'good enough' to meet his wealthy friends?

She tried to shake off her insecurity as he took her to a darkened store somewhere near Hatton Garden, which didn't really look like a jeweller's from the outside, and he and the owner began speaking in a language she barely recognised as English. They spoke of *cushion* and *marquise* and *princess*, which she gathered were cuts of diamonds, though when she emerged from the store an hour later, it was with an enormous rock called a *round brilliant* dripping from her finger.

As they were leaving, she saw a woman in the street do a double take when she spotted the size of the jewel. But all Hollie could focus on was the sobering thought that the entire purchase had been conducted with zero emotion. There had been no joy on the face of her husband-to-be as he slipped the priceless ring on her finger—just a glimmer of quiet satisfaction in his eyes as the shop's owner informed him that he had just purchased the finest gem in his collection.

Because there *was* no emotion involved, Hollie reminded herself fiercely as they got into the waiting car. There might be mutual attraction and a determination to do the right thing by their baby, but this marriage was nothing but a solution to their *dilemma*, and she should forget that at her peril.

'So where are we going now?' she asked, slightly dazzled by the rainbow rays which sparkled on her left hand and wondering if she would have to remove it when she was cooking.

He glanced up from his phone, momentarily distracted. 'We'll spend tonight at the Granchester Hotel, for you must be tired after so much travelling?'

'A little,' she admitted.

'And tomorrow we head for the airfield where my jet is ready to fly us to Spain, because it's New Year's Eve and we have a big party to attend.'

'How big a party?' she said, suddenly nervous.

'Very big. The Spanish love to celebrate the start of the new year and since many of my friends will be gathered together in the same place, it means I can introduce you as my bride.' He glanced at his watch. 'We should arrive in Madrid in time for lunch.'

'And that's where you live? In Madrid?' It seemed crazy that soon she would marry him and she didn't actually *know*. There were so many things about him she didn't know.

'Yes, I have an apartment there, very close to the Retiro Park. I think you'll like it.'

Hollie felt dizzy. London for shopping. Madrid for lunch. And a massive New Year's Eve party with, no doubt, all the world's glitterati there. Was this going to be her life from now on? She supposed it was. Would she fit in? Or, even with all her fancy new clothes and hairstyle, would she still look like ordinary Hollie

Walker who worked in an office and baked cakes on the side?

But Maximo had put his phone away and was circling his fingertip over the palm of her hand and making her tremble, and her eyelids were fluttering to a close as he leaned over to kiss her. And really, what more could she possibly want?

# CHAPTER TEN

'AND THIS IS my housekeeper, Carmen. Anything you want—Carmen will be able to get for you.' Maximo's eyes glinted as he ushered Hollie inside. 'Within reason, of course.'

*'Encantada de conocerte,'* said Hollie, using one of the phrases her fiancé had taught her during the flight over from London that morning.

'I'm very pleased to meet you, too. I speak fluent English, by the way,' added Carmen, with a smile.

Hollie beamed. 'Thank goodness for that.'

'And congratulations on your engagement.' Carmen shot a brief smile in the direction of the knuckleduster diamond. 'The staff are all delighted for you and Señor Diaz.'

'I appreciate that, Carmen. And it's wonderful to be here.'

Carmen inclined her head. 'Welcome to your new home.'

'Thank you.' Hollie slid her tongue over her lips. Her new home—a huge and contemporary penthouse apartment overlooking Madrid's beautiful Retiro Park. It was terrifyingly immaculate, with not a single thing out of place, and as she shook the middle-aged housekeeper's hand she wondered if it would ever actually feel like home for her. But at least she was feeling calmer than she had done on the journey here. Their one-night stay at the Granchester Hotel had been unforgettable. Hollie had never stayed anywhere quite so luxurious and they'd been given an incredible suite with reputedly the best view over the London skyline, because Maximo was friends with the owner.

But butterfly nerves had been fluttering in her stomach as her fiancé's jet had touched down in Spain and they had been driven straight from the airfield to his apartment. It had been daunting at first, meeting his staff—Carmen, and a permanent cook as well as a daily cleaner. But they'd seemed very open and friendly, and genuinely pleased to meet her, and that gave Hollie a flare of hope.

*I can do this*, she thought.

*I will do this.*

'Would you like to see the rest of the apartment?' asked Maximo softly, once they were out of Carmen's earshot.

'Yes, please,' she said.

'And then, after lunch, I think it is time to introduce you to the very important Spanish tradition of the siesta.'

*'Maximo!'*

'You do realise that every time you whisper my name like that, it only turns me on some more, so you must never stop doing it? Now follow me and I will show you your new home.'

Hollie nodded, trying to concentrate on her surroundings, wanting to like them more than first impressions had suggested she might. Because although she was aware that she was in one of the most prestigious parts of Madrid, her initial reaction to Maximo's apartment had been one of disappointment. It was so modern and so *functional*. The spaces were vast and curiously impersonal, even thought they housed some pretty stunning furniture and artworks. Huge canvases adorned the giant walls and most of the furniture was dark, soft leather and almost tauntingly masculine. In fact, dark was the theme which predominated—apart from an illuminated wine cellar, which looked more like an art installation, a dining room which overlooked the city lights and a floodlit rectangular lap pool on the sprawling terrace, where Maximo informed her he liked to swim every morning before breakfast.

She tried to find the right words to say. Tried to imagine herself living here with a baby, with all these hard and gleaming surfaces. She thought about smudged little fingerprints clouding the acres of polished glass. 'It's lovely,' she said politely.

'There are plenty of good restaurants nearby and an interesting mix of people.'

'Gorgeous,' she said obediently, using the same tone she used to project in the office when a prospective vendor would canvas her opinion about the house they were just about to market. It wasn't a question of not being honest, it was simply showing consideration for other people's feelings. Because Hollie knew how a person could form a huge emotional attachment to their home. What right did she have to tell Maximo that she thought his apartment was a hideous monument to brutalism, when clearly he loved it? In England they often said an Englishman's home was his castle, well, maybe it was the same for Spanish men.

Yet all she could think about was a *real* castle, back in Trescombe, where they had shared that magical Christmas and candlelight had flickered intriguing shadows across the bare stone walls. Yes, Kastelloes could be chilly and, yes, the grounds were untamed and some of the interiors were crumbling away. But at least it had heart and soul and an artistic symmetry which took her breath away. Perhaps Maximo would capitalise on all those assets when he turned it into a luxury hotel to add to his existing group. She couldn't wait to see what he would do with it.

'Hollie?'

Maximo's voice interrupted her reverie.

'Mmm…?' she said absently.

'Weren't we talking about a siesta?'

She looked up, meeting the narrowed glint in his black eyes, and her heart turned over and melted. Who cared about bricks and mortar when a man looked at you that way? Who cared about anything when he could make her senses sing without even touching her?

'I believe we were,' she agreed and her answering smile seemed to spur him into instant and very masterful action. But she liked it when he made that soft roaring sound at the back of his throat and then carried her into their bedroom like a victor, carrying his spoils.

She liked it a lot.

Maximo watched Hollie's breasts rise and fall in time with her steady, even breathing. Her gleaming golden-brown hair was spread out over the pillow, her cheeks were lightly brushed with roses and she looked...

He swallowed.

Not beautiful, no. Her nose was a little too big and her lips not quite full enough ever to fit that imprecise and elusive definition which women craved and most men sought.

She looked sexy and serene. In fact, very serene and *very* sexy.

Once again he felt the tightening of desire low in his belly.

She had just flicked her tongue over his body and made his large frame convulse with spasms of delight he'd thought were never going to end. And afterwards he had done the same to her. Given swift featherlight licks against the hidden honey at the top of her legs, until she had clutched his bare shoulders with flailing fingertips and cried out his name.

But his remembered satisfaction was tempered by a sudden flicker of apprehension. She was the most perfect lover he could have ever imagined, and there had been a fair number during his thirty-four years of bachelorhood. But Hollie was like no other woman he'd ever known before. She was sweet and uncomplicated and innocent.

And she was having his baby.

His *baby*.

Didn't that give her a particular power—the kind of power he had vowed no woman would ever wield over him again? He could feel a sudden tightness in his throat. He had never wanted a child of his own, reasoning that someone who had never experienced parental love would be incapable of demonstrating any himself. He'd been scared of falling short and hadn't wanted another child to endure what he had endured. Plus, he'd liked his freedom and the ability to do what he wanted, when he wanted.

But now?

Suddenly he felt the winds of change upon him, and a feeling of inevitability blowing in their wake. He could sense a very different world opening up before him and simple, straightforward Hollie at the beating centre of it.

Hollie.

Hollie who seemed so soft and vulnerable. Almost *too* soft. *Too* vulnerable. He wasn't used to a woman looking at him that way, all wide-eyed and wondering. His mouth hardened. He would protect her and their child for as long as he lived, yes. He would give her whatever she wanted—hadn't he told her so just an hour ago, when he had carried her into the bedroom and stripped that provocative lingerie from her delicious body? She would have security for her and their child for the rest of her life, and he would put money in a trust to ensure that his son or daughter's future was secure. But those were practical needs he was able to fulfil, because this was a practical marriage and nothing more. He had made that clear to her when he'd asked her to be his wife and maybe now it was time to remember it himself. He wouldn't let her think this relationship was going to become any deeper than it already was, because that was never going to happen. Far better she get used to reality, rather than having her hopes raised and then dashed by unrealistic expectations. In the short term, wasn't it better to be a little cruel in order to be kind?

He stroked his fingers over the silky flesh of her cheek. 'Hollie?'

At the sound of his voice she began to stir, opening her eyes to find him watching her, and, almost shyly, she smiled. 'That was…amazing,' she said softly.

'Mmm. It certainly was, but now we must move. The party will already be in full swing and they're expecting us. Everyone's going to want to meet my fiancée.'

She bit down on her bottom lip. 'Have you told them we're engaged?'

'Not yet.' He lifted her hand and the dazzle of the large diamond shot bright fire over her hand. 'We'll let this ring announce it for us, shall we?'

'I'm nervous, Maximo.'

'Why are you nervous?'

'What if they don't like me?'

'Why wouldn't they like you? Now go and get ready and I'll ask Carmen to serve us a glass of *casera* before we leave.'

Hollie nodded and made her way towards the bathroom as Maximo's words echoed inside her head. Why wouldn't they like you? he had asked—because he had no comprehension of what it was like to be her. His world was very different and was inhabited by very different people. Would they welcome an unsophisticated stranger like her into their midst, or would they wonder if Maximo had taken leave of his senses?

She turned on the power shower and let the warm water bounce off her skin, telling herself she mustn't catastrophise the evening before it had even begun.

Maximo's staff had already welcomed her with open arms and there was no reason why his friends shouldn't do the same.

She was feeling much better by the time she emerged from the bathroom, to see Maximo already dressed in a dark evening suit—a delectable sight which made her heart twist with predictable longing. He was lounging back in one of the bedroom's dark leather armchairs and looked up from his phone when she entered, clad in nothing but a snowy bathrobe.

'I haven't a clue what to wear,' she said, rifling through the row of new clothes which someone must have hung neatly in the wardrobe while they were having lunch.

'Wear the black,' he said suddenly. 'And put your hair up.'

'I thought you liked it down.'

'In bed, certainly—but tonight, no. Stop frowning at me like that, Hollie. There's a reason.'

'Am I allowed to know what the reason is?'

'In time.' He smiled. 'Be patient, *mia belleza*.'

Hollie began to get ready, fixing her hair and pinning it in place. Half an hour later and she was ready, a loose chignon coiled against the back of her neck, the black silk dress skimming her knees, and a pair of strappy shoes adding extra height. As she leaned towards the mirror to apply a light coat of lip gloss, Maximo walked across the bedroom and placed a small box on the dressing table in front of her.

'Why don't you put these on?' he said.

'These' turned out to be two long and sparkling columns—a pair of exquisite diamond earrings—and she stared down at them in confusion.

'But you've already given me—'

'Put them on,' he emphasised softly. 'I bought them at the same time as we got your ring. It's your Christmas present, Hollie.'

'But…but I haven't given you anything!' she protested, surprised when he leant over and placed the palm of his hand over her still-flat belly and their eyes met in a silent moment, reflected in the mirror.

'Oh, but you have,' he contradicted softly. 'You have given me something money can never buy. My baby.' There was a pause as she was caught in the ebony spotlight of his gaze. 'Would it bother you if we announced it tonight? It would kill speculation and everyone is going to know about it sooner or later.'

Hollie didn't answer straight away. She wasn't sure she agreed because it still felt very…private, as well as very new. Yet it wasn't as though it were a guilty secret, was it? It was nothing to feel *ashamed* about. And if she was surprised by Maximo's desire to tell people, she couldn't think of any reason why he shouldn't— she was past the danger zone, wasn't she? 'No, I don't mind,' she said.

He turned away then, but not before Hollie saw the flash of something unexpected in his black eyes. A look which was hard and dark and very macho.

Was it triumph?

Was that why she felt a faint flicker of foreboding to add to all the others which seemed to be building up inside her? But she forced herself to push away her fears, determined to count her blessings instead. Tomorrow was the first day of the new year and the man she was going to marry was the father of her baby. Wasn't that good enough to be going along with?

He took her to the drawing room, which was situated at the very top of the large house, where they sipped glasses of *casera*—a simple bubbly lemon concoction, which Maximo said was rarely drunk outside Spain and which Hollie found delicious. Afterwards they were driven to the west of the city, to an upmarket area called Pozuelo de Alarcón, where the party was being held. The house was large and modern and surrounded by enormous grounds, with clever lighting focussing on beautiful outdoor statues and surrounding shrubs. Coloured bulbs were looped through the branches of trees, and as the line of luxury cars progressed up the long drive Hollie could see people laughing and drinking through giant plate-glass windows. It looked just like a commercial and Hollie would have defied anyone not to have felt intimidated by it.

Did her shoulders stiffen with tension—was that why Maximo ran a reflective finger over her palm? 'Everything okay?' he verified.

'I'm still nervous,' she admitted.

'Don't be, *mia belleza*. Your innocence will be like a breath of fresh air.'

'Not so very innocent any more,' she reflected ruefully.

'Everyone has to lose their innocence some time.' He reached up and touched his fingertip against one of the diamond strands which dangled like a spill of stars from her ear. 'You know that at midnight we have a big tradition in this country?'

'Like the siesta, you mean?'

'In its way, *las doce uvas de la suerte* is as important as the siesta, *sí*—because, to the Spanish, all traditions are important.'

Hollie nodded, wondering if that was because he'd grown up without any real traditions of his own.

*As had she.*

'Everyone eats grapes at midnight on New Year's Eve,' he said. 'One for each stroke of the hour—twelve grapes in all.'

'Why do you do that?'

'To bring us luck.' He smiled. 'Rare is the Spaniard who will poison his fate for the following year by failing to complete this simple task.'

'In England, we might be tempted to call that superstition.'

'Then I shall have to persuade you otherwise, won't I?' he said softly as the limousine slid to a silent halt, and she shivered as he whispered his fingertip over her thigh, as if to remind her of what delights lay in store for them later.

Heads turned as they walked into the party—where even the people serving drinks and canapés looked as if they had stepped from the pages of a fashion bible.

*Please don't let me make a fool of myself,* Hollie prayed.

There was a split-second pause and then conversation resumed as a tall and very handsome man extricated himself from a group of people and came over to greet them.

'Maximo,' he said. 'I'm glad you made it, though I confess to being a little surprised.' His black eyes gleamed with curiosity. 'Since the word is out that there are going to be a lot of very disappointed women here tonight.'

Hollie felt Maximo's fingertips touch the base of her spine.

'Javier, I'd like you to meet my fiancée, Hollie Walker. Hollie, this is Javier de Balboa, a very old friend of mine, who will probably do his best to cause mischief.'

'Pleased to meet you,' said Hollie, her hand straying to her cheek to push away a dangling strand of hair.

'So it *is* true,' breathed Javier, and Hollie knew she hadn't imagined the surprise which flickered in his dark eyes as he spotted the large diamond gleaming on her finger. 'Wow. I am delighted to meet the woman who has tamed this black-hearted rogue after so long. You *do* realise what you're taking on, don't you, Hollie?'

'I think so.'

Her tentative words made both men smile and suddenly Hollie felt a little more comfortable as she asked for a glass of *casera*.

'You won't have champagne?' asked Javier.

'Hollie's pregnant,' Maximo cut in.

'Ah. Of course she is. My congratulations to you both. In that case, I will have someone prepare you a *casera*.'

After he had gone, Hollie just stood very still for a moment, breathing deeply and trying to compose herself. What had Javier meant—*Of course she is*? That it was inconceivable the powerful bachelor would be contemplating marriage unless he was being shotgunned into it? And wasn't that the truth? She could see people watching them and wondered how they saw her. As an

upstart who had managed to get her claws into one of
Spain's most eligible bachelors? One who was clearly
out of her depth, despite her designer dress and the jewels which hung from her finger and her ears?

Maximo turned to talk to someone and, although
a nearby couple were eager to chat to her, Hollie felt
strangely isolated. She watched as Maximo seemed to
command the attention of everyone in the room. People
were trying to get near him and she felt as though she
were melting into the shadows and gradually becoming invisible. She realised that for him this was truly
home, and always would be.

She did her best to join in with the lively party but
couldn't quite contain the nerves which were growing inside her. She saw a huge dish of purple grapes
gleaming rather menacingly in a corner and prayed she
would be able to match everyone else in the room—
although eating twelve grapes in such a short space of
time did seem a big ask, particularly of someone who
was pregnant.

She glanced around the room, thinking that she'd
never seen so many stunning women congregated in
one place, and found herself remembering what Maximo had once said. He'd told her that if ever he met a
woman he desired more than her he would tell her immediately and their relationship would end. Looking
around at the model-perfect array of females, she failed
to see how that could *not* happen. Surely once the allure
of their brand-new sex life wore off, wasn't it inevitable
he would be tempted?

She wasn't much of a drinker but right then she
would have given anything for a small glass of wine

to help quell her spiralling nervousness, but of course she couldn't do that because she was expecting a baby.

*And that was the only reason she was here.*

All of a sudden Hollie felt as if she were adrift on a life raft, floating on a wide sea. Lost and all alone—despite the proud-featured man at her side who drew the gaze of every woman in the room.

# CHAPTER ELEVEN

HER NIGHT WAS RESTLESS—her sleep broken by ill-defined dreams which somehow scared her—and when Hollie awoke it was to find that Maximo had gone. She sat up in bed and blinked, glancing around at the unfamiliar space of his vast Madrid bedroom. Gone where?

As if in answer to her thoughts he walked into the room, dressed in his habitual black and talking on the phone on what was clearly a work call. He palmed her a wave but continued talking in Spanish, obviously distracted—and when Hollie emerged from the bathroom he was still speaking. She walked over to the window and stared out but, despite the beautiful Retiro Park being so close, all she noticed were the buildings and busy roads. She kept telling herself the problem lay with *her* and not the famously beautiful city of Madrid, but that didn't alter her fundamental fear about whether she'd ever get used to living here after the quiet of Trescombe.

Maximo cut the call and walked over to the window to stand beside her. 'You're awake,' he murmured, snaking his arm around her waist, his thumb stroking a slow circle. 'I thought I'd let you sleep. It was a late night. Did you enjoy the party?'

'It was certainly very lively.'

'Who was that woman I saw you talking to?' he enquired, his fingers reaching up to comb through the tangle of her hair.

'Which one? I was talking to lots of people.'

'The one in the green dress. She had blonde hair, I think.'

'Oh. You mean Cristina.' Hollie smiled. It had been one of the highlights of a very challenging evening. An elegant woman had walked across the crowded room and given her a warm and friendly smile. More than that, she had seemed instantly understanding, telling Hollie that she had once been the newcomer at a similar, glittering party. 'It can be a little overwhelming at the beginning,' she had said softly. 'They are a wonderful but rather intimidating crowd. Just give them a chance.'

'Who is Cristina?' prompted Maximo, breaking into her thoughts.

'She owns a shop on the…' she frowned as she tried to remember '…the Calle de Serrano, and wants me to have lunch with her some time, so I gave her my number. I explained I was going back to England tomorrow to work out my notice, but said I could meet her at the end of the month.'

'Good, good,' he said, as he linked his fingers with hers and began to lead her back towards the bed. 'It's important for you to make new friends.'

'What…what are you doing, Maximo?' she questioned, as he laid her down on the mattress and then began to peel off his clothes with impatient fingers.

'What do you think I'm doing? I'm going to make love to you because I am aching to be inside you again.'

'B-but, you've only just got out of the shower.'

'Then I'll just have to get right back in it, won't I?'

She felt the silky collision of his flesh as their bodies collided and heard the deepening of his voice as he brushed his lips over hers.

'Do I taste good, *mia belleza*?'

'You do.' She shivered. 'You t-taste very good.'

His mouth moved to her neck, her belly and then—most daringly of all—between her legs and Hollie's eyes fluttered to a helpless close as she felt that first deliciously precise flick of his tongue. Pretty soon her body was clenching with the explosive pleasure which was now part of her daily life.

How could I have lived without this for so long? she thought dreamily as she lay cradled in his arms afterwards.

How could I have lived without *him*?

But that was a dangerous way to think. Especially when the next few days made her realise that something fundamental between them seemed to have shifted. At first she thought she was imagining it, but gradually she realised that, on some level, their relationship had changed. It was difficult to define but it was definitely there. All the closeness and banter they'd shared over Christmas seemed to have evaporated. It had become functional. She told herself not to keep analysing the situation, but couldn't seem to stop herself. Because despite the undeniable intimacy she felt whenever they were having sex, hadn't Maximo been noticeably more distant with her ever since they'd arrived in Madrid? Hadn't he been obsessed with his work in a way she hadn't witnessed before? He seemed to be out at the office most of the time and when she had questioned him about it, he hadn't been in the least bit contrite.

'Surely you must understand that I have to work, Hollie,' he had replied, with a shrug. 'I am the head of a very big organisation and a lot of people rely on me.'

'And when the baby arrives? What then? Will you still be working around the clock?'

'Who knows? It's possible.' His black eyes were clear and gleaming. 'I'm not going to make any promises I won't be able to keep, *querida*. I'm planning to do the best I can, but I don't know what form being a husband and a father will take. Is that fair?'

It might have been fair, but it wasn't what Hollie wanted to hear—and while his honesty was admirable, it failed to reassure her. It felt to her as if he had achieved what he had set out to achieve—by offering her marriage—and was now free to turn his attention to other things. Would she be expected to build her own separate life here—a life which touched his only in parts? It wasn't what she had envisaged when she had agreed to marry him...

And before she knew it, it was time to fly back to Devon to work out her notice—an intention she had proudly insisted on but was now beginning to regret. Surrounded by luxury, Hollie stared out of the window of his private jet, wondering if Maximo would be relieved to have the apartment to himself again now she'd left. He certainly hadn't given any indication that he was going to *miss* her. And even though he made love to her that morning, and afterwards held her trembling body very tight, she could never remember feeling quite so alone.

It was weird being back in England. Weird yet strangely comforting—like climbing into a warm bath at the end of a long working day. As the limousine purred along the high-hedged country lanes, Hollie realised that people knew her here in Trescombe. She belonged in this little town. When she stopped at the local store to buy some provisions, the owner did a double take before her face broke into a huge smile.

'It *is* you! Why, for a moment I didn't recognise you, Hollie!'

Hollie blushed, realising she hadn't even considered the impact of leaving a fancy car sitting on the kerb waiting, while she purchased her pint of milk wearing a whacking great diamond ring, and a cream cashmere coat which must have been achingly expensive.

She would need to go back to her trusty skirts and blouses tomorrow morning when she started back at work. Her mind flitted over different possibilities as she wondered how she was going to explain what had happened to Janette. Was she going to give her boss the whole story, chapter and verse, and tell her she was engaged and pregnant in a single sentence?

Her boss was so…probing. She would almost certainly pry and ask Hollie what it was like being engaged to someone as charismatic as Maximo Diaz. She might even ask her details about how it had happened.

And Hollie would say—what?

That it had been a one-night stand with far-reaching

ramifications, hence the Spanish tycoon's shock proposal of marriage? She certainly wasn't going to hint at her growing insecurities about her place in Maximo's life or confess that he seemed to be pushing her away from him. Hollie bit her lip. He'd made it clear he didn't want deep, or mushy, or lovey-dovey from their relationship—yet despite knowing those things, it made little difference to the way she felt about him. She still felt dizzy with longing whenever she thought about him.

Perhaps it was the thought of how it had been before which kept her snared—all those evocative memories of a snowed-in Christmas, which had led her to believe in all kinds of possibilities. The way he'd taken her into his confidence and the way he made her feel when she was in his arms… Perhaps it was her lack of experience of sex which made her ultra-susceptible to its influence. Because sometimes, when she was lying close to him, with the powerful beat of his powerful heart slowing in perfect time with her own, Hollie would feel something close to…

Love?

She swallowed. Was it possible to love someone even if you knew that was the last thing they wanted from you?

Was it?

Yes, of course it was possible. People had been falling in love indiscriminately since the beginning of time. And, despite all her mixed-up feelings, Hollie's heart still lifted with joy when she answered Maximo's text asking whether she'd settled in and saying he'd call her later. His brief message made her think. It made her look at the situation from a different viewpoint. Back in Madrid she had convinced herself she was missing her simple life in Trescombe, but the irony was that she was missing Maximo a lot more. Didn't she ache for him with a fierce longing which was almost visceral? And if that was the case, then surely fitting into her new world in Spain wasn't only preferable, but achievable. All she had to do was to give it a decent chance, and that meant giving it time. Couldn't she choose her moment to suggest that he didn't have to work quite so hard—and couldn't they get back the kind of closeness they'd had before?

Feeling suddenly light-hearted, she made herself a sandwich and sat down at the table munching it as she looked around. Her little pine tree was wilting and had deposited most of its needles onto the rug, and two of the baubles had fallen to the floor. Christmas really was over and she was going to have to think about taking all these decorations down before Twelfth Night.

She was just about to leave for work next morning, when she heard her phone vibrate and she slid it out of her handbag to look at it.

It was a number she didn't recognise. An international number—Spanish, she thought. And when she clicked on the call she discovered it was Cristina, the woman she'd met at Javier's party. The woman with the potential to be a new friend. The blonde in the green dress.

'Hi,' said Hollie, a smile entering her voice. 'How lovely to hear from you! How are you?'

'I'm…well. You have returned to England, I think?'

'That's right. I'm just about to go to work. I'm flying back at the beginning of February.'

Cristina's accented voice dipped by a fraction. 'And Maximo. Is he there with you?'

'No, I'm afraid he's not. He's coming over at the weekend.'

'I see.' There was a pause. 'I understand you're pregnant, Hollie? I really should have congratulated you at the party.'

'Yes, I am.' Hollie felt her heart give a little kick. 'I'm twelve weeks along. The scan is on Wednesday.'

There was another pause but this time, Cristina's voice sounded different. It quivered with the air of somebody who knew something. More specifically, who knew something you didn't.

'I like you, Hollie,' she said slowly. 'And I have learned something which is difficult for me to tell you, but which I feel you ought to know.'

'You're scaring me now,' said Hollie, only half joking. 'What is it?'

'It's about Maximo.' There was a pause. 'About the real reason he's marrying you.'

It was an extraordinary thing for someone to say out of the blue like that—especially someone who didn't know you—and for a moment Hollie's only response was silence. Her fingers tightened around the handset and she could feel her throat constrict. She felt faintly disappointed. As if she had misjudged Cristina, who perhaps didn't want to be her friend at all. If she were a different kind of person she might have frostily retorted that it wasn't any of the other woman's business. But she wasn't going to hide from the truth, and if Cristina was expressing what everyone else was thinking, then maybe the subject would be better addressed head-on. 'I'm not naïve enough to believe the wedding would be happening if I weren't pregnant,' she said quietly.

'I'm sure you're not. But he's not just marrying you in order to maintain respectability,' Cristina said, and then the words came out in a rush, as if she was embarrassed to repeat them. 'He's marrying you because he stands to inherit the family business, which will be put in trust for your child. Only the will stipulates that the child must be born within wedlock.'

Hollie froze.

*But Maximo had been estranged from his father since the age of fourteen. He'd told her that.*

With her free hand, she gripped the back of a nearby chair. 'I don't believe you,' she whispered.

'I'm afraid it's true, my dear,' said Cristina. 'I heard this through Beatriz, one of his stepsisters. It was a hotly contested clause in the will, although the lawyers assured them it was watertight. They are obviously angry that their father's illegitimate son stands to inherit one of the most profitable companies in Spain. I'm sorry, Hollie. I felt it best you should know, but this is not news I would ever wish to be the bearer of.'

'No. Thank you.' Hollie's voice was brisk now. Polite, even. 'I appreciate it, Cristina.'

With a few more robotic words she cut the call, though all the time she was berating herself. How *stupid* she had been. Sorrow clamped its way around her heart like a vice and then she gave a bitter laugh. She might have lost her virginity but that didn't mean she wasn't still laughably naïve, did it? She had stupidly imagined she had no illusions about the opposite sex, but it seemed she was still capable of being blinded by the stars which had temporarily danced in front of her eyes. She had wanted love so badly that she had been prepared to overlook what was blazingly obvious. Because she didn't know Maximo at all, not really. The man she saw was the man she had wanted to see, not the one with hidden depths which he kept concealed from her. He was marrying her to gain control of one of Spain's most successful companies. Of course he was. Although he certainly didn't need the money, maybe he felt it was a justified legacy—to make up for his father's rejection. Payback time. But it didn't alter one key and painful fact...

*That he had betrayed her, just as her father had betrayed her mother.*

Her knees felt weak and she gripped the back of the chair even harder, afraid they might buckle. But the weirdest thing was that after that moment of dizziness had passed, Hollie felt calm. Icy calm. Almost as if she had been expecting this. As if things had always been too good to be true.

Because they were, weren't they?

Plenty of women got pregnant without getting married. Did she *really* think that someone like Maximo Diaz would ask someone like her to be his wife if he didn't stand to gain something from it, especially when he'd told her right from the start he didn't want a baby? Or had she walked into the self-deceptive trap of thinking they had something special between them, just because she'd fallen in love with him?

She had fallen in love with him.

Well, more fool her.

*He stands to inherit the family business.* Cristina's words were branded on Hollie's brain like fire.

If he'd told her himself, she might have understood. If he'd said *Look, this baby means that I can get something I've always lusted after*, she probably could have accepted it. If he'd kept it coldly businesslike from the beginning, then perhaps she wouldn't have built up all those fantasies in her head. But he hadn't and that had given her imagination a free rein. No wonder she thought she'd seen a look of triumph on his face when he'd asked if they could announce the pregnancy. He was probably rubbing his hands with glee at the thought of all that new power.

She picked up her phone, turning it over and over in her hand before finally tapping her fingers over the keypad. It took longer than it should have done but that was because her hands were trembling so much. She kept the message short—because, really, it all boiled down to one simple fact whichever way you looked at it.

Maximo...

A tear dripped onto the back of her hand and, impatiently, she shook it away before continuing to type.

Being back in Devon has given me a bit of time to reflect on things and I just don't think it's going to work out between us.

Her finger hovered as she battled between the desire

to put as much distance between them as possible and the knowledge that she needed to act like a grown-up.

If you like we can talk in a couple of days. Hollie.

She didn't put any kisses, and that drove home the realisation that there had never been any of the stuff which defined most *normal* love affairs. No letters or texts of undying devotion. Just sex and a baby and a big diamond ring. She thought about the turrets and towers of Kastelloes and the thick snow which had trapped them there. She remembered how grateful she had been to that inclement weather, because it had brought her into Maximo's arms. She'd been blown away by her Spanish lover, and hopeful when he'd opened up his heart to her. The world had felt tinged with magic, when all the time...

*All the time he had been using their marriage as a way of getting his hands on the family business.*

What a trusting fool she had been.

Well, not any more.

She had once told Maximo that she could do all this on her own and she would—with or without his financial assistance. Because anything would be preferable to a lifetime of deceit.

She tugged the heavy ring from her finger and it clattered as she put it on the table and then, letting out a shuddered breath, she laid her face against her cradled arms and wept.

# CHAPTER TWELVE

A THIN DRIZZLE of rain coated the windscreen in a slimy film as the car turned into the wintry English road. Maximo eased his foot off the accelerator, bringing the powerful vehicle almost to a halt so that it crept along at a snail's pace. He stared fixedly ahead, not caring if he was wasting time. Because he needed time to work out what he was going to do. To assemble his whirling thoughts into some sort of order before he saw Hollie.

To say what?

He still didn't know.

He thought about the bald little message he had received from her.

I just don't think it's going to work out between us...

He had been taken aback by the dark surge of pain which had flooded through him.

He had wanted to lift the phone and demand to know what had made her write it, but something made him change his mind—though he didn't stop to think what that might be. Instead, he sought a solution in action, because that was how he operated. He had ordered his jet to be made ready and within hours had flown into Exeter airport, planning his movements with the precision of a cat burglar.

Unobserved, he had watched Hollie leave the office and a wave of relief had swamped him as he'd seen her familiar figure walking towards the bus stop. And although every part of him had ached to drive up and tell her to get in the car, he'd resisted the powerful temptation to do so, because he didn't want any kind of confrontation or public spectacle. He didn't want to run the risk of her refusing to travel with him.

He had seen the chill wind blowing at her hair, but the tresses were no longer unfettered and free as he liked them. They had been tamed beneath a hat he'd never seen her wear before, and the coat she was huddling into was not one of the items he had bought her, but a well-worn relic from her old wardrobe. It was as if she had embraced her old life and cut him out completely, he thought, and his heart gave another painful clench as he increased the speed of the car.

Once he had vowed never to let a woman close enough to hurt him. What had happened to that fervent vow from which he had never wavered? The vow he'd made on his knees on that snowy Christmas Eve in Spain, all those years ago.

*You could leave now while there's still time*, a cold and pragmatic voice in his head reminded him.

But he ignored it.

His car slid to a halt outside her tiny cottage and he crunched his way up the gravel path. Ignoring the twee little bell which dangled in the porch, he lifted his arm and began to pound on the door and the mighty sound created by his fist echoed through the still night air.

Someone was knocking at her door and Hollie paused in the middle of washing up her teacup. No, it was more like a pounding. The sound which someone who was in a hurry—or a temper—would make. Someone autocratic and powerful who wouldn't think twice about making enough noise to wake the dead.

Her throat dried. There was only one person she knew who would knock like that. Was that why her heart started racing as she put her teacup down and headed for the door? Or was it just that deep down she'd been expecting this visit and now the moment had arrived, she felt a terrible fatalistic sorrow washing over her?

Drawing in a deep breath, she pulled open the door and there stood Maximo. His hair was windswept and he was dressed in the black clothes which were so familiar, but Hollie had never seen that expression on his face before. It was tense. Brittle. As if he were holding something dark and unwanted inside him. His eyes narrowed, and then he spoke.

'Can I come in, please, Hollie?'

Did he really think she would refuse him entry? That she would *want* to? Because even though she recognised that the final minutes of their relationship were ticking away, Hollie wasn't feeling the things she wanted to feel. Despite the fact that he had used her as a pawn in his ambitious game plan, she wasn't hating him, or not fancying him. Her stupid stomach still turned to mush when he brushed past her, forcing her to shut the door on the drizzly evening outside.

For a minute she was tempted to throw herself into his arms in an effort to blot out all those things she'd discovered. Or even to ask if he'd like some coffee after his long journey, in a futile desire to put off the inevitable. To act as if she were still going to be his wife and make like they were going to be a happy family.

But she couldn't do that any more. She couldn't pretend—not to him—not even to herself.

Especially not to herself.

Uncharacteristically, he seemed almost hesitant as his gaze swept over her. 'Is the baby okay?'

Of *course* that would be his number one concern. 'Everything's fine,' she answered briskly. 'I'm having the scan the day after tomorrow.'

There was a pause, and now the light from his eyes was very hard and very bright. 'Do you want to tell me why you sent that text?'

Hollie tried to think of the right words but there were no right words. Only wrong ones. Harsh, discordant words which had the power to destroy everything and now she was going to have to say them out loud and make it all real.

'Do you want to tell me why you asked me to marry you, Maximo?' she questioned quietly. 'Only give me the *real* reason this time!'

His frown deepened. 'But you know the reason.'

'Yes, of course I do. Because of the baby. Or so I thought. We were supposed to be completely honest with each other, weren't we? We said that truth was going to define our relationship. Yet all the time…'

She swallowed. 'All the time there was this great big secret bubbling away in the background, which you failed to mention.'

'What *secret*?' he echoed. 'You've completely lost me now.'

'Please don't treat me like an idiot!' she snapped.

'Then why don't you stop speaking in riddles? I told you. I don't know what you're talking about.'

'I'm talking about inheriting your father's business!'

He shook his head. 'Nope. Still confused.'

His words sounded genuine but Hollie steeled her heart against them, because men could lie, couldn't they? In fact, men *did* lie. Her father had rarely spoken a true word in his life, according to her mother.

'Cristina rang me up. The blonde in the green dress at the party,' she continued. 'She knows your stepsister, Beatriz.' She heard his sudden sharp intake of breath, which she interpreted as guilt.

'Beatriz,' he said slowly. 'Well, well, well. Now it really *does* get interesting.'

Hollie sucked in a ragged breath. 'Cristina told me about the will. About how your father left you controlling shares of his business, but only if you have a child born within wedlock. So why didn't you tell me that, Maximo? If you'd told me the truth in the first place then maybe I could have lived with it. It's the lies I can't stand.'

But there was no guilt or resignation on his face. No sense of having been found out. In fact, there was nothing on his sculpted features but a look of growing comprehension.

'This is all news to me, Hollie,' he said slowly. 'If there is such a bequest then it has never been on my radar, because I have been estranged from my family for many years and in all that time I haven't spoken to my stepsisters—not since they decided that cruelty towards an impressionable young boy was a sport they relished.' His voice harshened. 'Do you really think I would conceal something like that from you?'

'Yes! If you want the truth, yes, I do!'

Maximo flinched as if she had hit him, but through the slow burn of injustice came a powerful rush of feelings. Uncomfortable feelings he had buried for years and if it had been anyone else, he would have slammed his way out of there and taken his outraged pride with him.

But this wasn't just anyone. This was Hollie. Hollie who knew more about him than anyone else did. He remembered when he'd told her about working on the roads as a teenager and she'd asked him if he had lied about his age, as if it was important. As if it had meant something. Because it *did* mean something. She was used to men lying to her. Her father, for one. Did she think he was cast out of the same mould and that he would deceive her about something as big as this?

And then he wondered how he dared be such a hypocrite. Why *wouldn't* she believe that, when he had done nothing but push her away since she'd arrived in Spain, and maybe even before that? He had been so damned keen to create barriers between them and to ensure she knew never to dare cross them, that he had succeeded in destroying all the ease and the intimacy which had once existed between them. And now she was looking at him warily, with sadness and mistrust written all over her lovely face, and although he knew he deserved all of that—and more—suddenly he couldn't bear the thought that he might have sabotaged, not just his own future, but that of his family. *His family with her.*

'I repeat, I knew nothing about this legacy, and even if I did, do you really think I'd want his damned business? If I had, I might have stayed on in that heartless mansion—enduring the taunts of my stepsisters and the sniggers of the servants who surrounded him. Do you really think that even if I were poor—*even if I were poor*—I would accept the charity of someone who had never wanted me during his lifetime? Do you, Hollie?'

The fierceness of his tone must have convinced her, for she gave a brief and reluctant shrug. 'I guess not.'

But the wariness was still there and Maximo knew he had a long way to go. He could feel his jaw hardening—locking so tight he could scarcely grit the next words out, but then he'd had a whole lifetime of suppressing stuff instead of articulating it.

'I didn't lie to you about the will,' he said slowly. 'But in a way, I was lying to myself.'

Her eyes widened. 'What…what are you talking about?'

'I lied about the way you made me feel. I refused to acknowledge that you touched something deep inside me right from the start. And as that feeling grew, it scared me. It made me feel…powerless—and I had vowed that nobody was ever going to make me feel that way again.' He expelled a long and ragged breath. 'I thought when I took you to Spain—that if I could get back to the way I normally felt, I could deal with it. I was stupid enough and arrogant enough to believe I could just slot you into your own little compartment in my life and you would be content with that. But instead, I drove you away—'

'Yes,' she said. 'You did.'

'I shouldn't have done that,' he ground out.

'No, you shouldn't.' She hesitated. 'But we all say and do things we shouldn't, often because we're scared. You're not the only one, Maximo.'

'Hollie—'

'No, wait.' Her firm tone belied the sudden trembling of her lips and, suddenly, her voice was trembling too. 'Let me confess something to you. Something I'm only just starting to realise—which is that I felt almost *relieved* when Cristina told me about the will.'

'Relieved?' he verified incredulously.

She swallowed and nodded. 'Maybe it suited me to believe that all men were fundamentally liars and you could never trust any of them because that way…' Her eyes had suddenly become very bright and her words tailed off as she looked at him.

'That way you'd never get hurt?'

'Yes,' she whispered. '*Yes.* I didn't want to get hurt and I didn't want my baby—'

'Our baby.'

She bit her lip as if she was about to cry. 'I didn't want our baby to grow up the way I did,' she said huskily. 'In a world of broken promises and no real love. Or one-sided love. I thought it would be easier to go it alone than to do that. Because I want a *real* family, Maximo—not something which just looks like it from the outside—and I'm not going to accept anything less than that.'

This still sounded like bargaining to him and was

not the instant capitulation Maximo had expected to hear. It still felt as if someone were squeezing his heart with their fist—and it hurt. It *really* hurt. He'd spent his whole life avoiding emotional pain and maybe that was why he had built up no resistance against it. Because suddenly he realised that if he wanted Hollie, he needed to really put his feelings on the line. To say things he'd never expected to hear himself say and make sure she knew he meant them.

'I've never told you that I love you, have I, Hollie?' he questioned unevenly. 'I've never told you that first time I lay with you, it felt as if you were touching me with flame? As if you'd unleashed the lick of a potent fire which threatened to melt the coldness deep inside me, which I'd lived with for so long? I'd never felt that way before and it made me feel vulnerable. That's what made me want to push you away.'

'Maximo—'

But he silenced her with a shake of his head because he couldn't allow her forgiving nature to let him off the hook. Not this time. 'You withstood my appalling attitude when I discovered you were pregnant—as if I had nothing to do with it!' He gave a bitter laugh. 'And then you created the kind of Christmas I'd never had and never thought I'd wanted, but it seems I did. For the first time in my life, I discovered what people meant when they talked about coming home. You are my home and I love you, Hollie, and I want to share my life with you and our baby.' He shrugged. 'It's as complicated and as simple as that.'

'Oh, Maximo,' she said, so quietly he could hardly hear her.

He opened his arms to her and she went straight into them, like a bird arriving back on the nest after a long flight away. She buried her head against his shoulder and he held her until she had stopped crying and then he turned her face up towards him, tracing his fingertip over the tracks of her tears. 'But I've been thinking about my bachelor apartment in Madrid and I've recognised it isn't really suitable for a baby,' he mused.

'But it's right next to that beautiful park.'

'*Sí*, it is, but I got the distinct feeling that you're not much of a city girl, which was one of the reasons you left London, wasn't it?'

She shrugged. 'I guess.'

'When I took you there, I felt as if I had plucked a wildflower from a country meadow and transplanted it into a hothouse. Which is why I'm planning to fit into *your* world from now on.'

Her brow creased into a frown. 'Now who's talking in riddles?'

'There's something else you need to know,' he said suddenly. 'Something I should have told you a whole lot sooner. I was never planning to turn the castle into a luxury hotel. That was just an assumption local people made and I didn't bother to correct them. I had planned to demolish it and turn it into a quarry—to use the valuable stone it was built on to build a railway track.'

'You…you were planning to destroy hundreds of years of history just to build a railway?'

'Don't knock railways, Hollie, because we need them—now more than ever.'

'Why didn't you say something before? Why didn't you tell anyone?'

'Because I knew if that fact got out, it would drive up the purchase price.'

She punched a half-hearted fist against his chest. 'That is the most hard-hearted thing I've—'

'I'm a businessman, Hollie,' he interrupted gently. 'And that's what businessmen do. I'd planned to stay there over Christmas because I knew it would provide the solitude I was seeking, and then to sell it in the new year. I wasn't expecting to meet a woman in this one-horse town, and have my life turned upside down by her. You were the reason I couldn't go through with the sale, not when I saw how much the place meant to you. I realised I couldn't take a wrecking ball to the heart of this little community in order to steamroller another money-making scheme.'

'Oh, Maximo,' she said, lifting her left hand to her heart, making him notice she wasn't wearing her engagement ring.

'I have been thinking that we could keep the castle and turn it into our family home, if that's what you wanted. Or maybe turn it into a hotel and buy a big house and garden for our family instead, if that's what you'd prefer. I was waiting for the perfect moment to tell you, only perfect moments have a habit of being elusive. But those things could only happen...' His words tailed off and somehow he was finding it impossible to keep the sudden break from his voice. 'They could only happen if you still wanted me. If you still wanted to be my wife.'

Hollie put her arms around his neck and pressed her face very close to his as a powerful shaft of joy and gratitude shot through her. 'Of course I still want to be your wife. Because I love you,' she whispered. 'I love you in a way I never thought possible, but I never believed you might feel the same way about me.'

'Believe it now.'

'I do.' She looked into his black eyes and saw a look of true understanding, but she knew there was more to tell him. 'When I thought you'd lied to me, I took the coward's way out. I was trying to protect myself against hurt and pain. That's why I sent you that text instead of waiting until you got here and talking it out with you, face to face.'

*'Querida—'*

'No, let me finish.' That was easier said than done when tears were starting to stream down her cheeks— big and wet and salty and dripping on her sweater. 'But the worst hurt and pain I've ever experienced was imaging a life without you...' Once again her words tailed off and it took a couple of moments before she could catch her breath to speak. To articulate the emotion which Maximo had never been shown as a child and convince him that she meant every single word. They had both been damaged in the past, yes, but love was the true healer. Some might say the only healer. 'I love you with all my heart, Maximo Diaz,' she whispered. 'And I'll never stop loving you. Believe me when I tell you that, my darling.'

His slow smile was like the sun coming out and the glint in his eyes warmed Hollie's heart. And when he caught hold of her she felt as if she'd been reborn. As if he were breathing new life in her, to join the life which grew beneath her heart. Blindly, her lips sought his and as they kissed, the salt water of their mingled tears slowly began to dry.

# EPILOGUE

*'SLEEP IN HEAVENLY PEACE...'*

The poignant last notes of the carol seemed to hover on the still night air as, fortified by a pitcher of mulled wine and a platter of home-made mince pies, the group of singers began to make their way down the hill towards the town. Hollie glanced up at the sky as several large, feathery icicles drifted against her cheek. The bright moon of last night was obscured by cloud as the first fat flakes of snow started falling. There should be a thick covering tomorrow, she thought with a glow of satisfaction, as she closed the door of her castle home.

In the wood-panelled hallway stood a tall fir tree, decked with plain white lights and tartan ribbons and topped with an organza-robed angel. There was another tree in the library, where tomorrow they would eat a late lunch, illuminated by as many candles as she could lay her hands on, as had now become a yearly festive tradition. Mistletoe dangled in the hallway and there were bunches of holly and fragrant green garlands strewn everywhere. In the kitchen, a large pot of Cantabrian mountain stew was quietly bubbling away—also a tradition. It was Christmas Eve and it was perfect.

'Will Father Christmas come tonight, Papi?' asked a little voice from behind her and Hollie turned around to see her sleepy son nestled snugly in his father's arms.

'*Sí*, he will come to visit every child in the world tonight,' murmured Maximo, meeting her gaze over Mateo's tousled black head. The smile he slanted her was full of promise and Hollie felt a delicious shiver of anticipation. 'But only when you're asleep. So I'm going to take you up to bed right now, which means morning will come faster.'

'*Oh!*'

'Would you like Mamá to come, as well?'

'Yes, please.'

'Come on, then. *Vamos!*'

Mateo giggled as, going past stone walls now covered with artwork, they mounted the beautiful curving stone staircase to his room, which was just along the corridor from their own. Silk rugs lay scattered over the floors, the draughty windows had been fixed and hung with sumptuous drapes and the building was gloriously warm. In fact, Hollie never stopped marvelling how cosy the place felt after its costly refurbishment, which had started just over three years ago.

Work had begun on the neglected castle soon after she and Maximo had vowed their love and commitment to each other, when they'd married in Trescombe's small church, with its sweeping views of the sea. It had been a small and simple ceremony. Hollie had worn a long dress of fine white wool, with a hooded and feather-trimmed cape, to keep out the bitter winter winds. And although they had been well into January, and it hadn't been Christmastime, her bouquet had nonetheless contained sprays of mistletoe, holly and ivy. Maximo's friend Javier had been best man and the ancient church had been filled with the competing sounds of Spanish and English chatter—though the Spanish had undoubtedly been the louder of the two. It had been, everyone said, the most beautiful wedding.

And they had made their life here, in Devon. Maximo continued to run his empire from this rural base—though they kept apartments in New York and Madrid. But he hadn't forgotten his vow to serve the community of his newly adopted home. He had completely refurbished the rather tatty hotel where first they'd met and the resulting five-star establishment now came under the umbrella of the Diaz group and brought many tourists flocking to the small town which nestled between moorland and sea. It had put Trescombe firmly on the map, although the narrow and winding access roads ensured that it was never going to be *too* much on the map, as Maximo drily commented.

Once their son had reached a year, Hollie had opened her tea shop—though someone else ran it for her. She'd fished out her best recipes and helped with batch cooking whenever she got the opportunity. She'd had the jaunty café painted in ice-cream colours of pink and lemon and spearmint, there was mismatched bone china on the tables, the waitresses wore old-fashioned frilly aprons and people came from miles around to taste her featherlight scones.

Her thoughts dissolving, Hollie sighed with pleasure as she watched her husband tuck his lookalike son into bed before going through the various night-time rituals they had evolved, including a very special one tonight, which involved the reading of Clement Clarke Moore's famous Christmas Eve poem. And when the story had finished, and Mateo had fallen sound asleep, Hollie and Maximo crept from the room and into the corridor outside.

There she turned to him, looping her arms around his neck—unable to resist the temptation to plant a kiss on his lips and then to linger there. A feeling of excitement was bubbling up inside her and it was making her heart beat fast. There was something she needed to tell him and she wanted to find the right time, but for now she just kissed him.

'Everything's *almost* ready, I think,' she whispered, drawing her mouth away from his. 'The stockings have been hung—and Javier's room is prepared. I'm sure he's going to cause something of a stir when he arrives in Trescombe tomorrow morning.'

'Like I did, you mean?' he teased.

'I doubt it. Javier's not quite as arrogant as you,' she advised primly.

He laughed as he curved the palm of his hand over her buttock. 'And don't you just *hate* that arrogance, *mia belleza*?'

'Maximo.' Her throat dried as his fingers continued on their inexorable journey. 'What do you think you're doing?'

'What does it look like I'm doing?' His voice was careless, his arms strong. 'I am picking up my beautiful wife to carry her into the bedroom, because I know that kind of macho thing turns her on, and once we get there I am taking her to bed, where I intend to ravish her.'

'But it's Christmas Eve! And we haven't—'

'Haven't what?' he questioned as he kicked open their bedroom door.

'Finished wrapping all the presents, or—'

'Shut up,' he said gently, laying her down on the luxurious red velvet cover she'd bought in homage to their first night there. 'And come here.'

He undressed her, slowly and reverently, and just before he entered her Hollie almost told him. But passion was a strange and beautiful thing. It stopped you having coherent thoughts. It blotted out the world so that all you could see and feel was that person in your arms, and all you could hear were soft moans which gradually became more frantic. And then it was happening, just as it always happened, and she was pulsing around him and his powerful body tensed for one exquisite moment before, finally, he collapsed into her arms.

Her heart was thumping heavily, her head was lying on his shoulder and all Hollie wanted was to go to sleep, but there wasn't time. 'Maximo…' she murmured lazily.

'Mmm…?'

'I've got something to tell you.'

'I know you have.'

'It has nothing to do with wrapping presents.'

'I know that, too.'

She rolled over to look at him and his black eyes were crystalline, hard and very bright. 'What do you know?'

'That you're having my baby again.'

'Yes, I am,' she breathed, slumping back against the pillow. 'But how did you *guess*?'

Maximo smiled, for this was the easiest question he'd ever had to answer. He didn't even have to think about it. 'Because I love you and because I know you. I know the look in your eyes and the smile on your lips when you have a new life growing inside you. And both of them are there now. Or at least, they were until a couple of minutes ago. Hollie, *querida*—what's the matter?' He frowned and smoothed his finger along the line of her quivering lip. 'Why are you crying?'

'You obviously don't know me that well at all! I'm crying because I'm happy, of course!'

And Maximo laughed softly, a feeling of pure joy wrapping around his heart as he brought her soft body closer to his and kissed the top of her silken head.

He had once thought there was no such thing as a perfect moment, but he had been wrong. Because this—*this*—was the perfect moment. These days his life was filled with them.

'And you spread happiness wherever you go, *mia belleza*,' he said softly. 'Happy Christmas, my beautiful wife.'

\* \* \* \* \*

# HIS MAJESTY'S
# FORBIDDEN
# TEMPTATION

## MAISEY YATES

Thank you to Mills & Boon for 100 books.
Here's to 100 more.

# CHAPTER ONE

"WELL, I THINK the paperwork speaks for itself. Marriage is the only course of action."

Alexius de Prospero, Lion of the Dark Wood, Hope of the People, King of Liri, looked across from him at the small, plain woman. He was standing, which made her quite literally beneath him. She was sitting in a floral, overstuffed armchair looking frizzy and distressed.

In fairness, he had never seen Tinley Markham looking anything other than frizzy. It was hoped, on the day when the engagement had first been arranged between her and Alex's younger brother, that she would have been tamed into something quite a bit sleeker and more fitting for a princess of Liri.

But it was not to be.

For Dionysus had died before they could ever be married. Which had shifted her from the category of *future Princess*, to *unwanted ward*.

Dionysus's death had also hastened the demise of their father, his health failing him shortly after his youngest son died so tragically.

Which had moved Alexius from Prince to King.

Alex's duties as King had been immediate and pressing. The matter of Tinley not so. Her father was dead, and as she was the daughter of his father's most trusted advisor, her welfare had mattered a great deal. But it was nothing that he had to see to in the day today. However, now he was butting up against the reality of the will her father had left behind.

Alexius loved his father. And he had been very fond of Tinley's father as well. But it could not be said that either man was deeply entrenched in the modern era. No. In fact, it might be said—affectionately—that both men were a bit medieval. Again, not a problem for Alex. Until recently. But now that Tinley was approaching her twenty-third birthday, and about to go over the prescribed deadline for marriage, it was a problem. For he was tasked with finding a husband for Tinley.

The consequences of failing were unacceptable.

And he had vowed that he would take care of her. He had sworn it. His father had been on his deathbed when Dionysus had passed. And though he had not made accusations, the ferocity in his father's leonine gaze had sharpened as he looked at him.

For King Darius had been blessed with three sons. And only one had survived to the end of his life. Only one stood a chance at inheriting the throne. For Dionysus was dead, and Lazarus long before him. And the weight of the deaths of both rested on Alexius's shoulders.

The firstborn son in Liri was named successor to the throne at birth, as it was with most other monarchies. But owed to years of war and corrupt leadership, there was a tradition.

All heirs of the King could issue challenges for the throne.

So while Alex had been born King, either of his brothers could challenge him at any time. Either to a battle, with the victor—either the last left alive, or the last to surrender—taking the throne.

Or there was the Dark Wood.

A week spent there, the last to surrender, or the one to emerge alive, named King.

The Lion of the Dark Wood.

And it was rumored that Alexius, even as a boy, had sought to end potential challengers to his throne.

King Darius had never accused him of such. His mother, on the other hand...

Things had changed.

And for all his life after, Alex had felt the distance between him and his mother. And the tension it had put between his mother and father.

What if he had been watching Lazarus more closely? What if he had stopped Dionysus that night he'd gone off drunk into the forest, rather than heeding his own selfish desires?

What if.

Some of his people revered Alexius as a god. He had, after all, met the challenge. Others saw him as fallible. A man who'd let those who should have been in his charge come to a tragic end. A man who had, perhaps, been born a ruthless, power-hungry monster.

Alexius had never known what his father believed. But the King had said to him, with a ferocity in his voice, that Tinley was now his responsibility. For her father was dead and her mother had never truly had the best interests of her daughter at heart.

*I had thought for her to marry Dionysus. To honor her father's position in the country. But she was suited to be the wife of the spare, not the heir. She is fragile, that girl. Sweet. She needed your brother. Her father's wishes were that she marry, and the estate and money is tied up in his wishes. Find her a husband. Ensure she never wants for anything.*

Alex had spoken nothing of Dionysus's flaws, for what would the point be? The King had had a blind spot when it came to his youngest son. He saw only the son, and none of the ways his selfish actions might have harmed Tinley.

But he'd asked Alex to ensure she wanted for nothing, and she hadn't.

Not a thing. In fact, he had made sure that she was able to attend a very prestigious University, where she had gotten a degree in social work. She currently held a position working for a charity, and he knew that while money meant very little to her on a personal level, she appreciated what she might accomplish with it in the broader world.

There was a clock ticking down. Tinley had to be married in her twenty-third year. If she was not, her father's money would be given to her next male relative.

It was funny to him, that his father thought Tinley suited Dionysus. Alex hadn't thought so. Tinley, though, had idolized Alex's brother. Had loved him. In the way a puppy loved its master, he'd often thought.

She'd had no idea he was dallying with other women, and happily, while Tinley was trailing after him, a flurry of ginger hair and pure devotion.

Watching it had made Alex's stomach sour.

"Yes," he said, his voice firm. "I was happy to allow you to live your life, but you have not come any closer to securing a marriage in the last four years than you were as a girl of eighteen."

"I was engaged at eighteen," she said softly.

"Younger," he said.

He looked around the cottage, which was something like a mishap out in the middle of the forest that had collected itself into four walls and a roof. There were baskets stacked in every corner, filled with yarn and what looked to be unspun wool.

The kitchen itself, which occupied the same space as the living area, was in a tip. There was a pie sitting on the counter, and there were baskets of blueberries, and flour sprinkled everywhere.

The woman herself had a bit of flour on her face.

As if the picture of spinster had not been painted well enough, a very large, fat ginger cat chose that moment to saunter into the room.

"To my point," he said. "You are no closer to finding a husband than you were four years ago. And I fear that you must. I wanted to keep my intervention to a minimum. But that is no longer practical."

She narrowed her eyes. "To *what* point?"

He let his gaze travel to the cat. "Nothing."

She frowned deeply and stood from the chair, making her way over to the beast. "Algernon is a rescue."

"I would've expected nothing less."

The cat walked by her, making a beeline straight for Alexius. The beast wove itself through his legs leaving behind a smattering of orange hair on his black pants.

"Retrieve your creature."

She huffed and crossed the space inelegantly, her softness amplified by her movements, her red hair a wild curl as she bent in a huff to pick up the massive mammal. "Leave the mean man alone, Algie. He hates cats. And sunshine. And rainbows. And everything good and proper in the world."

The problem with Tinley, the problem that had existed with Tinley since she'd begun to blossom into a woman, was that she was improbably beautiful. To him, at least. Her figure lush and soft, her hair untamed. She was unpredictable and unquenchable. She had freckles on her face and a gleam in her eyes that always seemed to hold a secret bit of humor. Her lips were full and quick with a smile, a wide smile that creased her cheeks and eyes and would make lines there when she was older.

She didn't seem concerned by it.

She rarely seemed concerned by anything.

And there was a part of him that had been drawn to that for years.

It was untenable. She was nothing like what he needed or wanted.

His body, though, had other thoughts about her, ridiculous though she was. A perversity in his nature.

"Need I remind you, Tinley. I am King. I am *your* King."

Tinley whirled in a circle, still holding her cat. "And I was going to be a princess."

"Not anymore."

Her mouth snapped shut, and her skin went waxen. "No."

"I'm not trying to be cruel, Tinley."

"Of course not. You don't have to try."

The moment stretched between them and he allowed it. She could despise him all she wanted. It wouldn't change the circumstances.

"So that's it. I marry, I get my inheritance. I don't marry. I don't get my inheritance. And not only do I not get the inheritance, my horrible cousin will get it, and he will likely spend the money on liquor and whores."

"That about sums it up."

"Well, that's just excellent. Anything more?"

"Yes. You leave Liri, and the palace withdraws its support."

The color drained from her face. "You would do that to me?"

"It's not I who wrote this will out, but your father, and mine."

"So what? They're dead, and you're the King. Surely you can override all of this."

He could not believe this *child* was arguing with him. He couldn't recall a time when anyone had dared. "I cannot. Because it was signed by the previous King. And these things are not that simple. And when it comes to you and your well-being, it is a matter of honor."

"Certainly not a matter of affection."

"Affection between you and I is inconsequential to me. But what is not is honoring that which my father has demanded of me. You must be cared for. And this is the way your father demanded you be cared for. I owe my father."

"Why, because you lost his other sons?"

She threw the challenge down with a resounding echo. She was the first one who had dared to lob such an accusation at him in a very long time. It was notable for that reason alone. And if he'd had a weak spot in that wrought iron chest of his it might have hurt.

But he was beyond hurt now.

Beyond feeling.

He was a man with drive, purpose. A man determined to become that which Liri required he be. He was prepared to do what needed to be done to honor his country and his father.

He too had a marriage time line. Though he was able to wait until thirty-five.

He had a prospective bride selected. A beautiful, frosty socialite who had been trained for just such a position.

The very opposite of the explosion that was Tinley Markham. Tinley had been given every advantage that a socialite would have been, but she had always been... Well, she had always been unruly. The only child of

Barabbas and Caroline Markham, she had been practically raised on the grounds of the palace. But her positioning as the future wife of his brother had certainly been more about his father's feelings regarding her father, than it had been about her particular suitability. The engagement had been cemented before Tinley had hit puberty.

And Tinley had… Well, she had worshipped Dionysus openly. And he had thought nothing of her. And why would he? She was a girl, and his brother Dionysus, four years her senior, was a renowned playboy with a voracious appetite for lush women. Blonde and ceramic or raven haired and brown skinned, he didn't much care. But he'd favored a particular sort. And in mass quantity. He had also favored drink.

It had been viewed as a lark. By his father, by the country. He was lighthearted. A man who knew how to enjoy a party.

Alexius had seen the darker side of Dionysus, even if no one else had.

It would be easy for Alex to name alcohol as the primary culprit in the death of his brother. Dionysus's obsession with sex and alcohol.

But then, Alex himself had known of those weaknesses in his brother. Had known what weaknesses they were.

And when, at a party where Tinley was in attendance, foxed out of his mind with a doe-eyed beauty clinging to his arm, Dionysus had claimed that he was going into the woods to face the spirits that had taken their brother, Alex should have known it would end badly.

He *had* known. On some level. For Lazarus had been lost in those same woods two years before Dionysus's birth and Alex should have had it in the forefront of his mind.

Instead…

Instead, that night, he'd made a different choice. He'd fallen prey to his own weaknesses. He'd sought to appease his own selfish desires. For the first time in his life, he'd truly thought only of himself. Consciously. Willingly.

And it had ended in tragedy.

His father had often said that his remaining sons were two sides of one coin. Their core was the same. Royal and resilient. They had the same golden eyes as their father that had earned him the name Lion of the Dark Wood. One that had become a title, along with King.

But Alex had always been missing the humor. The levity. And Dionysus had loved nothing more. He was named for the god of drink and revelry, after all.

It was their beautiful Greek mother who had named them, and she had done a fair job.

Except Lazarus was dead and wasn't returning.

And Dionysus's love of excess had in fact been his demise.

Alexius was simply…

He was simply King. And the rest was rumor, speculation, and in the case of Tinley, an inconvenience.

She held the cat clutched to her chest, and the creature left a gingery trail on her sweatshirt.

"I do hope you washed your hands before you made the pie."

"It's a cat friendly house."

The cat really was enormous. It spilled from Tinley's arms. "I suggest you find lodging for the beast. For you are returning to the palace with me."

He would not be ferrying himself back and forth between the palace and this badger's den she called a home. She was his project and he would have her in a convenient space.

Her eyes went round. "I will do no such thing."

"Leave your animals?"

"Return with you!"

"You haven't a choice, Tinley. I will see the stipulations of my father's last wishes fulfilled, and quickly."

She frowned. "And if I don't?"

"I will think nothing of using force, Tinley."

She frowned yet more deeply. "I am certain you would. All right. I will come. But my animals—"

"You cannot possibly think that you're bringing that into the royal palace of Liri."

"I fully think it. Your father had dogs."

"He did. Dogs that would have...eaten *that*."

"Algie is coming with me."

"Algie," he repeated, the word dripping with disdain.

"They're *all* coming with me."

He narrowed his gaze. *"All?"*

"Yes. Peregrine, Alton and Nancy."

"Are they all cats?"

"Don't be ridiculous."

He regarded her expression, which had gone mulish. "I'm sorry. I don't know how to respond to that."

"Peregrine is a ferret. Alton and Nancy are hedgehogs."

"I live in a palace, not a menagerie."

"I thought my happiness was important to you. I have a life. I have a charity to run. I have rescue animals."

"I suggest you open the cages and release the animals into your garden. Hedgehogs are often quite happy in gardens. I have it on good authority they can often be heard rutting beneath windows, so it must be a happy place for them."

Tinley's face went beetroot. "You of all people should know that it's dangerous out in the woods." Her eyes clashed with his, sparks in their green depths.

And he was done sparring with an impotent creature.

"I will bring my men in to pack up your detritus." He looked around at all of the baskets. "Do you require... everything?"

"Yes," she said. "I do require everything. If I don't have my yarn I won't be able to knit."

"God forbid. We cannot have a knitting crisis."

"Indeed. You say that dryly, but you have no idea. Also, we should bring the pie."

She looked around. "I'm able to work on my charity remotely."

"It will please you to learn the castle has Wi-Fi."

"Really? I'm somewhat surprised."

"Why are you surprised?"

"Because nothing about you seems modern, Alex."

Though on the outside, he remained stone, her words hit him strangely. He could not recall the last time a person had called him *Alex*.

His brother had done. Everyone else referred to him as Your Majesty. No one was so bold as to be quite so familiar with him. But of course, Tinley would be.

She would have heard her father refer to him as such. Alex walked to the window of the cottage and waved his hand. It was a signal for his men to come, and come they did. They descended on the small cottage and made quick work of everything in it. But by the time they had done so, he and Tinley, and a carrier that contained Algie, were bundled up in the back of the sleek black town car.

"He does not like to travel," she said. "If he couldn't hear my voice he would be very cross."

"Tinley, do not mistake me, I am doing this for my own convenience. You have to marry."

"Have to. So much have to in your world and I would have thought I'd escaped it when your brother died, but no. Here we are. Trying to get me to conform with all this protocol."

A wealth of memory flashed between them. Every time he'd ever scolded her for breaking that protocol.

He could remember clearly the time she had come with his family on a vacation to the Amalfi Coast. And she'd worn some swimming costume that was horrendously inappropriate. One piece but plunging down to her breast bone, the cut around her legs coming up over her hips.

He'd been entranced by her body.

And it had angered him.

*The press makes it their mission to get photographs of our family outings. You must be conscious of that, Tinley.*

*What's wrong with this? It's not a bikini, and this isn't the Dark Ages! Should I make sure I'm covered from crown to ankle?*

*You are to be my brother's wife. You must conduct yourself with a bit of decorum.*

*Then perhaps you ought to cover yourself. What will the world do if it gets a glimpse of your royal chest hair?*

She'd planted her palm in the center of his chest to give him a shove and he'd caught her wrist, their eyes locking together.

And he'd nearly been lost then. He'd been able to see clearly that Tinley had no idea why their eyes made sparks when they clashed. Why the air suddenly felt thick.

But he knew.

He knew and she didn't. And it was all the reason he'd needed to release her.

Protocol had not come into it.

"Well. It's a shame that your protocol wasn't functioning when you let Dionysus get lost in the woods."

"I did not over consume alcohol on my brother's behalf. Neither did I beseech him to try and impress the equally drunk and luxuriously curvy woman he was with." He knew that was unkind. To bring up the woman. That betrayal had hurt Tinley then. He didn't care. He couldn't afford to care. And he had no patience with her accusations. "And finally, I did not direct a pack of wolves to tear him limb from limb."

He felt something in his chest that might have been pain once. But the years had left him too hard and scarred to feel it.

He wore grief like a cloak. As much a part of him as the crown. It was not painful. It was not sad. It simply was. There was a weight to it, but it was not unbearable.

The grief for Dionysus, though, it was tinged with anger.

For he should have known better.

He knew the stories of how Lazarus had vanished.

He had gone in anyway. Brash and bold to impress a woman. For the forest would surely deem him worthy. As everyone had deemed that golden child, born after the King and Queen's first loss.

Worthy, more than worthy. Invincible.

But it had proven not to be so.

Dionysus had been lost in the wood, cementing Alex's reign as inevitable. Cementing his reputation as a fated ruler.

It was the Lion who remained. The Lion who claimed the throne.

The Lion who now found himself alone with the woman who had once been his brother's. Soft and delicate. And not for him.

It was all a bit gothic.

"How can you talk about it like that? You don't have a heart."

"No," he said, and that at least was true. It had been replaced with granite long ago. And without a heart, all he could fathom was duty.

Tinley was a duty. No matter how she might try him.

Her animals, her yarn, everything she came with. They would be his problem for just a little while longer.

"But I do have the means to find you a husband. And I will do so, Tinley, you have my word. I will return to you that which I stole from you. I will find you a husband. You have my word."

# CHAPTER TWO

TINLEY HADN'T BEEN back to the palace since King Darius's funeral. It had been just two weeks after Dionysus's funeral and she'd been shocked the palace hadn't crumbled around them all.

To lose both of them so quickly had been… It had been unthinkable, and yet it had been real.

Her life had felt like an absolute parade of grief. One blow after another. Her father. Her fiancé. The man she'd thought of as an uncle.

Her mother was still alive. She had her mother, but… they had never been…close. She had always been such a disappointment to her mother.

When King Darius had told her that she would marry Prince Dionysus she'd been so honored. She'd been young enough she hadn't fully understood what married meant. But she'd felt…approved of. She'd felt special.

Her mother had been so upset. Why Dionysus? Why not Alexius? Why not the future King?

A princess, not a queen. A slight, her mother had said.

Because of her tromping footsteps, frizzy hair and dizzy demeanor.

That was the first time she'd realized her mother had had loftier plans for her than she would ever reach. The first time she'd realized she would never be what her mother wanted.

Their distance had not improved in the years since.

Tinley had felt like she might as well not have a family, while her mother had gone to Italy and joined a fashionable crowd there.

Her engagement then might not have been all her mother had wanted, but it had brought Tinley into the fold of the royal family and from the time she was eight onward she lived in the palace part-time, along with her father who acted as advisor to the King. When he was there, she was too. They went on family vacations, attended royal balls and ate dinner with the family.

She'd been besotted with Dionysus from the moment she'd learned he was to be her husband.

He was beautiful, and kind. Closer to her age than Alexius, who frightened her. And who never smiled. Who always seemed to disapprove of her and who had not gotten less forbidding, but more so once she became a teenager.

Still, she'd been happy with her engagement.

But second best would never be good enough for her mother.

Her parents had been older when her mother had finally fallen pregnant with her. She'd been like a fairy tale gift and her mother had built up a store of expectations for what that might mean.

But she had been her father's pride and joy. Just as she was.

Then she'd lost him. And the other two men in her life who'd meant the very most to her.

Illness had taken her father, and the King.

Dionysus had been taken so cruelly she…she couldn't

even allow herself to think of that night. It was too painful.

So she had left Liri. She had immersed herself in her new life. In University. In the friendships she'd made there. The new hobbies she had discovered.

She had joined clubs. She had learned to bake. She had taken knitting lessons from an older woman who lived near the University. She had enjoyed her years in Boston. She had experienced new food, new culture, and she had escaped.

But it had never been real. Because marriage was the end destination for her, whether she wanted it to be or not.

Or else she'd be exiled in poverty, which wasn't a great option.

She had returned to Liri six months ago somewhat reluctantly, but there was a cottage there waiting for her, and she had known that. She had also been given the opportunity to head up a charitable foundation that contributed to the education of special needs children. The combination had been irresistible. So home she had gone.

Home.

After the death of King Darius, that final loss of the familiar life... Liri hadn't felt like home.

But the cottage had begun to feel like home.

This palace...

She had spent weeks at a time there sometimes.

It was a second home, and she had moved between her parents' grand manor home in the Lirian city of Tanaro and this castle with ease.

She'd felt happier here than there. For a time.

Coming back she felt nothing like happy at all.

It had been strange to come back to Liri at all, moving into the cottage near the edge of the wood.

There was dark magic at the center of the wood, and she knew it. Every Lirian child knew it.

And the palace overlooked the Dark Wood. This forest that had taken the love of her life away.

Even now, it made her heart ache.

She had been promised to Prince Dionysus since she was eight years old, and he was twelve. She had fallen in love with him when she'd turned fourteen.

A smile from him had been worth a pound of gold. More. She had thought he was the most beautiful, brilliant man. She had tried to explain her situation to some friends when she'd been at school, and they had all been horrified, that two children had been promised in marriage to each other. But they didn't know the truth of it. They didn't know him. They didn't understand how handsome he was. They were imagining some kind of medieval arrangement, but it hadn't been. The affection between their fathers had been real.

The honor it had been, for her anyway…it had been real.

And the way that she had felt for him had been… Well, it had been equally real.

The idea of getting married now…

She didn't want to. Her life was a monument to the loss of Dionysus. She was trying to be useful in the position she found herself in. In many ways it was better that she not be a princess, she supposed.

She knew he hadn't been… She knew there had been other women.

And yes, she'd been disappointed there had still been other women, even when she was old enough that he might have turned his attentions to her.

But he was gone. And there was no real reason to hate him for being with another woman when he died.

He'd never been with her anyway. He'd never made any promises.

She chose to remember the things she'd loved about him.

She wouldn't have been suited to being a princess, though. And she wasn't really suited to marriage at all, she didn't think. Her path had been determined for her from a young age, and because of that there were some things she'd never really thought about it.

Really, she had never thought of what it meant to be a princess. Only what it would be like to walk down the vast Cathedral aisle in a white dress toward the man her heart had longed for ever since she had understood why men and women were different.

The reality of it… Well, it fairly horrified her.

She had discovered that she liked to work behind the scenes. Doing hair and makeup just frustrated her. It reminded her of how frustrated she made her mother. Whenever she and her father had been back in residence in the family home, or when her mother had come for stints at the palace, her mother had picked at her.

Reminded her of all of her shortcomings.

She'd told her King Darius and her father might have been accepting of her in the role of Princess, but the press would have been vicious. She would have been subjected to millions of people scrutinizing her as her mother did and the idea of that was…intolerable.

Apart from the reasons she didn't like the idea of being looked at, she had also discovered that she liked quiet evenings at home. That she was good at particular things, just not socialite and royalty things. She had an artistic flair that she didn't discover until she went to University, and she expressed that through her baking, and with her knitting.

Losing Dionysus had been a tragedy. But from that, she had discovered some deep and important parts of herself. And somehow coming back here... It made it feel like that new creation she'd knit herself into was all beginning to unravel.

She was wearing leggings and a sweatshirt.

She hadn't been expecting Alexius to come to her house today. But Alexius didn't announce himself. He didn't ask permission, and he didn't make plans. He simply was.

It had been like that when she'd been at University. He'd come to see her three times, with no warning each time.

And good luck explaining why a man who radiated regal bearing and who was so handsome he made women swoon in the dorm halls, had come to see her.

Well, she'd had to just explain.

She was the ward of the King of her home country. As simple and complicated as that.

Just like the current situation.

She had seen the paperwork, and there was no use arguing.

She needed the money. Not for herself, but to fund the charity. Well, she did need to live, as well. Have money to feed her animals...

But the idea of a husband...

She was well used to the idea of an arranged marriage. It was just that the first one that had been arranged had suited her so much.

"I have a few requests."

Alex turned and looked at her, and there was something about that stark, rock carved expression that made her stomach feel hollow.

He was such a large man. Having him in her cottage had been strange and disorienting. He was so firmly associated with a life that she had left behind. With the forbidding palace walls.

That was why he made her feel so strange.

He always had. So grim and dark and brooding. A long shadow cast over her sunny days at the castle. He had never thought she was good enough for his brother. Her mother was angry with her for failing to be good enough to be Queen.

Alexius had never even thought her good enough to be Princess.

She doubted he thought she was good enough to scrub the floors.

"Requests?"

He was looking at her as if she'd grown a second head. One he didn't like any more than the first.

"If you're going to help me find a husband…"

"It isn't going to just be any husband. He must meet the requirements that I know your father would have."

She could say no. But he would only force her to go with him. There was no point opposing him here and now. Maybe she would be able to regroup at the palace, or perhaps they could come to an understanding after she met with some of his suggestions. But arguing now would get her nowhere.

She was too familiar with the brick wall that was Alexius to bother trying.

"Fine. But find me…the most bookish aristocrat you can. A man with a library. A man who likes to stay home in the evenings. A man who likes cats."

"I'm afraid our criteria are different, Tinley."

"*My* criteria have to matter," she said.

"I could easily find you a noble who doesn't care what you do."

"True."

The idea of that kind of marriage filled her with a great unease. Her parents had been a bit like that. Tinley was absolutely wild about her father. Her mother had always been untouchable. A beautiful doll in a glass case. There had been a distance between the two of them that could be felt when you were standing with them.

She had never wanted that. And she had been convinced that she and Dionysus wouldn't. Because he had looked at her and her insides had lit up.

Given the way he'd died... She knew that there were other women. She hadn't thought about it, not until then. Not until that poor traumatized girl in the woods, who had watched him die while she'd hidden.

But before then she simply hadn't thought about that. She'd considered the chasteness in their relationship a sign of his respect for her. Their engagement had felt like something enchanted, just like the forest.

But the forest had swallowed him whole.

The magic had not been with them after all.

She had been so sure that things between them would be different. And then she had been ready to spend the rest of her life... Well, not alone. She had friends. She had a calling, more than a job. She had found a niche. She had found some happiness.

Alexius had come in and upended it.

*It's your father's will...*

She couldn't even take that on board.

Alex was also sadly right. Of course there were any number of aristocratic men who would be happy to have a distant relationship with their wife. Who would expect to continue having affairs in the way that they saw fit.

Who would maintain cordial politeness, and allow her to use their money and her money.

"I fail to see how that's me being taken care of. And I feel certain that if my father were alive…"

"I cannot negotiate with a dead man, Tinley. This document is written as law."

The car stopped, but it wasn't the driver who ended up opening the door for Tinley, but Alexius himself. She moved slowly out of the vehicle, staring up at him. He was more than a head taller than his brother had been, and much, much broader. Dionysus had been a manageable fantasy with an easy smile.

Alexius was not a fantasy. He was a mountain.

One she had no desire to be standing at the base of.

She moved quickly, clutching Algernon's carrier to her chest.

"Wait," he said, his voice weighted with authority. And she had no choice but to stop.

There was something about that voice. It traveled down her spine like lightning and immobilized her.

"I will accompany you."

He held his arm out to her, and she, out of force of a long forgotten habit, looped her arm around his, and allowed him to lead her toward the front doors of the palace. She felt ridiculous. She was wearing trainers, leggings and a sweatshirt, next to a man in a bespoke suit. She was holding a cat carrier.

And this had once been her life. This place. There was a time when she had been the presumptive Princess and…

She could hardly reconcile it with who she was now.

The palace loomed before them as they walked up the brick path, and the wind picked up, wrapping her in a breeze that seemed to be full of memory, grief and a strange longing that seemed to well up from deep inside of her.

She wanted to hide. She wanted to jump in the cat carrier with Algernon.

But she didn't. She kept her gaze steady, and she kept walking. Like she didn't look a ridiculous mess. Like she wasn't a frizzy-haired woman walking with a polished king.

She felt like she was living in an alternate moment. And when the grand doors opened wide, and they entered the great antechamber that she knew led to the throne room, her heart squeezed so tight she thought she would choke.

"Welcome back," he said.

She looked around the space, and she felt decidedly...

It was a strange feeling. It wasn't bad or good.

"Charis," he said, as a woman entered the room. "Please show Tinley to her room."

The momentary relief that she felt over being out of Alex's presence was completely replaced by the disquiet that she felt moving through the once familiar hallways.

She could see her father everywhere. She could see King Darius.

She looked up at the walls, and she saw portraits of the family. Hanging on those marble walls.

She had never known Lazarus. He had died long before she was born.

But oh, she remembered the rest of them.

The Queen had been beautiful, but frail. And everyone said that she wasn't the same after Lazarus disappeared.

They had also said that it was a blessing she had died before her youngest son.

Before her husband.

Because the grief would have just been a cruelty she could never have borne.

As she moved down the hallway, looking at all the portraits, her gaze kept landing on those of Alexius. He was intense. Dark and brooding, even in these depictions. He was so different than Dionysus. And she had never really felt like...

Not that either of them had ever been her playmates, or anything of the sort. She had been an inconvenience, underfoot to them. Dionysus had been kind to her, likely because he knew that she would be his wife someday. Kind, a bit indulgent.

Alexius had always been...remote. Distant.

In fact, he reminded her of the wood.

And it seemed fitting, because it was the wood that had consumed the man that she was meant to marry.

And it was the man who seemed like a personification of that dark, demonic place that had brought her here.

The room had a familiar feel to it, but she couldn't quite be certain that she had ever stayed in it before. But it had a massive canopy bed. And it overlooked the lake, not the forest. For which she was grateful.

"Charis," she said to the woman, as she retreated. "Can you please make sure that my... That my other animals are brought to me." She paused for a moment. "And my yarn."

"Of course," she said.

When the woman retreated, Tinley put the cat carrier down on the bed and opened the door.

Algie did not come out. In fact, he seemed peevish over the change in scenery. "This is a palace," she said, keeping her voice soft. "You're supposed to like it better than the cottage."

He meowed plaintively.

"I know," she said softly. "I don't either."

When her things were brought to her, she was all ready to settle in for the evening. But before Charis left her with Nancy, Alton and Peregrine, she paused at the door. "I'll be back in a moment with your dress. We are going to have to get you ready for dinner."

## CHAPTER THREE

SHE WAS LATE. And Alexius did not like to be kept waiting. At least, he didn't *think* he liked to be kept waiting.

No one had ever dared do it before.

If he were not so angry, he might find it extraordinary.

Of course for Tinley it was par for the course.

She always dared.

His mind flashed back to her pushing him. Her hand on his chest…

The door to the dining room opened, and the creature that appeared there was nearly unrecognizable. That cloud of carrot hair had been tamed into something sleek. He could not see her freckles, smoothed by some sort of makeup. Her lips were painted a pink color that should have clashed with her hair, but somehow didn't.

Her gown was much the same. A daring shade that went off the shoulder and revealed far more creamy skin than he was comfortable seeing on her.

He hated it.

It was not Tinley. And yet it was. Her voluptuous figure on display, her full lips dewy from some gloss that verged on pornographic.

She was a nightmare. Tinley made visually acceptable as if to mock the fact he found her attractive even when she didn't. And to present to him a vision of her as the sort of sleek trophy he was seeking in a queen.

She couldn't know, and yet there was a light in her green eyes that spoke to him. That said: Where are your excuses now?

Not a girl.

Not dizzy.

Not frizzy.

"Good evening," she said, edging slowly into the room and taking a seat a comical ten chairs away from him.

His body relaxed into the relief of the distance and he tightened his fist. Unwilling to cede that he needed her to keep distance.

"Tinley," he said. "We will not be able to discuss anything if you are half a league away from me."

"Sorry," she said. "I didn't know the appropriate distance to keep from a king."

He thought of the times they had all been forced to dine at one end of the table, with their fathers down at the other talking about matters of state.

She knew well enough.

"When you are dining with a king you must sit close enough to converse with him," he said.

"Well, your voice *does* carry."

"It shouldn't have to."

She stood, hardly the picture of lithe grace and dignity. No. She was nothing half so basic.

*You want basic. You need it.*

She walked slowly over to where he was. And then she sat, her posture remaining comically rigid.

"I'm surprised you didn't bring the cat."

She rolled her eyes at him. Like a bratty teen. "I'm not ridiculous."

"Good to know."

Those same eyes now narrowed at him. "Was that a joke?"

"No. It really is helpful to know that you're not ridiculous. It's valuable to know exactly what it is I'm working with."

"It may have escaped your notice," she said, folding her hands in front of her on the table and staring him down. "But I am not eighteen. I'm not eight years old, either. I run and coordinate a charity. I manage events, fund-raisers. I'm not going to bring a cat to the dinner table."

And in those words he saw a spark of something. Not just the dizzy, frizzy hair that he had noticed earlier. But the light deep down inside of her that he was certain she must show in other areas of her life. She had to. If not, then how could she run a charity.

When he had arrived at the cottage and seen it in disarray, when he had taken a look around at all the homey things that—in his opinion—were a study in superfluity, he knew that many people saw the life of a Royal as one of potential excess. Of privilege. And it was true, there was a great deal of power and privilege to be had when one was royal.

But in Liri, at least, the tradition of royalty ran much more toward stark. The King was the protector. Liri had mountains to the north, the sea to the south, and thick forest to the east and west, guarding the borders, with Italy on one side and Slovenia on the other. They were small, but they were powerful. And the ruler of the country had always been a part of that power.

It was not power to be taken lightly.

His father had taught him that a king must rule with a firm hand.

He and Dionysus were different people. He had always

been more serious than his brother. And it was entirely possible that… Perhaps his brother would have brought some much-needed lightness to the country.

His father had been an only child, and Alex knew it had been his hope that his sons would help one another. That they would not have the competition seen in family generations past, but that Dionysus would be the piece Alexius might be missing on his own.

The world was not as it had once been, after all.

The Lion of the Dark Wood had been necessary across the history of Liri. They'd had conflict with other nations. They had struggled financially in the beginning. War, famine.

These things were not so in the twilight of his father's reign, and they were not so for Alexius.

But he was what the people had gotten. Even if he was not what they deserved.

And he was what Tinley had to contend with as well. Whether she liked it or not.

"It is true," he said, "that you have managed to tame yourself into an image that will be easier for me to pass off to another gentleman."

"That's very sweet that you think of yourself as a gentleman."

"A figure of speech, more than an actual commentary on my beliefs regarding myself."

Her eyes glittered.

She was a strange and fascinating creature. She seemed hapless, and yet he could see that wasn't the case. Her choices, her animals, her hair…

There was a deliberateness to her. To the hodgepodge of her house and the whirlwind of her movements. And he realized she wasn't dizzy at all.

She was like a carnival ride, flashing and spinning

and lighting up the night. Seemingly random and reckless, but in fact spinning in perfectly calculated time.

It was like he was seeing her for the first time. Not as he wanted to call her. It was easier to just see her as accidental, for that made her less than she was.

And she was already far too much.

But she was right. She could not do the job she did, couldn't have graduated from University, if she were truly haphazard.

"Tell me," he said, the command in his voice like iron. For his every command was iron. "What was it like to grow up with your father?"

She blinked. "Why?"

"Because I'm intrigued. I'm interested in what exactly has made you…this. You were raised practically in the palace, as I was."

"As was Dionysus," she said. "But the two of you could not be more different than… Well, a Ferrari and a lion."

"Those comparisons have nothing in common."

"To my point," she said, dryly mimicking something he'd said to her earlier. "You know, one is machinery. Modern and sleek and shiny. The other is a bit toothy. Dangerous. Ancient."

"If that's a joke about my age…"

"Oh, no." She waved a hand. "It's definitely about your personality."

"So tell me. How is it you managed to grow into… what you are?"

"You saw me grow up. I was here most of the time."

"And when you weren't?"

She blinked. "I don't know. I guess… It was difficult with my mother. Always. I think she loves me."

She looked away, her eyes downcast.

"You *think*?"

She looked back at him, her expression defiant. "Yes. I think she withheld her praise because she thought if she gave it I might not try. And in her opinion I never tried hard enough."

He felt…he didn't like it, for he *felt*. But he knew what it was to be denied your mother's love. He knew.

"Tried hard enough for what?" he asked.

"To be… Well, to be her, I suppose."

Her mother had always seemed spoiled and selfish to him. Certainly nothing like Tinley. And nothing she could ever want to be.

"If I remember correctly. You really are nothing like your mother."

She shook her head. "No. And I also think she was very disappointed that I wasn't… Well, that I wasn't asked to be your wife."

"My wife?"

"Princess is a bit below Queen, particularly in the estimation of my mother, who I think believed that our fathers' connections would benefit us more than she believed it did in the end."

"So my brother wasn't good enough for her?"

"Mostly, I'm not good enough for her. But the thing is, I was more than good enough for my father. I loved him so much. And he loved me." She looked down at her plate. "Your father picked me for Dionysus just like I was. It was much easier to be more of that person than the woman who could never be the Queen my mother wanted me to be."

He knew what it was to disappoint a mother. More than disappoint. He might as well have taken a knife and cut his mother open.

He should have been the one to be keeping an eye on his brother.

They had been outside playing on the palace grounds, and it wasn't until he realized he no longer heard his brother laughing that he realized something was wrong. He had lifted his head to see the back of his brother as he disappeared into the Dark Wood. As the trees seemed to swallow him whole. He had run after him. With all of his speed and might, but he was nowhere to be found.

Not a trace of Lazarus had ever been found.

He had only been seven years old, but Alexius had searched for his brother in the wood with the men until he had nearly fallen off the mount with exhaustion.

And then, he had gone back out the next day, after forty-five minutes of sleep, to continue searching. He had gone into the wood, and no harm had become of him.

The Lion of the Dark Wood. Or, a failure who had allowed his brother to die.

Opinion was divided.

Not with his mother, though.

He was thankful yet again that she had not lived through the death of Dionysus, for her opinion would've been confirmed then.

"And you...you were born a mountain?" She asked.

"I was born to be King. But time changes us all."

She shook her head. "You've always been like this."

"Regretfully, I cannot speak to the way that you've always been." But he could. For he could remember her, a ball of energy and light and noise.

And could remember her as she grew older, watching the energy shift and change into something that shone from her eyes, rather than exploding into uncontrolled movement.

That was when the feeling in him had begun to shift. From a fascination that verged on horror that his father had chosen her as wife of the spare, to an attraction that felt like an abomination.

It felt no less so now.

"Why should you?" she asked. "I was nothing more than a child to you. But of course when you're seventeen or so you don't think you're a child, do you?"

He locked his jaw tight. "I wasn't."

That truth stood stark between them. "I don't suppose you were."

"We do a great deal of supposing between the two of us."

"No need," she said. "We can confirm. That's my origin story. A girl who was told she would be a princess at eight. Whose mother found that to be a disappointment. Who was frizzy and loud, and still is." She reached up and touched her sleek locks. "Your staff did sort of an amazing job fixing me up. I can't take credit for it. I've never known what to do with my hair."

"Well, if you marry wealthy enough you shall never have to. You either hire the appropriate staff who will enable it to look however you wish, or you'll be able to keep it as is and call it a trend, as your husband will be influential enough that you will command such public opinion."

"Not a dream that I've ever had. But I would like very much to command influence to help with my charity."

"Why does that charity matter to you?"

"I was very lucky. No matter who I might have been born, or how, I would have been able to get an education. My safety net has always been…well, you. A king. When I left this country, when I began talking to people about their different experiences, people from all over the world who I met at school, I realized that that wasn't true for most of them. That if they were there, it was often through great financial expense of their parents, or an immense amount of effort. More than a normal person could ever give. If a person has learning disabilities, or special needs, the fight that they're engaged in to get the kind of education that will work for them is intense. And it's education that enables them to take their place in the world. We want people to work. We want them to be productive members of society, but we don't care to give them the building blocks in order to make that happen. I do care. For people who are not as fortunate as I've been."

"I hope that's the speech that you give at events for your charity."

"More or less."

"It's very affecting."

"Thank you. I've discovered that I care quite a bit about it as a topic. Accidents of birth shouldn't be the deciding factor in your potential."

"Neither should accidents of death. But my life has certainly been changed by them." Normally, he would not have made such a comment, but he was struck by the strange realization that he and Tinley shared commonalities he would never have imagined.

Though, she had not earned her mother's disdain.

She looked at him, those green eyes full of a deep, round emotion he couldn't put a name to. A suspicious sort of question that stopped short of accusation, but held no small amount of censure.

She looked down, her neat white teeth closing over her lip. "Why didn't you stop him from going into the woods?"

She could have been speaking of either of his brothers. Either of his historic failures.

"Should I? That is a common take, Tinley, and you're not the first to express it. Though most don't express it directly to me. I should have stopped both of my brothers from going in the woods, shouldn't I? And yet, I did go in after them. And I seem to have emerged unscathed."

"So, you believe that you're the Lion of the Dark Wood? The born leader of this nation? Fated to rule and any potential competition removed?"

"I believe nothing of the kind. I believe that if you're drunk and a fool and you go running into the woods where your older brother previously disappeared, and where you know there are packs of hungry wolves, you are perhaps taking your chances."

"That's a disrespectful way to speak of the dead."

"The dead got themselves eaten by wolves. The dead must be strong enough to cope with the fact that unflattering things will be said about them."

She frowned deeply. "The dead is not here to defend himself."

"If he were, do you think he would defend himself? No. He would smile, and he would take another drink. For all that I find him frustrating, I cannot hate him. For he is entirely who he is. At least, he was."

"It's what I liked about him," she said softly. "There was a freedom to him that I admired. And I tried to carry it forward in my life. I did. I tried to be… I tried to be someone he would have liked."

"He was young. And I do not believe he knew quite what he liked, or what he would have liked had he been able to grow more. I think eventually, he would have liked you quite a lot." Those last few words were rough in his throat. Painful.

Their food arrived at that moment, wheeled in on carts by members of his staff. And as her plate was set out before her, he continued. "In any case, I've taken you on."

"Wonderful," she snapped. "So, I've gone from prospective Princess to charity case. Unless of course you want to make my mother's hopes and dreams come true and make me your Queen?"

She was being provocative on purpose. And she didn't think he'd rise to meet her.

"And if I did?"

His words were like a gauntlet thrown down between them and their eyes clashed for a moment and something…electric passed through the air.

Down his spine.

He resented it. The tightness in his chest, his gut. That she should have the power to change the air around him. That the air would change without his permission.

"No thank you," she said.

He was nearly disappointed that she backed down.

She looked down at her plate.

Then she looked back up at him, delight suddenly shining from those green eyes.

He felt that delight pour through him like melted gold. Hot and precious and dangerous. Something strange that went off low in his stomach. Like a bomb bursting.

The food. The food had made her light up like a switch had been turned on and there was something inescapably compelling about her simple joy.

No.

She was in love with his dead brother.

He was the King.

She would never be his Queen.

"Dinner looks amazing," she said. "Is that puff pastry?"

She poked at the top of the meat pie sitting on her plate. *Poked* at it.

He said nothing.

"It's lovely," she said, cutting through the top of it, and closing her eyes when the crust made a sound. "Amazing." She hummed as she took a bite.

There was something to the excitement in her. The warmth. This castle was ancient, a stack of stones that had come from a cold earth. And she infused them with… her. He could feel her. Surrounding him. How long had it been since he'd seen someone take pleasure in such a simple thing?

There was a purity in her that ran through his veins and twisted. Turned from that bright innocence of a woman enjoying the flavor of her dinner, into something dark and tortured in him.

She looked up at him. "What?"

"Absolutely nothing," he said.

He looked away. Perhaps it had been too long since he'd had a woman. He had been focused on the practicalities of striking a deal with Nadia. The two of them had no connection, physical or otherwise, and she had been out of the country for the entirety of the negotiations. Given that he was in the process of negotiating a marriage agreement, he had not thought it prudent to take a lover. But perhaps in this case a discreet lover would be the better part of valor.

He could not endure this. This proximity to her.

It was a sickness that should have died the night his brother did.

But here it endured.

"Next week. Next week we will have a ball, and we will invite all of the eligible men in the higher echelons of society, from all nations friendly to Liri. And there, we will find you a husband."

"That makes me a bit like Prince Charming, doesn't it?"

"If any of the men arrive in a pumpkin I'll be sure to let you know."

"You know, I would quite like that. Because not only would he come with a pumpkin, he would come with a couple of fat rats. And I assume his suit would be tailored by birds."

"That's absurd."

"It's been said, on more than one occasion, that I myself am slightly absurd. So, that bothers me less than you think it might."

"Your cat would eat them," he pointed out.

"We can't have that. Though, he has not eaten the hedgehogs or the ferret yet."

"A relief to all involved."

"You know," she said, and impish expression taking over her face. "If it happens now, I'm going to blame the change of venue."

"The death of your rodents will weigh heavily upon my conscience."

And he realized that perhaps it was a poor choice of words, considering there were two deaths that did weigh upon his conscience. Deaths that the passage of time would never ease the wounds of. Deaths that had caused deep and abiding division in his country. Between the people who supported him still, and the people who thought him a murderer.

Division that he was having to work now to ease.

"End of the week," he said. "There will be a ball. You will behave. You will comply."

"What if I didn't?"

The question was asked so simply, the expression on her face not angry or inflammatory in any way. Rather it simply was. A sort of innocent wonderment that he had only ever witnessed in Tinley.

"I would throw you in the dungeon."

"You could just marry me and save us the trouble."

"In the end," he said, his stomach going tight. "Dungeon or marriage to me. Is there a difference?"

She shook her head slowly. "No. There isn't."

After that, there was no more conversation.

And by the time she left the dinner table, a knot had begun to form in his chest that only expanded with each passing moment. And when she left the room, it did not ease.

The sooner he had Tinley Markham married off the better.

He got up from his seat and went over to the bar that was at the far end of the massive dining room. He took out a bottle of scotch and poured himself a measure of it. He downed it in one gulp.

The sooner she was dealt with, the sooner he could get on with the business of ruling Liri.

And the sooner he would have fat cats and hedgehogs removed from his castle.

That would be a blessing indeed.

# CHAPTER FOUR

COMPORTMENT LESSONS BEGAN the next day. Tinley was horrified. Why was he so hell-bent on changing her? Yes, there had been a presumption that if she was going to be Princess she would have to conform in some way. But she had assumed that her basic raw material was decent, considering she had been chosen to be the Princess of Liri at a very early age.

And anyway, that future was gone. She wasn't supposed to be a princess. She was simply looking for a... for a husband.

She looked around the ballroom, empty except for the older woman that Alex had assigned to be her mentor.

She had been walking with a book on her head for half an hour.

But for some reason, every time she got midway through the room she would imagine Alex's dark, disapproving gaze boring a hole through her, and she would stumble.

She really didn't like him.

Their conversation last night had been strange. It had affected her in unexpected ways.

It had been easy to cast him as the villain in Dionysus's death. Though the ferocity of her anger had waned over the years.

She had gotten older, and as she had borne witness to rowdy, drunken behavior in college, she had been forced to ask herself many times who needed to bear responsibility for that behavior.

And every time, she could only ever bestow the responsibility to the people engaging in the behavior.

Which meant Dionysus bore the weight of his own rash act.

He had been twenty-two years old when he'd died. He had seemed such a man to her. Now that she was the same age as he'd been when he passed it seemed…strange. Because they were on equal footing now.

And she… Well, she would not have done the things he did. She wouldn't have drunk to excess and put herself in danger like that.

She would never have cheated.

The thought of that was like a knife twisting her chest. Not because she loved him so much. Not now. It was just…she'd excused it. A great many times, because it hadn't suited the vision she'd had of him, of her feelings for him, to be angry about the other women.

But it had been wrong.

She couldn't imagine Alex behaving in such a way. Never.

Alex had been in his own stratosphere to her when Dionysus had died. In his thirties already and so remote and responsible. She'd been certain then it was all age, and now she knew better.

She didn't know why she was comparing the two of them. Dionysus had been fun. Dynamic. He'd had plans for the country in his role as Prince, and when he had spoken, it had been electric. He had been a firm favorite of the people for a variety of reasons. He had established festivals and parades. He had brought a much-needed levity to the culture.

She loved her country. She always had.

Her mother was American, and she had spent a great deal of time in the States as a girl, and had also been privileged enough to travel around the world. She felt that gave her the context to truly appreciate Liri and what was unique about it. But she could also appreciate the fact that it had an old-fashioned feel to it, that there was a sense of seriousness derived from years spent with the people in poverty, and with uncertainty surrounding them while war had raged.

There had been generations of that sort of unrest, all resolved when King Darius had been in power. But the psyche of the people was rooted in that, and those things did not change overnight.

Dionysus had seemed like the medicine the country needed.

It had seemed as if he had been born not feeling the weight of the potential crown. And it had been a good thing.

Alex himself seemed to bear the weight of a mountain on his shoulders. And he walked straight and tall all the same. But there was…a gravity to him that seemed to affect the rotation of her when she was around him.

It was disconcerting at best. But then, this entire situation was disconcerting. Because she had spent a few years feeling like she might be a normal girl. Not one who had been set on the rarest and strangest of paths as a child, only to be completely derailed from it, then spat out into the real world alone and aimless.

But she'd had a chance to rebuild herself from the ground up. In Boston, there had been no expectations, no decisions about her future made anymore.

And in the back of her mind she'd known about the stipulations in her father's will but it had seemed so distant.

She hadn't imagined they would be enforced.

But now she was back. A reminder that she was part of a relatively old-fashioned system, and that she was the daughter of a king's advisor.

*But what if you did walk away?*

She would walk away with nothing. And she had no idea what she would do with that. What would she be able to offer…anyone? How would she take care of herself? The job that she had at a charity was fulfilling, but it didn't make a large amount. And she had always known that she would have an arranged marriage. It was just that…

It was just that she had wanted the marriage that was arranged.

"I can see it's going well."

She whirled around, and the book flew off of her head. And there he was. Standing in the door, the object of her consternation.

"Very well," she said dryly.

"Concentrating hard in your lessons?"

"Thinking about running away."

He began to move closer to her, and her heart beat faster in response. She didn't know why she found him so… So.

"There will be none of that," he said.

"Why?"

"You know what happens when people run into the woods."

But he was not teasing her. His voice was heavy.

"I'm not going to run into the woods."

"A relief. Good to know that you do have some sense in your head."

"I was actually beginning to wonder if I do. I could go back to America."

"You could," he said. "With nothing."

"I don't need a lot of money."

"But your charity…"

"Yes. It's an astronomical waste of privilege, isn't it."

"Interesting that you think that way. When it isn't as if you have a whole lot of choice."

"I don't. But I do have… I have benefited very much from all the money that has surrounded me my entire life. To completely disregard it seems shortsighted."

And she realized that she stood there, staring up at him, that she also had no idea what her life looked like if she cut ties with Liri. With her homeland.

With this palace, and with this man.

No, she had never been close to Alex. But he had always been there. He had been there during her years at University, however distant.

It hadn't been her mother who had supported her then. But the palace.

Her mother had gone off to find a way to keep herself in the lifestyle she was accustomed to, at least from Tinley's point of view. She'd found lovers who aided in that pursuit.

She'd told Tinley she couldn't understand why she didn't find a rich husband.

Why she needed school.

Why she needed to make her own life.

Even being responsible and independent, Tinley was wrong.

The palace was the reason she had the cottage. She doubted Alex had overseen any of it personally, but her connections to the royal family had been a safety net for her.

And even now, this palace—though she had avoided it for many years now—was a particular sort of safety net. And she supposed that in some ways going along with all this was a bit of cowardice. But she couldn't… Couldn't fathom simply deciding to cut herself off from this. Her final connection to her father. Her final connection to the life she'd been meant to have.

She had a chance here, to have a say in her future. And no, not in the way other women did, it was true. But she could choose her husband. She could find someone who did suit her.

It was archaic in some ways, she knew. Or it would seem so to other people. But she'd had a husband chosen for her as a girl. To have an actual selection now seemed nearly decadent.

And marriage… This was the key to her succeeding, she knew it was.

She'd given up pleasing her mother.

But she could *show* her.

With the right husband she would have the assets she needed to make a difference in the world. The right husband would like her as she was. And she could show her mother that she could make a success of herself.

That she didn't need to be a queen or even a princess.

"I don't need to be turned into a robot. I want whoever I marry to marry *me*, not some elegant lie." she said. "This is ridiculous."

"Now," he said, his voice stern. "That isn't terribly polite, considering Madame Dansforth makes a living at this ridiculousness. It is her life's work."

Tinley turned to her instructor. "I didn't mean your life's work is ridiculous." She turned back to Alex. "What I meant is it's ridiculous to try to make me into something I'm not. I'm never going to be able to maintain anything like this." She held her foot out, displaying the impractical high heel she was wearing. "I'm not going to be swanning around my house wearing things like this. So if I managed to impress a man, it's going to be based on nothing but a lie that I will never be able to keep up for more than a few hours."

"Best foot forward."

She wiggled her toes. "Clumsy foot."

She hated this. Because it reminded her so much of what it was like to be a clumsy, sad girl who couldn't do anything right as far as her mother was concerned.

She took in a long, slow breath. And it caught, somewhere in the center of her chest, as her eyes met his.

"I am supposed to find a husband for you," he said. "And I will do it by the means that I consider to be best."

"And you never question your opinions?"

"I question them often," he said. "Any leader should." And she felt something bloom there at the center of her chest. Hot and reckless and strange. Irritation. Because it could be nothing more.

Because she resented him. Resented him, and the fact that he lived and breathed and stood there disapproving of her while his brother was gone.

That he had taken her here and manipulated the connection she still had to this family, to this place, against her.

*That isn't fair. You chose this. You chose this because you're afraid to do anything else. Because you want to show your mother...*

She shut that thought down.

Along with the reckless heat inside of her.

"How is dancing coming along?" he asked, not directing the question to her at all.

"We haven't begun," Madame Dansforth said.

"Then we will begin now."

"The girl has not managed to walk across the room with the book on her head," the madam snapped.

"Will she be walking across the ballroom with a book on her head?" Alex asked, his tone dry. "Because she will be dancing. So it is perhaps in her best interest if she practices one above the other."

Madame Dansforth looked exasperated. "I have a method, and you did hire me to use it."

"Yes," he said. "But I'm still the King. And I'm over-riding you now."

There was a pause and if Tinley wasn't mistaken, a hint of frost in the air. But the good madam knew better than to argue with a king.

"As you wish, Your Majesty," the woman said.

It really was amazing how people deferred to him, even if they were irritated, as Madame Dansforth visibly was. It was only that no one dared say it to his face. That he was being high-handed. That he was overstepping. When he so clearly was.

When the music started, Alex turned to her.

"Dance," he said. He extended his hand, and she looked at it, having the feeling that he had offered her a live spider.

"With you?"

"Yes," he said. "I will be dancing with you the night of the ball. It is my job to present you."

"That seems a little bit much."

"It's a dance," he said. "Not a siege against your person."

But for some reason, as she reached out to take his hand, slowly, ever so slowly, she felt as if they might be the same thing.

She thought of another moment. Another time.

She'd been nearly eighteen and standing against the wall during a ball. Dionysus had danced with two other women then slipped off to get drunk. She felt numb and she'd tried to tell herself it was only that he hadn't known how she felt. That their relationship had not yet become a romantic one, not for him. Still, it had hurt.

She hadn't known quite what to do with herself and Alexius had come over to her, dark eyes alight with black fire.

*We will dance.*

*Oh, no I'm fine.*

*It wasn't a request.*

And she'd found herself swept up into strong arms that had made her feel small, fragile and safe, all at once.

His hand on her waist had burned and she'd been able to think of nothing else the whole time he'd twirled her around the dance floor. She'd been holding her breath and the relief she'd felt when he'd released her had been beyond words.

Because she hated him.

Because he hadn't done it for any reason other than because he was Alex, and when it came to duty he'd do it whether he wanted to or not.

But in the present, when their fingers connected, something shot through her midsection, down between her thighs.

And it made her wonder if what she'd felt back then had been hate at all.

It reminded her of a time she had gone on a hike when she'd been at college. They had gone up to the very top of a ridge, and she had stood on the edge, looking down, and she felt it. That kind of terror. That resonated in her core. In her teeth.

Fear. That's what this was. She feared him.

The Lion of the Dark Wood.

Except, to her, he would always be entangled in the wolves that had eaten his brother.

Somehow, to her, they had become one in the same. This forbidding older brother whose job it was to protect an entire country, but somehow hadn't protected his blood.

He had become the villain of the story. And she couldn't quite figure out why. Because of course it wasn't his responsibility to monitor every movement of his younger brother. It was even more ridiculous than the blame he took from the public, for being a boy, a small boy, who had failed to supervise another child. There should have been nannies. There should have been guards. His parents. Why was Alex the one who seemed to take the unequal weight in all of this?

And yet, she tended to think of him in that way as well. As the responsible party for something that had gone wrong.

And maybe it was because of everything that had come before, more than legends and curses. Because in her memory, the palace had been wonderful. And Dionysus had been wonderful. But Alex had never approved, and it had been transparent, at least to her.

Alex had always felt like their villain.

He had that way of stealing her rose colored glasses.

It made her feel raw and wounded and fragile. Because her advocates were gone. And it was he who remained.

And then, it wasn't only her fingertips that touched his. His large hand enveloped hers, and he pulled her against his body. She stumbled in the high heels, falling against that hard, broad chest. With her free hand, she braced herself, and then removed it as if she had been scalded.

"Dance," he repeated.

Then he swept her into his arms, and he took the lead.

He was strong, and steady, but her heart was beating at some erratic, ridiculous clip, and she could not manage to keep her feet beneath her. She kept slipping, tripping, trembling.

Madame Dansforth was shouting out instructions, and Tinley could feel herself failing. Alarmingly off rhythm.

She hated it. Hated this. It reminded her of being at home. Her mother had tried to get her dancing lessons and she'd failed. She'd been awful at piano. Her mother had placed coins on the backs of her hands to get her to play with her hands held just so, and they'd always clattered onto the floor. She'd had her sit in a dining chair with a scarf tied around her shoulders to improve her posture.

Even dinner had to be a lesson, because she couldn't even eat right.

She couldn't do this right, and Alex's disapproval burned even deeper.

"Leave us," Alex shouted.

They stopped moving, and his voice echoed over the music. Madame Dansforth looked at him, her expression blank. "Leave you?"

"I do not think my order was ambiguous."

The woman paused. "Of course it wasn't."

"Good."

She left them, leaving them alone. And Tinley simply stood, standing in front of Alex, feeling small and inadequate and *angry*.

"Dance again," he commanded.

"You've dismissed the instructor."

"She wasn't helping you. I am your instructor now."

"You don't know that she wasn't helping. You don't know me."

"I do know you," he said. "You are the girl that my father matched up with my brother simply because he thought the world of your father. It had nothing to do with you. It had nothing to do with him."

"How dare you?"

"It is the truth," he said. "I'm sorry if you find it inconvenient."

"I didn't ask for this. Not any of it."

"And yet, there are hoops we all must jump through in order to fulfill our destinies, are there not? What is my life but a public performance? But a show. And it is not the most important thing that I am. For a show will not run a country. I must do that. I must keep the people secure. Keep them safe. I must fulfill the destiny of the nation. I must do it while instilling confidence in myself as a leader."

"Difficult to do. You're a walking PR problem."

He smiled. A predator's smile.

Lion or wolf, it didn't matter.

It was still all the better to eat her with.

"Dance."

"On my terms." She kicked her shoes off, which was not the power move she had hoped, since that put her directly in the line of sight of the center of his chest. And then, in a state of rage, she grabbed hold of the band that held her hair in place, and pulled it free. "Now I'll dance. As me. Not as this…trussed up turkey on stilts."

She found herself back in his arms, and this time, when he began to lead, his strong arms nearly lifted her off the ground.

They moved in time with the music. Rough. Angry. Intense. But she didn't feel off rhythm now. For she moved with him. As if their rage had twined together, flowing through them both.

Her every move was now in time with his. Her heart thundered, her body quaking as they did. She had never been this close to a man before. She had danced light and carefree at parties. The way that young people did. Holding hands, and not inviting any intimacy.

She had danced with Dionysus and he had kept that sort of distance. Out of deference to her father and her age.

He had treated her as a perfect gentleman.

And Alexius was as well. He certainly wasn't taking liberties. It was simply a dance. But her breasts were crushed against his chest, and it felt like a sin. And the most disturbing thing was she had a feeling that sensation of sinning came from inside her own body. And the expression on his face sharpened, turned to stone.

It wasn't disapproving anymore.

It was something else. Something she couldn't pin a name on. But it echoed inside of her. She knew, somehow, that it matched. That it matched the reckless feeling that was riding through her like a rhythm all its own. One that overrode the music. One that sounded a call to a different kind of dance.

*You know.*

Something inside of her whispered that. From a place deep and hidden.

And she felt horribly exposed. Bright and sensitive, and like exactly what he thought she was. Something untamed and coarse and unworthy.

A woman who had kicked her shoes off in his presence, and unbound her hair.

And yet, he held her. Yet, he didn't let her go. It was an anomaly. One she could not put a name to. They twirled around the ballroom floor, and while the thick, leaden sensation that was so foreign to her pooled in her stomach, created alchemy and heat inside of her, she didn't notice she had been lifted off the floor. That she was spun so her back pressed against the wall, and even more hard and unyielding than the marble behind her, was the man at her front.

His dark eyes blazed down into hers, and she lost the ability to breathe.

But he didn't move. A sense of wretched desperation filled her. But it could not be. It could not be that this quickening of her heart, that the sensitivity she felt in her breasts, down between her legs was anything like desire.

Desire for this man who was wrapped in the most painful memories she possessed.

The brother of the man she'd been so certain she loved.

And he wouldn't answer the question of what this dark, terrible beast inside her wanted. He wouldn't do anything to ease her suffering.

Had he moved away from her, or had he closed the distance, she might have found some clarity. But he refused to do either. He held them both there, frozen, poised as if on the edge of a knife.

"Learn to dance in shoes," he said finally. And then he moved away from her.

And he left her feeling…cold. Bereft of something that she would have denied she wanted unto death.

And she was helpless to do anything but stare as she watched him walk out of the ballroom.

She leaned against the wall, collapsed, sliding down to the floor. And she stared at the book she had been balancing on her head only moments ago, lying in the center of the room discarded.

What had she done? Or worse still, what hadn't she done, that a piece of her seemed to want.

"This is the problem," she whispered. "Yarn and cats can only take you so far. And loving a dead man doesn't do much for pent up physical desire."

She had always thought that maybe... That maybe her desire was low. That maybe she didn't have all that much. She had found Dionysus beautiful, but she had been young.

She hadn't had...fantasies about him.

But she had felt comfortable with him, and she had liked him. She'd told herself that made their feelings pure, for it wasn't clouded by anything base.

She hadn't felt that great weight of discomfort in his presence like she had done with Alexius. But tonight that discomfort had twisted into something else, and she despised it.

She despised herself.

She needed to untangle it, but she didn't want to.

And the truly terrible thing was that she was quite stuck with the man for a bit of time yet.

"It's nothing," she whispered.

And she whispered it again when she was shut up in her room, lying on the bed and scratching Algernon behind the ears.

Restlessness rolled through her. She got up off the bed and walked over to her little pet cages. Offering both Peregrine and the hedgehogs a treat. She felt a deep, enduring sadness. And she couldn't pinpoint quite why.

It was an ache that started around her heart and spread, affecting her breathing.

*You're lonely.*

She was. Lonely and a coward, and it was all kind of sad.

If she left here…if she left Alex…

The idea made her feel devastated and she didn't know why.

"But if I get married, I won't be lonely," she whispered into the room.

Except she knew that wasn't necessarily true. And the weight of that truth filled her with a sadness so profound she found it difficult to breathe past it.

# CHAPTER FIVE

ALEXIUS WAS IN his office the next day when she appeared unannounced.

The sight of her was like a physical punch straight to his gut.

She wasn't dressed up. She had no makeup on, her freckles in full view. She had on a pair of jeans, and a soft-looking T-shirt that molded itself to her full breasts. Her hair was in a state, and he found himself wishing he could sink his fingers deep into those tresses.

He gritted his teeth. He had very nearly made a mistake with her when they had danced in the ballroom.

He was not accustomed to this. To this feeling.

The sort of reckless, out-of-control sensation.

*Temptation.*

In his world there was no temptation.

He did not act in a way that might endanger Liri, and if he did want something, and it did not endanger the future of his country, then he set about getting it.

He was a man who conducted his business in matter-of-fact ways.

But Tinley lived in an astonishing gray area.

Having her would cause an endless stream of problems. An array of issues that would echo throughout his life. The first issue being that her father would likely come back from the dead and haunt him. The second being… He could not marry her. Neither did he want to. He had arrangements made. She had been his brother's fiancée, and the optics of taking her as a wife…

The entire country had perceived the match between Tinley and Dionysus as a love match. To take his dead brother's future wife, particularly when his own failures were mixed in to the cause of his brother's demise…

No matter what he thought about her ability to fulfill the role as Queen, it was something that simply could not be borne.

And there would be no touching her without a commitment.

*Except you could. She wants you. You could, and no one would know.*

No. Only his conscience. Only his honor.

Walking that line was why he remained.

And he would continue to walk it still.

Atonement for past sins that could never truly be forgiven.

"What is it you want?" he asked.

"I want to discuss the logistics of this ball."

"There is nothing to discuss. It will happen. A husband for you will be found."

"Who is doing the choosing?"

Frustration shot through him like an arrow.

"I feel it will be apparent who is right for you when you're both in the same room."

"Are you playing Cupid?"

"Nothing of the kind."

"Do I get to choose?"

"You get to choose," he said. "I'm certainly not frogmarching you down the aisle."

A thoughtful expression crossed her face. "And who

will be in attendance? Will there be anyone I can look at beforehand?"

"You make it sound as if you're buying a used car."

"Well, it seems only right that I be able to kick the tires of my future husband."

"Certainly," he said. And then he realized that he had not personally overseen any of the guest list. He had handed it off, as was his typical practice when he felt a deep aversion to something.

And he shouldn't.

*You don't want to share.*

"Well, tell me about them."

"Of course."

He pulled out a file for the event, and perused the guest list. He found he did know a few of them.

"Robert Martin," he said. "He's an American philanthropist. Very wealthy. You'll like him."

"How old is he?"

"Near my age, I believe."

"Does he have all his teeth?"

"I've never asked."

"Who else?"

"Marcus Weber. He's British. Descendent of some minor nobility or another. An innovator in green technologies."

"Well, I like the sound of both of them."

"So there. You will be quite happy."

"When am I expected to make a decision?" She asked. "Do I have until midnight on my birthday?"

"Tinley," he said. "It is not so easy."

"You're the one who came in issuing commands. I want a timeline. Don't you have…a way that you think this will work?"

"We will evaluate after the ball."

"You're very cavalier with my life."

"I'm not being cavalier. I can assure you that I never have been, not for one moment. You have me confused with someone else." He let the words settle between them.

"No," she said softly. "I would never confuse the two of you." She began to move away from his desk, and then she stopped. "You're a king. You're kind of…all-powerful. You don't know what it's like to have this much of your freedom tied up. I can leave, but I'll leave with nothing. You don't have any clue what that's like."

She had no idea. None at all. He'd had to live under the shadow of two deaths. He'd had to hold himself back when he'd wanted nothing more than to destroy the agreements made between their families.

She knew nothing about his life.

About the curse he lived under.

"I know all about not having freedom," he said, rage pouring through him. "Do you think that if left to my own devices I would've chosen to live as I did? Of course not. I was born a man like any other, but I must be a king instead. Do you not think I would've enjoyed womanizing and drinking as my brother did? Perhaps I would have. But I had to be strong. I had to be a symbol, not a human being, and I continue to act in that way. Do you think that I'm choosing my own wife now? For sentimental reasons? Or even for the reason of desire?" He stood, and rounded the desk, which he knew was a mistake, even as he did it.

He knew it was a mistake. A dark thrill worked its way through his body. For he did not make mistakes. But he made this one, and deliberately. Because the word *desire* arced between them like an electric current, and he could feel it, resonating down below his belt. Throbbing there.

He had sex. And plenty of it. With women who were

willing. With women who knew the score, absolutely and completely. All of his decisions about sex were made clearly and consciously. He did not act on impulse.

The first time he had realized he wanted to deviate from that had been when he had cornered Tinley in the corridor of the palace once, at barely eighteen. When that initial kick of desire he'd tried to push off as an aberration when he'd seen her in her swimsuit had turned into something darker, sharper.

Something he couldn't ignore.

She and his brother had caused some sort of spectacle at a state dinner, and he had felt compelled to scold them both. But her before Dionysus, and he hadn't immediately known why. But he had followed her, that trail of red hair and humor, down the hall from the dining room, and when she had turned and looked up at him, those eyes had been wide. And then she had licked her lips and he had felt it like a glide of her tongue against his manhood. And he had known then. What forbidden was. What desire was. And why those two things together created something delicious that he would never be able to explore.

His brother was a known womanizer, so even then, he doubted that Tinley was a virgin. Would it be so bad then for him to touch her?

He had entertained that, if only for a moment.

For virgin or not, she was his brother's. If he'd decided that he wanted her, and then desired to return her to Dionysus, he would be within his right to do so. He was the King. The future King. And no one could tell him he could not. His weight and rank far outstripped his brother. And there was nothing his brother had that he could not.

He knew the true temptation of an abuse of power then as well.

And none of it would have been half so dangerous if he hadn't seen a strange, innocent desire in her eyes too. The sort of desire he imagined she didn't quite understand.

But with the right touch, the right kiss, she would have.

And that was when he took a step back. Because he was pondering violating everything that he was supposed to be for the chance to touch a woman who was unsuitable. A woman who should not possess the ability to tempt him. And she tempted him now. Still. Four years later.

A glaring testament to the weakness that lived inside of him.

To the dark terror he truly suspected. That the world was random and he was the lion of nothing. Not chosen for any one particular thing. Just alive.

A man who had let his brother wander into the woods so he could have a taste of what his brother had. Who perhaps had wanted to ensure that he could never be challenged by this spare who had no true responsibilities. And who had a woman that made Alex's heart beat faster and his blood run hotter.

She reminded him of all those things, of all those potential shortcomings, even now. And it ate at him like acid in his gut.

But worse, the look on her face set a fire to his blood, made it flow hot and fast and low, pooling below his belt. Making him hard.

"I'm engaged," he said.

"You are?" The question came out a hoarse whisper.

"Perhaps not in the way you might think of it. But I'm in the process of drawing up an agreement with an Arabian socialite. Nadia is exactly what I want in a queen.

She is everything suitable to this position. The position of Queen. And that is why I have chosen her."

"I…"

"You must marry in your twenty-third year. I must marry by my thirty-fifth. And so, we are both in the middle of the deadline, you see."

"And you just chose someone. Just like that?"

"Yes."

"What about love?"

"What about it?"

"Did your parents love each other?"

"I don't know. I never asked."

"I didn't have to ask mine. They didn't. And it made the lives of everyone around them quite miserable."

"No one is around me."

The truth of his own words struck him then.

"What are you talking about? You have an entire household of people around you."

"It is not the same. We are separate. By station."

"And when you have children?"

He did not like to think of such things, nor of the future. Living here in this palace on the edge of a forest that had consumed so much. But it would be different. He would be different. "We will have nannies. Guards."

"And you won't do any parenting?"

"It won't be necessary. I am King, and I will protect."

She reached out, and her fingertips made contact with his suit jacket sleeve.

He shrugged her off. "Do not test me, Tinley."

"What would I be testing?" She took a step toward him, and the expression on her face reminded him so much of when he had caught her out in the corridor four years ago.

Hours before his brother's death.

"If you don't know," he growled. "Then you should truly think before you put a hand on me."

"Why have you always hated me? I know you never thought I was worthy of him."

"I don't hate you. It would be simpler to hate you. And as for worthiness? It is not as simple as that."

"What is it then?"

"You stand out. That is not in the job description for a princess."

"That will always be the issue, won't it? My standing out. I'm sorry that I was born objectionable. But your brother did not seem to find me objectionable at all."

Rage poured through him. At him, at her. At Dionysus. At everything. He hated it. For it was grandly out of control, because it made him like her. And he was different. He had to be different. For the weight of the crown rested on his shoulders.

And the minute he took his focus away from what mattered, everything could be so easily destroyed.

But his focus was off everything but her. Everything but those glimmering green eyes, and everything that seemed to shimmer beneath the surface of her skin. Everything he wondered about, but had taken steps not to.

She haunted him.

And he mourned his brother, but he saw him for who he was. She still defended him. Above Alex.

As everyone did.

"My brother found every woman who would warm his bed acceptable. And believe me when I tell you he had counted on a life where he could have you and whoever else he fancied. Do not think my brother was going to promise you fidelity. Do not think that you were some great love of his. It is a shame that you build your life as a monument to him when he would never have done the same for you."

"You don't know," she said, color rising in her face. "He was my friend."

"Friendship does not keep a spark alive in the marriage bed."

"And you speak with such great authority on marriage? On relationships? You're brokering a business deal for your own."

He scoffed. "What makes you think yours was any different? Business between our fathers. A reward for time spent serving in my father's court. Your mother might have found you unsuitable, but your father found you an easy pawn."

"He didn't," she said. "He loved me." Her voice faltered there.

"There is no question he did, Tinley, but he was a man. Flesh and blood mortal. And we all of us are subject to the weakness inherent in that state. And perhaps in part for all that he could gain from having a daughter. Most men would want a son, but not a man with the ear of the King. For his daughter could marry into our family."

"Even if that played a role in my relationship with my father," she said, her tone dripping with disdain as she took a step toward him. "It is no different than you. Your father had three sons. An heir and two spares. How lucky for him. Except your family is cursed. Strife between brothers or death. You're no less an accident of birth than I am."

"An accident of death spared you." He reached out and grabbed hold of her chin. Her skin was impossibly soft beneath his own, and it reminded him of yesterday's dance. Yesterday's failure. "For you would have wasted away here. Bored. Your bed empty while your husband went and amused himself elsewhere. You could have become a jaded courtier. Entertaining extra lovers as you saw fit while the staff raised your children."

He had let himself think, for years, she might have been happy with Dionysus. But he'd been lying to himself. Not Tinley. Tinley would never have sat back and been contented with that life, not forever.

He'd thought because of how she'd been during their engagement she might be.

But she'd been young. That was all.

And now…now less so.

"Why are you like this?" Her eyes glittered, not with anger, with unshed tears, and it was that show of emotion that saw him dropping his hand to his side and taking a step away.

"You have to believe it, don't you? You have to believe all those things about him. Otherwise you might feel truly guilty for the fact you didn't protect the remaining son your parents had that wasn't you. That wasn't anything more than an icon of the crown. Dionysus was a person. You're… You're not a man. You're a beast. At best. A rock at worst. Stone. Unfeeling and cruel. You have to believe Dionysus would have disappointed me because otherwise you don't know how you live with the guilt. It doesn't matter if he could have been responsible for his actions. You're the King. Even if you weren't on the throne then, you always had that power in you. You should have stopped him. You were his older brother and you didn't. You had the power to remove me from my home and bring me here. To demand that I marry. You had the power to stop him that night. To stop himself from making a fool of the family and wandering into his certain death. You certainly could've stopped him from having another woman at the party. But you didn't want to, because you didn't want me with him anyway. Is that the truth of it? That you liked him parading that other girl around on his arm? Because you knew it might get back to me?"

"I didn't think it would hurt you to know the truth."

Her words cut deep, because there was a truth to them. His brother had been more and more careless with his whoring. And there was a time when it had mattered little, because Tinley was young and he wasn't going to be in an intimate relationship with someone her age. But they were at the point where their marriage would have been coming soon, and the engagement had been officially announced. And that meant there was no excuse for him appearing in public with other women.

The fact was she wasn't wrong about any of it.

He had been angry with Dionysus and he had been happy to allow his brother to make a fool of himself so that he actually had a mess to clean up.

He had been happy to give himself a moment to indulge himself in what he wanted most of all.

Dionysus had female company for the evening, and it wasn't Tinley so why shouldn't Alex have…

And had it gone that way, he would feel no guilt. But the consequences for allowing him to go off on his drunken night had been permanent and irreversible. He was only grateful the woman who had been with Dionysus had not been an unintended casualty. She had been traumatized, certainly. But not harmed.

"If you consider it my job as King to conceal people from the truth, then you're correct," he said, his voice stone. "I was lax in my duties. I thought he was your friend. I thought you knew him. You certainly weren't my friend."

The truth of it resonated between them. They'd known each other years, and they were not friends.

They never would be.

"I wouldn't be surprised if you didn't have any friends."

"Kings don't have them."

"Your father did. So I suppose that's just a lie you tell yourself to feel better about living here. By yourself. With no one. At least, no one who likes you." She turned to leave and that same recklessness that was only ever present when Tinley was near fired through him. He reached out and grabbed her arm, stopped her from leaving. She turned around, her eyes wide, her lips parted softly. He could see her breath coming shorter, harder. Faster.

"You might not like me," he said, his voice like gravel. A stranger's voice. "But you feel something else, something more than hate, and I think you find it disturbing."

"What do you think I feel?"

He reached out and touched a lock of that unruly hair, and the fire inside of him nearly exploded. But outwardly, he kept himself still. She was frozen, like a startled doe caught in the headlights. The pulse of the base of her throat beat rapidly. He moved his hand, cupping her face, sliding his thumb along her cheekbone, then tracing the line of her lower lip.

She was so soft. Impossibly so.

The beach.

The ballroom.

The corridor.

It all burned between them now.

Those moments filled with anger and recrimination and resistance.

"You're not so naïve that you don't know what this means."

His words broke the spell, and she jerked away from him.

"Nothing," she said. "I find you disgusting."

"So disgusting that your heart is beating fast, and your pupils have dilated so that your eyes are nearly black."

"Fear," she said, her voice breathless.

"You don't fear me. You should. But you don't. Perhaps that's the problem, Tinley. You're a woman who wants a challenge. I'm the biggest challenge around. Perhaps what you really want is to test your strength against mine."

"There's no way I could fight you. You would destroy me."

"I don't mean a fight. Perhaps you wish to test your strength against mine. In a bed."

He could see the moment he had pushed her too far, and he realized he had been trying for just that. Because if she took one step toward him they were both lost. So he had no choice but to try and force her into taking a step away.

"Why would I want that?"

"I've heard that sex often holds more appeal when the object of desire is forbidden." And then she did something he did not expect. She turned and she ran. She left his office door wide open as she did, not even taking the time to close it behind her.

He had done it. He had pushed her away. And he supposed he should feel some triumph in that.

Instead he just felt the ache in his gut widened.

He had won nothing.

And for a man in his position, it was unacceptable.

But he had been unacceptable for a very long time. Without even a hint of satisfaction to make it bearable.

# CHAPTER SIX

SHE STOOD THERE on the edge of the wood.

The Dark Wood.

Her cottage was on the other side of it. And she knew there was no way she could ever pass through and make it out alive.

But as she stared into the dense green wildness, she wondered if this was what had driven Prince Lazarus forward when he'd been a boy. She wondered if even drunk, this is what Dionysus had felt the need to test himself against.

This deep, dark forest filled with secrets. Filled with danger.

It was a mystery.

She wondered, sometimes, why the royal family had not cleared the wood. Knocked it over.

But there was now, and had always been, such a strange relationship with the royal family and this enchanted place. They had won wars there, bolstered against their enemies by their knowledge of the forest. They had lost kings, sons, daughters to the dangers of the wood. Generationally. It was as if the source of their power came from it, as well as the source of their potential demise.

And what of her own demise? It seemed to be back there in the palace.

He'd said all those things to her, and they had cut her deeply. His words were sharp knives, and she had felt the cut of every single one of them. And then he had touched her. And his skin was so warm and enticing. A temptation, even as his words caused harm.

He'd spoken to her of dark things that she barely understood.

And she had felt no less like she was standing on the edge of a perilous wood in his office then she did now. In fact, the Dark Wood seemed safer.

For Alexius contained mysteries. She suspected there was a dark magic beneath his tailored suits. Shattered things brought to light resting in the palm of his hand. If he touched her, would he light up all those things that were still hidden from her?

When he touched her, she felt bright.

Even as anger simmered through her blood, there was something else that he had ignited over the surface of her skin.

*I've heard that sex often holds more appeal when the object of desire is forbidden.*

Her breath caught.

She wasn't running from him. She was running from herself. Perhaps that was what brought everyone to the edge of this wood. Fleeing yourself.

For that's what it had to be. You had to be more frightened of the monsters outside of it, than the monsters that might be within. Otherwise… You would never set foot in it.

"What are you doing?"

She whirled around to see a mountain of large, angry alpha male coming her way. His expression was thunderous, filled with rage.

"Nothing," she said.

"Get away from there." He closed the distance between them and grabbed hold of her, physically moving her a foot away from where she had been standing. "Don't be a fool."

"I'm not being a fool. Running away from you is the first sensible thing I've done in days."

"And so you would run into the wood? You would never come back out."

"You think you can survive the wood, but I can't?"

"You think Lazarus and Dionysus can perish there but not you?"

"I guess my arrogance matches yours."

"Do not be a fool," he said again, his words carrying a veil of threat over them.

"If I'm a fool it's because you chased me away. Perhaps you should reflect on that."

It was a lie. And she spoke those words with no conviction, and she knew that he heard it.

"I think," he said, his voice soft and deadly, "*cara mia*, that you were running away from yourself."

And that was when she found herself being hauled toward him, and when his lips crashed down on hers it was like the whole mountain had fallen over the top of her.

His mouth was hot and firm and certain as it moved over hers. And she... She was lost.

She had shared pleasant, nice kisses with Dionysus that had felt nothing like being wrapped up in fire.

But that's what this was. Licks of flame moving over her skin as he parted her lips and licked into her mouth.

She had never seen the attraction to kissing like this.

With all of yourself.

With the full weight of your body pressed against another person, and your lips parted, gaining them access to taste you. She had never understood why the scrape of someone's teeth against her lips might be erotic. But it was. Everything about this was. And she realized then that she should have just gone straight into the Dark Wood, for she had a better chance of emerging unscathed than she did from this kiss.

But he was uncompromising.

He did not allow her to rethink. Not because he was holding her with his strength, but because he immobilized her, in thrall because of his mastery of her body.

She was cocooned in his arms. He was so big and hard and he lifted her up from the ground with no effort at all. One large palm was pressed between her shoulder blades, the other low on her back. And he kissed her. Like a beast.

Like a wolf.

Set on devouring her.

She couldn't breathe. She was dizzy with it. With the slick glide of his tongue against hers and the heavy strength of his hands weighting her to the earth.

For if he wasn't holding her she was sure she would fly apart into a million pieces and be lost as a mist in the air. There was salvation in this devouring, and she could not explain it any more than she could understand it. But she could feel it.

Oh, she could feel it.

And then, as suddenly as he had caught her up, he set her back down onto the ground. The rejection was startling. Verging on terrifying. For somehow, the world had been tilted on its axis and she didn't know who she was when she wasn't in Alex's arms.

*Alex.*

Alex, who had always felt like a dark, forbidding figure in the corner of her world. But the lens had shifted now and he felt like the center of it. No less dark, no less forbidding. But more tempting than the wood itself.

"You," he said, his voice low. "You have tempted me for far too long. And it is unacceptable. I am not tempted. I do not deviate from the path."

He turned away from her then, and walked back toward the palace, leaving her standing there, shattered.

He had been tempted by her?

He had been tempted by her. Those words echoed inside of her like dark magic.

He had wanted her. All those years when he had been disapproving? She could remember when he had come after her one night, there had been a dinner party, and she and Dionysus had been laughing at the end of the table. She knew that Alex had disapproved of their behavior, found them disruptive. Treating them like naughty children rather than the young adults they'd been. She had been annoyed with him, as she always was. And her annoyance with Alex always felt large. It was never simple.

It always seemed to take up every available space inside of her, then expand.

There was something about Alex that always did that to her.

And she could remember him cornering her in a corridor, his dark eyes blazing with black fire.

*That is not the behavior of a princess.*

*And is this but the behavior of a future king?*

*You should show me more respect.*

*You should give it.*

*Earn it. Though I would prefer you did it as an occasional houseguest, and not as the future wife of my brother.*

*Do you not wish to be my brother-in-law, Alex? Is our relationship quite so damaged?*

She remembered how his irritation had flared up.

But something deeper. Something more.

And now she wondered.

She wondered now if the feeling inside of her whenever she had been alone with him had not been fear. Had not been irritation at his disapproval, but a desire to...

As he'd said. To test herself against him.

Because he wanted her.

And if he wanted her, in this state that he disapproved of so...

Didn't that make it powerful?

It was like the sun had risen on a personal darkness inside of her, and lit it all up.

She could not be controlled. Any more than her hair could be. She wasn't tamed.

And that was what her mother hated. It was what bothered Alex.

She was chaotic, it was true. And she could be messy. And most of all, she simply wasn't that which all the people around her seemed hell-bent on making her into.

And they couldn't force her to, not with the whole weight of their disapproval.

And Alex wanted her anyway.

He wanted to marry her off, he wanted to get rid of her.

He wanted to do his duty and not have to face this big, bright thing between them that was wrong in every single way.

Wrong.

Yes, it was wrong. That Alex had the power to ignite this thing in her blood that no other man had. Not even Dionysus, who she had been certain she loved.

Perhaps it was just age. Perhaps she was coming into herself a little later than some.

Maybe now any man would have the power to invoke this kind of response in her.

But she didn't think so.

Her body felt overly sensitive the entire day following the incident. And it was the eve of the ball, and a team of servants were sent to her room.

"You must be prepared," Charis said.

She was led to a place in the palace that she had never been before. Down a winding staircase, all the way down to the bottom of the palace, where she would have assumed that a dungeon might exist. But there was no dungeon here.

Instead, it was nothing but marble tiles, intricate mosaic inlaid into the floors. Jewels.

A spectacle unlike anything she had ever seen in Liri. The country tended to be more Spartan than this. Everything quite medieval, rather than ornate.

"What is this?" she asked one of the women.

"The baths. The royal family has a long tradition of preparing for either war or celebration in the private baths."

Tinley had never heard of such a thing. It seemed rather a luxury for the royal family, as she knew them. For with the exception of Dionysus, they had been austere, not given to indulgence.

"There are several rooms," Charis told her.

"How will I know what to do?"

"I can stay and guide you if you like."

The thought of being assisted with bathing made Tinley uncomfortable. "No."

"I thought not. The first is cold. It will bring the blood closer to the surface of your skin. You can move through it quickly. Then there is a tub that's very hot, you go into that next. And finally, you'll find the perfumed pool. It has been prepared with essential oils to perfume your skin. There will be sugar scrubs and other products to make your skin glow. It is how the Queen always prepared for parties."

"Really?"

"Yes."

"Why is this so secret?"

"I think rather it's…humanizing. And the royal family always does resist being seen as human."

A very insightful comment, Tinley thought. For it was true. They were a lineage wrapped in legends that had survived centuries, and they seemed to do nothing to try and dispel it. "How long have you worked for them?"

Charis frowned. "Ten years. I remember you. As a girl. Just like I remember Dionysus. And the Queen." There was something in the way she said *the Queen* that stuck out to Tinley and she couldn't quite place it.

"Did you like him? Dionysus. Only, sometimes I don't think his brother did."

"Alex loved his brother very much," the woman said. "I think he doesn't know how to show it."

"Oh. That being human again."

She laughed. "Yes. I think of all of them, he resists it most of all."

Tinley was bundled into a robe, her clothes taken from her, and then she was sent into a small room with glimmering, clear gemstones on the wall. They reflected in the water, made it look like ice. Which was appropriate, because when Tinley slipped her robe off and got into the water, she was certain that her skin would not survive. It was freezing. She moved through the pool quickly, getting out on the other side. Her robe was back where she had entered, but it was too late to do anything about that.

Her skin burned, and felt bright. Tingling from the

water. She couldn't tell if her blood felt closer to the surface of the skin, or if it had frozen right in her veins. She passed through to the next room, which had red gems inlaid, glittering on the walls like fire. And so, she didn't have to guess what she would feel like when she entered and exited this pool.

The scalding heat of the water was nearly unbearable, particularly after her ice bath, and Tinley was wondering if the royal family was human after all. She moved through that pool quickly as well.

After that, there came a long corridor. The rock laid into the wall was blue and jade, like swirling waves all around her. She walked on a narrow path, with water on either side of it, as if a river flowed underground here. It made shifting, moving reflections on the wall. There were pedestals on either side of her at the center of the corridor. In one bowl, there was a textured looking substance. She put her fingers in it, and found it was the sugar scrub Charis had spoken of.

There was a smaller bowl next to it, and she put a small measure of it inside. Then she smelled it.

It smelled… It was not floral, nor was it feminine. There was a rich, spicy scent to it, and she realized it reminded her of Alex.

Unbidden, she had an image of him walking through here, naked. Of him scrubbing this onto his skin, for he must.

In the bowl on the other side was a cream, and she took a small measure of that as well.

Then she continued on her way, walking naked through the hall.

She didn't know what she expected of the grand pool she'd been instructed was waiting for her, but it was… Something else entirely. It was not a large rectangle, no, rather it was a winding, organic looking body of water that extended around the corner she could not see. The entrance had a slow slope into deeper water, like the ocean, but here, the sand was made from marble, precious stones and gold.

It illuminated the water from beneath, and overhead, the glittering stones cast fractured light all around.

It was like being in a sparkling cave of gems, in a river of light. She stepped into the water slowly and sighed when she found the temperature perfect. She set her bowls down on the edge of the winding pool, and slid beneath the surface. She allowed the silence to envelop her. The solitude. These last days had been... She could not recognize her life. Or rather, she could, but it was a strange, twisted mirror, showing her the past while driving her on toward a future she could not envision.

Was she really going to marry a stranger? Was she truly going to meet that man tomorrow, choose him, and...have Alex arrange it?

*Alex.*

The mention of his name made her skin burn hot and bright and it had nothing to do with the water.

She came up for air, no longer feeling cocooned by the water.

She swam over to the edge of the pool and put a bit of the sugar scrub on her fingertips, working it over her body, grimacing at the roughness.

But part of her welcomed it. For it felt a bit like a punishment, and she was angry with her skin.

Her breasts.

That treacherous place between her thighs that she had never given much thought to until *him*.

Her heart, which was filled with fear and trepidation.

Which lacked the courage to run away, but also the courage to embrace where she was with any full passion.

The heart stuck in limbo.

And had it not been for years now?

She had been certain of a path, and then it had vanished, and she had tried to find something new.

And instead hadn't she just sunk into some kind of strange rebellion at her mother.

Choosing to live in a tiny cottage and take a job where she worked from home so she never had to concern herself with her image?

An image that felt so short of what she knew her mother wanted it to be.

So it was so much easier to pretend she didn't care.

And in many ways she didn't.

But part of her yearned for an acceptance she would never have.

And even now it made her chest ache.

*But Alex wants you.*

Even thinking it made her nipples go tight, even as she scrubbed that punishing mixture over her skin.

She finished quickly, touching herself only creating more problems. Then she submerged herself in the water again, rinsing it all away.

She swam forward, the warm water a pleasant glide now over her skin as she went. As she tried to school her mind into something blank.

The pool wound on, and she could sense the many feet of the palace above her, all stone and stark and intimidating. And now she would never not know that this was here underneath.

This enchanted river that was something so different than the enchanted wood that stood all around.

For this place did not offer certain death. But a strange

kind of pleasure that seemed absent from everywhere else on these grounds.

She came around another bend, and stopped.

For there he was.

She knew it was him. It took only a glance for her body to react in the most violent fashion. Her stomach seizing tight, her heart slamming against her breastbone. He was facing away from her, and he lifted his arms, running his fingers over his hair, water sluicing down his back. His every muscle moved and flexed as he did so. And she was enthralled.

His shoulders and back were so broad, his waist narrow. He was like a god.

Or a wolf.

The moment she had thought it might all be safe.

She had forgotten.

That the deadliest predator was in the palace walls, not beyond them.

She could slip away. She could. She should. But she was frozen.

Just as she had been on the edge of the Dark Wood.

So close to danger and unwilling to turn away from it.

*Your heart lacks courage.*

Her heart lacked courage and it was why she lived in a tiny cottage. Her heart lacked courage and it was why she was here. Moving toward a future that she wasn't sure she wanted.

It was why she had never gone to see her mother, not since college, and asked her why she never seemed to think she was enough. Not as a princess, not as a student, not as the head of a charity.

Why her hair was so wrong, and why her laugh was so loud, and why everything she seemed to do held them at further and further distance.

She was suddenly so very tired of herself.

And whatever happened at the ball tomorrow night, it needed to happen because there was conviction in her heart, and not simply fear of what might happen if she didn't do as Alex bid her.

And she…

She wanted something. She wanted something she didn't have a name for. She wanted more of what he'd made her feel yesterday. Desired. For what she was. As she was before any makeovers or scrubs or whatever else was going to become of her before tomorrow night. All the comportment was certainly leading up to a fair amount of oil masks and waxed body parts and scrubbings and makeup.

And here she was, in this grand bath washed clean of anything. She had on no clothes, nothing that signified her as the former future Princess, the woman who had arrived at the palace in leggings. And he had on no suit. Nothing that made him King.

Except all the *everything* about him.

She was a virgin.

What had surprised her most about going to college was the fact that it wasn't all that rare. Even a lot of the boys she knew hadn't actually been with anyone yet. Though, by the end of the four years there, almost everyone had dealt with it. She was in the minority, but not alone, and none of her friends had ever mocked her for it. They had all known about Dionysus. And while they could certainly all relate to feeling awkward, or not finding the right person, the grief of losing someone they were in love with was unique to her, and as a result, no one had ever pressed her. But she knew plenty about sex.

She had one roommate in particular who had been quite active and comfortable with her sex drive, and she brought a fair amount of men back to the dorm. Her other roommate had been a bit more reserved, but by the end of school even she'd had a boyfriend who'd spent the majority of his nights there.

She also talked with enough of her friends about first times to know that while every experience was different there were certain things to expect.

And nerves was one of them. But they all survived it.

And maybe this was simply... This was right.

Maybe this was what the royal family owed her.

Because she had been bound up in them for so many years, and maybe... Maybe she would decide to marry no one. Maybe she would decide to walk away with nothing and no money.

And maybe that would mean never returning to this place, never being here where she had felt so accepted. Her father had been happy here, and that had spilled over to her. Dionysus had been kind. The King had treated her like another child.

But Alex, the man who had made her feel like she might not be enough, wanted her. And maybe that was the ending she needed. Maybe this was the courage her heart needed.

To be big and fierce and bold.

She wanted to be.

She played at it in her own little world. Rescuing animals and heading up a charity that spoke to something in her heart, and made everything she did feel natural. Doing the things that mattered to her without having to put herself out there. But she could certainly exploit her position as Dionysus's former fiancée. As the once-and-no-longer-future Princess of Liri.

Maybe she didn't need her family's money. Maybe she simply had to be bold enough to put herself forward.

Yes, she had rebelliously dug into her image, but she had still kept it to herself.

And perhaps the key to that lay on the other side of this mystery. On the other side of this man.

Dionysus had been a dynamic, and obvious, influence on her life. But Alex had always been there.

Alexius. Tall and broad and imposing and creating wide, sweeping feelings inside of her.

She had felt uncomfortable around him. Always. And when his lips had met hers yesterday she had to wonder exactly why.

If perhaps she didn't truly understand the real reason she felt uncomfortable around him.

If it had never actually been fear.

No. It was fear. And the fear heightened inside of her as she stepped toward him.

It was fear. But it was something else as well.

She had never felt afraid of Dionysus.

But she had never felt this mounting, terrible excitement either.

Alex had given her a deep, trembling excitement over the years that had frightened her unto her core.

She could remember being on the beach with him in Italy. Him being angry at her for her swimsuit...

It all came back in a rush. What the undercurrent of that anger was.

And she'd touched him...

This was like standing on the edge of a cliff and trying to bring herself to jump off of it. Having to trust that somehow the bottom didn't hold doom, but escape.

He turned suddenly. His dark eyes connected with hers, and she felt her nipples go tight. For she was exposed above the hips, hiding nothing from his sharp gaze.

And he was...

It was only a fleeting moment that she felt embarrassed over her own body, because then she was consumed with the look of his.

He was…

She had often thought of him as a mountain, and she was correct. His chest was broad and heavily muscled, covered with dark chest hair.

He was a man.

That word emblazoned itself on her mind, her soul.

He was not a boy. Not a young man her age. A man with strength and depth and vast experience. And he would not give quarter if she took a step toward him and then decided she was too frightened.

She knew. In that moment. She had to make a choice now, and there would be no reversing it. And so, with her heart pounding sickeningly in her ears, she took a single step toward Alexius. She took a single step toward courage.

# CHAPTER SEVEN

SHE WAS A WITCH. There was no other explanation for it. He had been here in the baths, doing his best to scrub her from his skin, doing his best to scrub this unwanted desire from all that he was, and she had appeared. A siren in the water. Naked and glistening and far beyond the beauty he had ever allowed himself to imagine she might possess.

Her breasts were full and plump, rosy tipped and delicious.

Her waist nipped in gently, then sloped outward, rounding into luxurious hips that would be perfect for a man to hold on to. She was the embodiment of his temptation. Of his weakness. And when she took a step toward him, he knew that his fate was sealed.

He had spent much of his life denying a belief in fate.

For the legends about his family and fate were dark indeed, and they suggested that there was no hand stronger or mightier than that of an invisible, immovable force that might decide to rearrange the whole kingdom on a whim.

To kill young princes and leave but one remaining.

In his position, a belief in fate had always felt somewhat grim.

That he was chosen for some reason beyond anything

he had done or could do. But his brothers had been cho-sen for death.

That belief did not make him stronger or better. That belief meant that trying was truly a pointless exercise. And so he had rejected it. But Tinley. Tinley had gotten under his skin for all these long years, and he had con-vinced himself that there was nothing in this world that was inevitable.

Here she was, a slick, bare inevitability that seemed to make a mockery of the idea that he could outrun any-thing. Her red hair hung damp and curling down her back, a couple of stray locks falling into her face. And as she walked toward him, the water moved around her, concealing the most womanly part of her from his view. It changed nothing.

It changed nothing and everything.

It simply was.

And down here, in this ancient, traditional place, cer-emonial in many ways, and important to the royal fam-ily, it felt sacred.

A confirmation.

One he might have tried to outrun, but he…decided not to.

And so he stood firm and fast as his doom closed the distance between them.

He looked down, saw that her nipples were hard. That her breathing had gone shallow.

"You're right," she said. "I'm not afraid of you." She reached out, delicate fingertips touching the side of his face. They drifted downward slowly, making contact with his broad chest.

Like on the beach. But this time she did not touch him in anger. And this time she didn't stop there. Her hand went down farther. He breathed hard, his stomach pitching as her fingertips ended where the water began. Just above where he was hard and aching for her.

"I didn't understand," she whispered. "But I want to."

"Do you know what you're doing?"

Those green eyes, always filled with challenge, with rebellion, sparked. "Of course I do. I'm not a child. I know what it means to walk into a room with a naked man. To touch him. I know what I'm asking you for."

"But do you know how it will change things?"

For it would. It would change the entire way he had arranged the world.

It would have to.

Damn it all. *Burn* it all.

Tinley Markham was his. Everything else could go straight to hell.

He'd made this choice once before and as he looked at her…he had the sense he would make it again and again until the end of days.

So why not make her a duty, rather than a sin in waiting?

Why not embrace it, and her.

Her body. Her lips. He would sink inside of her and claim her. And he did not care if his brother had had her first. He didn't care how many men had had her since. She was his and had been from the beginning. Fate.

Destiny.

He alone survived. He alone remained. How could this destiny be denied? How?

It could not be.

He was the Lion of the Dark Wood, and he would devour that which wandered into his path.

He would devour her.

"Yes," she said, her voice thin and breathless.

"And you accept that? All for this? All because your

body craves mine?" He studied her closely, the crimson stain in her flushed cheeks. "Do you even like me?"

She shook her head. "No. I don't. But yesterday you made me feel more beautiful than I ever have in my life. I don't *like* you. That's an insipid word. I feel…tormented. My body is not my own. My skin is not mine. It blushes at the memory of you, and becomes sensitive at the thought. Every time my heart beats it's sore. Because it wants to be with the excitement of the touch of your hands. My lips feel swollen, changed. How can I go on if it isn't completed? If this is unfinished?"

There would be no *finish* to this. Not one that either of them would like, not one he was even certain he could live with.

But there was nothing to be done.

There was no turning back.

"You're walking into the wood, little girl? Tell me you understand that."

There was half a breath, a heartbeat, where he thought she might turn away. But then she nodded. "I have to know. I have to know what's on the other side."

It was decided.

He reached out and hooked his arm around her waist, bringing her slick, naked body up against his. Her lush breasts pressed against his chest, and he could swear he almost felt the rapid beat of her heart against his own. He knew that she would be able to feel the hard, insistent length of his arousal pressed against her body.

He was so hard he could scarcely breathe.

He rocked his hips forward, making sure she knew.

And he could tell, by the widening of those eyes, that she felt it.

"I am not an easy man," he ground out. "In this or anything."

"I know."

"You're soft, Tinley. And you have been swaddled and cosseted and protected for all of your life. But I will not do that. No harm will come to you." He slid his thumb over her cheekbone. "But this will not be gentle."

"I don't need gentle." Tears filled her eyes, but he knew they weren't tears of fear. They were defiant. They were angry. "I just need real." She tilted her chin upward. "Tell me that you want me. Tell me that I'm beautiful. Even like this."

"Is that what you need to know? Is it?" He moved his fingers over the freckles on her cheeks, then pushed his fingers through her wet hair. "This. All of this, it tempts me. When you were a girl of eighteen all I wanted was to press you up against the wall and claim you as mine." She was the source of his greatest sin, that girl. And yet she doubted him. But she could never know that. She could never know the truth. "Even when I was angry. Even when I was telling you how unsuitable you were. What I wanted was to sink myself into you and make you mine. You were unsuitable for him. You were supposed to be *mine*."

The words, the ferocity behind them, shocked even himself.

"But not suitable enough to be Queen," she said breathlessly.

"Not suitable for any damn thing. I am a king. And I must keep my head. I am a king, and I must have supreme control over myself and all that I do. And you test that. I am at my end. If you had not been his then…" But it was a lie. He very nearly had. And all that had protected Tinley was his brother's death. "It didn't matter. In the end it didn't matter, did it?"

"You sent me away."

He remembered when she'd come to his office—formerly his father's—after the funeral.

*What will I do now?*

*Anything you wish.*

*School?*

*If you desire. There is no more need for you to be here. Of course the palace will care for you, but this is no longer your home.*

Guilt and the desire to be rid of her had spurred him on.

"You were happy enough to go."

"I was," she said. "But the speed at which it happened... I had to make a lot of choices and it was overwhelming."

"I was not going to debase myself, or the position of Queen, with my brother's leftovers." Lies on his tongue, bitter. "I was not going to be slave to these feelings."

"And here we are."

So simply she spoke of his failure. So simply she laid out the inevitable.

"I want you," he said. "You must understand, it is not easy."

"I know. It isn't easy for me either."

He didn't have to explain this dark, tortured thing that aided him. Of course he didn't. Because it was like that for her too. There was nothing sweet or simple about it. Nothing misty or magical. This was not fated mates. It was deeper than that. A fated, tortured attraction that existed to make a mockery of all that he was. To make a mockery of whatever power he thought he might possess.

Their desire was the wolf pack. Come to devour them both.

And he surrendered.

He lowered his head and kissed her, harder, darker

than yesterday. He plunged his tongue deep into her mouth, wanting to consume her. As she consumed him. Would that it were so simple as want. Would that it were so simple as sex.

Sex was easy. He'd had sex.

This was something else.

This was shame and need and torture all wrapped in a soft, delectable package that he could not turn away from.

He moved his hands to her breasts, cupped them, teased her nipples. For why hold back? Why make slow what had been on the verge of boiling over for all these years?

She gasped, and he took advantage of that. He ate deeper into her mouth, before abandoning her lips and blazing a trail down her vulnerable throat. To her collarbone. He kissed one rounded curve of her breast before taking her nipple deep into his mouth and sucking.

She whimpered, spearing her fingers through his hair and holding him there. As if he would abandon her. As if he would abandon her now that she was finally his.

The only sound in the echoing chamber was their breathing, the gentle sound of the water lapping against their skin. He moved his hands down her body, to her hips, and then, between her thighs where he found her wet and slick and perfect, just waiting for his touch.

His own body pulsed with need. He had never known anything like this. It consumed him.

It was a temptation that surpassed anything he had thought was possible. And the fulfillment of it was beyond anything he had imagined.

Centuries of duty could crumble all around him, he didn't care.

He didn't care.

He moved his hands to her thighs, lifted her up and

urged her legs around him, carrying them both up out of the pool.

He walked them both round the bend, to the end of the winding pool. There were low cushions, a cabana of sorts with plush pillows and fabric draped around.

Privacy that was unnecessary, here in this place shared by no one other than royalty.

And as he lowered her down onto the cushions, he asked himself… He asked himself if perhaps he had known that she would be here.

For of course he had given permission for her to use this place to ready herself for the ball.

He had not known when…

But it would stand to reason that she would have been down here. And perhaps he had known.

Perhaps he had always known that in this place, for royalty alone, he would send her to meet her fate.

For if he must be damned by it, then perhaps she should be too.

He stood, looking down at her, her skin pale against the dark red of the cushions. The thatch of curls between her legs aroused him beyond the point of reason.

All of the blood in his body had flowed into the source of his desire, and he felt that he would die for not having her. Which was exactly why he was going to make himself wait longer.

Years.

There were spare few things in this world that he had ever wanted and not been able to have.

He wanted his brothers back, and he could not reach beyond the veil of death to make it so.

And he had wanted Tinley Markham.

Beneath him, astride him, in front of him. However he could have her.

From the moment she had become a woman.

He had wanted her in spite of the fact that she had worn his brother's ring, in spite of the fact that their fathers had decided she would be most suited to marry Dionysus, and not Alex, because God knew the men could've made that determination. It was what Tinley's mother had wanted.

She was correct, in that, the cold hard facts were neither man thought she should be Queen. For had they, she would have been put in the position to be Queen.

And still, he wanted her.

But he was savoring the moment. Savoring the moment where control failed and desire ruled. For this time…this time nothing would stop him. Not when she wanted him as he did her.

Only her.

He knelt down before her, a king on his knees, and brought her body to the edge of the raised cushion, pressing a kiss to her ankle, to her calf, the inner part of her knee. To her side, where she shook beneath his lips.

"Alexius?" She said his name like a prayer, like a question.

Supplication on her lips.

"You know what I intend to do," he said, his voice a growl. "I intend to devour you."

He knew then, that when she had been standing on the edge of the wood, she had been weighing these things. Whether to run into the forest and be devoured by what awaited there, or stay here and be eaten by him.

He was very glad she had chosen the latter.

"I bet you taste sweet," he said. "I have wondered. These long years, I have wondered, what it would be like to feast on you. What it would be like to hear you call out my name, and I intend to. You know how long it has been since anyone has called me Alex? Until you. I would hear that name on your lips as I pleasure you."

He moved higher, his breath on the heart of her now, her sweet scent inflaming him.

Then he lowered his head and slid his tongue over her swollen flesh. Her hips bucked up from the cushion as she whimpered. And he pinned her there, consuming her like a man starving.

For he was.

Starving for her. For all that she was.

He consumed her like he would die if he did not, because he thought he might. Gorged himself on her. On her beauty. On her essence.

He pushed two fingers deep inside of her and found her tighter than anticipated. So he teased her, toyed with her until he began to feel her internal muscles quiver around him. Until he could feel her orgasm building.

Then he sucked that bundle of nerves at the apex of her thighs, and he felt her break. She twisted and writhed beneath him, her release a relief to them both. For he had little control left, and none he could exercise anymore.

He moved up her body and kissed her, deep and long, and then, finally, he thrust inside of her body.

## CHAPTER EIGHT

TINLEY WAS STILL trying to recover from the earth-shattering pleasure that Alex had given her, when he breached her.

It *hurt*.

It nearly took her breath away, as powerful as the pleasure that had come before it.

He was so big. When she had seen his body, she had been terrified for a moment, but then he had begun doing all those wicked, pleasurable things to her and it had been difficult to think. No, not difficult, impossible.

And everything he had done to her felt so lovely, his tongue slick and perfect, his fingers knowing and deft, and he had penetrated her that way, and she had thought perhaps it would take some of the difficulty away from their actual joining.

It did not.

Panic rose in her breast.

*Courage.*

It was a strange thing, to call out for courage for something she was the one who had initiated. Something she had chosen to do.

But it was frightening. And it was all a bit too much. And he was…

He was so large and hard and everything. And having

him inside of her was beyond anything she could have imagined. For she had known that it might be intense, but she hadn't really known.

It was as if he was inside of her, not just in a physical sense. But in all the ways he could be. As if he inhabited her soul.

It was terrifying. And so was he.

His expression was intense, his big body frozen atop her.

"Tinley?"

"I… I didn't know."

*"How?"*

Confusion swarmed her. "I… How could I?"

He looked tortured then, his dark brows locked together, his teeth clenched.

"Are you all right?"

"No," she said.

"We'll stop."

"No," she said.

*Courage.*

"I want this."

Because she had to do this. She had to. He was the lion. The wolf pack.

The dragon.

And she was not a virgin sacrifice. She was a knight, needing to slay him.

Needing to slay this.

So that she could become… Whatever it was she needed to be.

But if she backed away now, then it would still be unfinished. If she backed away now then she would never know.

And she had to know.

She had to.

He pushed deeper inside of her, and she hadn't known it was possible. But finally, some of the pain began to recede, and it gave way to pleasure.

Or, if not pleasure, then something infinitely better than what had come before.

This was different, though, from the easy pleasure she had found from his mouth.

This was something more. It went deep inside of her, and seemed to weave itself in the fabric of her soul.

Created in her a symphony of desire that wrapped itself around her every cell, her every vein, every fiber of what she was.

Until she became part of him.

And he became part of her.

There was a depth to it she could not fathom.

An intensity she could not pin down.

And somehow she knew, this wasn't about sex. This was about the two of them.

About the things that had existed between them for all time.

About fate.

And when he began to move, all the glimmering strands of pleasure that had woven themselves through her began to sparkle. Shimmer.

They warmed her and filled her, changed her. Consumed her. Until she was a creature made entirely of need.

Alex's creature.

But when she saw his face, when she saw the cords in his neck standing out, when she saw the intensity in every line of his big, muscled body, she realized that he was her creature all the same.

That they were one with this, and with each other.

This man who was so different than she.

Who was duty and honor and perfection.

They were the same.

In this, they were equal.

In this, they were remade.

His thrusts were deep, consuming, and she wrapped her legs around him, urging him deeper now, for the pain was gone, and all that remained was wonder.

She didn't think she could possibly be stretched any tighter, didn't think she could possibly scale to higher heights, but she did.

She did.

And each movement of his body within hers did it.

Each rush of his hands over her curves, his lips on her neck, on her mouth.

And then, he lost the rhythm entirely. Splintering into something golden and bright and sweeping her up and all of the fractured edges. And when they broke for the last time, it was together, harsh cries escaping them both at once as he pulsed inside of her and she gripped him tight, wringing every last bit of pleasure from each other as they found their ultimate release.

And then she lay there, knowing that she had been utterly changed.

Knowing that she had lied to herself when she had said she was simply on a quest for courage and closure and an end.

For she had begun something here in this place, and had seen herself utterly changed as a result.

And she did not know how she would find a way back from it.

*You won't. You'll have to find a new way.*

Everything made sense then.

For that was the truth of it.

She had been trying for all of these years to make sense of an old path that no longer went anywhere.

To go over old wounds, over and over again without actually finding a way to heal them.

To sink into a life that she cared about—undoubtedly—but in such a way that she held herself back for the simple reason of wanting to show her mother she was wrong about her. That she was wrong about her needing to change in any way at all.

There were things she needed to change.

And it might not be about hair or any of the shallow things her mother had fixated on, but there was truth buried beneath the criticism, and being angry about it wouldn't do anything to change that. And rebelling against it for the sake of it wouldn't fix anything either.

He moved away from her, his expression grim.

"Why didn't you tell me?"

"Tell you what?"

"You hadn't had a lover."

"I thought… I didn't think it would be terribly surprising."

"My brother slept with… Anything and everything. The fact that he did not sleep with you is unfathomable to me."

"All you would've had to do was ask. I wasn't ashamed of it. I assumed… I assumed for a long time that he didn't out of respect for my father. Because he was… I don't know. It was some kind of virgin bride thing, I figured. Now I just think maybe we didn't have chemistry." She felt humiliated and small. And it wasn't about the fact that she hadn't had sex with Dionysus. That didn't embarrass her.

It was that she didn't recognize all she hadn't known.

She felt ignorant, and ridiculous, and she hated that most of all.

"It would never have occurred to me he would not have had you the minute it was justifiable."

"Well, he didn't," she said. "You don't have to rub it in."

"Does it bother you greatly?"

"No. I said it didn't. I mean it. I've never been… wounded about that."

He frowned. "You loved him, and you were never sorry that you missed a chance to be his lover?"

"I was young," she said, her face hot. "I didn't know. I don't want to talk about this with you minutes after losing my virginity to you, thank you."

"You should have told me. I would've been more gentle with you."

"All the more reason to not tell you. I didn't need you to be gentle with me. I just needed this to be done."

"Oh, is that all you needed? Was I an itch you needed to scratch?"

She didn't like the sound of that. And she could tell by the disdain in his tone that he did neither. But he wasn't being nice to her, and she found that she perversely wanted to exercise the power that she seemed to have to upset him. Because she felt vulnerable. And she didn't like it.

"I guess so. A question I needed answered. Something owed to me by the royal family, after all. I haven't had a lover. It seemed time that I did. I didn't really want to be trotted out to a roomful of men that I might be married off to not knowing exactly what I was agreeing to. I had never even seen a naked man until you. So, now I know more or less what to expect."

He chuckled. The sound dark. "No. Trust me, *cara*, you don't."

She narrowed her eyes. "Oh. Are you one of those men quite confident in your singularity?"

He lifted his dark brow, and as she was fully able to gaze upon his singularity in the moment, and as he stood there naked, unabashed and unashamed, she was certain that most men did not match him for size. They couldn't possibly.

He was far too…much to be anything beyond above average.

"Now I know," she said. "I thank you for that."

Her clothes weren't here, so she gathered up her dignity as best she could, and walked away, knowing that he could see all of her bare skin as she tried to keep her head high and walked next to the winding pool, back toward where she had abandoned her clothes. It meant going through that hot water again, and back through the ice.

And by the time she was in her room, she was shivering and miserable, and felt nothing like the luxuriously appointed Royal she was sure she had been meant to feel like by the end of an afternoon spent in that spot.

No. She felt ruined. Unmade, without being remade all the way.

She felt…

Broken.

With a spirit of rebellion, she put her leggings and sweatshirt on, refused to put any product in her hair, knowing it would dry frizzy.

With Algie safely in his carrier, she took Nancy and Alton out of their cage, and placed them on the bed, letting them both trundle around while she tried to find enjoyment in their cuteness. She had been effortlessly charmed by them before.

She was not charmed now.

Peregrine chattered from his cage in clear indignation. *Join the club.*

"I can't please everyone," she threw a hand out wide.

"You don't get along." She frowned deeply at the ferret and added, "And it's not my fault you're mean."

She would've liked to shout that at Alex.

"It's not my fault you're mean," she repeated again. "And completely unreasonable. And… And… And *why did it have to be you*? Why did it have to be you that I wanted so much? Why couldn't it have been anyone or anything else? And why didn't you warn me that it would…"

Her stomach hollowed out suddenly and she lost all her anger, overtaken completely by abject misery.

She slowly unfolded herself onto the mattress, pressing her face firmly against the bedspread. One of the hedgehogs crawled up onto her back, and over the other side.

It summed up her feeling perfectly.

She had thought she would come out the other side of this feeling empowered, courageous.

Like a woman.

Instead, she rather felt like a hedgehog doormat.

It was not empowering in the least. It wasn't anything except for sad and tomorrow… Tomorrow she was supposed to go into a ball and be presented to all these men. And decide who she was going to marry.

A flame lit itself in her breast. And that was when she knew.

That she had needed to do this. She had. Because she might have balked if she'd not had this experience. She might not have been able to be brave enough.

For tomorrow, when she was introduced, she was going to make the announcement that she was not going to marry anyone. She was going to find a way to make a life on her own terms.

And the one thing she had done for herself…

She had made it impossible to stay here. Impossible to stay connected to Alex.

He was engaged to another woman. However unofficially as far as a love match went.

She would never be able to face his wife. Not after she had seen him naked. Not after he had been inside of her.

And there was no question of her marrying another man. None at all.

She had sealed her own fate, and even though much of what she had done had been foolish she could not regret that. At least, in the story of her life, she had been the author of this particularly inglorious moment.

She would not pawn the credit off to fate.

She would take it all.

And she would take it with pride, even if she couldn't take it with happiness.

And she would have to hope that someday she could.

Even if it would be someday very far away from here.

Even if it would be a someday without Alex.

# CHAPTER NINE

HE HAD HANDLED the aftermath of their encounter badly.

But his thoughts had still been swirling with the truth of it all. That Tinley had been a virgin. That she was his, and only his. That she had not been with his brother.

He did not know why he should care, except that he felt no man particularly wanted to have a woman after his brother had had her. For a variety of reasons. And he was no different.

And there was something… Something extraordinary about it. His.

Except, he had wounded her gravely, and now the time of the ball was drawing near and he had not had a chance to speak with her. But perhaps it was better for that. Perhaps, the time for conversation was over. They didn't do well when they conversed with each other, but they did quite well when their bodies met.

Being inside of Tinley was unlike anything he had ever experienced before.

It had been a baptism. A revelation.

It had been…

It had been wrong. But it had also been something to chart a course by. It had made decisions out of problems, and for that, he was grateful. For that, there was nothing to be but grateful.

He was certain that his decision would cause irritation, after all, his PA had certainly made it clear to some of the men that the reason for coming to this event was to look for a prospective wife, one who had the full support of the crown of Liri, but... No one would express their displeasure, for Alexius was the King. And in the end, that was all that mattered.

The King would do what he willed.

And there would be whispers. For there always were.

He was done trying to silence whispers.

He was done denying that which he desired.

He came around the corner, toward the ballroom, just as Tinley came around the curve of the sweeping staircase that led to the antechamber.

His heart stopped in his chest. And then raced forward, as if it was on the verge of exploding.

Her red hair was loose, save for two small strands which had been woven back, and twined together. It was full and curling, and devastating. Her body was wrapped in a gold gown, which made her curves look gilded.

She had barely any makeup on her face, gloss on her lips and something shiny on her cheeks, but her freckles were still clearly visible. She looked like a nymph, a fairy. Something that had come straight from the Dark Wood.

An enchantment.

Or a curse.

She tilted her chin upward, her expression proud.

"You look beautiful."

She stopped. "I do?"

"You know you do. You're a triumph."

He took her arm, and he could feel her resist his hold.

"We will go in together."

"All right."

There was a determination about her, that light in her

green eyes that he knew well, and he had the feeling that she had a plan of her own.

Whatever it was, it didn't matter to him. For his course was set. And he was the King. And so his course was the course for Liri.

They walked into the ballroom, which was already filled with guests. It was customary for the King to arrive late, as a formal presentation of his royal personage.

But he had a feeling that what Tinley did not understand was that she was being formally presented as well. And not as a mere ward of the crown.

When the double doors opened and they walked into the room, everything stopped. He looked out over the crowd of people. "Good evening. On behalf of the royal family of Liri, I welcome you." It was a customary greeting, but one that was grim these days, considering he was the last remaining Royal.

"Tonight is very special indeed, as I am presenting to you my future Queen. Ms. Tinley Markham of Liri."

Tinley could hardly believe what she had just heard. The future Queen? There was no way. She had been about to tell him that she was going to marry no one.

That she would be presented to no one. That she would go off on her own and start afresh. And he was engaged to someone else. She turned her head sharply, and met fierce, dark eyes that invited no argument at all.

And she had no idea what she was supposed to do. What she could do. For he was the King, and she could hardly defy him openly in his own ballroom. And soon, they had been swept away from the staircase that acted as a stage, and he drew her out to the center of the room. To the dance floor. He looked at her, his gaze uncompromising. And it reminded her of that moment in the baths.

They had not seen each other in the hours since, much less touched, and now she was in his arms. And any ferocity or resolution was quashed by the fact that being in his arms stole her ability to think.

*Have courage.*

That voice echoed inside of her, and she had no idea where it came from, or how it applied now. What courage was there to have? She was in the arms of a king, held prisoner in a room full of hundreds of people, all who glittered. It was a spectacular, gilded show of imprisonment.

And it wasn't fear of reprisal that stopped her. For part of her sensed that it would be easy to speak up now and burn it all down.

To shout that she had no intention whatsoever of becoming the wife of Alexius. That she was not going to be Queen.

Oh, the idea of being *Queen.*

Of being paraded around in front of people at all times. Influence.

The power to make change.

A queen had that. She also would have the eyes of the world on her.

Yes, it would be easy to run away. It would be easy to defy him, as she did it at every turn. She knew Alex well enough to know that it wasn't exactly like he was going to shift her off to the dark forest and have her executed by a wolf.

No, he wouldn't do that.

The much more terrifying thing was seeing where this might go.

As she had done in the baths.

For she couldn't run then. She could have told him that she didn't want him. That it was a lie. That whatever he thought was happening between the two of them, it wasn't.

That she was naked by circumstance, and not because she had chosen to come down there and seduce him.

And she hadn't.

But she had taken a step toward him because that step put her on the path to a different life.

And this one…

She looked up at him, at this man that seemed as if he were carved from granite.

He was the more dangerous choice. Not defying him. Staying with him.

And when they began to dance, she didn't feel clumsy. She didn't feel awkward. And she didn't know if she was truly skilled all of a sudden or not. It was entirely possible that the sensation she had that she was flying had nothing to do with reality, but only the fact that she was in his arms.

She hadn't the faintest idea why that suddenly made a difference.

Hadn't any idea what it might mean.

That she suddenly felt right, in place, in his arms in spite of the fact that everyone was staring. In spite of the fact that, to an extent this was adjacent to her worst nightmare.

And so they danced, with all eyes on them, but she didn't feel it at all. She felt nothing but the strength of his hold, the warmth of his body.

"Alex," she whispered. "Why didn't you tell me?"

"Why would I?" The question was spoken with such finality, such authority. And there was a faint undertone of…wonder. As if it would never occur to him to consult her on the subject of marrying him.

It was so very Alex.

"To give me some warning."

"And to give you a chance to leave?"

"What if I wanted to leave? Would that matter to you?"

"I am not a man who makes decisions lightly." As if the very fact he'd made a decision was the only thing that truly mattered.

He didn't care what she wanted, only what he thought was best. She thought of the other woman he'd told her he was going to marry.

"What about Nadia?"

He twirled her, and then brought her back close to his body. "She has been informed. Our arrangement was only ever one on paper. It was not a matter of the heart."

She moved her hand from his shoulder, down to his chest. He looked at her, the glint in his eyes sharp. She wondered if she had gone too far. If touching him this way in a room full of people was too…

But the spark in his eyes smoldered, and she leaned into him, into this.

She could feel his heart thundering beneath her palm.

"Ours is a matter of passion, don't you agree?"

Not the heart. *His* heart, which she could feel even now.

"What does that have to do with the royal marriage?"

"There are certain things that are unacceptable to me," he said. "Certain things I will never be able to reconcile. I could never condone infidelity, not in a marriage. Though I considered making the arrangement. Once." That last part was spoken softly, deadly. And the way his dark eyes settled on her made her feel…

*"Me?"*

"I wanted you when you were his. And I could've taken you. I could have." There was an intensity to his tone that echoed inside her. In her soul.

She knew that it was true. For he was the future King, to Dionysus's future Prince, and Alexius's authority would always be superior. And she…she would have been unable to resist the temptation. She knew that now. For all the simmering fire inside her when she looked at him wasn't hate and it never had been.

In her innocence, she'd thought that discomfort had to be anger. But no. It was desire. Desire for a man she knew she couldn't have. And what would have happened if he'd made it known he wanted her?

The same thing that was happening between them now, and there was no use denying it.

"I was tempted," he said. "But fate…had other ideas. And I'm not the man I was then."

The little bubble of hope that had welled up inside of her fizzled out. It didn't die, because she was much more resilient than that. If she were so fragile that mere words could kill every ounce of hope inside of her she would have lost it, all of it, long ago. At the hands of her mother. Who had been nothing but scathing about her and her accomplishments ever.

Alexius didn't love her. He didn't care for her. If he could have justified sex without marriage he would have done so.

But he couldn't.

So here she was. Not subject to the whims of fate, but to his medieval code of honor.

And as small as it seemed, in this moment, the worst part of all was that her mother would win, her mother would get what she had always wanted. Her daughter as Queen. But under the worst circumstances possible. Her mother, who wasn't even here. Who Tinley hadn't seen in years. Because her father had died, the King had died, Dionysus had died. Every link her mother had to power in Liri was gone, and so she had just… Well, she'd gone off and made another life. A better one.

For Tinley, enough on her own wasn't enough.

And now, by default, she would become the thing that her mother had always wanted.

She wanted to reject it. She wanted to turn away from it. She didn't want to give her mother the satisfaction.

But she also didn't…

She didn't want to live for her mother. Or against her.

She wanted Alex, but she couldn't explain what that meant or why.

It wasn't just sex, but a threat that seemed to bond them together, deeper than she could explain even to herself.

She searched his dark gaze, looking to see if she might find something she recognized there. Something she felt echoing inside of her own chest.

She saw nothing but darkness.

Like standing on the edge of the wood.

"You know, usually a man asks the woman if she wants to marry him," she said softly.

"That implies you have a choice."

"I could leave. You act like I'm more afraid of having nothing than of all this. And that isn't necessarily true."

"And will you leave? You're right. I would not stop you. I would not imprison you. Walk out the door. Tell everyone here that you will not be my Queen."

"No," Tinley said. "I will be your Queen."

Something shivered inside of her. It terrified her. Unto her soul.

"I'm glad we could come to an agreement."

"Good. Think of it as an agreement. Because you should understand that I do have a choice. I had a choice when I went to you yesterday. It was my choice to stay there. It was my choice to take a step toward you, rather than run away. Just as this is my choice now. Don't mistake me, Alex. I'm not afraid of being left with nothing. There are things far worse in the world."

Like trying and failing. Wanting to live up to the standards of another person, only to find that it was impossible. And this put her square in the path of all those fears.

But deeper than her fear she wanted... What she wanted was to explore the dark link she felt with Alex.

It was something new and exciting and magic.

Or perhaps it was old magic.

That truth echoed inside of her.

This thing between them wasn't new at all.

He'd said that he'd nearly claimed her. Taken advantage of his power and taken her back when she'd been with his brother.

And what she had always deemed to be dislike felt like it was something else altogether.

She had been so convinced that she *loved* Dionysus, but here she was agreeing to marry his brother.

His brother who was different from him in every way.

She did not understand herself.

And she needed time to understand herself, and running away wouldn't help.

She'd been running for years now.

They finished the dance, and the rest of the evening went by in a strange blur.

They were on the receiving end of many congratulations, though some of the interactions were with men, and they were quite strange.

"They thought they were coming here to view you as a potential bride," Alex said at one point, as he handed her a glass of champagne.

The glass was crystal, the stem a tree, the branches

wrapped around the cup. It reminded her of the wood, encroaching on her.

"And you announced that you were going to instead."

"Yes."

"What must it be like, to wander through life without fear of reprisal. Most people would never be so bold."

"I am not most people."

"No indeed. Sometimes I wonder if you're a man at all."

His dark gaze burned into her. "Do you? Perhaps I have not made it sufficiently clear."

A thrill raced down her spine. She was frustrated with herself. That she would be consumed with his brand of sexuality while there were much larger things at stake.

But there was only so much that could be spoken about here, in a ballroom full of hundreds of people. There was only so much that could be said.

For she had discovered more about herself and more about him and the time they had spent with no words at all.

Everything that had happened after they'd had sex had been... Wrong. It had driven a wedge between them.

She had felt vulnerable and hurt, and small because of what he had said. And then he had surprised her by declaring that she would be his Queen.

She could not join up the two moments. But she had a feeling that the truth, the answer, was somewhere in that physical connection they shared.

It had to be.

For there was something between them that burned hot and bright, and there was no explaining it. No untangling it with mere words.

They had known each other for years. They had not managed it.

And when the evening wound to a close, she did not know what to expect. For it was late, and there were so many unspoken things between the two of them, they could fill a novel with it.

"I'm hungry," she said.

"You're hungry?"

"I never got a chance to have anything during the ball. People kept talking to me."

"Something we will solve," he said.

He strode toward the dining room, and she lifted her dress up off the floor so she could try to keep up with him. He sat at the head of the table, and she took a seat next to his right.

"Food will arrive soon."

"You didn't…ask for any."

"I am here," he said. "Seated at the dining table. My request is clear. And it will be met."

He wasn't wrong. Moments later, trays of food were brought out before them, savory and sweet, more than she would have ever thought to ask for.

"This is… This is a bit much."

"This is what it is to be royalty."

"Yes. I'm seeing that. I spent a lot of time in the palace but not… There's so much that I don't know. Alex, I've known you for years, but I don't know you." She put her hand on his arm, and his gaze burned with unspoken things. "I want to know you, Alex."

# CHAPTER TEN

"A KING IS not meant to be known."

"But I can't live that way. I can't live not knowing you. We are going to be married, and I need to understand you."

He frowned. "There's nothing to understand. I'm a king. You will be my Queen."

"Those are both labels, not personalities." She looked at him. Hard. "I'm Tinley. You think that I'm too loud, and a bit clumsy. I like to knit. I enjoy baking. I hope I'll be allowed to do some of that even after we've married. I like animals. The charity that I'm affiliated with is very important to me." Her heart squeezed. "Because I know what it's like to have my mother look at me and think that there's something wrong with me. And the children my charity benefits live in a world that isn't made for them. And in every way, big and small every day, they are made to feel like they're wrong. Because they have neurological differences. Because they have different ways of thinking and learning. Because nothing in the world, in their school, is made for them. And I'm passionate about creating ways for them to be able to feel like they belong. Because all I have ever wanted is to feel like I belonged. It isn't the same. I don't have the same challenges they do. But I understand the feeling. And if I can help spare even one person a measure of that, then I will. I hope in my position as Queen I can further that."

"Undoubtedly," he said, visibly unaffected by her speech. "As Queen of Liri you will have money and influence at your disposal. Invest in whatever you like. You will be able to raise the profile for your convictions with ease."

"Well. Good."

She studied him, trying to see if what she had said had... Meant anything to him. Sunken at all. Because it felt important that he understand. She was... She was so tired of being alone.

A feeling...

Nobody knew her. Not really.

She'd made decent friends when she'd gone away to school, but none of them could really understand what her life had been like. Many of them were from privileged backgrounds, it was true, but none of them had been engaged to a prince.

She had experienced a measure of pretty intense grief at only eighteen.

She had lost the future she'd been dreaming of. She had rebuilt herself to an extent. But the more she thought about it the more she realized that in every space she'd ever occupied, from being Dionysus's fiancée, to being a college student, to working at a charity, to being here now, she had only ever given pieces of herself in those places.

No one had all of her.

Sometimes she wasn't even entirely certain she had all of her.

"Were you not hungry?"

She nodded, and reached out and took a stuffed date from one of the trays. It was good, but her hunger was no longer the most pressing issue she faced. It was this strange, desperate feeling of isolation, and the desire to be rid of it.

"What do you care about?" she asked.

"Being the King my country needs."

It was like flinging herself at a brick wall. "But what do *you* care about. You're not just a king, Alex. You're a man. And I can't... Nothing in this castle is yours. It's all your father's. All your ancestors'. Even the scolding you gave me that night at the state dinner back when I was engaged to Dionysus... That wasn't yours either. It was what you thought you had to do to behave in a way that fit the crown. But what do you care about?"

"You're wrong about one thing, Tinley, King is not just a title. It must be who I am. All of who I am. It is essential. For it is in the man that you find weakness. I can afford no more weakness."

"If you mean Dionysus... It's ridiculous that anyone blames you. And I'm sorry that I've been one of them. I felt... I cared about your brother very much. And for a whole lot of my life I was convinced that I loved him. He was easy to love. I got angry at you yesterday because I had to face how foolish I was to not realize that he didn't love me back. The things that I excused, and the things that I decided had explanations... They were born of naivety. Nobody wants to believe that they are naïve. But I was. I am. I felt like a silly child next to you yesterday, and I hated it. Because we were naked together. I didn't want to feel that gulf."

She took a deep breath. "You're not responsible for what he did."

"When Lazarus disappeared, it's because I... I forgot myself. I was more interested in fun than doing my duty. We were playing together in the yard. He said he saw something in the forest. Something that moved. And

he wanted to see. I… I was tired of him. He was bad-
gering me. I got angry. We were supposed to be playing
ball, and it had gone the opposite direction of the wood,
and we couldn't find it. I told him to go on then, and he
would have to deal with Father. I left him. I went to the
hedge to search for the ball. When I turned back, he was
gone. Because I was selfish. Because I didn't want to deal
with him. Because I didn't want to do my duty. It doesn't
matter how old I was. I had a responsibility."

"Alex, you know that's just kid stuff, it's not anything
you can be held responsible for."

"Dionysus. I knew he was drunk. You had left the ballroom by that point, so you won't remember this. He was
making grand claims about how he was going to brave the
wood. About how it was clear he was the real lion. The
true heir. He had a woman with him, and he was bound
and determined to show off for her. And I… I didn't stop
him." There was something strange in his voice. As if
he was holding something back, but she couldn't figure
out what it might be.

"His decision is not your responsibility."

"I am the King. I am the King and in those moments
of weakness, when I was simply a brother, simply a
man, I allowed petty things to get in the way of what I
knew to be better. What I knew to be true. I did it twice,
and the consequences were fatal. No, a man should not
blame himself for the actions of others, but a king has
no choice. For I hold the future of the nation in my hand.
For the responsibility of the people is mine. My brothers were my people. And I did not serve them. I did
not protect them. I failed. I made a decision then. To
be King. Not Alexius and a king. But King Alexius of
Liri. There is no other identity. There is no other piece
of me. There cannot be."

"I don't believe that."

"Believe it. It is a decision I made with great weight."

"I can't be just a queen. I can't. I can't disappear behind a façade."

"I would not ask it of you."

"I feel like it puts you on one side of the glass and me on the other."

"I never expected to know my wife."

"And is your… Is your temptation toward me something of the man or the King?"

His posture stiffened, his face turning to stone.

"You're to be my Queen. You are not a temptation."

It was like a brick wall had gone up between them.

Like he was intent on proving something to her. On distancing her.

But she had agreed to marry him. He could not do that. And she couldn't live this way. So near to him, and yet so far.

"Then tell me something else," she said. "If you will not talk of temptation."

Her heart beat a sickening rhythm at the base of her throat. Her hands were damp. Shameful excitement bloomed in her midsection.

And she cast her mind back, to all the times she had catalogued with him over the years. And there was a catalog of encounters, to be sure. She remembered each and every one of them, as if they happened only recently.

"Dionysus made me feel warm. Happy. Accepted. And I understand now that…he had a different plan for our relationship than I did. I understand that what I thought was love between the two of us was… It was not love for him. It wasn't even love for me. I confused friendship for love. And I didn't consider desire at all." She swallowed hard. "That day that you scolded me in the corridor. I felt very upset. My heart beat fast, and my stomach twisted. I thought I was angry. I thought I was furious with you. I wanted to get closer to you. I wanted to hit you. Something. Make contact. Did I want you? Is that what was happening?"

His face seemed to turn to stone, and a muscle in his jaw jumped, the only sign of life. "I cannot answer that question."

"Your cold fury, your disapproval... I thought about it all the time. Your eyes. The way that you looked at me. It upset me so much, Alex, that I could not make you like me. Dionysus was so easy..."

"There is no benefit to this discussion."

"Was it always going to happen? We'd have found ourselves alone after some party, me the Princess, married to your brother, and... Would we have touched? What about if I had been with him, and what transpired between us didn't make me feel half so much as what looking into your eyes did?"

"Tinley, it doesn't matter. He's dead." Those words came out raw. "You were never with him. And you will be with me."

"I think it matters. Because I want to understand. I want to understand desire. And why it doesn't seem to make sense. Why sometimes it makes it seem like the world is turned inside out. Is it why I make you so furious? Is that why you had to marry me? Because you are afraid if I was wandering around out there married to another man, and you married to another woman that we might... That we might violate who we want to be in order to be with each other?"

"I turned temptation into duty. All in all, I feel it was the best decision I could've made."

"So you were afraid of that. You were afraid of me.

Were you always? Is that why you opposed me so very much when I was engaged to Dionysus?"

"None of this matters."

"It matters to me."

"I told you. I made the decision to be a king, and not a man."

"You outran temptation rather than being potentially subject to it. You would bind yourself to me forever so that you don't ever have to feel weak again."

"If it is a weakness that you're looking for, Tinley, then look no further than this moment here. Does that make you happy? You are correct. What you're reaching around for, searching for... It's true. I made the decision to marry you so that I would not be fallible. Now your body is my duty. Your children will be mine. And there will be no vows to violate."

Her heart pounded in her ears.

"Why does it make you so angry?"

Because that was one thing she couldn't understand. Hadn't he won in some respects, gaining her as a wife? If the temptation of her had vexed him all this time.

"Because nothing should test me in this way."

"Why is that? Does it bother you so much because of the temptation in general? Or because... Because it's me. Because I'm so unsuitable."

He closed the distance between them, cupping her chin, forcing her to look into his eyes. "It is that the strength of my desire for you makes me unsuitable."

And this was it. A window into the man. The man that she was going to marry, for whatever he said, it was not simply the King she would bond herself to for her entire life. For it was not a king looking at her now. He needed to believe it, and she understood that. She understood that the blame that he carried around was heavy on his shoulders. That he believed he couldn't want things for himself. That he couldn't want fun. That he couldn't want pleasure. And he had moved her into the category of duty to sidestep that, and he recognized it was a side step. He had also tried to make it as a grave decision. One that seemed a better choice than simply pining and taking chances.

She wanted to believe it meant there was more, and she couldn't even quite say why, for she was only just beginning to wrap her mind around the fact that she had wanted Alex for quite some time. That Alex was something uniquely special to her. It occurred to her then that maybe there was a difference between the disapproval that her mother had shown her, and the actual feeling Alex had given her when she was near him. Perhaps it wasn't disapproval at all. Perhaps the real issue was that Alex made her feel like she needed to be different, and the idea of having to try like that terrified her. Yes, it was rooted in what her mother had made her feel, because she had gone into her awkward phase, her teenage years, already feeling at a deficit. Already feeling like there was no possible way for her to triumph over the awkwardness she had been born into.

But there was a difference between that, that shallow disapproval of her mother, and limiting herself because she was afraid to be disapproved of. Because she was afraid of trying her absolute hardest and failing.

What an easy thing it was to fail at having straight hair when your hair was frizzy and curly. What a difficult thing it was to try your absolute hardest to be the best, to try to be the Queen and not manage it. It was such a vastly different thing than failing at living up to a standard her mother had invented for her that she didn't even want. One showed her a glimmer of the feeling.

Of feeling like a failure. Of feeling not quite good enough.

The other would be… It would be devastating. To well and truly be rejected by someone she really wanted. Doing something she really wanted to do. Something that mattered.

She had hidden herself away because it was easier.

And this desire to know him… It was deep and real, and it meant she couldn't hide. Not anymore.

So, she clung to that thing he'd said. To that one honest thing. To the fire burning in his eyes.

That to him, the way he wanted her made him unacceptable.

For that was real, and it was human. It was the man and not the King.

And it was what she was desperate for.

It was, she was certain, the place that she would find the answers to what she desperately needed to know.

And so she stood from her chair, and positioned herself in front of him.

"Is it how you want me now?"

"You're to be my Queen."

"Then I'm yours. And you can take me if you want. You can do whatever you like. Because I belong to you."

"Say that again," he said, his voice like iron.

"I belong to you."

He growled, wrapping his arm around her waist and drawing her down onto his lap, she could feel the hardness of his arousal pressing up against her behind.

"You're mine," he said, kissing her jawline. "Mine at last. I've wanted you… It has been like a sickness. But now you belong to me. And no one else. Do you have any idea how intoxicating it was to discover that no other man had ever touched you? Not just my brother, but none of the men at your University? No one. As if you were waiting for me."

She turned to him, conviction burning in her breast. "But I imagine I don't have the same sort of gift. I imagine there have been women. You weren't simply waiting around for me. So, are you to be mine? As I'm yours?"

His eyes went flat. "I belong to Liri. My first service must be to my country."

"So I'm to share you with a nation? While I belong solely to you? That doesn't seem fair."

"Everything here is mine. You among them. It is as fair as anything."

"You belong to me," she said, pressing her forehead to his.

She could never have imagined doing this even weeks ago. Touching Alex like he was a human. Pressing her face to his. So close that she could see the lines at the corners of his eyes, the deep grooves that bracketed his mouth. That she could see the beginnings of his evening beard, dark and heavy on his jaw.

She knew how it felt to be kissed by those firm lips. What it was to feel those whiskers on his face scratching at her skin.

She had been afraid of him. Or rather…wary, because somewhere inside of her she had always known it could be this way. Yes. She had been wary. Desperately so.

And now, it was as if a wall had come down. And she could see him, truly. Challenge him. Touch him.

"You're mine," she whispered. "And I don't care if you believe it. I don't care if you'll admit it. You belong to me, Alex. Me. I had your body inside mine, and I don't care if there have been other women. They weren't me. I'm the one that tempted you. And you don't succumb to temptation."

"Must you believe that?"

"I know it," she said, her voice barely above a whisper. "I know it." She repeated that again.

He growled, cupped the back of her head and brought her in for a kiss, hard and ferocious. He might not admit to being hers, but she could feel it. Every move of his lips over hers, and the slide of his tongue against hers. The way his hands moved over her body. He was trying to claim possession, but he had already done so. It was that she could feel her own possession in the way they touched. In the way he tasted her. For there was a care in the way he handled her that spoke of someone taking great pains to be gentle with something that was precious to them. Precious belonging.

But there was something deeper and richer underlying it, and she knew. Knew that it was flowing both ways. Knew it to be true.

And if he wouldn't admit, it was all right. She would simply know it in her heart until he could.

And she would try. With everything. Not in the way that she had been.

Not sliding under the radar, hiding out in a cottage in the woods.

No. With everything.

She reached behind her back and undid the zipper on her dress, let it fall to her waist.

The undergarment was built into the gown, and un-zipping it left her breasts bare.

"These are yours too," she said, a small smile tugging at her lips. "My body is yours."

It was sort of cheesy, and she felt half silly saying it, but his response wasn't silly at all. He gathered her up in his arms and kissed her. With everything.

It was a claiming. An absolute devastation.

And she loved it.

"Do you have any idea how beautiful you look tonight? Coming down the stairs with your hair loose? It's everything I was afraid to see in you. Your wildness. Your beauty. Because I was afraid that if I thought, I would not be able to resist it. Disapproval was so much easier."

"And running away was always easier. Pretending that what I felt was fear."

It was true. It was so much easier than this. Than diving headlong into a flame that might consume them both, reduce her to ash, leave her less than nothing.

He was the King, and in the end he would stand, even if he was reduced. But she… She would not. She knew it. With everything inside of her she knew it.

He shifted her on his lap so that she was astride him, so that the very heart of her was pressed against the hardness in the front of his slacks. Then he reached between her thighs and began to stroke her there. He pushed his fingertips beneath the edge of her lace panties, teasing her, finding her wet and ready for him.

She had been ready for him. For so much longer than she'd realized. And she felt no shame at all, golden and brazen in the great dining hall of this palace.

"You were so scathing of my being loud at this table some years ago," she said, wickedness overtaking her. "What do you suppose you would have thought of such a display?"

"I wanted it then," he growled. "Make no mistake. I wanted it then."

Pleasure bloomed low in her stomach and he continued to stroke her, gliding through her pleasure, using his fingers inside of her and tormenting them both. She tilted her hips against his hand, moving with the rhythm of his strokes. Then she reached out and curved her fingers around him through the fabric of his pants, squeezing him before unbuttoning the pants, drawing his zipper down and freeing his hardened masculinity.

He was glorious. The feel of him in her palm satiny and hard. Hot.

"I did not know a man could be so beautiful."

"How can you speak of male beauty when you are here? When you are golden? When you are every fantasy a man could ever possess. Tinley," he said, her name a growl on his lips.

And she burst into flame.

Her climax overtook her, suddenly, radically.

She hadn't been expecting it. Her name on his lips. Her. He wanted her.

King Alex de Prospero wanted her. She was not a second prize, nor was she simply his responsibility, his ward. He wanted her. It was laced into every word he spoke, but most especially into her name.

For she wasn't only a generic woman to him. She had cost something.

And perhaps she wouldn't be able to lay sole claim to his body as he could to hers, but she had that. And it mattered.

He gripped her rear end, pulling her hard against him, his flesh pressed against her aching cleft. He rocked against her, eyes blazing. And she gasped. A pulse beat between her legs, and she felt hollow, desperate for his invasion. But he only teased her, his masculinity growing slick with her desire as he teased them both.

She was gasping, weeping, barely able to breathe as he continued to rock in a maddeningly slow rhythm against her.

With one hand, he gripped the back of her hair, forcing her to keep her gaze steady on his. Then he leaned forward, kissing her, the edge of his teeth scraping her chin, her neck, making his way down to her breasts.

And she felt beautiful. Perfect. Cherished. As he held her like this she felt like everything.

And for a girl who had constantly felt small, diminished, like nothing, it was the most erotic and incredible experience to be had.

He lifted her then, as he stood up, and deposited her on the table. Then he repositioned himself, sliding slowly inside of her. And when he was buried deep, he kissed her. Hard.

She cried out, bucking against him, the pleasure that was pouring through her almost too much to bear. He barely moved, and he sent her straight over the edge again. The climax shocked her, so hard on the heels of the other, and it left her gasping, begging for more. He cupped her breasts, riding her hard, the sound of their mutual need filling the room. He was fully clothed, and she resented it. She wanted him. All of him. Wanted to touch his body. Wanted to claim him, consume him as he was doing her. She ripped his shirt open, wrenched his tie free of his neck. She couldn't stop touching him. Moving her hands all over that golden skin. Every masculine inch of him, as the thickest, hardest part of him filled her to the brim.

"Alex," she called out his name.

"Yes," he growled. "You know who this is. Inside of you. Claiming you."

*"Alexius,"* she said.

The sound of his pleasure became a fury, driving them both to the brink.

"No," she whimpered as she felt another climax rising inside of her. There was no way she could survive it. "I can't. Not again."

"You will," he said.

He reached between their bodies, and closed his thumb and forefinger over her slick lips, pinching the source of her pleasure, and she cried out. "Alex!"

She shattered completely. She couldn't stop. It seemed to go on and on. Over and over again, when surely she must have reached the end of pleasure. The end of being.

The end of the world.

But there at the end, was Alex. His strong arms, his stern face. And it wasn't disapproval that she saw there. It was passion.

It was what always had been there. But it had been banked before, controlled. And now it was rampant. Free. Rioting through them both.

Taking them both to a place she hadn't even realized existed.

*Alex.*

Of course she had feared him. She had been right to.

For this was blessing and curse rolled into one. This was more than anything had ever been.

Than anything ever could be.

And when he shattered, it sent her over the edge again. Left her a sobbing, gasping mess in his arms.

"My King," she said, putting her fingertips against his lips.

And he shuddered again.

Her King. Hers.

He might have mistaken her, might have thought she was simply using it as a title. But it wasn't. It was more.

*Hers.*

Her King. Her man.

And hovering around the edges was the truth that she didn't think she wanted.

The truth of her feelings. Of how she really felt.

She hadn't known love. Not before this.

*Love.*

It made her want to weep. And in her reduced state she didn't think she could handle it.

"Take me to bed," she said.

"As you wish." He righted her down, began to put his own clothes back together as best as he possibly could.

And he lifted her up in his arms. She reached down and grabbed a tray of cheese and meat, holding it in her arms as he held her.

"It seems a shame to waste it," she said as he carried her from the room.

"I doubt I will be hungry for it tonight. Not when I have so much of you to feast on."

Her face went hot. "Well. If it's all the same to you, I might want some protein later."

"Whatever you need to keep up your strength."

He carried her into his bedchamber. She hadn't been here before.

It was expansive and incredible, and the bed at the middle of the room was massive.

"You bring a lot of women here. Because it looks conducive to athletic…"

"No," he said. "This is my space."

"Good," she said. "I find that I'm possessive." He carried her partway into the room. "Go by the dresser."

He looked at her like she was strange, but he complied, and she deposited the tray on the top of it.

"Let it never be said you don't think of the practicalities," he said dryly.

"Well," she said. "I run a charity."

"Indeed," he said.

That stern face. She would give anything to make him

laugh, but she knew that he would resist it. With everything he had.

She wanted him to like her cat. To at least tolerate the hedgehogs and the ferret. Because caring for them was part of her. And she wanted to share herself, share her life with him.

But she didn't know if they would ever be able to bridge that.

As he carried her to the bed and set her down at the center of the large mattress, she found herself releasing that.

It may never happen.

They may never be able to find ground that common.

But they certainly seemed able to find common mattress. And dining table.

Perhaps that would be enough.

Because the naked connection she felt with him here was incredible. Was absolutely everything she could have ever asked for and more.

"My Queen," he said, before he entered her again.

And it wasn't the Queen part that mattered to her.

It was that she was his.

# CHAPTER ELEVEN

"WE HAVE CREATED quite a stir," Alexius said, walking into Tinley's bedroom the next day.

She was tucked up on the bed in sweats, her hair a tumble around her. And there was a ferret on the mattress beside her.

"What is the meaning of this?" He gestured toward the animal.

"He's having his exercise."

"Why is there a *rodent* on the mattress?"

"Ferrets are not rodents," she said, her indignance nearly humorous.

"Ferrets *look* like rodents."

"They don't. You can actually tell because of the teeth…"

"Ferrets look like rodents," he said. "In Liri, they are now classified as rodents."

"You can't do that. You can't…" She picked the white drapey animal up from the bedspread. "You can't reclassify an animal just because you want to."

"I think you'll find that I can." Now her fury was amusing.

"Well, it's stupid," she huffed. "And no one will agree with you."

"I think you'll find everyone will agree with me."

She sighed, exasperated, and draped the creature over her shoulder. "What is it you wanted to tell me?"

"We have created quite the stir," he said. "With our engagement."

"Well, that's understandable. Given I was previously engaged to your brother."

"Indeed. Though, the stir that I've created with your mother might be bigger than the stir created worldwide."

"That doesn't surprise me one bit. My mother is deeply avaricious. And I imagine she's thrilled."

"Yes. She misses you."

Tinley frowned. "She doesn't. She's only very happy that she's finally managed to get what she always wanted."

"And that is?"

"The potential position with me as Queen. You should hold him."

"I'm sorry, what?"

"Peregrine. You should get to know Peregrine." She offered up her pet, like a ropey, furry python.

"I will have to decline."

"He means a lot to me."

"How interesting for you."

"You know," she said, "when I came back from school I was feeling really low. And I found out about these animals, which were taken from an animal hoarding room situation. And being able to take care of them made me feel like I was doing something."

He was not interested in the getting-to-know-you thing Tinley seemed bound and determined to enforce between the two of them. But he found…he was interested in her. And that was something he had not anticipated. "You have a real obsession with feeling like you're doing something good."

"Why not? I get tired of feeling like I'm just another pawn. Like I don't really matter. It feels good to be able to actually make an impact. To do something good, rather than just worrying about myself. I've been through a lot of things that were really sad." Something in his heart went tight.

"Not to say you haven't," she said. "But, you have a whole country to do the right thing for. I've had *them*." She indicated her animals.

"And your charity."

"Yes. It's not because I'm very good. Or because I'm uniquely predisposed to being an altruist. It's just that... When things are sad it's very easy to sink into a space where you get tired of yourself. Tired of your own pain. Helping somebody else can take your eyes off of that for a while. It can make things feel better. I was deeply hungry for that when I returned to Liri."

"I can understand that," he said.

"Good."

She had so much passion in everything she did. It shamed him, in some ways. Because he didn't allow himself such measures of feeling. Such an indulgence.

Feelings... Feelings for him had only ever been a bad thing. When those desires began to outweigh his duty, it became a problem. A problem he couldn't afford.

And she had always been a problem.

He had her now, and as long as he kept everything in its rightful place, it would be as it should.

"You can hold him."

"I don't want to."

"For me?"

She smiled at him. And the strangest thing happened. He found himself smiling back. "I'll pet it," he said.

He reached out and brushed his hand over the animal's ears. Tinley lit up like a beacon.

"Is that a smile?" she asked.

"At you," he said, putting his hand back at his side. "And you didn't even get your way. I didn't hold it, I petted it."

"I knew you'd never hold him," she said. "I suggested that so you'd downgrade it to petting. I won."

"You look ridiculously pleased with yourself."

"I am. I only wish I had taken a picture."

"I would have you thrown in the dungeon."

"You're really not so scary."

"I am. I promise you. Ask my enemies."

"You haven't got any, have you?"

"None living. So actually, I suppose you can't ask them. Dead men tell no tales and all of that."

She rolled her eyes at him. "You try to make me believe you're that scary. But I know you're not."

"Do you?"

With an impish grin she reached out and pressed her palm to the front of his pants. "No."

He took hold of her wrist and moved her away from him. "Do not touch me while there are animals present."

She laughed, the sound infectious, and he found himself nearly joining her.

"So what will we do about my mother?" She put the animal back in his cage.

"I suppose we invite her to the wedding. She will know better than to make any comments that will upset you."

"I'm not sure about that."

"Does it bother you?"

"It doesn't bother me, really. That's another thing I realized recently. I spent a lot of time doing things to defy my mother. She had a low opinion of me, and there was a point where for the sake of rebellion, I decided that I wasn't going to try. Not to live up to her expectations. Not at all. And I think I became less than I could be trying to be the opposite of her, rather than just being myself."

"If you don't want her at the wedding," he said, "you only have to say."

"She can come."

Satisfaction burned inside of him. That suddenly Tinley had the power in the situation with her mother. That she was no longer a small child to be made to feel inferior.

It made him… Happy to give her something.

Whether it was holding her pet or giving her the chance to have a victory against the woman who had made her feel less.

Feelings. They had no place in this. Not anything that went deeper than a smile. Longer than a moment.

He pushed them aside. He pushed everything aside.

"We will marry as soon as possible."

As soon as possible still meant that it would take some time. But Tinley was okay with that. The sooner the wedding took place the sooner she would have to deal with her mother, and she wasn't looking forward to that. The sooner the wedding took place, the sooner they would have to deal with the public aspect of what they were doing. And she was just enjoying Alex.

He was adamant, of course, that there was nothing more to know about him. But being with him taught her things that words he spoke never could.

She slept in his bed at night and fell asleep in his strong arms. He saw her in the morning when she woke up, an absolute mess, but smiling. And he seemed to want her all the same. It didn't matter if she was dressed for dinner or in her pajamas that had little badgers all over them. Though, he'd made it clear he preferred her out of them, and typically stripped her naked the minute she appeared wearing the cozy garments.

She didn't mind.

Because she liked being naked with him. Because when she was naked with him, she learned things not just about him, but about herself.

She had always thought that she would end up with someone funny.

Dionysus had been like that. Funny and light and easy to get along with.

Alex was… He was dark.

But there was a gravity to his seriousness that made her feel anchored to the earth.

A loyalty in him that she had never witnessed in anyone else.

It made a deep quiet move in her soul.

A security that surpassed all she had ever known.

For when Alex said he would be true to her, she had no doubt he meant it.

She had no real doubt that Dionysus would have meant it either, it was just that she would've doubted his ability to keep his promise.

Alex's promises were part of who he was.

He was a rock, a mountain, a predator. All those things that she thought of him as before.

But she had missed a few crucial things about that characterization.

A mountain was strong, and it would not easily crumble.

Wolves, lions…they protected their pride. Led their packs. They were not solitary, and they did not turn and eat their own.

No. They were the leaders. The protectors.

That was Alex.

And he had brought her in and made her part of him, and that meant that he would die for her.

Kill for her.

She had been loved before.

Her father really had loved her, and she didn't doubt it.

But the arrangement he'd made with her and Dionysus had been about him. He hadn't thought it would make her miserable, of course. But Alex had said…her father was human.

This command that she marry Alex, though, it was about managing his own temptation…

It was about her. About who she was in the fact that he could not turn away from her.

And she wouldn't say that Alex loved her.

But she had become his.

And in his world she felt it was the same thing. If not more. If not deeper.

And tonight she had enticed him out to the garden. It was warm, and beautiful outside, the twilight settling down over them like a veil, the light strong overhead in the garden illuminating them.

She was letting Algernon pounce off some of his fatness, though mostly, the cat was interested only in rolling in the grass, and not actually getting any exercise.

Alex, being Alex, was standing there in his dark suit and shoes, his expression like stone.

Tinley was barefoot, wearing a dress, her hair loose. Her cat was currently on his back, wiggling around in the soft blades of grass, and Tinley giggled, lying down on the grass beside him and rolling onto her own back.

"What is it you're doing?"

"Enjoying myself," she said. "You know, you might benefit from enjoying yourself."

"I'm opposed."

She shifted, letting her dress ride up around her thighs. There was no one out here. No one but them. Well, and the cat. He did have a strict rule about the fact that she wasn't permitted to try anything when there were animals watching.

It was fair enough, she had to admit. It was a little bit disconcerting. But sometimes she forgot, and lost herself in looking at his stern male beauty, and the fact that there was a cat around was the furthest thing from her mind.

Anyway, the cat couldn't talk. It's not like he was going to tell tales.

His gaze sharpened, looking at her bare legs.

"You can come down here and join me."

"I don't…sit in the grass."

"You don't think you'd ever make love in the grass?"

The corner of his mouth turned upward, and she found herself pinned to the earth, his great, muscular form come down on top of her at the speed of light. "That is a different suggestion altogether."

The show of humor, playfulness, coming from Alex buoyed her. She lifted her head up from the ground and bit his lip. He growled, gripping her wrists and drawing them up over her head, flexing his hips forward and letting her feel his hardness.

"Very wicked," she said. "Much more wicked than I ever thought I could be."

"I always knew I could be," he said, his voice suddenly rough. "At least, I always knew I could be with you."

He said things like that, and it made her feel special. Made her feel like this was so singular and special nothing else could ever come close to it. Ever.

Which made her special, and that, above all else was a revelation. He was a mountain, it was true, and everything good that went with it. But he would also get down on the ground for her, with her. She made him smile.

She touched the stern lines around his mouth.

"What?"

"Nothing," she said. "Except you know I find you impossibly beautiful."

"Beautiful," he said, his voice filled with disdain.

"Yes, beautiful. Such a beautiful man."

"Tinley," he said, his voice rough. "I would have you…"

"People could come out," she said, feeling slightly nervous about being too much of an exhibitionist. The baths were one thing. The garden was another. "Too much staff and all of that. Oh, could we…? Could we have a picnic?"

"A picnic?"

"Yes. Come on. It will be fun."

"Fun? Eating out here on the ground?"

"Yes," she said. "I'll even put Algie back in his cage, and take him inside. And then it will just be you and I out here. And whatever happened after the picnic…"

"It would make you happy?"

"Yes," she said.

Something shifted in his expression. "It is so simple to please you?"

She reached out and touched his hand. "It can be."

She could see, for just a moment, emotion in his dark eyes. "I will arrange it."

He stood, and made his way quickly back to the castle, and Tinley laughed at his retreating figure. He wanted her. It was a wonderful revelation. Just then, something caught Algernon's attention, and he sat up, his ears facing forward. The little cat was never that alert, and Tinley thought it was odd. He was staring into the woods.

"All right," she said, "let's get you back—"

The cat sprang into action, and then ran into the forest, disappearing from view before Tinley could grab him.

She stood, staring after him. He couldn't have gone far. He was only capable of short bursts of speed. She sighed heavily and took a step toward the forest. Dread crept over her. She knew that she wasn't supposed to do this. Knew that she wasn't supposed to go here.

Alex would be furious.

"And I'll be back before he is."

And on a deep breath, Tinley slipped into the trees.

# CHAPTER TWELVE

WHEN ALEX RETURNED from the palace, he found the garden empty.

Tinley wasn't there. Her cat wasn't even there.

A wash of dread went over him.

And he knew. He knew exactly where she was and what had happened.

He had let his guard down.

And it happened again.

Fury rose up inside of him, and he charged headlong into the forest without thinking.

It was dark here under the trees. Completely black.

It was evening as it was, and here beneath the canopy of trees, there was nothing. Panic ate at him.

For he knew exactly what could happen here. And so did she. She knew better than this. She knew better than to play around with this.

Perhaps this is it. The end of the curse.

*Everyone who touches you dies.*

He gritted his teeth. There was no point in thinking that way. Not with Tinley lost in the woods, and with nothing to be done for her except find her.

He pushed through the trees, listening intently for anything he might hear.

He heard the howl of a wolf, and the hair on his arms rose on end.

He took two steps forward, found a large tree branch and held it like a club. An entire pack of wolves would be no match for his fury. Anything that dared touch Tinley was already dead. Man or beast.

There were no paths in the wood, and the trees reached out to grab him, and he elbowed his way through. Listening. He didn't want to call out, for some reason. Something inside of him prevented it. And he felt the need to trust that sensation.

For he always did.

The kingdom of Liri was an ancient one, and the only thing more feared than the wood itself was superstition of what might happen if it was destroyed. That sense of old-world magic was something he still carried inside himself, though he was pragmatic in many ways.

He felt the weight of the mystical here.

And if nothing half so fanciful as old magic lived here, then many animals did. Trees. A delicate ecosystem that scarcely existed anywhere in the world before. It was for men to be respectful of it. Careful of it. Not to destroy that which they could not dominate.

Even he believed that.

He heard another wolf howl, and that was when he knew the silence had to end. He growled in response, and pressed forward quickly, bursting through the trees and into a clearing. Tinley was sitting there, clutching her cat, looking wide-eyed.

"Get up," he commanded, reaching his hand out.

She looked up at him, a mixture of gratitude and fear in her eyes. "Come with me," he said.

She didn't need to be asked twice.

He hauled her up off of the ground and brought her up against his chest. "What were you thinking?"

"Can we get out of the terrifying forest, please?"

"Nothing will touch us." He looked around. "You're with me."

He propelled them both back through the woods, back toward the palace, and when they were on the grounds again, free of the oppressive darkness of the trees, he rounded on her. "What the hell were you thinking?"

"Algie… He went into the trees. I was sure that he was only just a little bit away, but then he was gone. I found him and that clearing, and I have no idea how he covered so much ground so quickly. But I was about to walk back out, when I heard the wolves. And I needed to figure out which direction they were coming from…"

"Every direction," he said, his voice hard. "You can never let your guard down like that again. Ever. You cannot expose yourself to such dangers, Tinley. I forbid it."

"I know. But it's… It's only a forest, and nothing is cursed. I understand that people have died going into it, but many people have gone into it and not died."

"It's only the people who have were my brothers."

"I know," she said. "I'm sorry."

"It will not happen again," he said, his voice stern.

"No, it won't. I… I'm sorry. But everything's okay." She looked around and saw the picnic that he had brought out for them. "Let's have dinner."

"No. There will be no picnic."

"Why not?"

"You're not to go in the garden anymore. Not for a while."

"Are you… You putting me under house arrest?"

"If I must. I will. It concerns me not in the least to

cut you off of the outside world if I have to do it to keep you safe."

"Alex…"

She could have been killed. The idea of coming upon her…her blood staining the ground. For the first time he was tempted to tear the forest apart. Raze it to the ground.

How could he have forgotten?

How could he have let himself slip into this fantasy?

This was not an old-world fairy tale. Where the crows ate your eyes, ships were dashed on the rocks and the dark magic won. This was not happy endings and true love.

Those things did not exist.

"I am the King. I am not… I'm not your boyfriend. We are not on a date. I forgot, for a moment, who I am and what I must do. But I will not forget again. My word is law, Tinley. We will marry next week. You will take your place as my Queen. You will do your duty. And that is all."

He marched her into the palace, up to her room. "Put the cat away."

Then he went furiously to his own chamber, slamming the door behind him and pacing the length of it.

He had forgotten himself. He had forgotten himself again. It was unforgivable.

And the exact same thing had nearly happened.

He had nearly lost her. Because of his own selfishness. Because he had taken his eyes off of his duty. And he had given in to temptation. It could not be endured. It could not be.

And it never would be. Never again. He was not a man, he was a king. And he would not forget.

It was only two days till the wedding. Alex had not come to her bed, and she had endured endless days of frost ever since she had gone into the wood. She knew what he was doing. It was all related to those things he'd said to her about not being able to be a man and a king. Not being able to have fun. To ever loosen the hold on his reins.

Because if he did, bad things would happen. And somehow, the picnic, all of that, had combined to create the perfect storm inside of him the other day.

She'd been so stupid going into the wood. She knew she had been. But she had been...

It was difficult to explain the journey she was on in herself, and it was not terribly compatible with the journey he was on.

But she was finding courage. Finding her own feet, and it made him want to lock down and control her.

There had to be a middle ground. Had to be something else. Had to be a path to freedom.

For both of them.

She made sure the animals were fed and happy, Algernon sleeping on the bed, the others in their habitats, and she decided that she was going to do something to breach the silence between them.

She walked down the hall, toward his bedroom. She had always let him determine when they might sleep together, but she was done with that.

She wasn't afraid to put herself forward. Wasn't afraid of being rejected.

She didn't know why.

*Because you know now it has nothing to do with you, even if he does tell you to leave.*

It was true. She did know that. And she knew it well. She had found a sort of comfort with herself here, in a place she would have said should've made her the most uncomfortable.

And it was magic.

She felt magic, even now in this precarious position. She slipped down the hallway and she paused in front of that family portrait she had looked at when she had first arrived.

Her eye went right to Alexius.

And she didn't feel lonely. She didn't feel isolated.

No, he wasn't quite where she wanted him to be. And she didn't know how long it would take for him to get there.

But he was… He was hers.

And she had found a way to open herself up, join all of the pieces together. No longer compartmentalized.

He understood her. Understood the life she had here at the palace, and he had gotten to know the person that time spent in Boston at school had helped shape her into.

He understood about the charity, and he tolerated her animals.

He knew her in a way that nobody else ever had. Perhaps in a way no one else ever would.

And it made her chest burn bright.

She'd made a mistake. Going into the wood had been a mistake, but she had a feeling it was one she had to make.

Without knocking, she pushed open the door to his bedroom. And there he was, lying on the bed, that lounging predator. His eyes were sharp, hard. "What are you doing here, Tinley?"

"I think it's past time we talked, don't you?"

"Why would you say that?"

"Well, because. Because we ought to, don't you think? About what happened."

"I wasn't confused about the incident that you might want to speak about."

"Good," she said. "I'm glad that you weren't confused. Because it's important. It's important that we have this discussion. I… I'm very sorry. I didn't think. I didn't think, and I should have. It was so important to me to go get Algie that I didn't think about my own safety. But I want you to know that I would've crashed in even if you were standing out there. You would have had to come after me either way."

"I would have stopped you."

"It doesn't matter. It doesn't change the fact that I would have needed to go in after him."

"I would've gone for you."

"All right. But you can't control me, Alex. I'm finding myself for the first time in my life, and I don't want to be married to a man who wants to control my every breath. That's a thing. I really don't want a king. I want you. And I know that you think they're one and the same, but they aren't. I belong to you. But you do not rule me."

"They're the same."

"They aren't. Because a king is born ruling over a people, royalty is inevitable. But love? I give you that. Freely."

"Love?" he asked, his voice deadly.

"Yes," she said. "Love. I… I love you, Alexius."

His eyes were flat, his chest pitching with the effort it took him to draw in breath. He looked angry. More than angry. He looked furious. This was the first time she had ever truly feared him.

"Love is not what a sane person would call this thing between us."

"Perhaps I'm not sane, then. It wouldn't surprise me overly much."

"Love is a distraction. Love is a lie."

"It feels very much like the truth to me."

"Yes, it was the truth to you when you thought you loved Dionysus as well. When are you going to accept that your naivety makes you believe things that simply aren't true?"

"You don't get to tell me what it is I feel. You don't get to tell me who I am or what I'm naïve about. I might have been wrong about Dionysus, but that doesn't mean I'm wrong about you. I'm not. I understand what this is between us. It's real. You cannot tell me otherwise."

"No," he said. "I trust my head. I do not trust my heart."

"Because of Lazarus? You were a boy, Alex, and you were forced to pay for sins that not even a man should have to pay for. Accidents happen."

"One time is an accident," he said. "Twice is not."

"It isn't the same. I understand why it feels that way, but it isn't. It isn't, and it never could be. Dionysus was responsible for his own actions, as a man. He might've been young, but he was still an adult man. What happened to Lazarus is a tragedy, what happened to Dionysus is… Idiocy. An idiocy that was not yours."

"No," he said, his voice harsh. "There is something you don't know."

"There's nothing you could tell me that would make me change the way that I feel."

"The night that Dionysus went into the wood I did not discourage him. In fact, I was glad of it."

"What?"

"I knew he was going to create a spectacle. Dragging that socialite who was with him off into the darkness. I knew it would create a sensation, and that you would know for certain what he'd been up to that night. And in fact, I was coming to tell you."

"You… You were?"

"Yes. I was intent on letting you know just how unsuitable your fiancé really was. That even now, so close to when the two of you were to be married, he was off with another woman, all showing off and being a fool. And I was going to seduce you."

"What?"

"Oh, yes," he said. "You see, I wanted you for myself. And as long as I thought my brother was keeping his vows to you, I wasn't going to touch you. But then he didn't. He didn't, and I thought that you deserved to know. And that I would make you mine. But Tinley, I was not going to offer you marriage. I was going to offer you the chance to be my mistress. Such is my weakness. I was going to take advantage of the fact that my brother was drunk, that he was a fool, and use it to maneuver myself into a situation where I might have his fiancée. His future Princess. I felt we could come to an arrangement that would be quite satisfactory to us both."

"But you… You didn't come to me."

"I was on my way, when I got the news of my brother's death. I let my brother go into the woods so that I could seduce his fiancée. There is no sugarcoating that. I let my first brother die because I wanted to go off and have fun. I let my second brother die for the same reason. Do you not see? I am selfish. I am weak. More than either of them could ever be. Though, they're dead. So it makes no difference, does it?"

"Alex…"

Shock slammed through her. She tried to imagine the self that she'd been then. Young and fragile. Naïve.

What would have happened if she'd found out before his death that Dionysus had gone off with another woman, even while she was in the palace? Feeling like she loved him? And what would she have done to the bearer of the news? And if he tried to seduce her?

She had thought then that she'd hated Alex. But she

recognized now that the intensity of emotion she felt in his presence was desire, and not hatred.

She had rejected it at the time because she had been young. But… But if he had kissed her? If he had offered her comfort in her moment of being made a fool of, would she have given him her virginity even then? And what would he have thought then? Discovering that she had never been with his brother?

And she waited. She waited to feel something. To feel disgust. To feel angry with him for that. For allowing that low moment to occur, so that he could try to take advantage of it, except all she felt was…

A sense of regret.

For it was possible that she could have been with Alex even then.

*Yes, and you would've felt guilt forever. If you'd been sleeping with Alex while Dionysus was being attacked.*

It was true. Any resentment that she felt toward Alex all these years… It would've been worse, would've been magnified had the things between them come to a head then.

And she'd…she'd needed those years away.

She'd needed to spend time on her own. To learn things, and find things out about herself.

For the woman she was now with Alex was not the woman she'd been then. Eighteen and full of doubt in regard to herself.

No, she hadn't been the same woman then at all.

She'd truly been a girl. And not ready for any of the situations she'd found herself in.

But she had become more. She had become stronger and better since.

And she knew Alex had too.

"Alex, no matter what… It was still his choice. It was still…"

"It was my weakness. My selfishness. And then, that same weakness nearly got you killed as well. For I do not know who I am when I'm around you. I do not know...

"I thought that I could turn you into a duty, and I thought that I could fix this. I thought you were more dangerous wandering around in the world belonging to another man than you ever could have been as my Queen. But I underestimate the power of this curse on my family. I underestimate the power of my own weakness."

"Look at me," she said, poking her own chest. "I am not eaten by wolves. I'm here. In front of you. I am the woman that you wanted then, but I'm stronger now. I'm choosing to stand here. Whatever you might think. I choose to be with you. We are stronger than this. What happened all those years ago was a tragedy. And I wish... I only wish that if we could have been together then, we were able to be strong enough to recognize the feelings we had. But I wasn't. I was young, and I was immature. And I couldn't figure out what I wanted. I was happy to go along pleasing my father because I could get no approval from my mother. I felt resentment toward you because you were the brother my mom wanted me to be with. And because you made me feel things I wasn't ready to feel. I wouldn't have been ready for your seduction then. It would've burnt me alive."

She blinked furiously. "And you... You were still punishing yourself. And you still are. But it has to stop. We are more than this. We can be more. I love you. And it doesn't matter what happened then. It doesn't matter who my father thought I should be with, who your father thought you should be with. It doesn't matter that my mother wants me to be Queen. I don't care about being Queen. But I do care about being your wife. I love you,

Alexius. King and man, it makes no difference to me, but you have to understand I would take you gladly without the title of King. But I could never take a king that wasn't you. So in the end, it's not all the same. It is the man that matters. For it is the man that makes a difference. It is the man I want. It is the man I need. And I don't care that you think you were weak. I find you to be strong."

"You don't care about the truth? You don't care about lies? That's all this is. Pretty lies you're telling yourself to make it all feel okay. Because you're drunk on sex and desire, and you don't understand the difference between that and love."

"No. You don't understand the difference between a curse and life. You don't understand the difference between a king and a martyr. You want to blame yourself for all of this, and for the life of me I can't understand why. Why is it so important to you that all of this is your fault?"

"Enough," he said, his voice hard. "If you wish to be my Queen, come here and demonstrate your supplication."

It was so clear what he was doing. What he had always done. This thing between them was so intense, so undeniable that he wanted distance. He'd done it by disapproving. He did it now with cruelty. But she could see him. She could see what he was doing. "Is that what you want? You want to degrade me?"

She took a step toward him, her heart thundering in her chest. "You can't."

He reached out and curved his hand around her throat, urging her toward him. The dominant hold sent a shock of desire, of excitement and trepidation through her. "I can degrade you. You have only seen a taste of my destruction, Tinley."

"The only person you're destroying is yourself. And you cannot degrade me if I choose everything that happens between us here." She dropped to her knees. "It's my choice. Does that make it degradation or worship?" She reached up, undoing his slacks, and freeing his manhood. She squeezed him tight, running her hand up and down his hard length. "Am I to feel degraded now?"

She looked up at him, at the torment on his face. "I think it's you who feels shame. I don't feel shame. I love you. And this thing between us could never feel wrong. Not to me."

He reached out and wrapped his fingers around her hair. "What do you know? You've gone from hating me to wanting me to loving me in the space of weeks. How will it change, then, tomorrow?"

"It won't."

"It will," he growled. "It will, because it inevitably does. I will fail you in some regard and lose your good favor. And once it's gone, it will be gone forever. Mistakes change you. And they change how you are seen. No one loves unconditionally."

"My feelings haven't changed. But I have. And I recognize now what burned within me all those years ago. But I couldn't have you, Alex. What was the point of feeling these things? What was the point when I could never have you? And so they sat inside of me, fuzzy and half realized, and nothing quite like what they are now."

"Do not test me."

But she did. She leaned forward and flicked her tongue over his heated length, desire gathering at the base of her spine. She loved him. Every inch of him. Strong and hard and masculine. Glorious. He was everything that she could ever want. Everything she could ever hope for. He was a man. Tortured, alone in a hell of his own making.

*His own making? Somebody put him here.*

It was true. And she recognized the truth of that as soon as she had the thought. As soon as it entered her head.

His hell had been created by someone. By Dionysus? Who had told him all these things? Who had given him love once and then taken it away?

And so she set about showing him that she never would. She took him deeply into her mouth, luxuriating in him. In all that he was. And all the two of them created together. The heat and the fire. The need too.

There was something blessed about needing another person like this. Something glorious and outrageous, and far beyond anything she had ever hoped to experience before.

It was a relief, actually. To need.

She couldn't explain it. Except that it made her feel more connected, more, than she ever had before. Except that it created in her a deep sense of purpose and desire.

It made her feel important. It was that belonging, and being belonged to.

That singular relationship she had found with him.

Fate, maybe.

Except… If they had always been fated, they might have found each other earlier. But even fate required a choice.

And she was grateful for the choice.

Grateful for the power that she found within it.

He was shaking beneath her, trembling with need. And oh, how she loved it. She pushed them both to the edge, until he growled and hauled her to her feet. "Enough. Undress me."

She removed the rest of his clothes, leaving him a

glorious, naked warrior before her. A man carved from stone, but a man all the same.

He wanted her. And he might hate himself for it, but he could not be icy when they were together like this. It was impossible.

For in this, there was power. Real power. And maybe here, she would be able to show him that she wasn't lying. That her love was unconditional. But there wasn't a horrible story about mistakes he made that he could tell her that would have her turning against him.

No.

He kissed her. Fierce and hard, with everything he had.

And she thought, for a moment, for a glimmer, that he might know. That he might feel it. He stripped her clothes from her body, his movements forceful, intense. And when she was naked before him, she opened her arms to receive him, and found herself being turned over onto her stomach.

"You say you want a man," he said. "But there is no man. King or beast. That's all there is. You may have the beast, since you seem so eager to test me."

He urged her up onto her knees, and she felt his hardness pressing up against the slick entrance to her body.

"Alex…"

And then he was inside of her, deep and rough, and she cried out, half agony, half ecstasy.

He gripped the back of her neck with one hand, and held her hip fast with the other as he poured his fury, his rage into her body.

He was trying to take their connection and twist it. Trying to turn it into something it wasn't. Trying to make them something they weren't.

She knew because for some reason it was important to him that this be a sin. That this be a failure.

Not a desire. Not love.

It was so important to him that this be a mistake, that she not love him, that he not love her.

He was determined to villainize himself, to weaponize this thing against himself.

And she could not understand why.

The reason was just out of her reach, and as pleasure built inside of her—in spite of the fact that this was rough and dizzying—the answer moved further out of reach.

She couldn't think when he was like this.

She could only feel.

*That's the answer. Feeling.*

He was thinking. He was doing mental gymnastics to come up with ways to explain away all that they were, but that wasn't right. It wasn't it. It wasn't them.

And so she closed off her mind, and she opened up her heart. A feeling.

"Alex," she whispered, his name on her lips the only sound in the room beyond the harsh slap of their skin as he pounded into her like an animal.

But it wasn't an animal. And he wasn't a beast. Just like all those disparate pieces of her needed to come together, so did his.

He wasn't a man. He wasn't a king. He wasn't the beast.

He was all of them. All at once.

He was desperate and sad and lonely and powerful and weak and vulnerable and dangerous, all at once.

He was everything.

Her world. Her potential destruction.

And it was all so much, so deep, so real and raw that

of course he was desperate to turn away from it, because this could be their undoing.

But it could also be their making.

She was certainly determined to have it be hers.

"I love you," she whispered.

He growled and slammed into her one last time, and it sent her over the edge, sparks bursting behind her eyelids. "I love you," she said again. "I love you."

"Stop," he growled.

"I love you," she said. "Why does it scare you so damn much?"

"You cannot love me," he snarled. "I am unlovable."

"You're not."

"My own mother didn't love me, Tinley, you can't. She loved her little boy that wasn't going to be King. The one she could have. The one who belonged to her. Not me. I belong to this country. To my father. She would not hold me at Lazarus's funeral, so little was I her child. I'm not a man. I cannot be. I cannot be yours."

"Alex…"

"The wedding is off."

"What are you saying?"

"The wedding must be called off. This cannot happen. It cannot be."

"Alex, it's too late to call it off. You said so yourself. Everyone is coming. My mother is coming…"

"And that matters to you so very much? I thought it didn't. I thought that you didn't care what she wanted."

"I don't," she said, desperation making her words flow out wrong. Desperation making her clumsy. "That isn't what I meant at all."

And she lay there looking at him, realizing that there was a gulf between them they would not be able to cross unless he chose to. Realizing that he didn't trust her.

And if he didn't trust her, there was nothing that could be done.

*It isn't you he doesn't trust. It's himself.*

Her heart squeezed tight. Burned inside of her chest.

"Alexius..."

"Dionysus was her new pride and joy. She didn't let him near me at all while he was growing up. She didn't trust me with her new son. How could she? I let Lazarus die."

"You didn't," she said, tears starting to fall down her face. Because she knew that whatever she said, it didn't matter. Because his mother had told him these things were true. His mother.

Her own mother had told her that she wasn't good enough. She had believed it. She had believed it because it was so easy. Because the person who taught you to speak, taught you to walk, taught you all those important things, taught you how to feel about yourself. And he was no different. King or not.

"She would rather I had died," he said.

"She would never say that to you," Tinley said, horror rising up in her breast.

"She did," Alex said. "She did. She wished so much that it were me. Lazarus would've been a better king anyway."

"You were a boy," she said.

"It doesn't matter. A boy in my position is never just a boy."

"Sometimes the world is just cruel. And we need something to blame so that we feel like we can control it. We need a villain. Your mother made you a villain. But you were just a child. You are not responsible for this. You're not."

"It doesn't matter. That's what she believed."

"So make a new story. About who you are. About who you can be. It's not too late for that. It's not."

"You are a sweet girl. And you see the world in a rosy sort of way. You care about too many things. Small things. But it makes you blind to the big truth that is right in front of you. I cannot love you, and even if I could, it would only mean destruction for you."

"No," she said.

"It's true, Tinley. You must be reasonable. About this. About us."

"Alex…"

"I will give you all the money you need to care for your charity. I will give you a platform. But you will not be Queen. We will not marry."

"But I want to marry you. Are you so perverse that now that I want it, you don't want to give it to me?"

"It is not about want. It is about what must be done. And about what I must be. You can tell me all you want what you believe to be true, but I've seen the opposite to be so. It isn't just general weakness. You are my weakness. And it cannot be."

"Alex…"

"Get out." He was a raw, wounded animal, his words shredded, his eyes haunted. And they hurt her, his words. But they were designed to. He wanted to hurt her, as he was hurt. Hurt her so she would run.

Knowing it didn't make it hurt less.

"You can't possibly be sending me away."

"I am. Because I must."

"You don't have to do anything. You can make a new choice. You can start over. Your mother is dead. She doesn't get to decide who you are."

"My brothers are also dead. And they can never decide who they want to be. And that's because of me."

"This is only impossible because you're making it impossible."

"If that's how you have to see it, then that is the way of it. I am the King. And if I choose for it to be impossible, then it will be impossible."

"Don't do this."

"It is done," he said. "And we cannot go back."

Despair broke inside of her like a dam. And instead of following orders, she dropped to her knees.

And she knew that she should be ashamed. Except… She wasn't. She felt brave, even as she was falling apart. She felt powerful. Because she wasn't scared to love in this capacity. With this depth that created despair in her that seemed to block out any and all hope.

He was, though. He was afraid of letting go of the past. He was afraid of what it would mean if he let himself love. He was lost in the middle of the Dark Wood, not her. He had never come back out the day he had gone to search for his brother.

"You have to choose to be found," she said softly. "Nobody can do it for you, Alex. You have to choose."

"I've made my choice."

A broken sob escaped her lips. "Very well," she said. "If this is what you want, I can't make you do anything else. I'm not a king. I'm just a girl who loves you. But think of all the things you have dominion over. Think of all the things you can buy, all the things you can control, and ask yourself if I'm one of them. You could not force this. You could not buy it. I had to choose it. And you have to choose it back. There is no fate. The only person keeping you from being happy right now is you. You can choose to be as good as you want to be. As happy as you want. As miserable as you want. You can choose to be defined by what happened. Or you can choose to move forward. It's up to you. You know where to find me."

She dressed slowly, then walked down the hall. She looked around her room, at the pieces of herself she had brought to the palace. Baskets of yarn stacked in front of ancient tapestries. A cat carrier on an antique highboy. A ferret and two hedgehogs in cages adjacent to an Oriental rug that was probably older than the Ottoman Empire.

And she smiled. In spite of the jagged pieces inside of her heart. She smiled because…she was good enough to be here. And she loved him enough. But she couldn't be healed for him. He had to heal himself. She had chosen to be happy. She had chosen to move on.

To decide that what her mother had told her about herself wasn't true.

And he would have to do the same. In his own time.

As for her part… She would leave. She would leave without taking his money. Because she would find a way. She would.

And she didn't want to use the King. Not at all.

Because she refused to contribute to the story that he told himself about what made him matter.

She could survive on her own. And no matter that she didn't want to, she could.

Without her mother's approval, without inheritance.

Without Alex, even, if it came down to it.

Because loving him had given her something that his rejection could never take away.

She had found herself.

And she had the hope that when he found a way to bring all those pieces of himself together, he would be brave enough to love too.

The gift that she would take away from this palace was that she was enough on her own.

And it allowed her to close the door on a lifetime of pain heaped on her by her mother.

And as she exited her room, and closed the door on this beautiful moment of her life, she knew that she would be taking with her more than she was leaving behind. Lessons and strength and powerful new truths about who she was.

It was just…that the difficult thing was, she was leaving behind one thing that was quite important.

Her heart.

And she didn't know if she would ever have a hope of getting it back.

# CHAPTER THIRTEEN

HE HADN'T HAD to check to know that she was gone. He had felt it. Had felt the absence of her as sure as he had ever felt the presence of her. She was gone, and it was a good thing. She was gone, and it was absolutely what he needed. What she needed.

*Is it?*

He thought that he'd banished pain from his chest as a boy.

For the loss of his brother had been great, severe and intense and it had torn at his tender, untried feelings. But more than that, the rejection his mother had given him after…

When Lazarus had died, he had been a boy mourning his brother. Above all else. And his mother had not held him. Had not comforted him.

*You did this.*

He could still hear those three words. Could see himself standing there with his arms outstretched and then she'd said that.

He'd needed her.

She'd turned her pain onto him like a knife.

He had learned then, what it meant to be a man. To take blame. To have to soldier on even with that blame resting on your shoulders.

*You were a boy.*

Yes, he had been a boy. But the end result was the same, whether he was boy or man, so he supposed it didn't matter.

He was the King, and he had to be King. He couldn't… *I love you.*

He could not accept her love. Any more than he could allow her to give it. It would be the end of them both…

*Would it? Or are you simply unable to put the ghosts of the past to rest? Just as she said?*

No, if she could love him then perhaps these dreadful and terrible things out in the world weren't his fault.

He looked out the window of his bedchamber. He looked down to the wood below.

That was it. It was the site of everything. The place of all his destruction. There were no answers up here, but perhaps…

He tore down the stairs, and out of the palace. He was not drunk, no matter how he had wanted to make the pain go away with drink.

He didn't allow himself such luxuries.

No, he was in his right mind. Utterly and completely sober.

Lazarus had been lost in the wood.

Dionysus.

His fear over Tinley, which had caused him to realize he was edging too close to his greatest fear, had happened because of the wood.

If it was magic, then it was a dark magic, and it wasn't going away. No matter how much he wanted it to. No matter how much he tried.

If there were answers, they would be there.

Through the darkness, through the mist, Alexius de Prospero, the Lion, charged into the wood.

Alex looked around at the eerie stillness in the trees. There was no sound. Not tonight.

Not even the wolves.

He didn't know what had called him into the forest tonight, but he trusted it.

Which was an odd thing to feel. To think.

For nothing the forest had ever done was particularly trustworthy.

But he was tied to it. Connected in a way he could not escape. And so he moved forward. Until he was back in that same clearing where he found Tinley and the cat. He heard a sound coming from the bushes, and he turned. But it was not a wolf standing there. It was a man.

Tall, his features obscured by shadow.

"State your business," Alex said.

"Do I need official business to speak to my brother?"

She had gone to her mother's house in Rome. She knew it was a strange choice, considering she was raw and vulnerable and it would be easy enough for her mother to take strips off her in her current state. Except... That would have been true if Tinley had been unchanged by her time with Alex.

But she had been. Utterly and completely.

Walking into her mother's drawing room, her inner sanctum, made Tinley's chest go tight, but she didn't feel nervous. She didn't feel cowed or afraid.

Her mother was lounging on a chaise, her red hair more a dark copper, sleek and twisted up into an elegant chignon. "Tinley," she said. "I'm quite surprised to see you here."

"Why is that? I am your daughter."

"You haven't been here for the past four years. Why would you show your face now? Especially in light of your broken engagement to King Alexius. It is being talked about in all of the important social circles. Soon to be in the news, I suspect. Though, I must admit, the dissolution of the arrangement surprises me less than the arrangement itself."

"How wonderfully predictable for you, then," Tinley said.

And if she meant that it was predictable her mother had said such a thing, and not that the turn of events was predictable, it was open to interpretation.

"Well," she said. "What will you do now?"

"I don't know. I'll continue to work with my charity. I'm going to be putting on more events. Speaking more."

"It's quite fashionable to be involved in charities, Tinley, but not really in the way you do it."

"I don't care about being fashionable."

Her mother's brows rose a fraction. "Oh?"

"Why does that surprise you? I've never done anything to indicate that I cared about being in fashion."

"I assume that you couldn't," her mother said, "not that you wouldn't."

It was a strange thing, because her mother was being hurtful, that was undeniable. But she was also being… genuine. And suddenly Tinley saw things through an entirely different lens. Her mother truly believed these things. That Tinley would be happier only if she found favor with the fashionable people. That she would be happier with a certain measure of status. That she would be happier if her hair was straight or her freckles faded.

"We don't want the same things," Tinley said. "I want… I want to make a difference. And I want to spend less than five minutes on my hair in the morning. I want to find a man who loves me." It made her chest catch to say it. "Who loves me as much as I love him. And I don't care if he's a king. A prince. A pauper. It doesn't matter. I just want someone to love me. With my five-minute hair and my unfashionable charitable pursuits. With my cat and my other animals. I just want to be me. I'm… I'm happy with myself."

"That's impossible," her mother said. "Nobody's happy with themselves."

Tinley's heart crumpled. "I… You believe that, don't you?"

"The public is never entirely happy with anything I do," her mother said. "How can I be happy with it, then?"

"There's always room for improving yourself, mom, and I don't mean looks. I mean your heart. What does it matter if your hair sits just right if the content of who you are is all wrong? That's what I work at. It's what I'm trying to find my way with. I want to be happy with the person I am in my heart. The rest of it doesn't much matter."

"The press doesn't care about your heart."

"And I don't care about the press. So it's all fine then."

"Tinley…"

"I love him," Tinley said. "I hope you know that. I'm actually heartbroken. Because I was in love with Alex. I've been in love with him for a long time. But I didn't care about being his Queen. That was why I was there. It was why I was with him."

"Love? Darling, in the grand scheme of all the years you will be joined to a man, love doesn't mean much of anything. You need to want the life that he can bring you."

"Things, Mum, you're talking about things. I don't care about things. I care about…" She imagined then, the way that he had lain on top of her in the grass. The way that he had come for her in the wood. How beautiful he found her in sweats or a ball gown. "It's not in the house you live in. It's in the small things between you."

"Small things won't keep you fed. I married a man with influence, in hopes that my child might have influence. Might have better."

"I do have better. It's just not the better you wished I wanted." She let that truth settle between them.

Staring at her mother now, she realized that it had been easy for her to make one parent a saint, and the other a villain. Her mother had hurt her, yes. But her father had not been a perfect man. He had controlled her life. Had wanted a very particular thing for her as well.

It was just he had known how to work with Tinley rather than against her to accomplish it. But even from beyond the grave he had dictated she marry and when.

He had not been a good husband to her mother. He had been distant, had taken Tinley to live at the palace part time.

He had allowed there to be distance in his marriage and all that blame could not fall on her mother.

For it took two people to be in a marriage, to be in a relationship, and now that she truly loved someone she could see that.

"I understand love. And I won't marry for anything less than that. I want better than the quiet, strained household that you and dad made. And now that I'm older, I can understand that it wasn't only your fault. For he was in that marriage too. And whatever he did to make you think… To make you think the most important thing between you was his status, he has fault in that. But I want better than that. And I found it. Even though things have fallen apart now, I know who I am. I know what I want."

"Wanting something you can't have isn't better," her mother said, and in that partially spoken statement was a wealth of truth.

Wanting a love her mother *couldn't* have. So her

mother had wanted *things*, because her marriage could not give her real love, real deep emotional satisfaction.

"You can want it now," Tinley said. "You could find love now."

"Well. You aren't going to find it with your hair looking like that."

She watched her mother close in on herself. Hide because she was... She was afraid.

In that moment, Tinley saw that if her mother admitted that Tinley was right, she'd have to admit she'd made mistakes when her daughter was young. And she couldn't do it. Not now.

And Tinley wasn't...wounded or angry or any of the things that she expected to be. Because she was too confident in the position she stood in now. Too confident in what she had been fashioned into.

Because of Alex.

And she felt bruised with not having him.

But not broken.

For she was able to stand before her mother now, and feel confident. Feel no shame. And see the wound in her mother, rather than just seeing her own.

"I will come to visit again," Tinley said. "But I hope... I hope things change for you between now and then."

And she walked out of her mother's house with her head held high, and a certain measure of confidence in her heart.

Her life might not look exactly how she wanted it to. But she had become the woman she needed to be.

And she would have to be able to find some solace in that.

# CHAPTER FOURTEEN

THE MAN STEPPED into the light, a pale beam cast there by the moon. Alex stared at this man, but he could not recognize him. Half of his face was scarred. He was as tall as Alex, but broader, his body that of a warrior's.

"Who are you?"

"It really spoils the theater that you haven't guessed yet. But who do you think? Mother named me to enable coming back from the dead in a rather dramatic fashion. Though she could never have planned such intense irony. Honestly I've been waiting for the reveal for a very long time."

"Lazarus."

"Yes."

"How?" It was the only question he could ask, because there were so many, and they were all trapped in his throat.

"That isn't the interesting part. Not really. Because the how is easy. Your assumption was that something killed me in the wood. That was the assumption of everyone. But I was taken. Not murdered. Though I suppose," he spread his arms wide, "the fact I wasn't murdered is fairly self-evident at this point."

"What are you doing here now?"

"Oh, I came to take your bride."

He said it with the casual arrogance that only Alex ever spoke with. Certain no one ever spoke that way to him.

"Why?"

"Revenge."

"Against me?"

"Yes. I… I hate this place," he said, looking around the wood. "Not the forest. I hate this country. And for years I've hated you most of all. I can't say you're my favorite person now."

"We were children," Alex said. "It devastated Mother that you were gone. It nearly destroyed Father."

"And you?"

"I couldn't let it destroy me. I had to be the King."

"That is the thing," Lazarus said. "I think you did let it destroy you. It's why I didn't take her."

"Who?"

"Your little fiancée. I was watching you both from the wood. It was easy enough to lure her cat into the trees, and once the cat was here, she followed. Predictable. I was going to kidnap her. But I realized something. In this dispute between the two of us, she's…innocent."

His brother seemed perplexed by the idea that Tinley's innocence had affected him.

"She is," Alex agreed. "And if you had put a hand on her… I would like for you to remain back from the dead, Lazarus, I would hate to send you back to the grave. And if you put a hand on her…"

"I thought as much," Lazarus said. "Though that is not what stopped me. The way she looked at you… She loves you. Alex, I was taken into a society of people who despised me. Love is a rare commodity in the world. Love like she feels for you."

"What does her loving me have to do with anything?"

The very question made a streak of pain tear through his chest.

"Because the way that I was brought up, Alex, there is little but hate in my heart for anyone or anything. I was created to come back and destroy you. But my captor died. And…" His brother looked into the distance. "I don't care. I don't want to be a pawn. Not of the crown of Liri, and not against her detractors. There are truths about our family that would be difficult for you to stomach, I've a feeling. Truths that go back further than Father. All those wars we fought for all those years, all those mysterious deaths in the wood. Why do you think people are kept out of here? It's not the wolves."

"It's not…"

"There are people here. Oppressed by this country. I was taken to be a symbol."

"But you weren't used."

"Things didn't go as planned. The woman Dionysus was with that night… She lured him into the wood. It was never wolves."

"Is he…"

"He's dead. I was not a part of that. You must believe it. And that, is where my fault lies. I cannot bring myself to kill you. Any more than I could've brought myself to kill him. Just as I couldn't take your woman. She loves you. And you love her. Those are gifts that I will never have, Brother, for they were stripped away from me a long time ago. And I let that fester into hatred, of you, of this place. Which was exactly what my captors wanted. But I… I see a different path."

"What path? I don't understand."

"You might be the Lion of the Dark Wood, but I am

the Prince. And I have my own people to protect. And you and I... Well, we have some negotiating to do."

"Surely that can wait."

"It can. Though... I heard that you broke your engagement."

"Yes. I did."

"Why? As I said, it was clear to me there was a great deal of love between the two of you. You don't have to stand in front of a fire to know it's warm. I don't have to be able to feel love to be able to recognize it."

"You might have been raised to hate me, Lazarus, but you... You cannot possibly hate me more than I was trained to hate myself."

"And is that why you can't be with her?"

"She doesn't deserve to be tied to someone like me."

"She doesn't deserve to be with a man she's clearly in love with?"

"It is not so simple."

"Life is actually quite simple," Lazarus said. "You must live. Whatever it is that's in front of you, take it if you can. For there are guarantees of nothing. I was born a prince in a castle, ended up raised in a shack in the woods. If you can have the castle, why are you choosing the shack?"

"What does that have to..."

"You can have love, you're choosing not to. Don't be a fool. You and I will have a meeting in a few days. But I expect you will have resolved things with your Queen by then."

And just as quietly and suddenly as he had appeared, Lazarus was gone. And everything Alex thought he knew about the world had been turned on its head.

Lazarus made it sound like a choice.

Lazarus was alive.

He was *alive*.

And if he was alive… If there was more to all of this than Alex had ever known…

But perhaps he didn't know everything.

Perhaps it didn't have to be the end of him and Tinley. Because they had something that had stopped Lazarus from taking revenge.

Something powerful.

And he… He was choosing fear instead.

He had hidden behind the title, because it meant he didn't have to feel. Not the grief over losing either of his brothers, or the pain of his mother's rejection.

But Tinley had asked for the man.

And suddenly, he realized, there wasn't only death in the wood, there was life too. And life was much the same. There wasn't only death. He wasn't only the King. There were miracles, and there were tragedies. There was pain and there was joy. There was hate, but there was love.

And as with Lazarus, love had won over hate.

Love had won.

He wished…very much that his mother had lived to see this. She had been hopeless, that was the problem. She had been hopeless and had seen no other way. And he… It had pushed him into that place too.

But there was hope.

There was life.

He no longer needed to carry the hurt his mother had put there. The sad thing was her life had ended before she could put it aside. But he could choose to. Now. He could choose hope.

He could choose love.

He needed Tinley.

Immediately.

* * *

Tinley was working on a sweater for her cat.

She felt that she had descended to some new low, but at the same time, it was so cute it felt like it could be a high. Life was funny.

She brought her needle around to the front of the yarn for a purl, when there was a knock on her cottage door. She shoved the work back onto the needles and set it down. "Yes?"

She wasn't expecting anyone, and it wasn't like her cottage was in the sort of place that got a lot of foot traffic. She stood up and peered out one lace curtain, and then her heart scurried up into her throat.

"Alex?" she called.

"Let me in," he said.

"I'll… All right."

She went and jerked the door open, and there he was, tall and broad as ever. But disheveled. He looked tired, as if he hadn't been sleeping.

*Join the club.*

"What are you doing here?"

"I have so much to tell you," he said. "The first of which is that Lazarus is alive."

"What?"

"He's alive. And… There is more to that story, which I will explain, but first… I was afraid. Because I thought there was no way you could possibly love me. Not when my mother seemed to see how unworthy I was."

"Alex, it's never been about worthiness…"

"I know. I do now. It was easier, though, to accept that. Because it required nothing of me. And I've experienced my share of loss. So it was easier to hide behind the title of King. To hide behind duty. When Dionysus died, when I made the decision to seduce you while he was away for the evening… I was acting with my heart. And over the years, I've dismissed it. As lust. Because it was easier than admitting that those feelings I had for you were complicated. But the timing of everything was complicated, and it wasn't evil of me to want you. Things happened the way they did. I will never be glad that he's gone. Ever. But I do wonder if I would have ever had the courage then to override what everyone wanted because love is stronger. I wonder if I would have been able to admit that I loved you." He moved closer to her, cupped her chin. "It doesn't matter now. What I would have done. What matters is that I'm here now. We cannot change the past. But we have a choice now. I have a choice now. And I choose to make the future the best it can be. I love you, Tinley. I want you to be mine. My wife. My Queen. Marry the man and the King."

"Of course I will," she said, love bursting through her chest like a flame. She wrapped her arms around his neck and kissed him.

"You're my lioness," he said, touching her hair. "How did I not see it before? The signs were everywhere."

"Alex. It's so easy to get caught up in the stories everyone else tells about you. But at some point we have to start telling our own."

"Yes. We must."

"Well, I suppose marriage is really the only course of action."

"I couldn't agree more. It's why I have brought the vicar with me."

"The vicar?" She blinked. "Now?"

"We can have a wedding for the benefit of the country. But I think we should have one now. For the benefit of us. Only us. This isn't for your mother. It isn't a symbol. It's not because I told my father I would take care of you, it's not because you will be a good queen—though you will. It is simply because I love you. And I will marry you here. With your animals as attendants."

"Really, that is the most ridiculous thing I've ever heard you say."

"I thought you would appreciate it."

"I do. So much."

"So will you marry me? Outside your cottage, on the edge of the wood?"

"I will. And we can have pie as a wedding treat."

"I can think of nothing better."

"I'm very glad we're writing our own story, Alex," she said. "Because I know just how I wanted it to end."

"Do you?"

"Yes. Happily ever after."

# EPILOGUE

OF COURSE THEY did have to have a wedding, for the benefit of the nation. Things had changed dramatically in the time since they'd had their private ceremony at the cottage. Tinley had discovered she was expecting the royal heir, a cause for celebration in Liri, but celebrated most of all in the palace, between the King and Queen.

Tinley's mother had fallen in love with an Italian count, and the man was her guest at the wedding.

And Lazarus was in attendance, along with his people. Reconciliation was being worked on, and the true history of Liri over generations was being brought to light. There were some hard truths to that. But Alex was passionate about making things right.

With his brother by his side.

But even more importantly, with his Queen.

When he spoke his vows to her, they came from his heart. The heart that was healing. That no longer felt so scarred.

The heart that had beaten for Tinley Markham from the very beginning. And he no longer looked back on those feelings as a sin, but a sign.

That love had always been there. And that in the end, love would always prevail.

For love was the source of all magic. Love could overwhelm curses.

Love was a light that no darkness could stand against. And for all his days Alex was committed to choosing love, with Tinley, forever.

* * * * *

# MILLS & BOON

## Coming next month

### THE COST OF CLAIMING HIS HEIR
### Michelle Smart

'How was the party?'

Becky had to untie her tongue to speak. 'Okay. Everyone looked like they were having fun.'

'But not you?'

'No.' She sank down onto the wooden step to take the weight off her weary legs and rested her back against a pillar.

'Why not?'

'Because I'm a day late.'

She heard him suck an intake of breath. 'Is that normal for you?'

'No.' Panic and excitement swelled sharply in equal measure as they did every time she allowed herself to read the signs that were all there. Tender breasts. Fatigue. The ripple of nausea she'd experienced that morning when she'd passed Paula's husband outside and caught a whiff of his cigarette smoke. Excitement that she could have a child growing inside her. Panic at what this meant.

Scared she was going to cry, she scrambled back to her feet. 'Let's give it another couple of days. If I haven't come on by then, I'll take a test.'

She would have gone inside if Emiliano hadn't leaned forward and gently taken hold of her wrist. 'Sit with me.'

Opening her mouth to tell him she needed sleep, she stared into his eyes and found herself temporarily mute.

For the first time since they'd conceived—and in her heart she was now certain they *had* conceived—there was no antipathy in his stare, just a steadfastness that lightened the weight on her shoulders.

Gingerly, she sat beside him but there was no hope of keeping a distance for Emiliano put his beer bottle down and hooked an arm around her waist to draw her to him.

Much as she wanted to resist, she leaned into him and rested her cheek on his chest.

'Don't be afraid, *bomboncita*,' he murmured into the top of her head. 'We will get through this together.'

Nothing more was said for the longest time and for that she was grateful. Closing her eyes, she was able to take comfort from the strength of his heartbeat against her ear and his hands stroking her back and hair so tenderly. There was something so very solid and real about him, an energy always zipping beneath his skin even in moments of stillness.

He dragged a thumb over her cheek and then rested it under her chin to tilt her face to his. Then, slowly, his face lowered and his lips caught her in a kiss so tender the little of her not already melting to be held in his arms turned to fondue.

Feeling as if she'd slipped into a dream, Becky's mouth moved in time with his, a deepening caress that sang to her senses as she inhaled the scent of his breath and the muskiness of his skin. Her fingers tiptoed up his chest, then flattened against his neck. The pulse at the base thumped against the palm of her hand.

But, even as every crevice in her body thrilled, a part of her brain refused to switch off and it was with huge reluctance that she broke the kiss and gently pulled away from him.

'Not a good idea,' she said shakily as her body howled in protest.

Emiliano gave a look of such sensuality her pelvis pulsed. 'Why?'

Fearing he would reach for her again, she shifted to the other side of the swing chair and patted the space beside her for the dogs to jump up and act as a barrier between them. They failed to oblige. 'Aren't we in a big enough mess?'

Eyes not leaving her face, he picked up his beer and took a long drink. 'That depends on how you look at it. To me, the likelihood that you're pregnant makes things simple. I want you. You want me. Why fight it any more when we're going to be bound together?'

*Continue reading*
THE COST OF CLAIMING HIS HEIR
Michelle Smart

*Available next month*
www.millsandboon.co.uk

# COMING SOON!

We really hope you enjoyed reading this book.
If you're looking for more romance, be sure to
head to the shops when new books are
available on

## Thursday 10th December

To see which titles are coming soon, please visit

**millsandboon.co.uk/nextmonth**

MILLS & BOON

# JOIN US ON SOCIAL MEDIA!

Stay up to date with our latest releases, author news and gossip, special offers and discounts, and all the behind-the-scenes action from Mills & Boon...

 millsandboon

 millsandboonuk

 millsandboon

*It might just be true love...*

# MILLS & BOON

## HEROES

### At Your Service

Experience all the excitement of a gripping thriller, with an intense romance at its heart. Resourceful, true-to-life women and strong, fearless men face danger and desire - a killer combination!

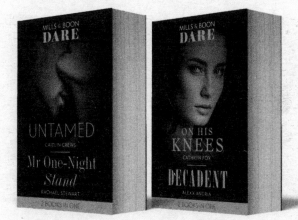